the LOLLIPOP KIDS

ADAM GLASS
writer

ADAM GLASS & AIDAN GLASS
story

DIEGO YAPUR
artist

DC ALONSO
colorist

SAL CIPRIANO
letterer

JUAN DOE cover
CHARLES PRITCHETT logo & book design
MIKE MARTS editor

CREATED BY ADAM GLASS & AIDAN GLASS

SEISMIC
PRESS

To dream up and then write THE LOLLIPOP KIDS with my son, Aidan, will always be a gift that I treasure. The adventure is just beginning for you, Aidan, and I'm so glad I get a front row seat to watch. Your mom and I love you to the moon and back.
— ADAM GLASS

SEISMIC PRESS IS AN IMPRINT OF

MIKE MARTS - Editor-in-Chief • JOE PRUETT - Publisher/CCO • LEE KRAMER - President • JON KRAMER - Chief Executive Officer
STEVE ROTTERDAM - SVP, Sales & Marketing • DAN SHIRES - VP, Film & Television UK • CHRISTINA HARRINGTON - Managing Editor
TEODORO LEO - Associate Editor • MARC HAMMOND - Sr. Retail Sales Development Manager • RUTHANN THOMPSON - Sr. Retailer Relations Manager
KATHERINE JAMISON - Marketing Manager • KELLY DIODATI - Ambassador Outreach Manager • BLAKE STOCKER - Director of Finance
AARON MARION - Publicist • LISA MOODY - Finance • RYAN CARROLL - Director, Comics/Film/TV Liaison • JAWAD QURESHI - Technology Advisor/Strategist
RACHEL PINNELAS - Social Community Manager • CHARLES PRITCHETT - Design & Production Manager • COREY BREEN - Collections Production
SARAH PRUETT - Publishing Assistant

AfterShock and Seismic Logo Designs by COMICRAFT
Publicity: contact AARON MARION (aaron@publichausagency.com) & RYAN CROY (ryan@publichausagency.com) at PUBLICHAUS
Special thanks to: ATOM! FREEMAN, IRA KURGAN, MARINE KSADZHIKYAN, KEITH MANZELLA,
ANTONIA LIANOS, ANTHONY MILITANO, STEPHAN NILSON & ED ZAREMBA

AFTERSHOCKCOMICS.COM/SEISMIC Follow us on social media 🐦 @SeismicComics 📷 @SeismicPress f @SeismicPress

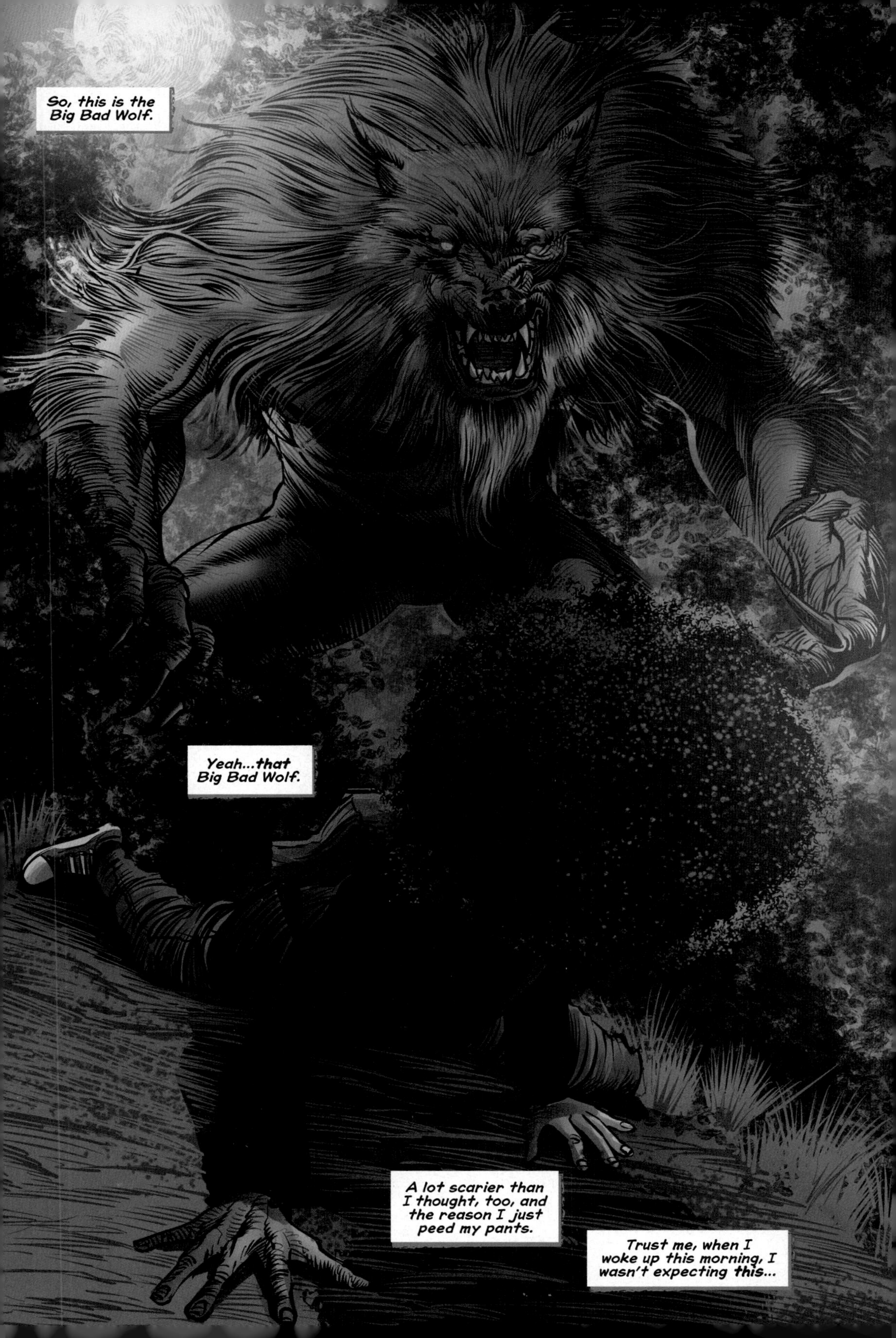
So, this is the Big Bad Wolf.
Yeah...that Big Bad Wolf.
A lot scarier than I thought, too, and the reason I just peed my pants.
Trust me, when I woke up this morning, I wasn't expecting this...

As long as I can remember, I have slept with my window cracked open.

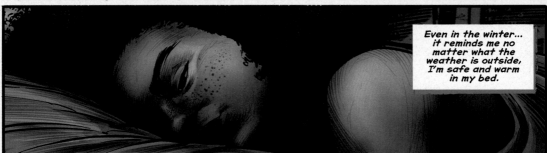

Even in the winter... it reminds me no matter what the weather is outside, I'm safe and warm in my bed.

This is much to the dismay of my roommate--

--and sister, Mia.

Who, it seems, didn't make it home last night.

That's not like her, especially when dad is out on his shift at the firehouse.

HEY, YOU'VE REACHED MIA, YOU KNOW WHAT TO DO-- BEEEEP!

Hmm...

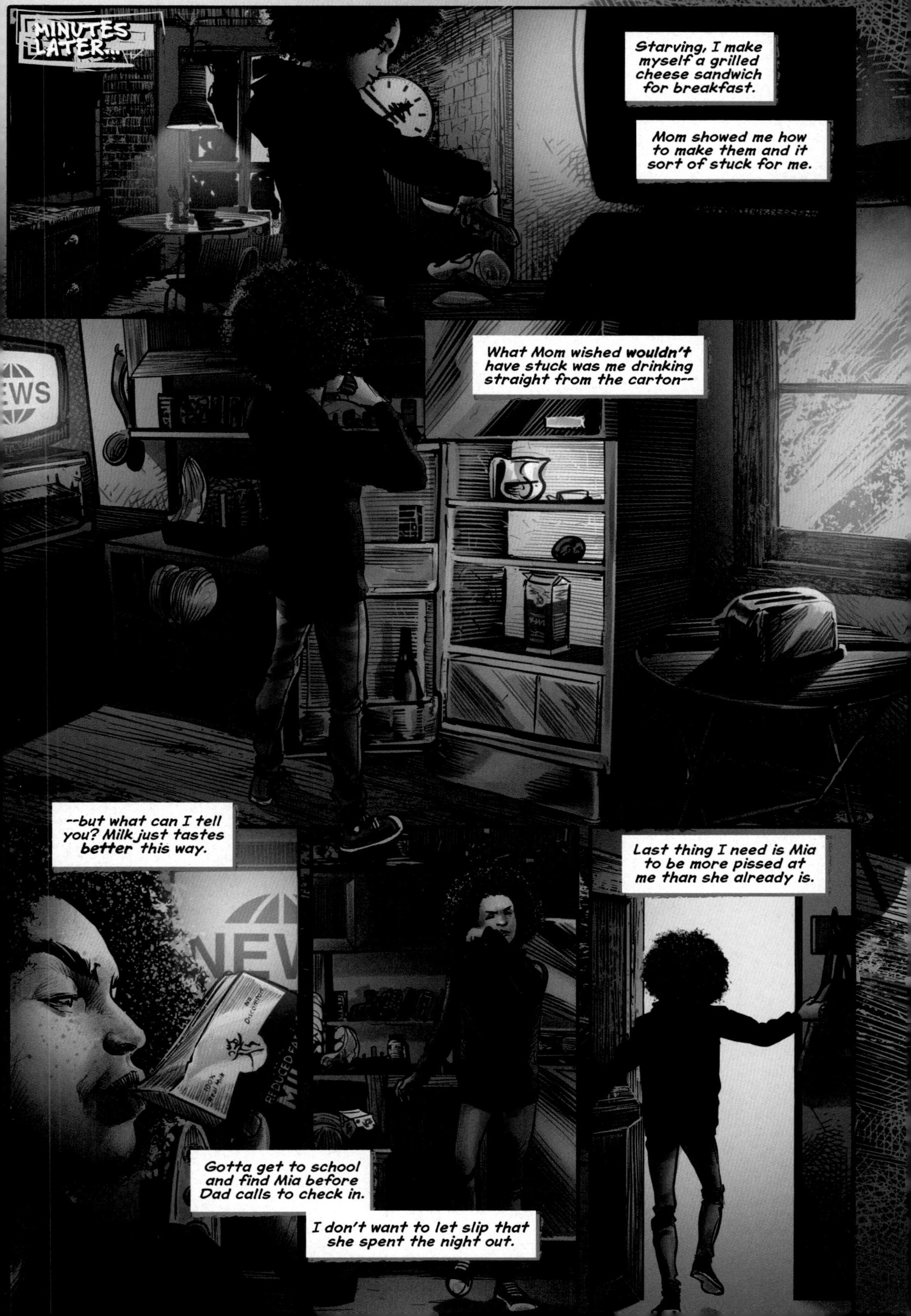
MINUTES LATER...
Starving, I make myself a grilled cheese sandwich for breakfast.
Mom showed me how to make them and it sort of stuck for me.
What Mom wished wouldn't have stuck was me drinking straight from the carton--
--but what can I tell you? Milk just tastes better this way.
Gotta get to school and find Mia before Dad calls to check in.
I don't want to let slip that she spent the night out.
Last thing I need is Mia to be more pissed at me than she already is.

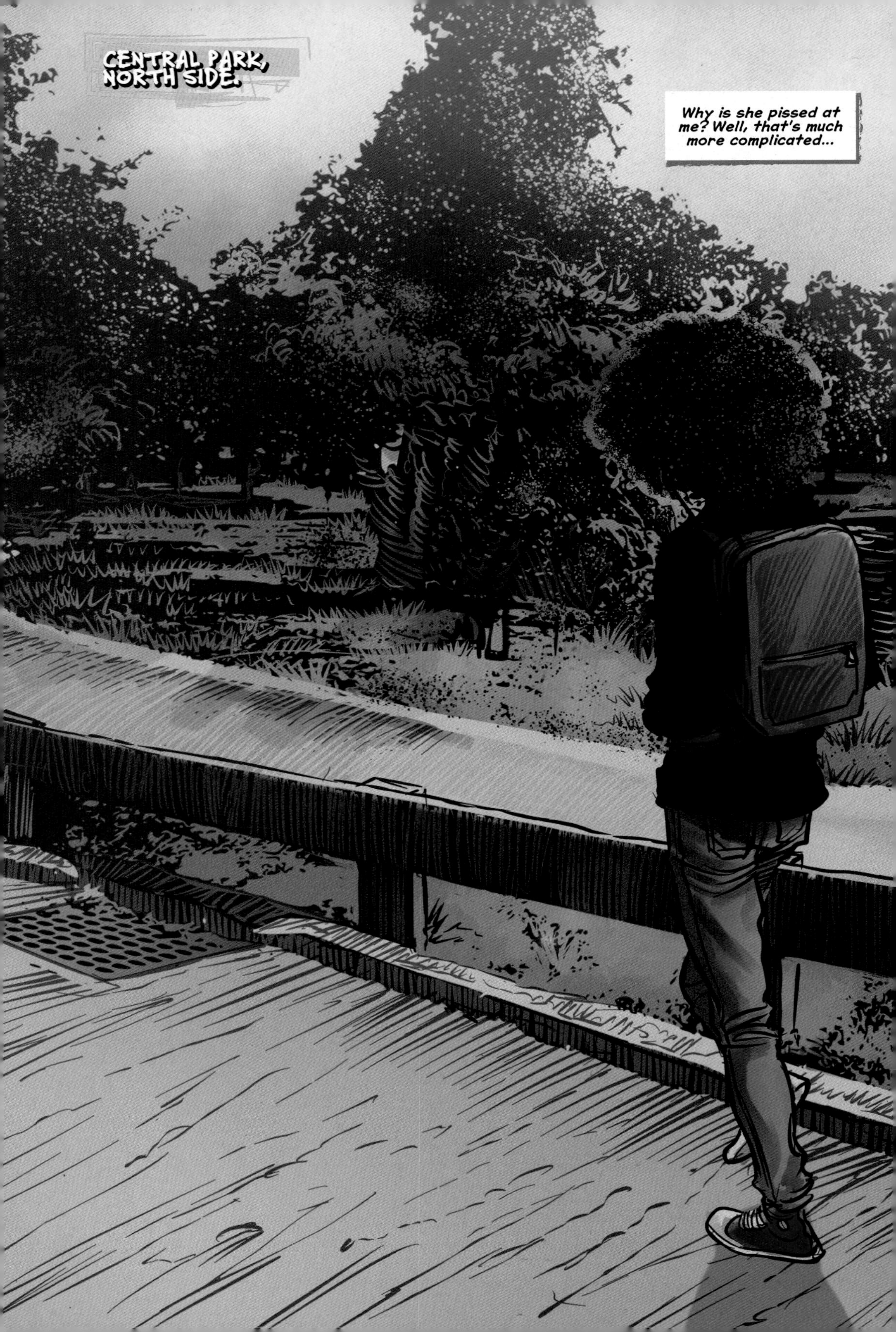
CENTRAL PARK, NORTH SIDE.
Why is she pissed at me? Well, that's much more complicated...

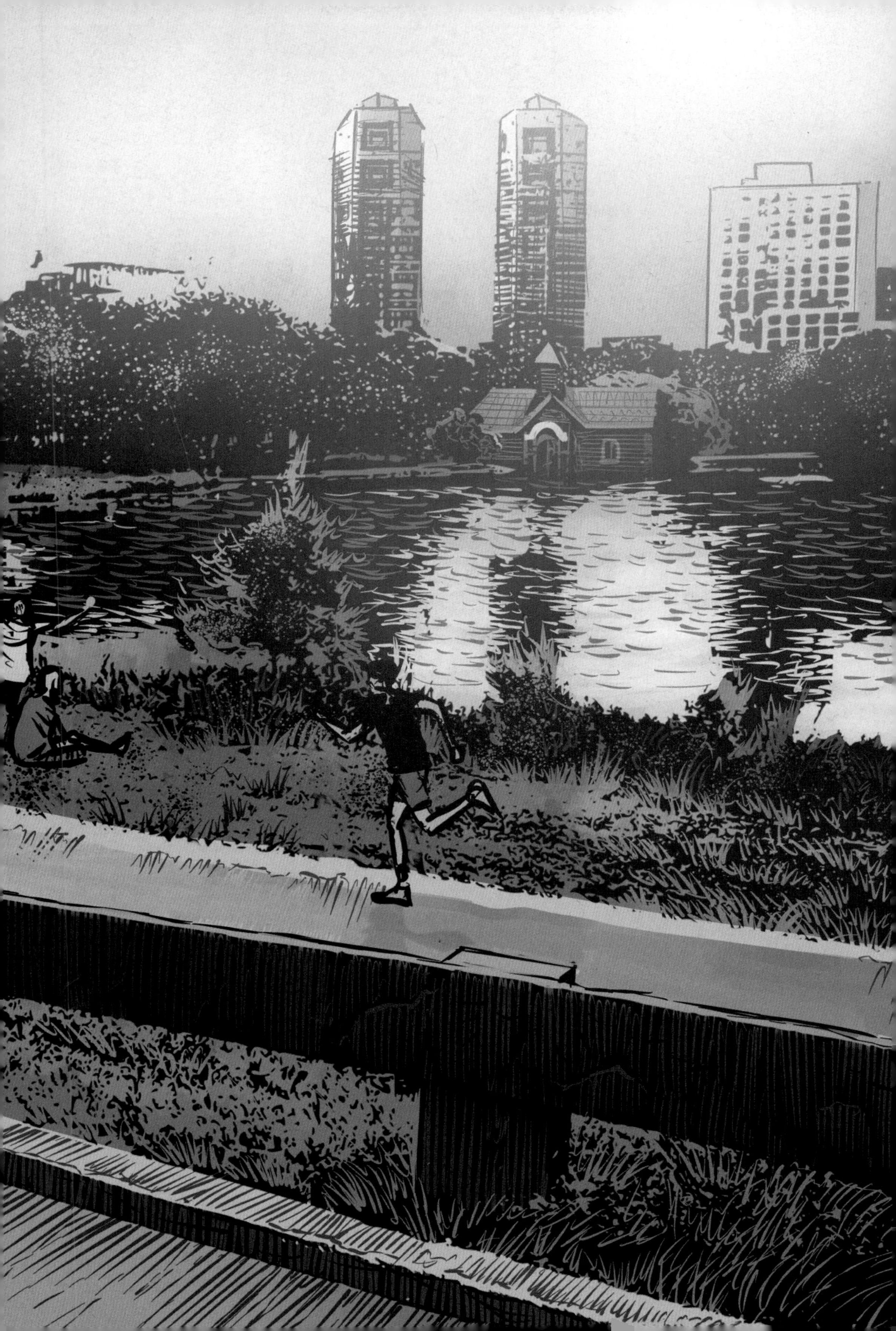

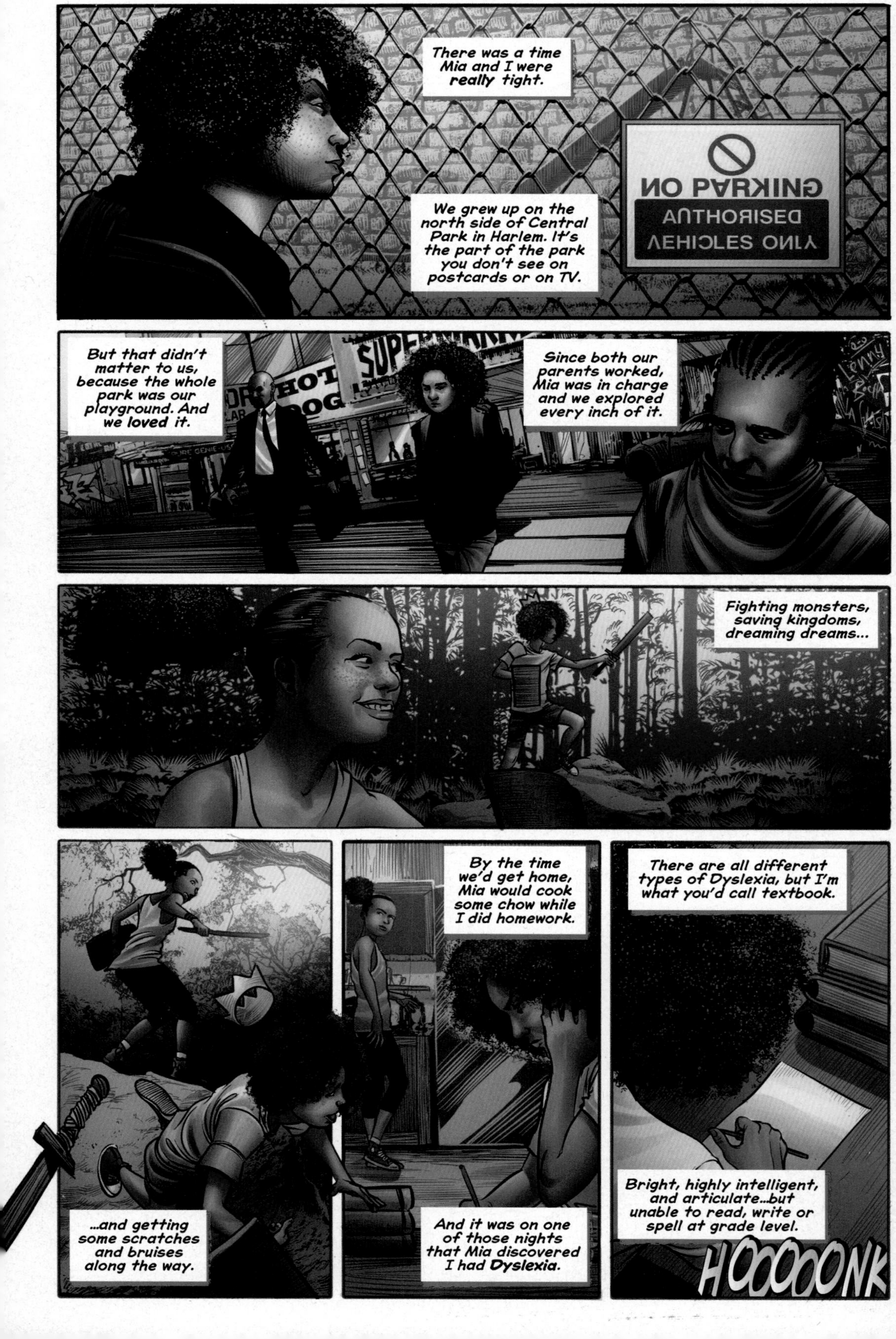

There was a time Mia and I were really tight.
NO PARKING
AUTHORISED VEHICLES ONLY
We grew up on the north side of Central Park in Harlem. It's the part of the park you don't see on postcards or on TV.
But that didn't matter to us, because the whole park was our playground. And we loved it.
HOT DOG
Since both our parents worked, Mia was in charge and we explored every inch of it.
Fighting monsters, saving kingdoms, dreaming dreams...
...and getting some scratches and bruises along the way.
By the time we'd get home, Mia would cook some chow while I did homework.
And it was on one of those nights that Mia discovered I had Dyslexia.
There are all different types of Dyslexia, but I'm what you'd call textbook.
Bright, highly intelligent, and articulate...but unable to read, write or spell at grade level.
HOOOOONK

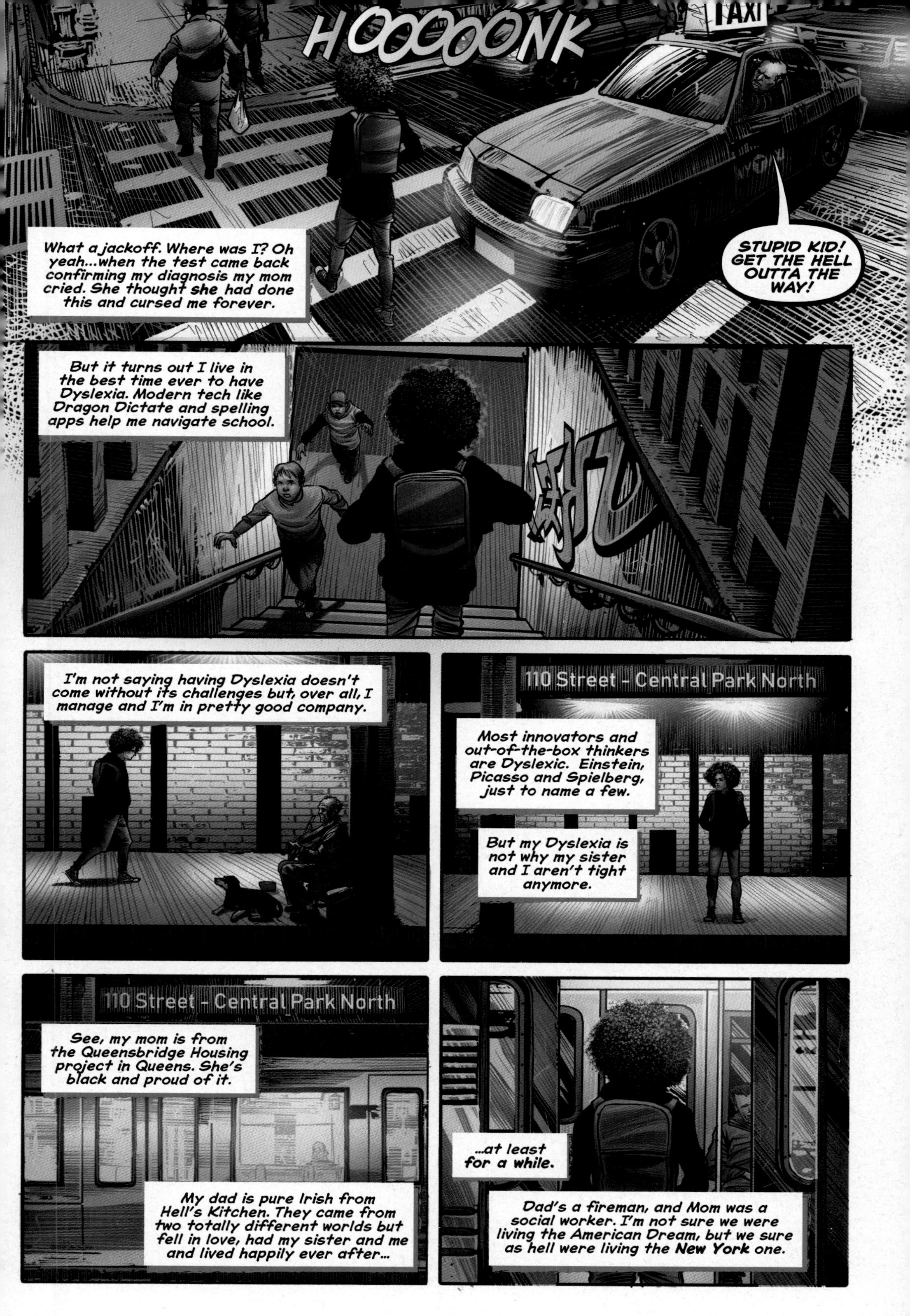
HOOOOOONK
TAXI
What a jackoff. Where was I? Oh yeah...when the test came back confirming my diagnosis my mom cried. She thought she had done this and cursed me forever.
STUPID KID! GET THE HELL OUTTA THE WAY!
But it turns out I live in the best time ever to have Dyslexia. Modern tech like Dragon Dictate and spelling apps help me navigate school.
I'm not saying having Dyslexia doesn't come without its challenges but, over all, I manage and I'm in pretty good company.
110 Street - Central Park North
Most innovators and out-of-the-box thinkers are Dyslexic. Einstein, Picasso and Spielberg, just to name a few.
But my Dyslexia is not why my sister and I aren't tight anymore.
110 Street - Central Park North
See, my mom is from the Queensbridge Housing project in Queens. She's black and proud of it.
My dad is pure Irish from Hell's Kitchen. They came from two totally different worlds but fell in love, had my sister and me and lived happily ever after...
...at least for a while.
Dad's a fireman, and Mom was a social worker. I'm not sure we were living the American Dream, but we sure as hell were living the **New York** one.

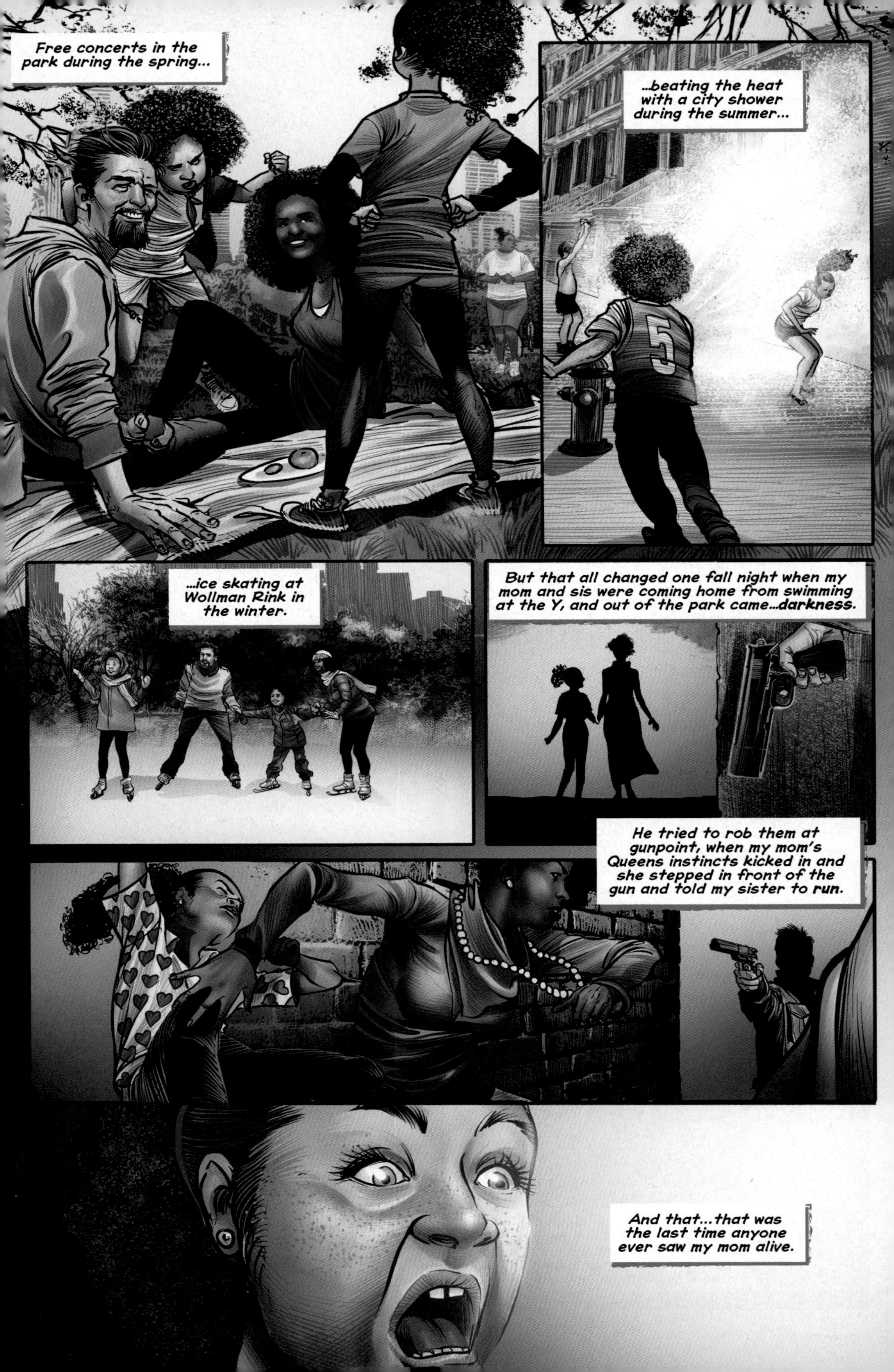
Free concerts in the park during the spring...
...beating the heat with a city shower during the summer...
5
...ice skating at Wollman Rink in the winter.
But that all changed one fall night when my mom and sis were coming home from swimming at the Y, and out of the park came...darkness.
He tried to rob them at gunpoint, when my mom's Queens instincts kicked in and she stepped in front of the gun and told my sister to run.
And that...that was the last time anyone ever saw my mom alive.

Dad being Irish Catholic and all, he wasn't exactly Mister "let's talk about it."

...but Mia was never the same. Always out, never wanted to play anymore and everything I did only seemed to annoy her.

Instead it was "God works in strange ways and all we can do is move on." So we did...

And the park, the only salvation we ever had, suddenly became a "bad place" that I wasn't supposed to be in anymore.

So I lashed out, which would lead to fights...and eventually we were living in the same apartment, sleeping in the same bedroom, but never speaking.

And that's the way it's been...but today that changes. I'm gonna show Mia how much she means to me.

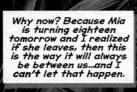

Why now? Because Mia is turning eighteen tomorrow and I realized if she leaves, then this is the way it will always be between us...and I can't let that happen.

I know what you're thinking--pretty mature for a fourteen-year-old. But I told you, us Dyslexic kids are wicked smart.

She wasn't in homeroom...okay, now I was officially worried.

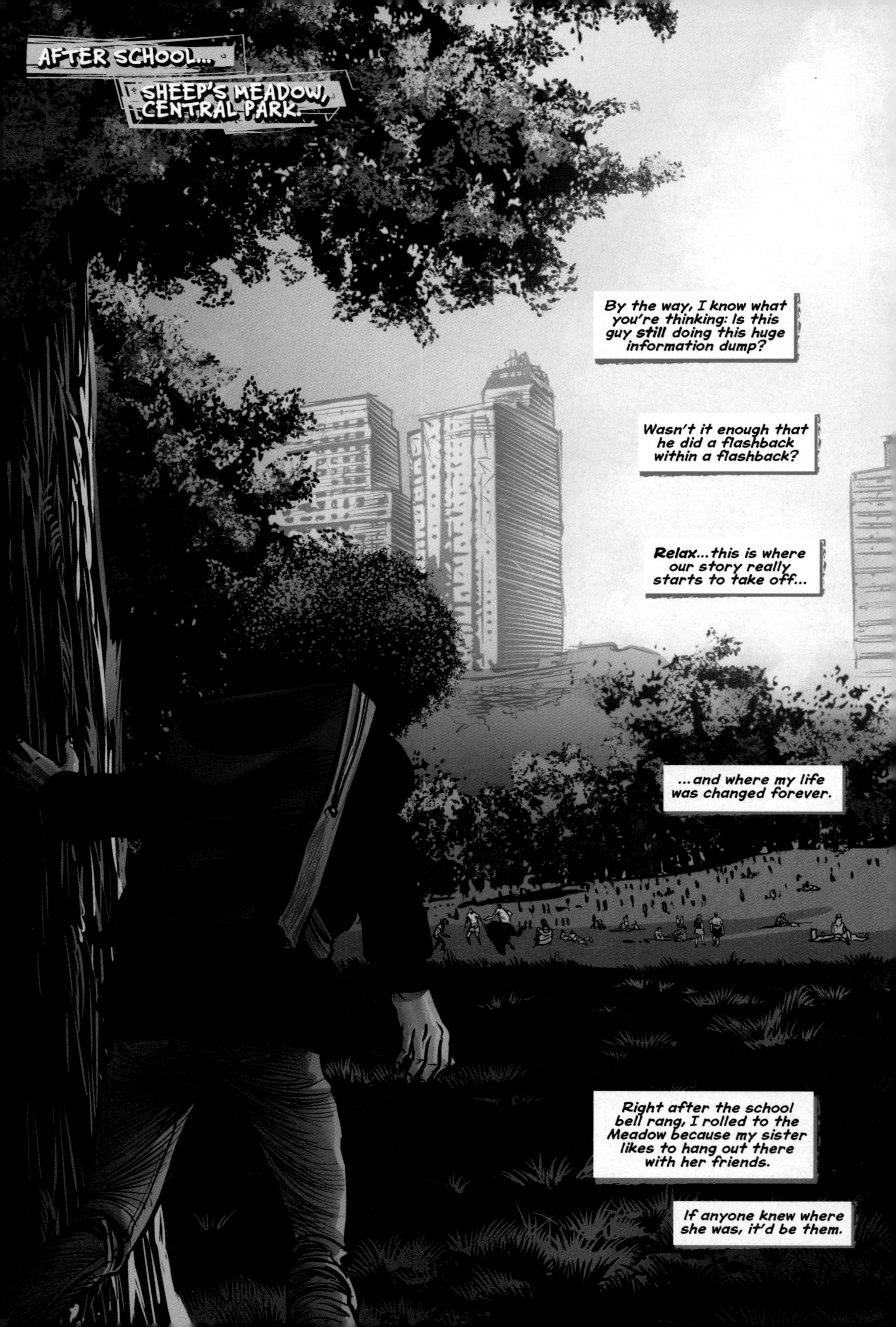
AFTER SCHOOL...
SHEEP'S MEADOW, CENTRAL PARK.
By the way, I know what you're thinking: Is this guy still doing this huge information dump?
Wasn't it enough that he did a flashback within a flashback?
Relax...this is where our story really starts to take off...
...and where my life was changed forever.
Right after the school bell rang, I rolled to the Meadow because my sister likes to hang out there with her friends.
If anyone knew where she was, it'd be them.

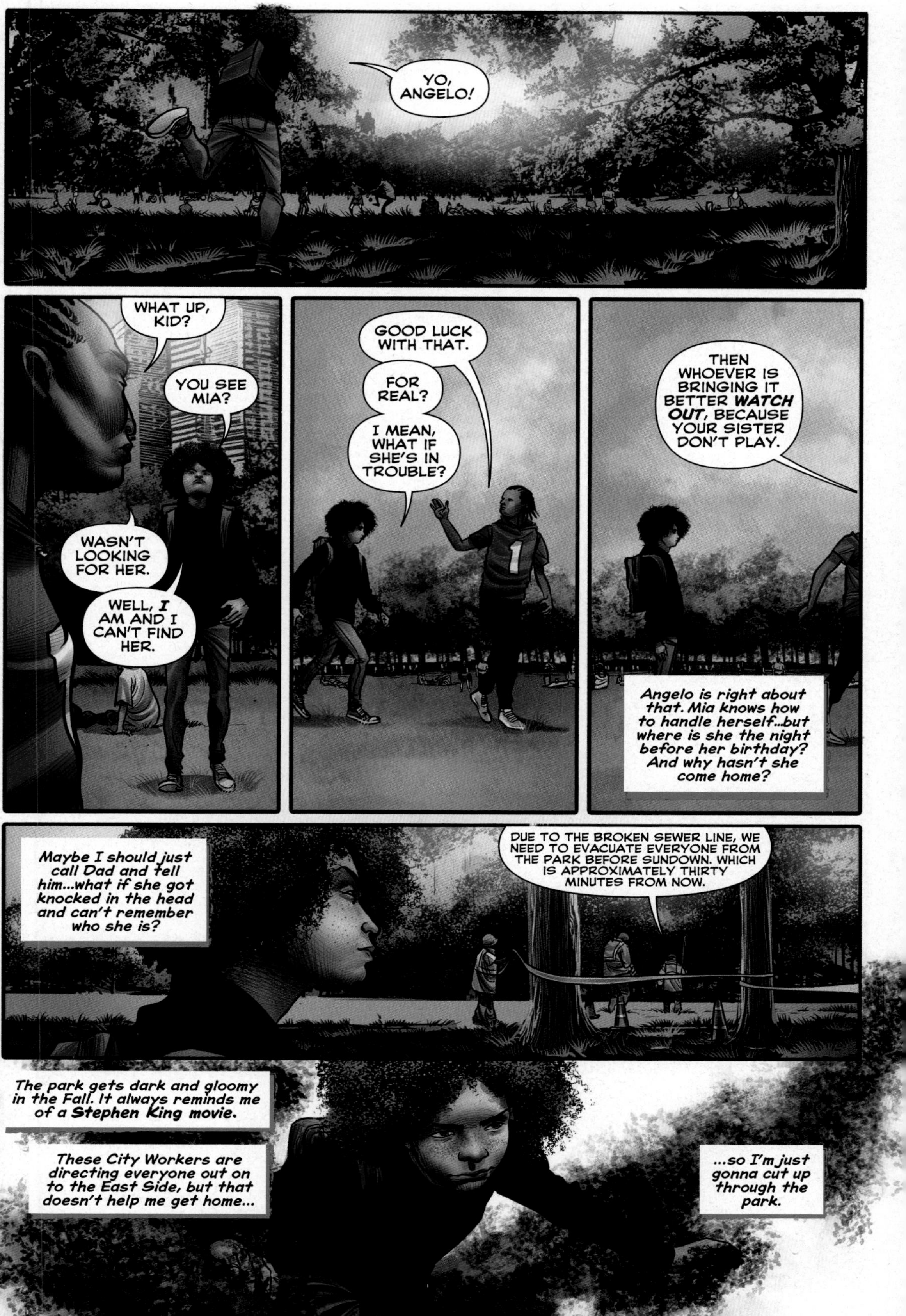
YO, ANGELO!
WHAT UP, KID?
YOU SEE MIA?
WASN'T LOOKING FOR HER.
WELL, I AM AND I CAN'T FIND HER.
GOOD LUCK WITH THAT.
FOR REAL?
I MEAN, WHAT IF SHE'S IN TROUBLE?
THEN WHOEVER IS BRINGING IT BETTER WATCH OUT, BECAUSE YOUR SISTER DON'T PLAY.
Angelo is right about that. Mia knows how to handle herself...but where is she the night before her birthday? And why hasn't she come home?
Maybe I should just call Dad and tell him...what if she got knocked in the head and can't remember who she is?
DUE TO THE BROKEN SEWER LINE, WE NEED TO EVACUATE EVERYONE FROM THE PARK BEFORE SUNDOWN. WHICH IS APPROXIMATELY THIRTY MINUTES FROM NOW.
The park gets dark and gloomy in the Fall. It always reminds me of a Stephen King movie.
These City Workers are directing everyone out on to the East Side, but that doesn't help me get home...
...so I'm just gonna cut up through the park.

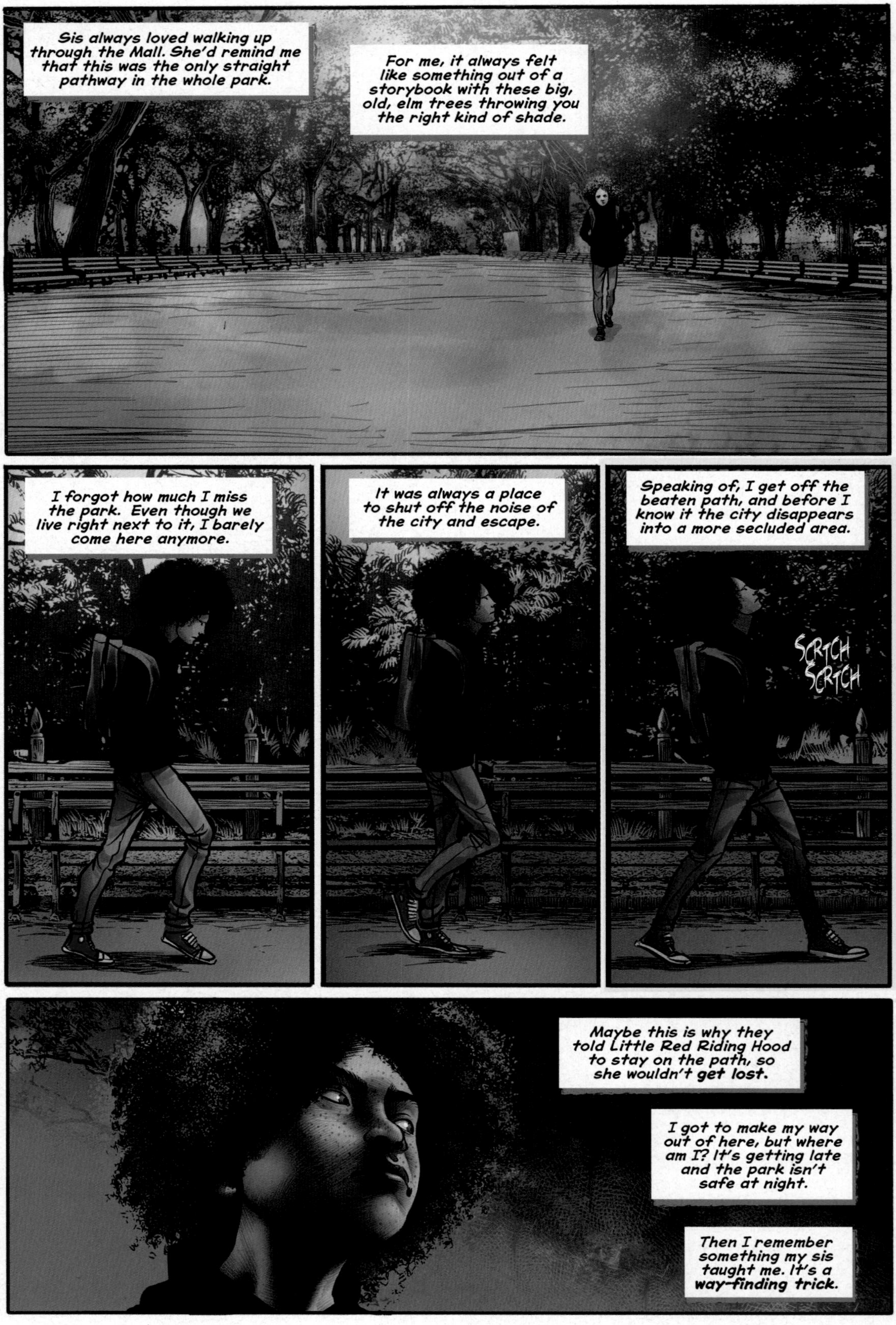
Sis always loved walking up through the Mall. She'd remind me that this was the only straight pathway in the whole park.
For me, it always felt like something out of a storybook with these big, old, elm trees throwing you the right kind of shade.
I forgot how much I miss the park. Even though we live right next to it, I barely come here anymore.
It was always a place to shut off the noise of the city and escape.
Speaking of, I get off the beaten path, and before I know it the city disappears into a more secluded area.
SCRTCH SCRTCH
Maybe this is why they told Little Red Riding Hood to stay on the path, so she wouldn't **get lost**.
I got to make my way out of here, but where am I? It's getting late and the park isn't safe at night.
Then I remember something my sis taught me. It's a **way-finding trick**.

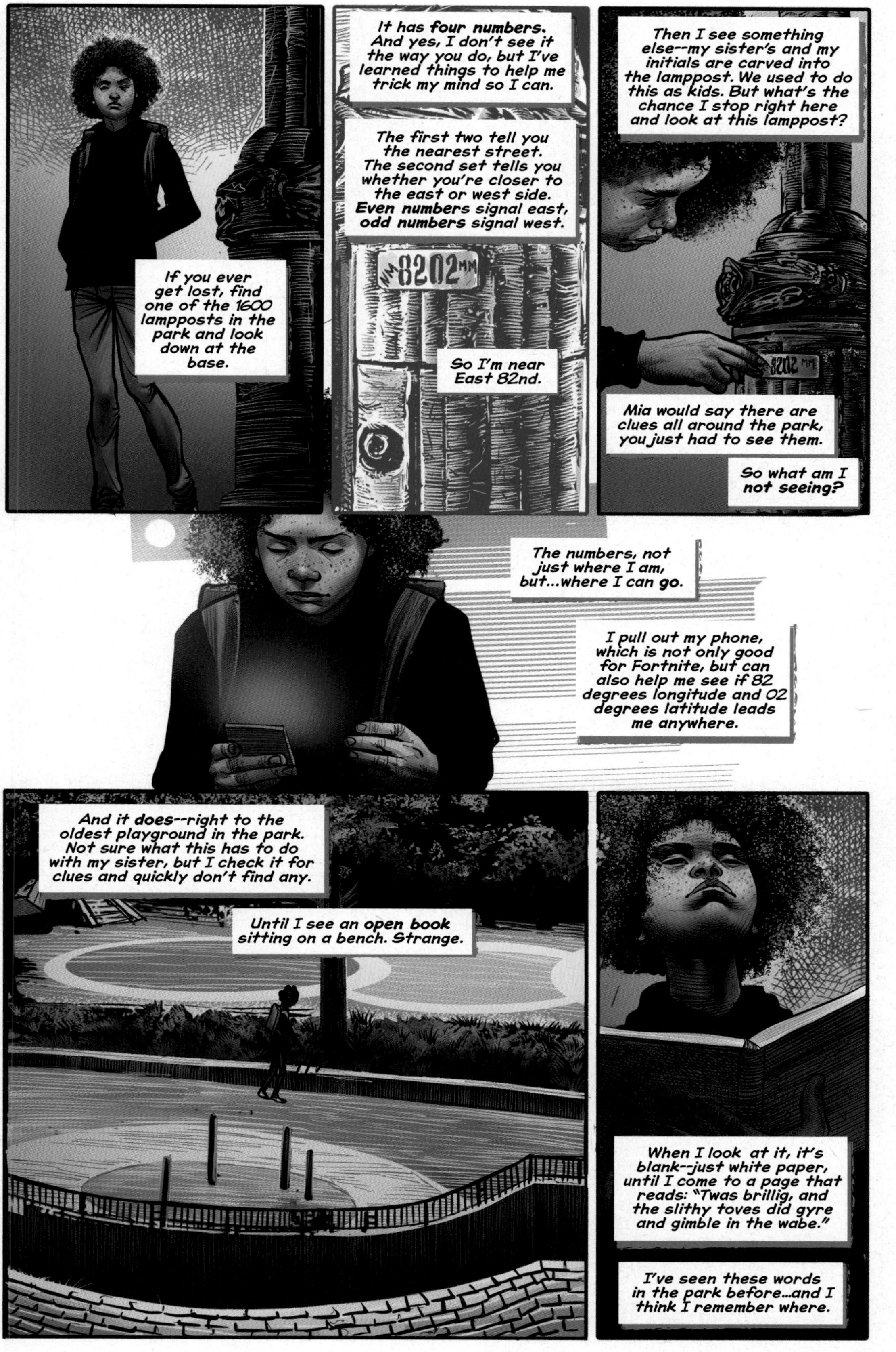
If you ever get lost, find one of the 1600 lampposts in the park and look down at the base.
It has four numbers. And yes, I don't see it the way you do, but I've learned things to help me trick my mind so I can.
The first two tell you the nearest street. The second set tells you whether you're closer to the east or west side. Even numbers signal east, odd numbers signal west.
8202
So I'm near East 82nd.
Then I see something else--my sister's and my initials are carved into the lamppost. We used to do this as kids. But what's the chance I stop right here and look at this lamppost?
Mia would say there are clues all around the park, you just had to see them.
So what am I not seeing?
The numbers, not just where I am, but...where I can go.
I pull out my phone, which is not only good for Fortnite, but can also help me see if 82 degrees longitude and 02 degrees latitude leads me anywhere.
And it does--right to the oldest playground in the park. Not sure what this has to do with my sister, but I check it for clues and quickly don't find any.
Until I see an open book sitting on a bench. Strange.
When I look at it, it's blank--just white paper, until I come to a page that reads: "Twas brillig, and the slithy toves did gyre and gimble in the wabe."
I've seen these words in the park before...and I think I remember where.

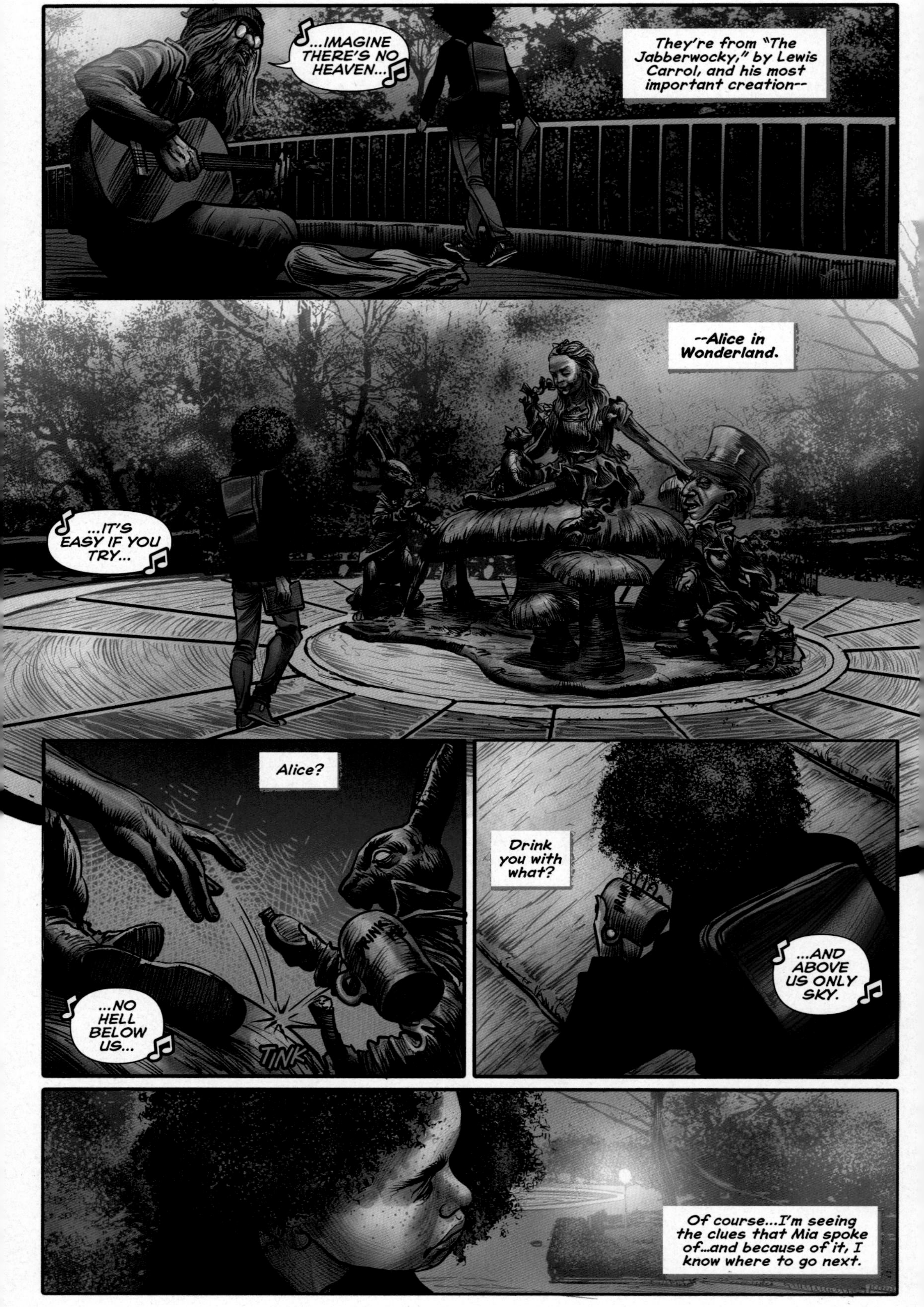

...IMAGINE THERE'S NO HEAVEN...
They're from "The Jabberwocky," by Lewis Carrol, and his most important creation--
--Alice in Wonderland.
...IT'S EASY IF YOU TRY...
Alice?
...NO HELL BELOW US...
TINK
Drink you with what?
...AND ABOVE US ONLY SKY.
Of course...I'm seeing the clues that Mia spoke of...and because of it, I know where to go next.

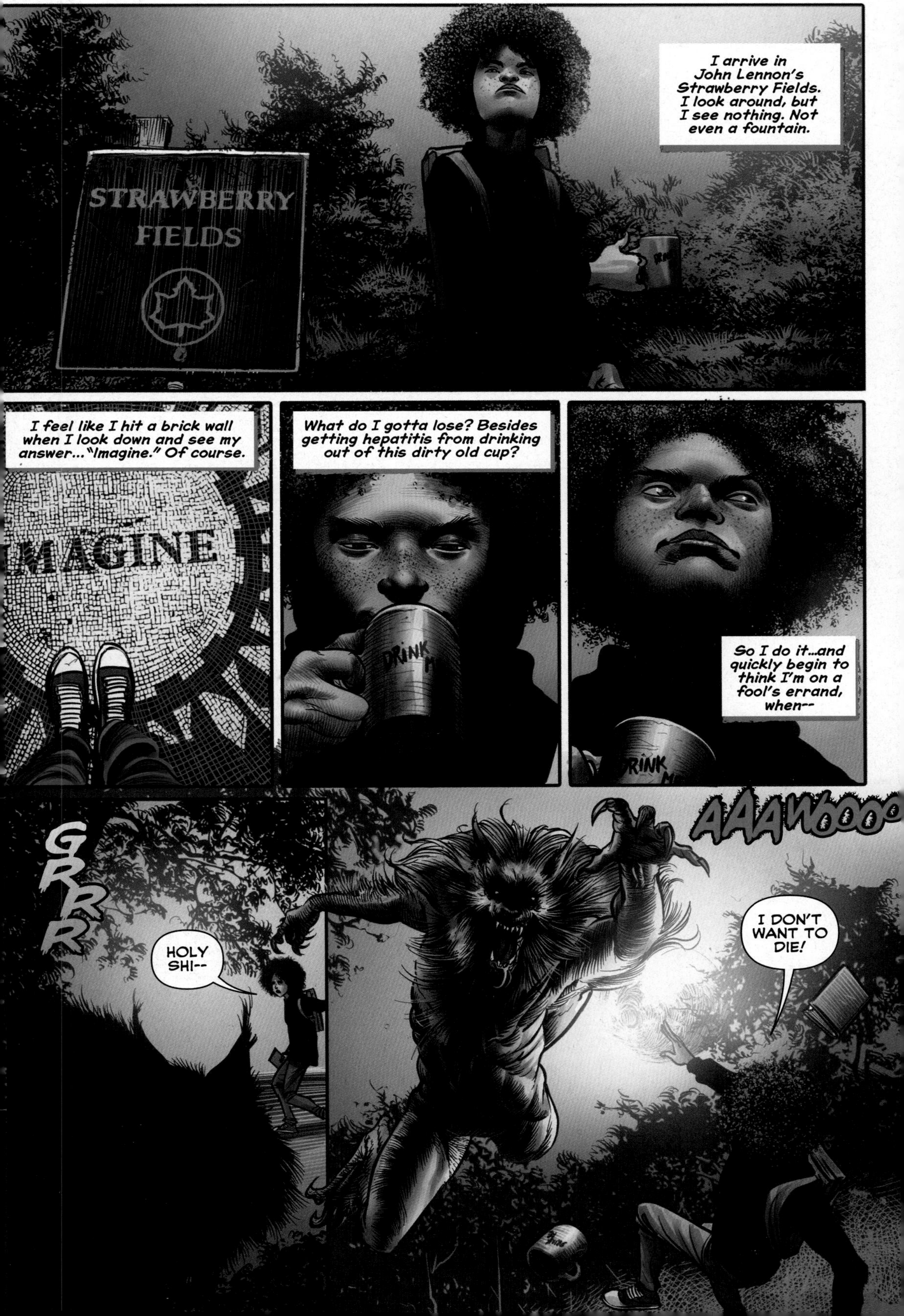
I arrive in John Lennon's Strawberry Fields. I look around, but I see nothing. Not even a fountain.
STRAWBERRY FIELDS
I feel like I hit a brick wall when I look down and see my answer... "Imagine." Of course.
IMAGINE
What do I gotta lose? Besides getting hepatitis from drinking out of this dirty old cup?
DRINK
So I do it...and quickly begin to think I'm on a fool's errand, when--
GRRR
HOLY SHI--
AAAWOOO
I DON'T WANT TO DIE!

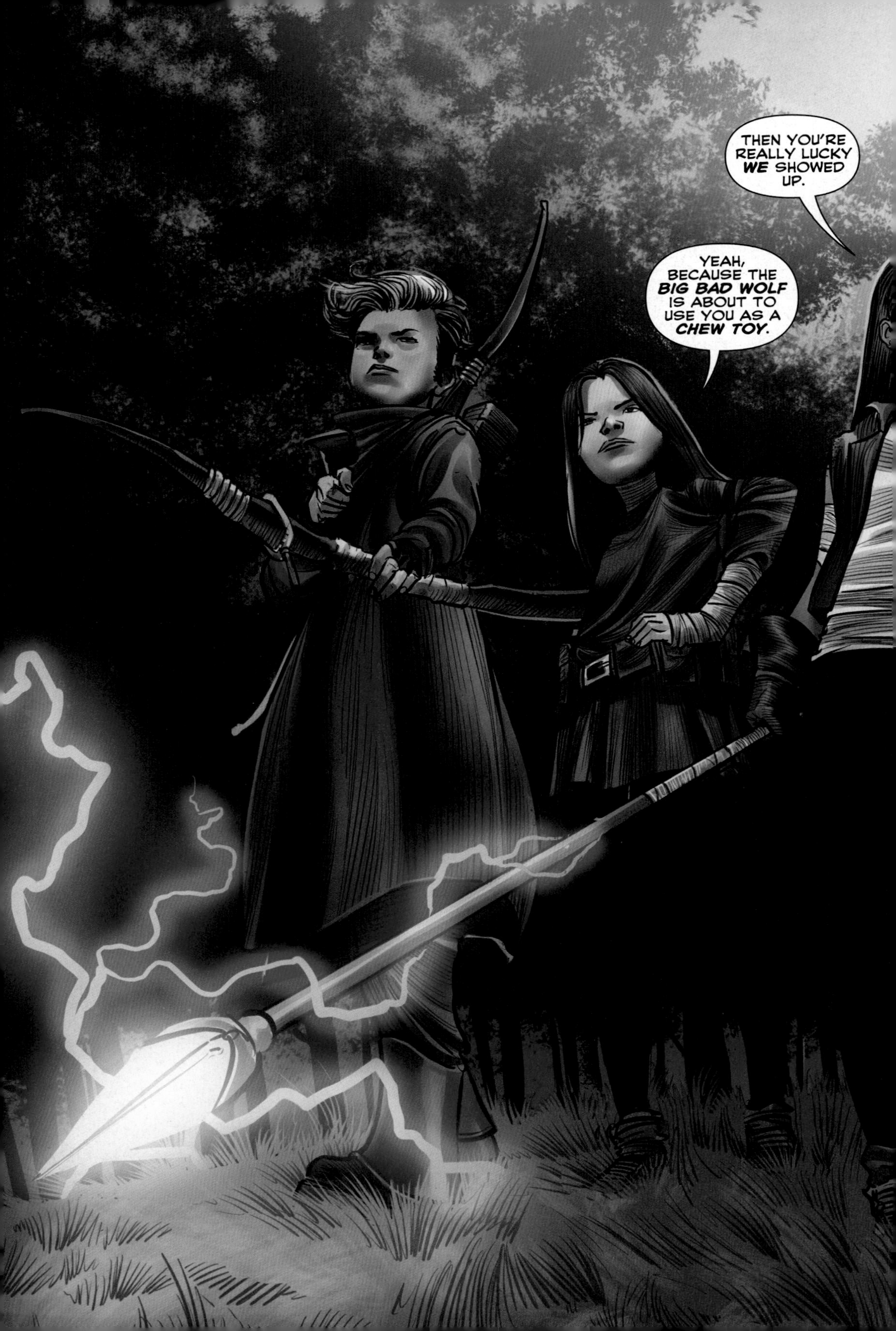
THEN YOU'RE REALLY LUCKY WE SHOWED UP.
YEAH, BECAUSE THE BIG BAD WOLF IS ABOUT TO USE YOU AS A CHEW TOY.

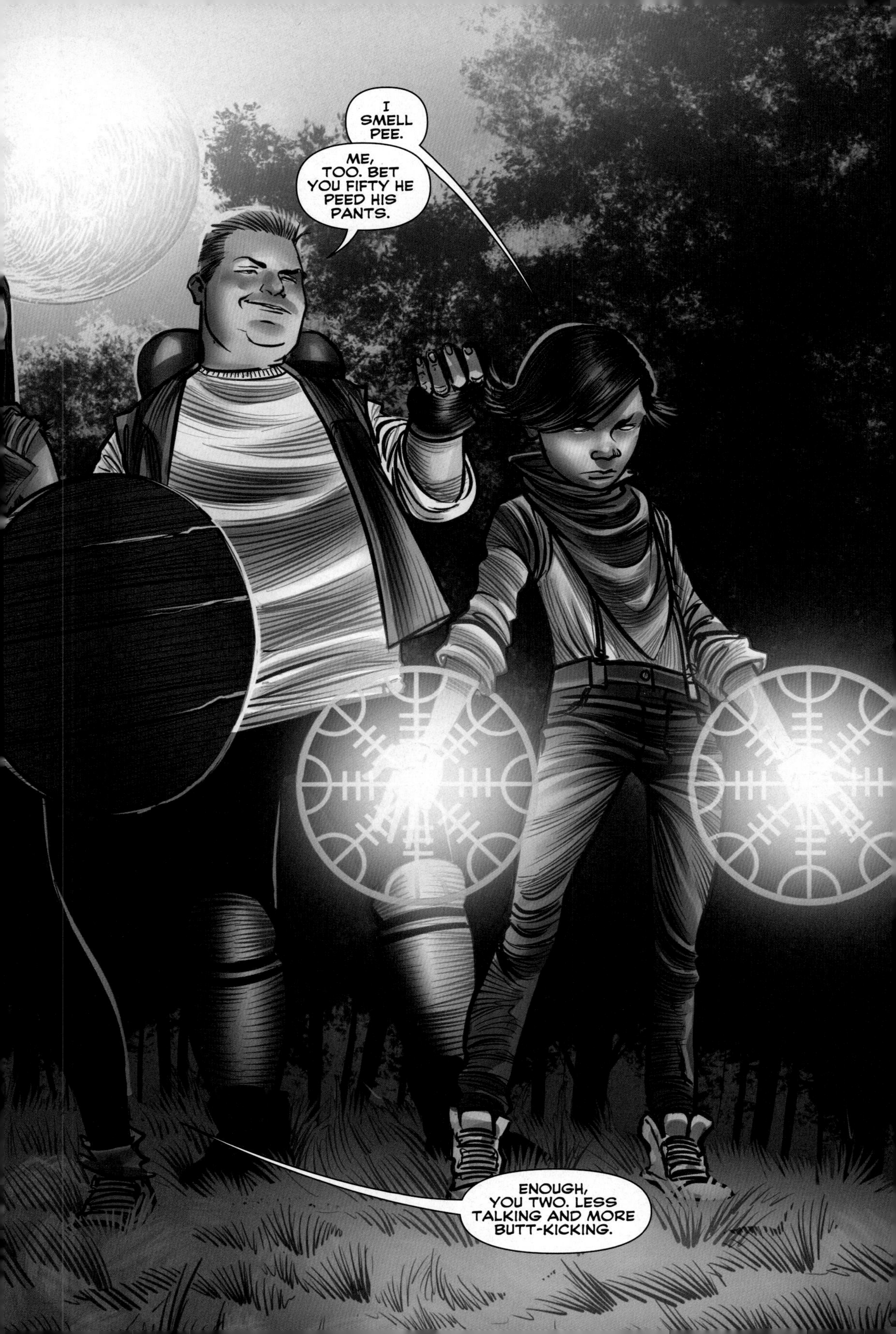
I SMELL PEE.
ME, TOO. BET YOU FIFTY HE PEED HIS PANTS.
ENOUGH, YOU TWO. LESS TALKING AND MORE BUTT-KICKING.

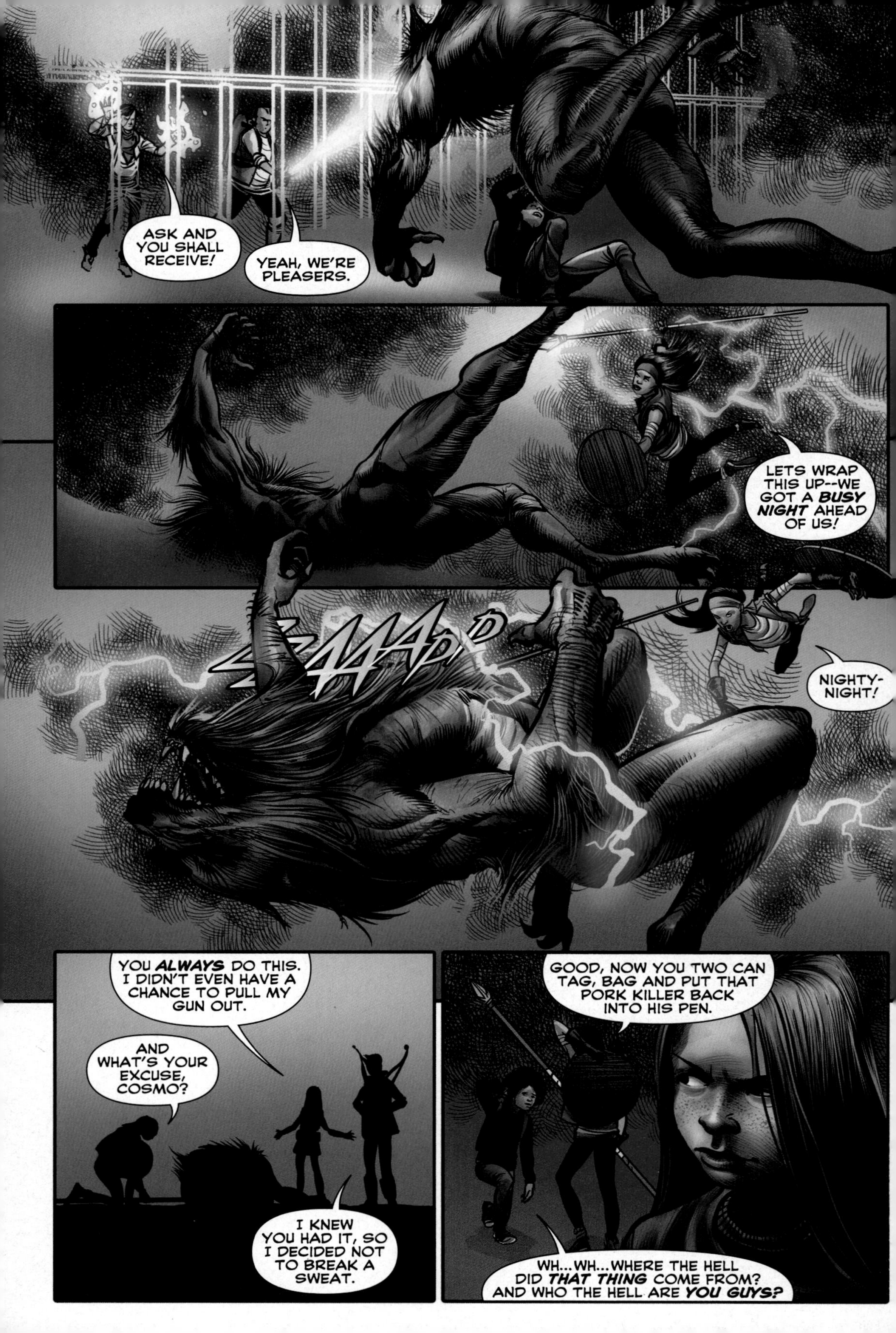
ASK AND YOU SHALL RECEIVE!
YEAH, WE'RE PLEASERS.
LETS WRAP THIS UP--WE GOT A **BUSY NIGHT** AHEAD OF US!
NIGHTY-NIGHT!
YOU **ALWAYS** DO THIS. I DIDN'T EVEN HAVE A CHANCE TO PULL MY GUN OUT.
AND WHAT'S YOUR EXCUSE, COSMO?
I KNEW YOU HAD IT, SO I DECIDED NOT TO BREAK A SWEAT.
GOOD, NOW YOU TWO CAN TAG, BAG AND PUT THAT PORK KILLER BACK INTO HIS PEN.
WH...WH...WHERE THE HELL DID ***THAT THING*** COME FROM? AND WHO THE HELL ARE ***YOU GUYS?***

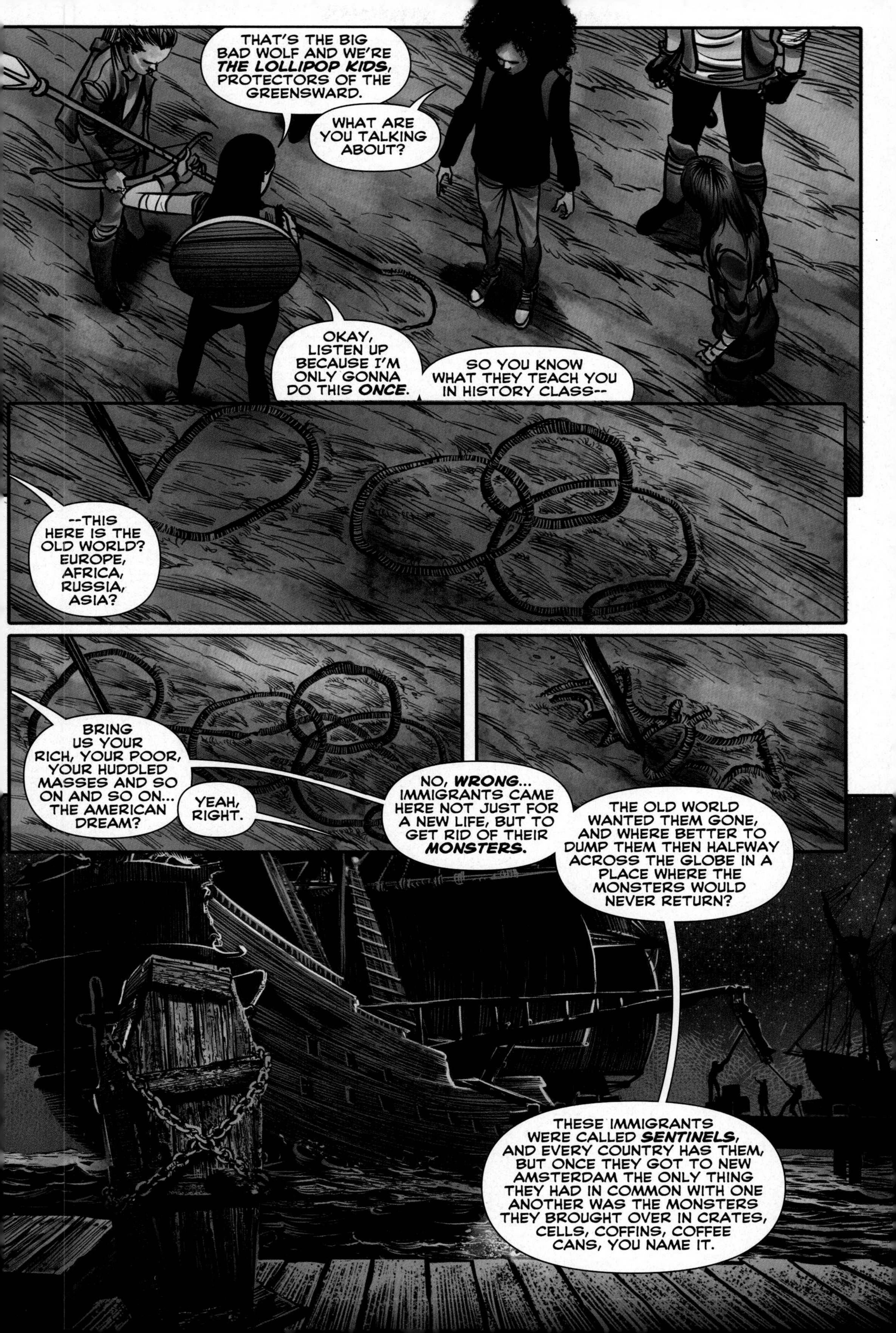
THAT'S THE BIG BAD WOLF AND WE'RE THE LOLLIPOP KIDS, PROTECTORS OF THE GREENSWARD.
WHAT ARE YOU TALKING ABOUT?
OKAY, LISTEN UP BECAUSE I'M ONLY GONNA DO THIS ONCE.
SO YOU KNOW WHAT THEY TEACH YOU IN HISTORY CLASS--
--THIS HERE IS THE OLD WORLD? EUROPE, AFRICA, RUSSIA, ASIA?
BRING US YOUR RICH, YOUR POOR, YOUR HUDDLED MASSES AND SO ON AND SO ON... THE AMERICAN DREAM?
YEAH, RIGHT.
NO, WRONG... IMMIGRANTS CAME HERE NOT JUST FOR A NEW LIFE, BUT TO GET RID OF THEIR MONSTERS.
THE OLD WORLD WANTED THEM GONE, AND WHERE BETTER TO DUMP THEM THEN HALFWAY ACROSS THE GLOBE IN A PLACE WHERE THE MONSTERS WOULD NEVER RETURN?
THESE IMMIGRANTS WERE CALLED SENTINELS, AND EVERY COUNTRY HAS THEM, BUT ONCE THEY GOT TO NEW AMSTERDAM THE ONLY THING THEY HAD IN COMMON WITH ONE ANOTHER WAS THE MONSTERS THEY BROUGHT OVER IN CRATES, CELLS, COFFINS, COFFEE CANS, YOU NAME IT.

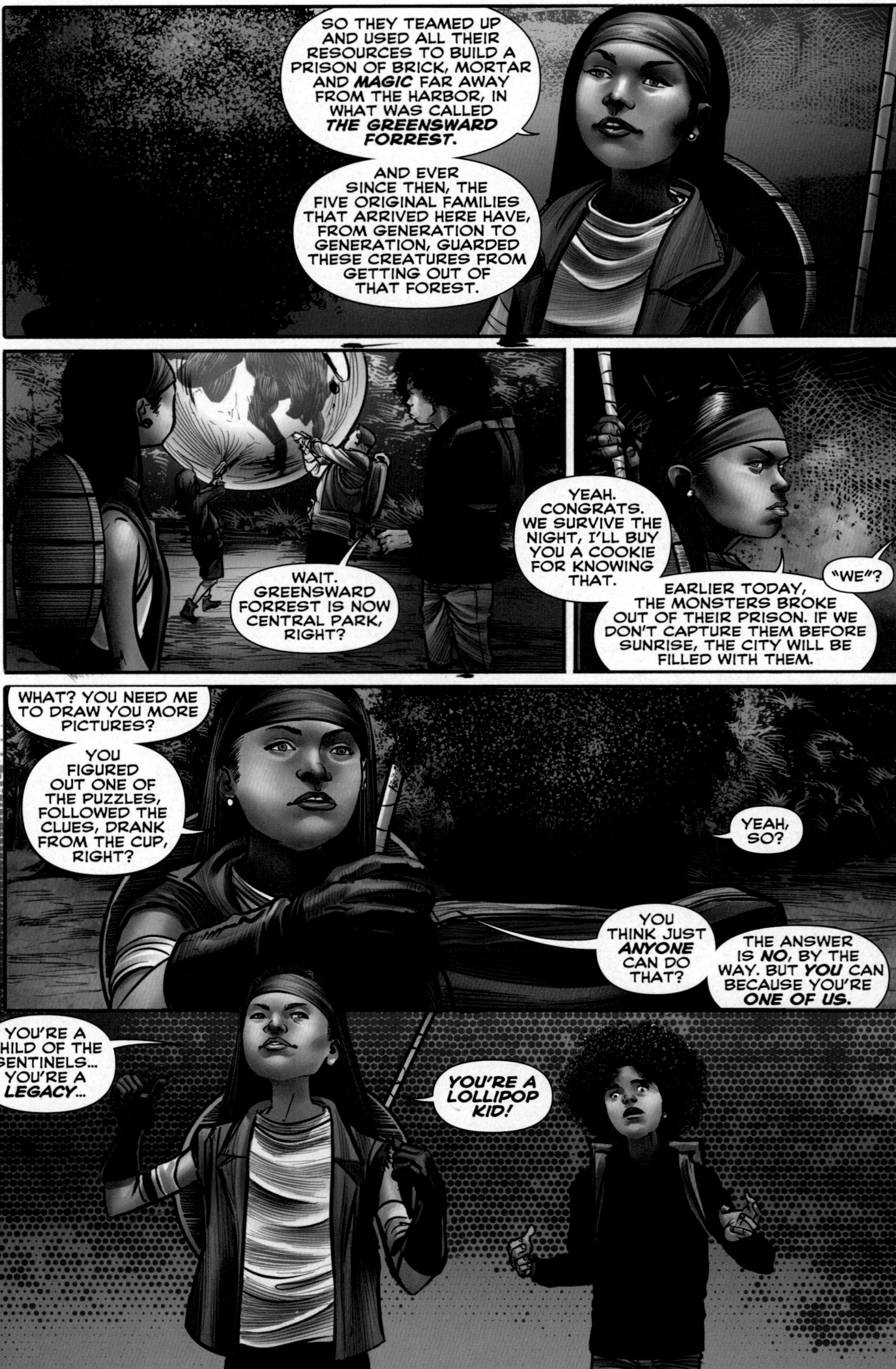
SO THEY TEAMED UP AND USED ALL THEIR RESOURCES TO BUILD A PRISON OF BRICK, MORTAR AND MAGIC FAR AWAY FROM THE HARBOR, IN WHAT WAS CALLED THE GREENSWARD FORREST.
AND EVER SINCE THEN, THE FIVE ORIGINAL FAMILIES THAT ARRIVED HERE HAVE, FROM GENERATION TO GENERATION, GUARDED THESE CREATURES FROM GETTING OUT OF THAT FOREST.
WAIT. GREENSWARD FORREST IS NOW CENTRAL PARK, RIGHT?
YEAH. CONGRATS. WE SURVIVE THE NIGHT, I'LL BUY YOU A COOKIE FOR KNOWING THAT.
"WE"?
EARLIER TODAY, THE MONSTERS BROKE OUT OF THEIR PRISON. IF WE DON'T CAPTURE THEM BEFORE SUNRISE, THE CITY WILL BE FILLED WITH THEM.
WHAT? YOU NEED ME TO DRAW YOU MORE PICTURES?
YOU FIGURED OUT ONE OF THE PUZZLES, FOLLOWED THE CLUES, DRANK FROM THE CUP, RIGHT?
YEAH, SO?
YOU THINK JUST ANYONE CAN DO THAT?
THE ANSWER IS NO, BY THE WAY. BUT YOU CAN BECAUSE YOU'RE ONE OF US.
YOU'RE A CHILD OF THE SENTINELS... YOU'RE A LEGACY...
YOU'RE A LOLLIPOP KID!

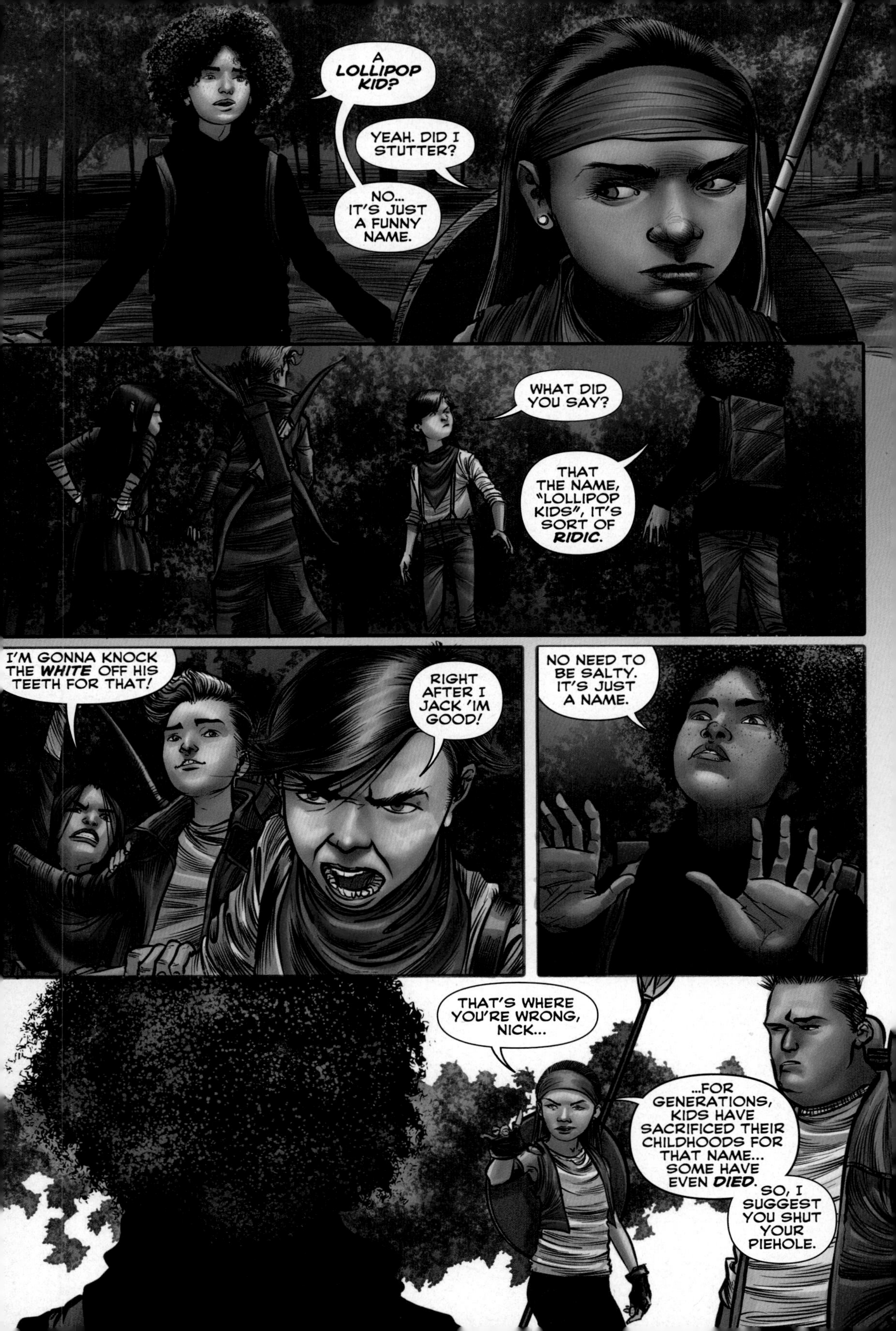
A LOLLIPOP KID?
YEAH. DID I STUTTER?
NO... IT'S JUST A FUNNY NAME.
WHAT DID YOU SAY?
THAT THE NAME, "LOLLIPOP KIDS", IT'S SORT OF RIDIC.
I'M GONNA KNOCK THE WHITE OFF HIS TEETH FOR THAT!
RIGHT AFTER I JACK 'IM GOOD!
NO NEED TO BE SALTY. IT'S JUST A NAME.
THAT'S WHERE YOU'RE WRONG, NICK...
...FOR GENERATIONS, KIDS HAVE SACRIFICED THEIR CHILDHOODS FOR THAT NAME... SOME HAVE EVEN DIED.
SO, I SUGGEST YOU SHUT YOUR PIEHOLE.

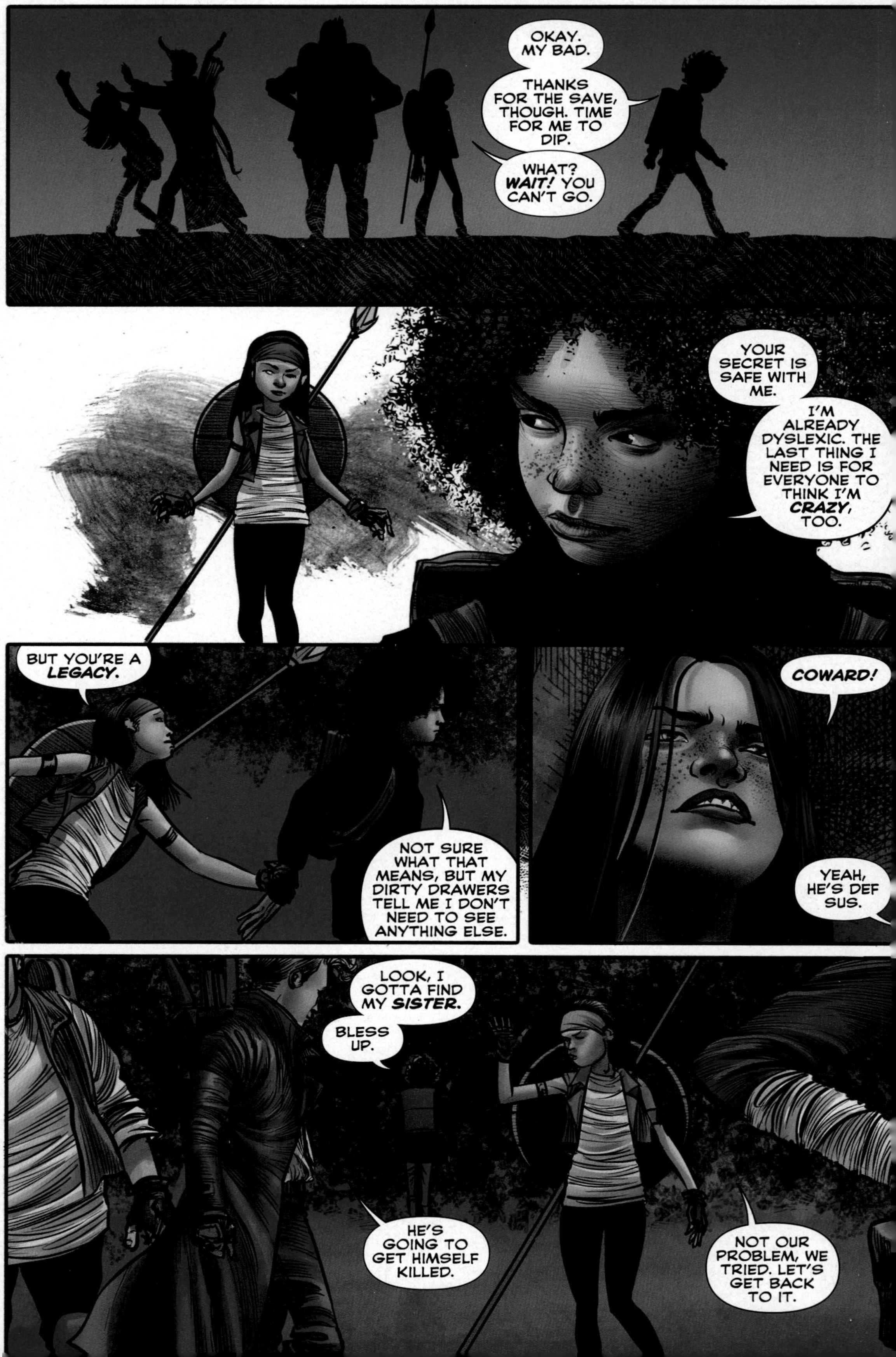
OKAY. MY BAD.
THANKS FOR THE SAVE, THOUGH. TIME FOR ME TO DIP.
WHAT? *WAIT!* YOU CAN'T GO.
YOUR SECRET IS SAFE WITH ME.
I'M ALREADY DYSLEXIC. THE LAST THING I NEED IS FOR EVERYONE TO THINK I'M *CRAZY*, TOO.
BUT YOU'RE A *LEGACY*.
NOT SURE WHAT THAT MEANS, BUT MY DIRTY DRAWERS TELL ME I DON'T NEED TO SEE ANYTHING ELSE.
COWARD!
YEAH, HE'S DEF SUS.
LOOK, I GOTTA FIND MY *SISTER*.
BLESS UP.
HE'S GOING TO GET HIMSELF KILLED.
NOT OUR PROBLEM, WE TRIED. LET'S GET BACK TO IT.

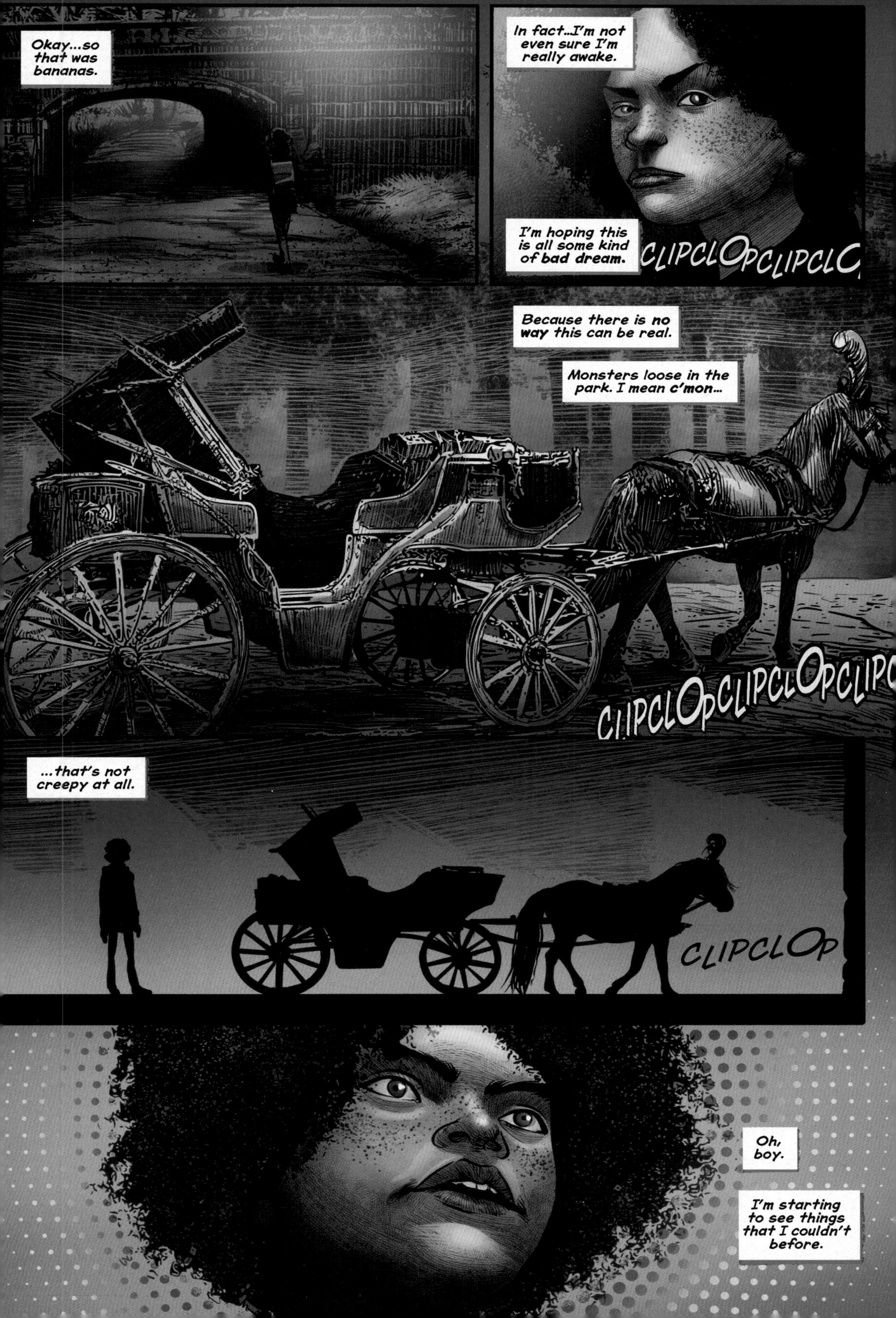

Okay...so that was bananas.
In fact...I'm not even sure I'm really awake.
I'm hoping this is all some kind of bad dream.
CLIPCLOPCLIPCLO
Because there is no way this can be real.
Monsters loose in the park. I mean c'mon...
CLIPCLOPCLIPCLOPCLIP
...that's not creepy at all.
CLIPCLOP
Oh, boy.
I'm starting to see things that I couldn't before.

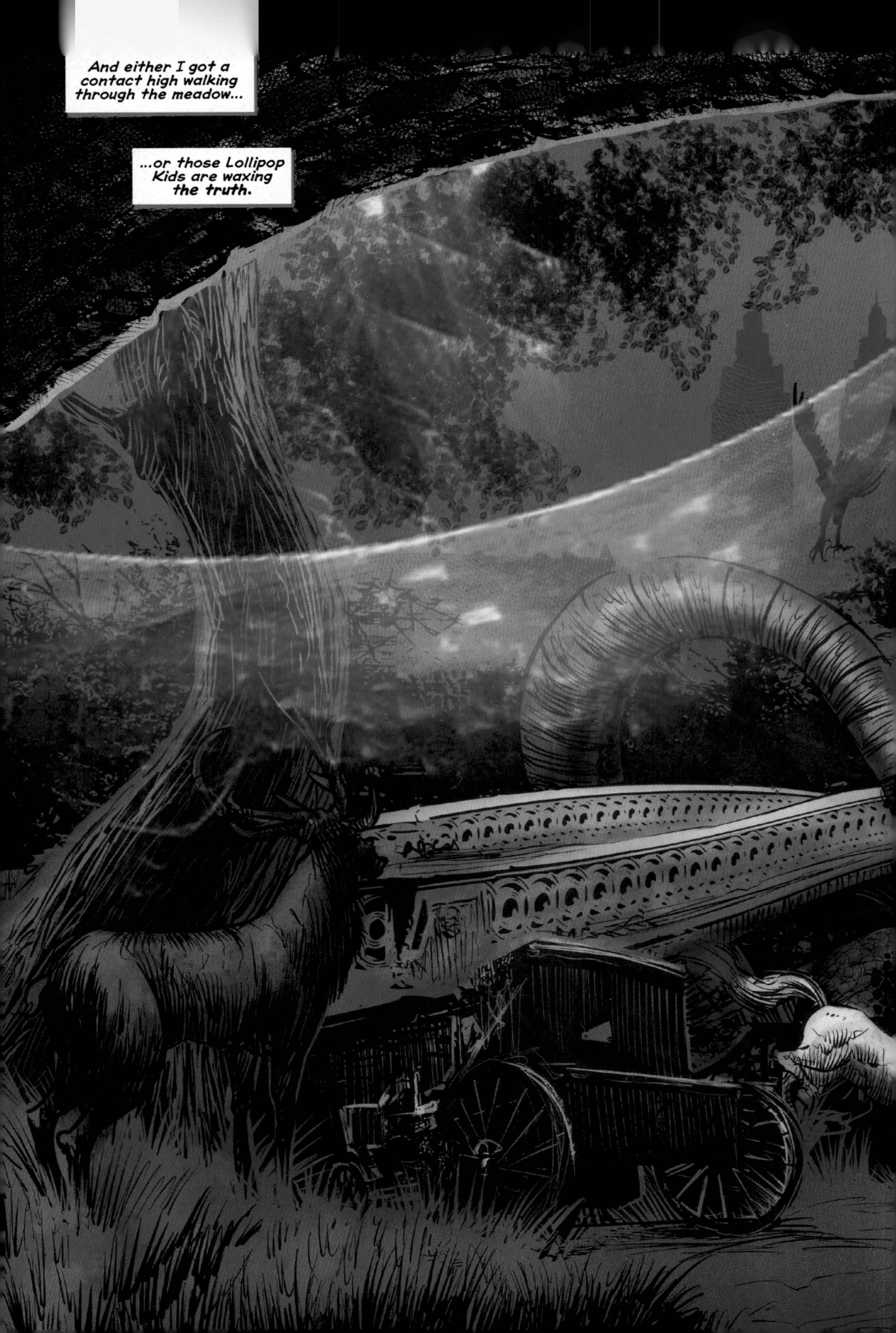
And either I got a contact high walking through the meadow...
...or those Lollipop Kids are waxing the truth.

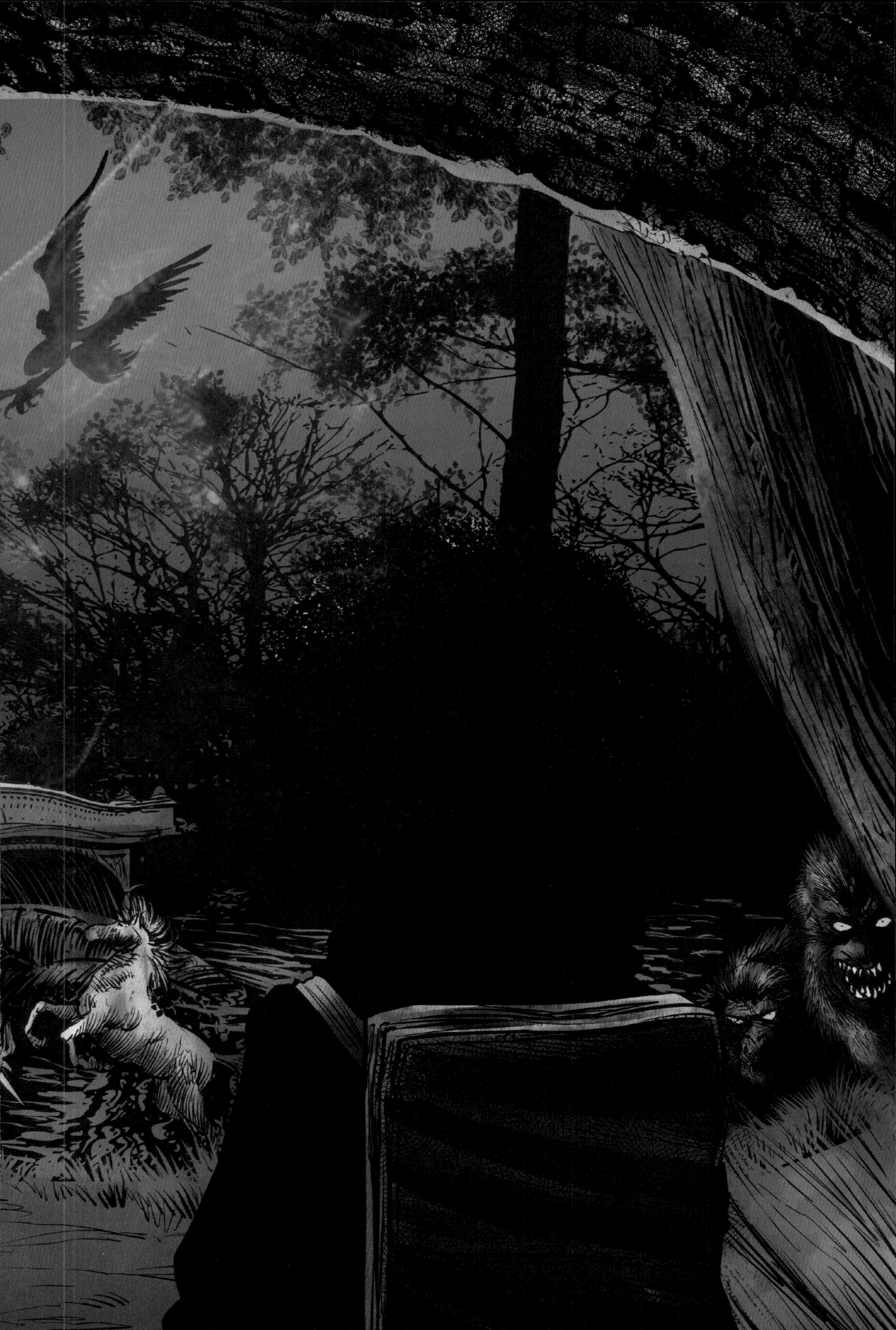

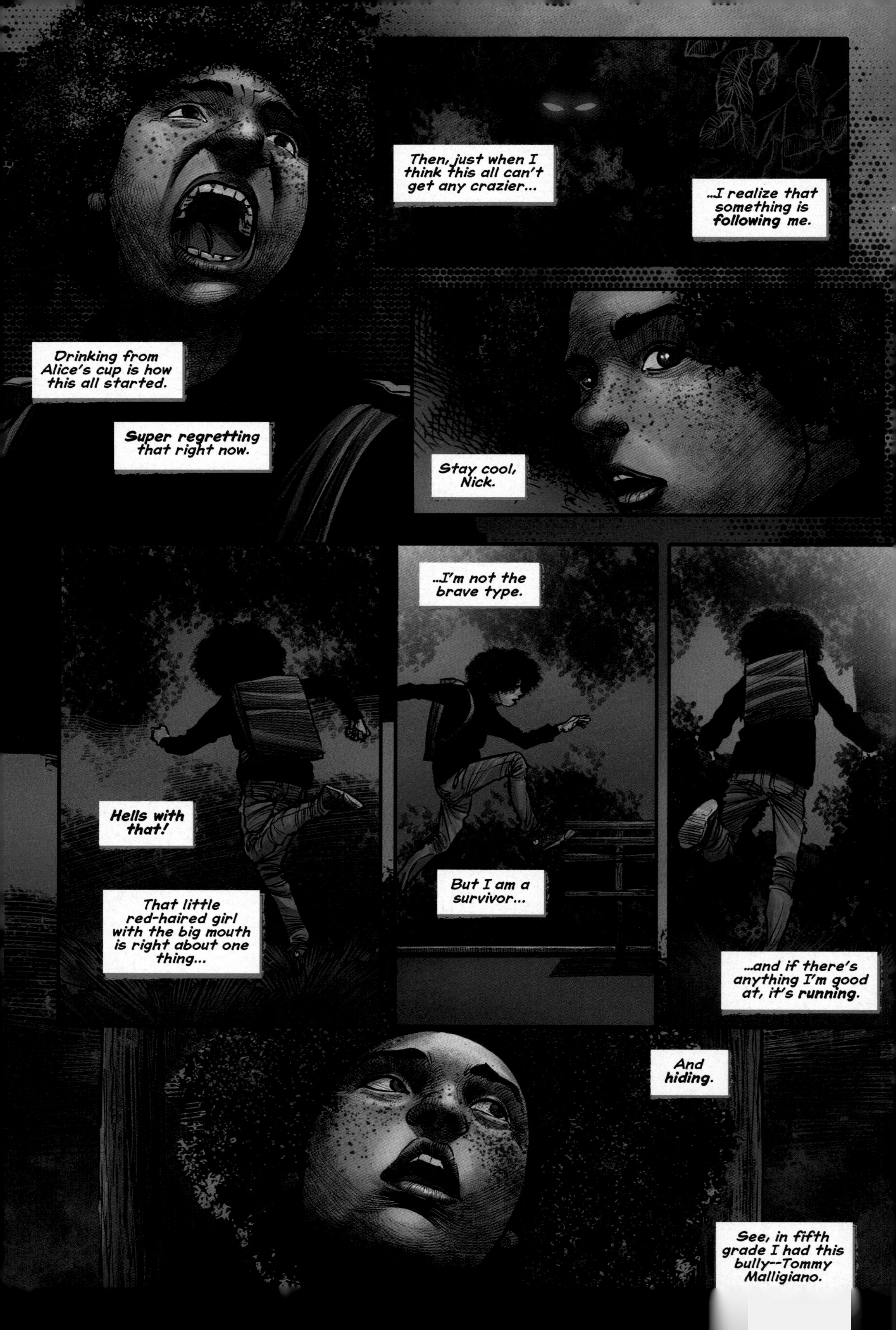
Then, just when I think this all can't get any crazier...
...I realize that something is following me.
Drinking from Alice's cup is how this all started.
Super regretting that right now.
Stay cool, Nick.
Hells with that!
That little red-haired girl with the big mouth is right about one thing...
...I'm not the brave type.
But I am a survivor...
...and if there's anything I'm good at, it's running.
And hiding.
See, in fifth grade I had this bully--Tommy Malligiano.

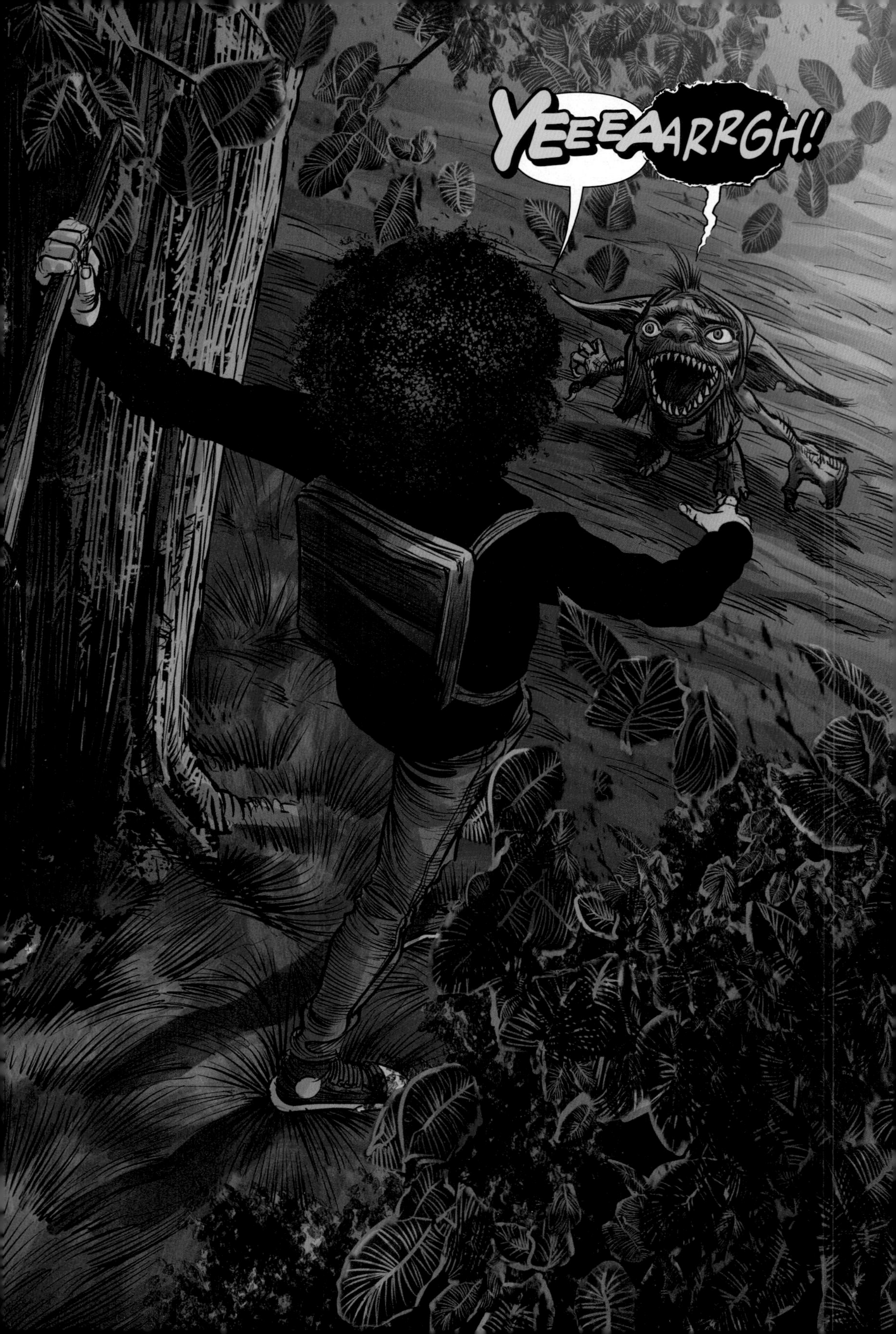
YEEEAARRGH!

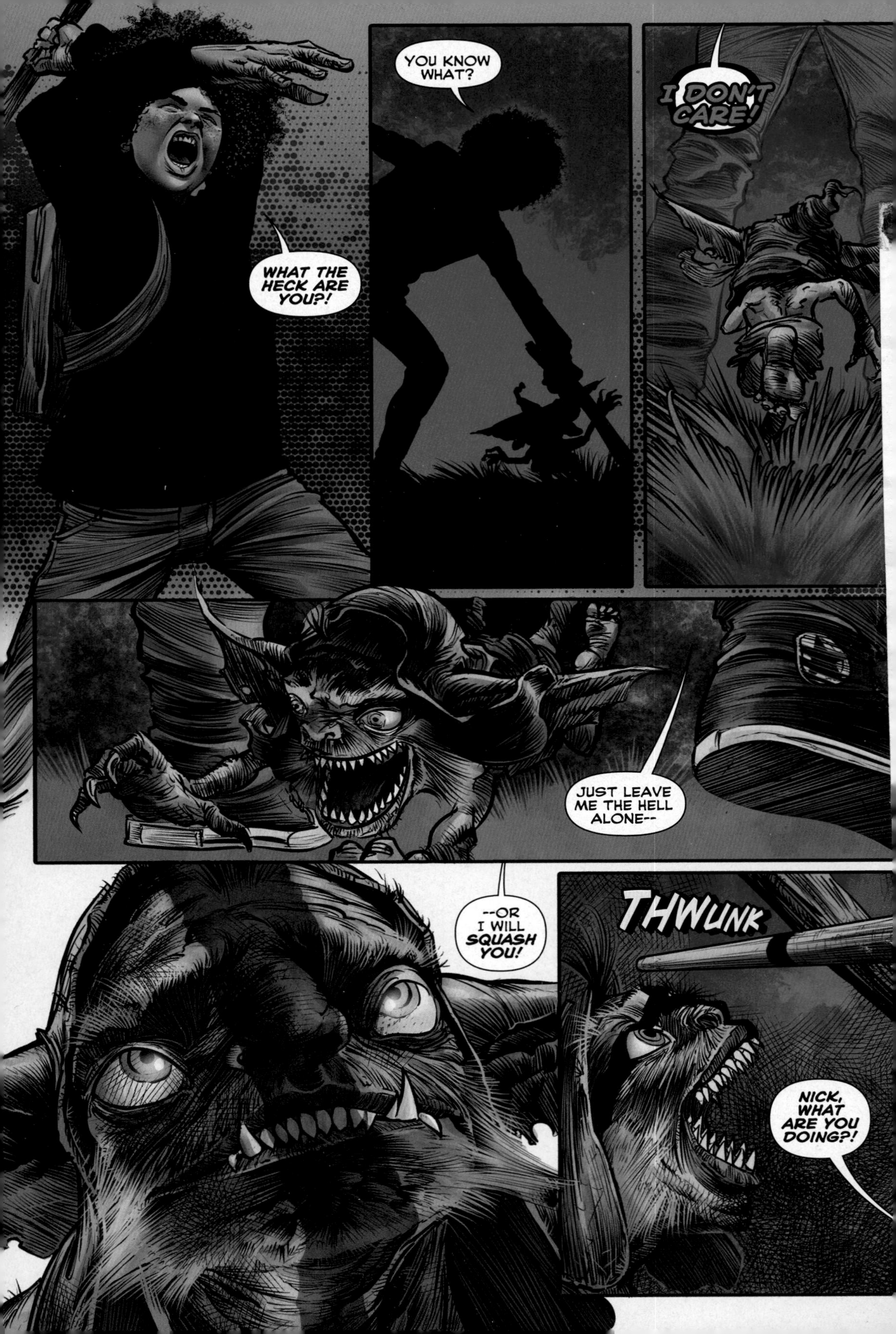
WHAT THE HECK ARE YOU?!
YOU KNOW WHAT?
I DON'T CARE!
JUST LEAVE ME THE HELL ALONE--
--OR I WILL SQUASH YOU!
THWUNK
NICK, WHAT ARE YOU DOING?!

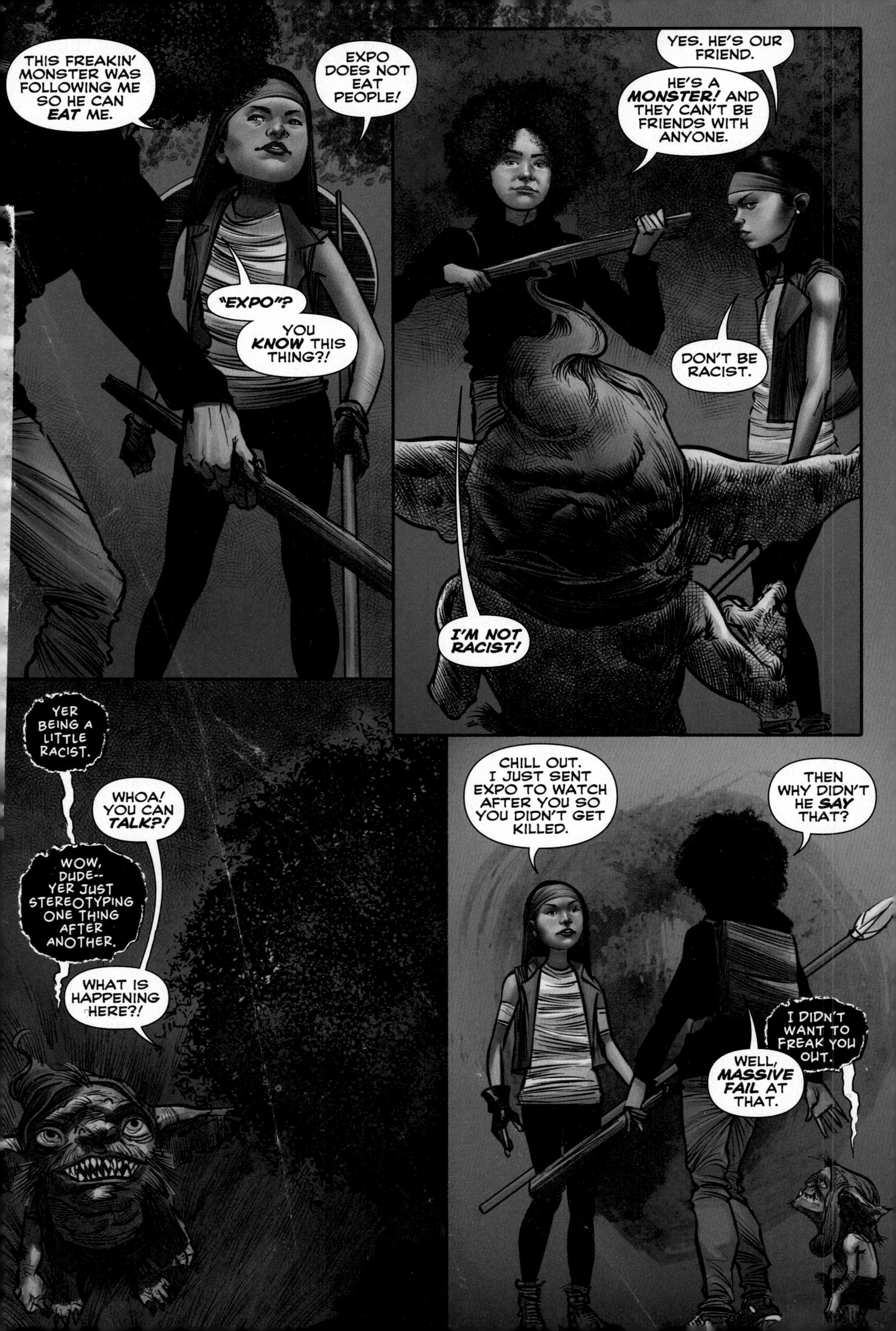
THIS FREAKIN' MONSTER WAS FOLLOWING ME SO HE CAN EAT ME.
EXPO DOES NOT EAT PEOPLE!
"EXPO"?
YOU KNOW THIS THING?!
YES. HE'S OUR FRIEND.
HE'S A MONSTER! AND THEY CAN'T BE FRIENDS WITH ANYONE.
DON'T BE RACIST.
I'M NOT RACIST!
YER BEING A LITTLE RACIST.
WHOA! YOU CAN TALK?!
WOW, DUDE-- YER JUST STEREOTYPING ONE THING AFTER ANOTHER.
WHAT IS HAPPENING HERE?!
CHILL OUT. I JUST SENT EXPO TO WATCH AFTER YOU SO YOU DIDN'T GET KILLED.
THEN WHY DIDN'T HE SAY THAT?
I DIDN'T WANT TO FREAK YOU OUT.
WELL, MASSIVE FAIL AT THAT.

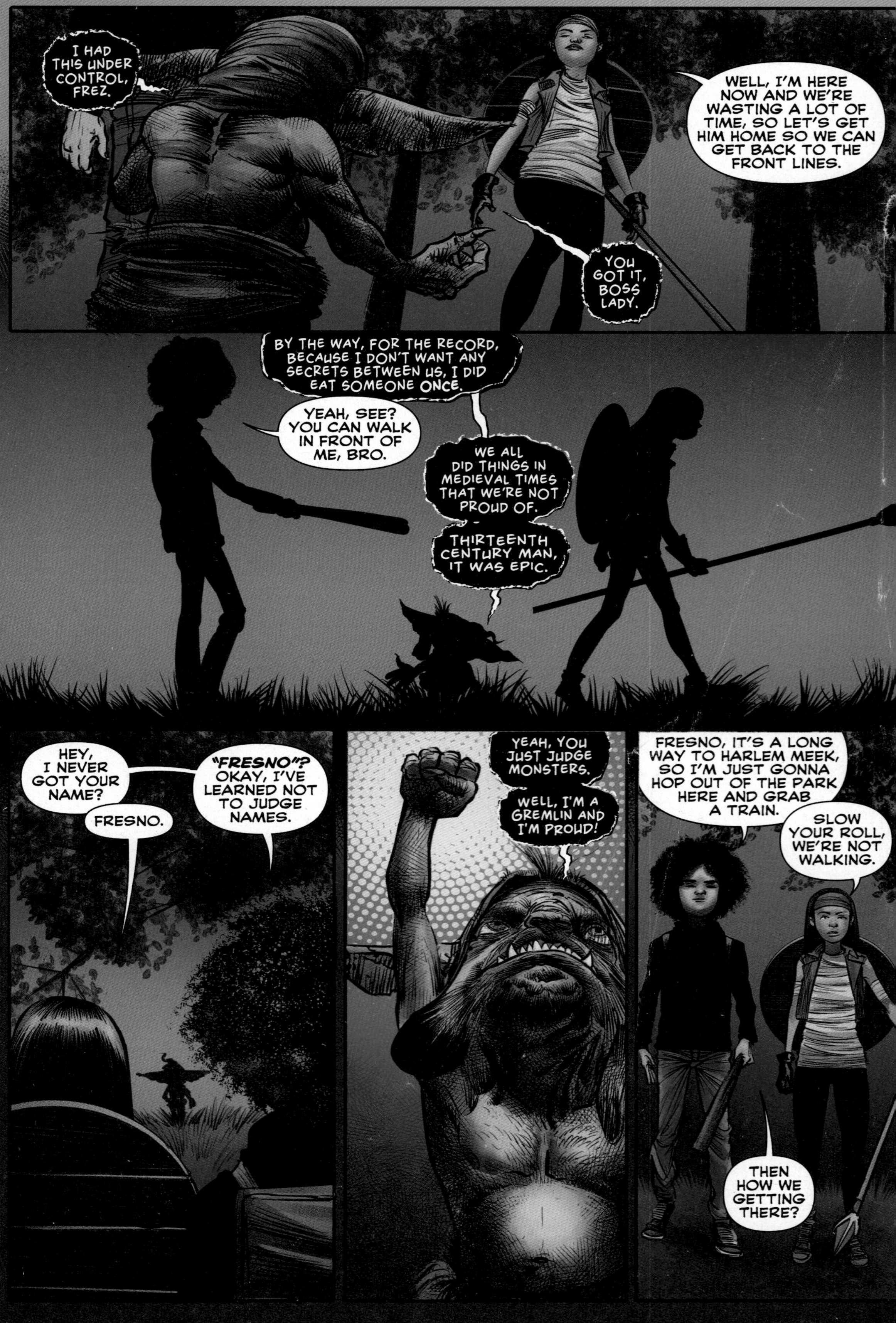
I HAD THIS UNDER CONTROL, FREZ.
WELL, I'M HERE NOW AND WE'RE WASTING A LOT OF TIME, SO LET'S GET HIM HOME SO WE CAN GET BACK TO THE FRONT LINES.
YOU GOT IT, BOSS LADY.
BY THE WAY, FOR THE RECORD, BECAUSE I DON'T WANT ANY SECRETS BETWEEN US, I DID EAT SOMEONE ONCE.
YEAH, SEE? YOU CAN WALK IN FRONT OF ME, BRO.
WE ALL DID THINGS IN MEDIEVAL TIMES THAT WE'RE NOT PROUD OF.
THIRTEENTH CENTURY MAN, IT WAS EPIC.
HEY, I NEVER GOT YOUR NAME?
FRESNO.
"FRESNO"? OKAY, I'VE LEARNED NOT TO JUDGE NAMES.
YEAH, YOU JUST JUDGE MONSTERS.
WELL, I'M A GREMLIN AND I'M PROUD!
FRESNO, IT'S A LONG WAY TO HARLEM MEEK, SO I'M JUST GONNA HOP OUT OF THE PARK HERE AND GRAB A TRAIN.
SLOW YOUR ROLL, WE'RE NOT WALKING.
THEN HOW WE GETTING THERE?

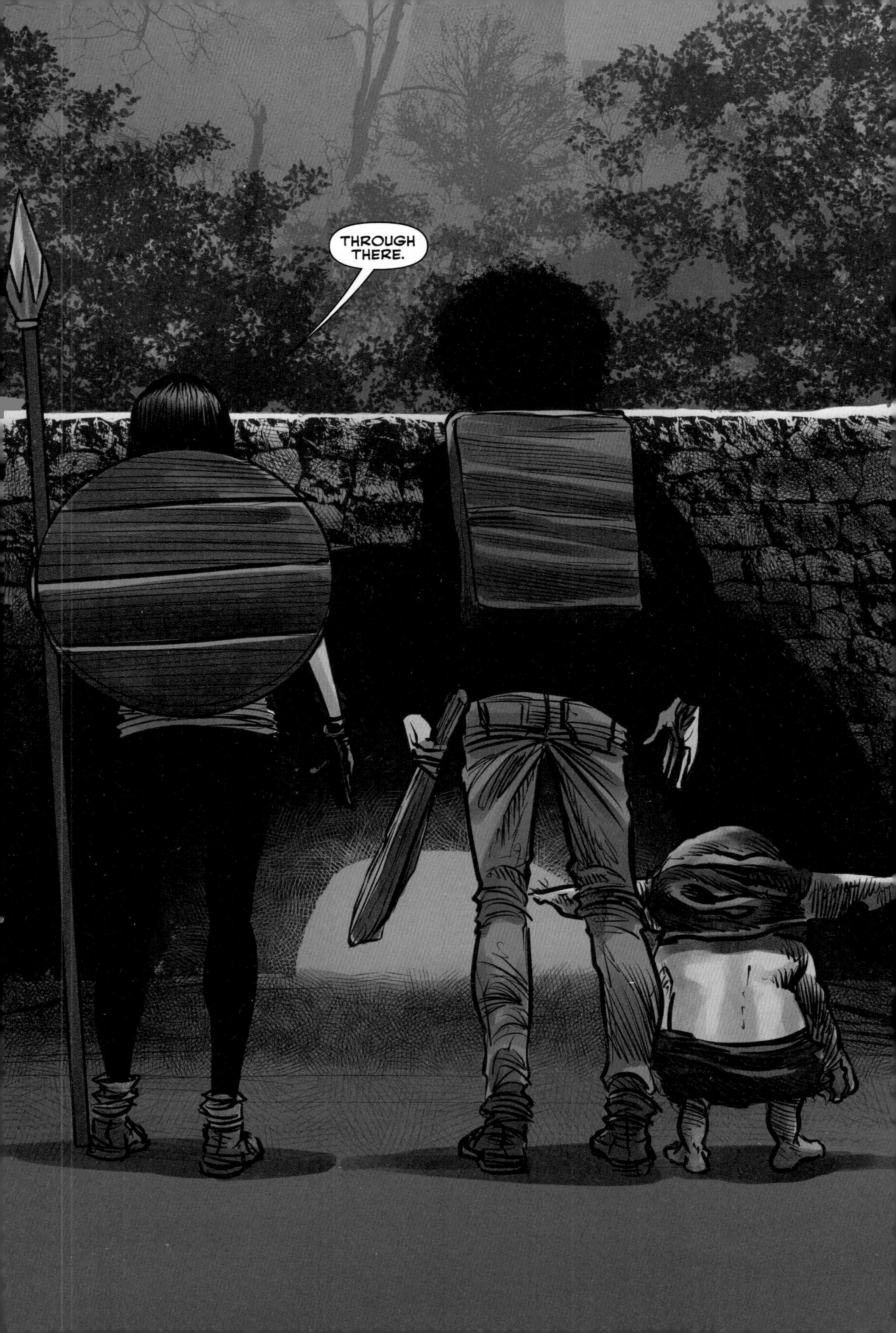
THROUGH THERE.

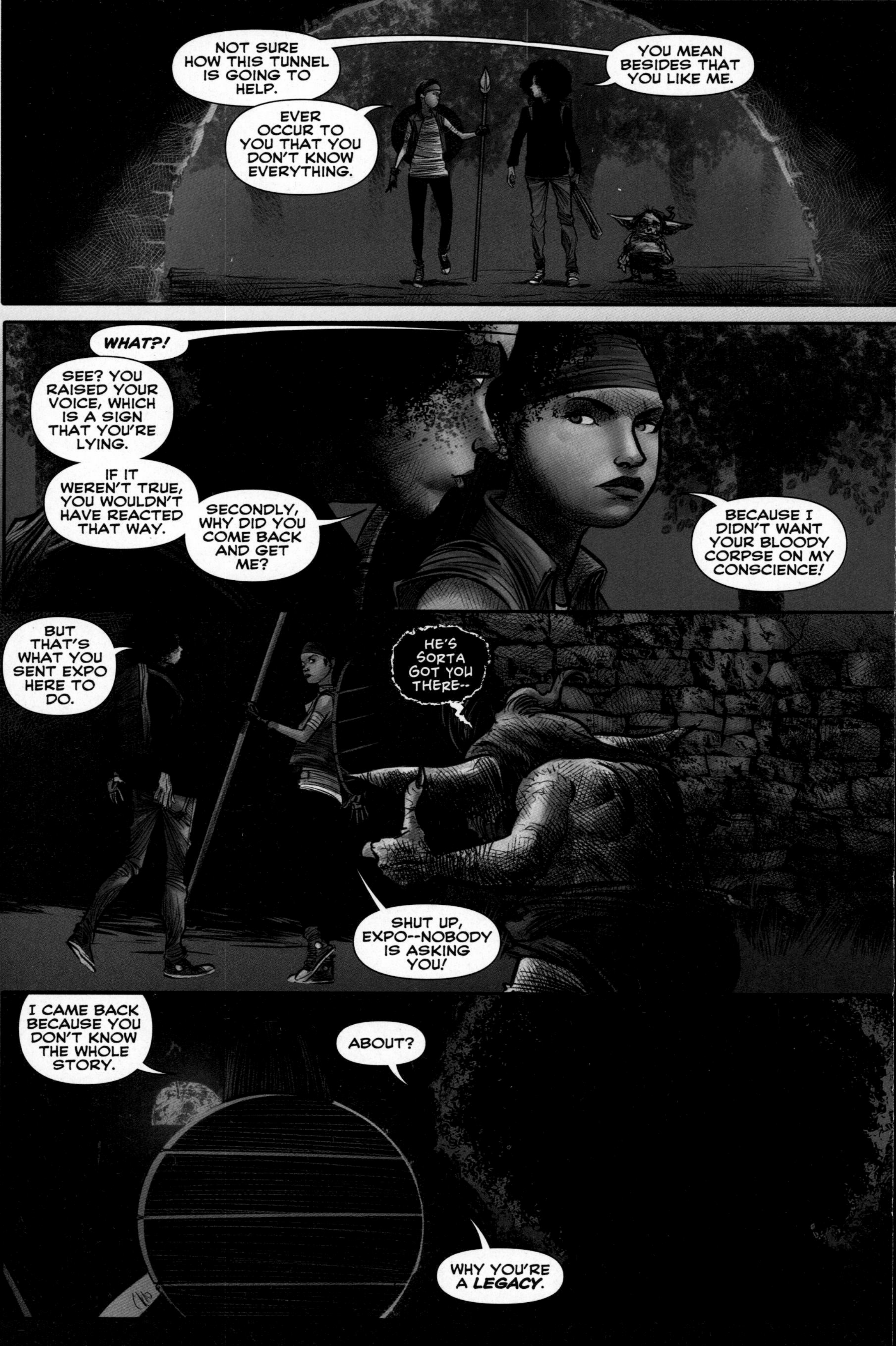
NOT SURE HOW THIS TUNNEL IS GOING TO HELP.
YOU MEAN BESIDES THAT YOU LIKE ME.
EVER OCCUR TO YOU THAT YOU DON'T KNOW EVERYTHING.
WHAT?!
SEE? YOU RAISED YOUR VOICE, WHICH IS A SIGN THAT YOU'RE LYING.
IF IT WEREN'T TRUE, YOU WOULDN'T HAVE REACTED THAT WAY.
SECONDLY, WHY DID YOU COME BACK AND GET ME?
BECAUSE I DIDN'T WANT YOUR BLOODY CORPSE ON MY CONSCIENCE!
BUT THAT'S WHAT YOU SENT EXPO HERE TO DO.
HE'S SORTA GOT YOU THERE--
SHUT UP, EXPO--NOBODY IS ASKING YOU!
I CAME BACK BECAUSE YOU DON'T KNOW THE WHOLE STORY.
ABOUT?
WHY YOU'RE A LEGACY.

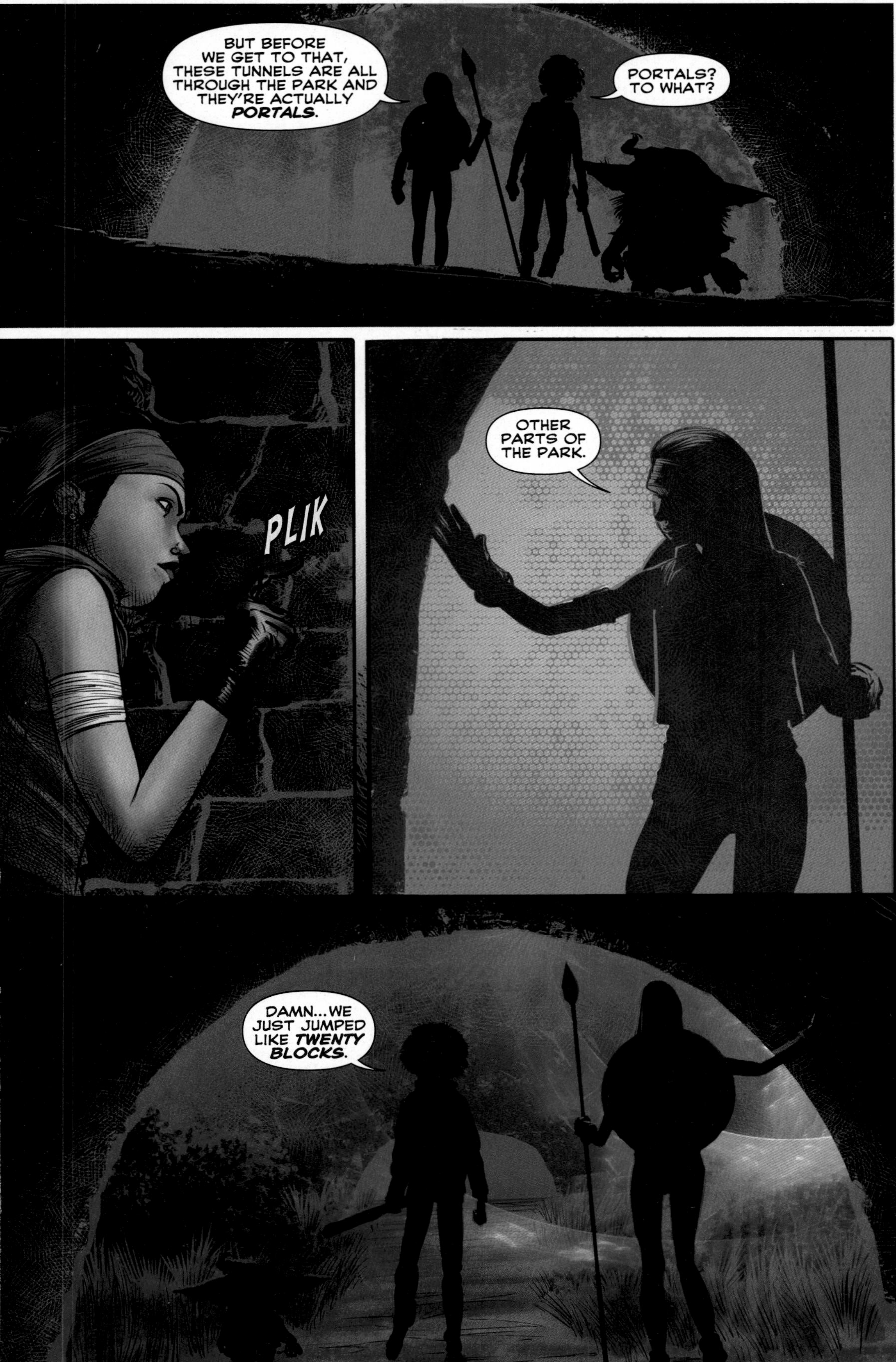
BUT BEFORE WE GET TO THAT, THESE TUNNELS ARE ALL THROUGH THE PARK AND THEY'RE ACTUALLY PORTALS.
PORTALS? TO WHAT?
PLIK
OTHER PARTS OF THE PARK.
DAMN...WE JUST JUMPED LIKE TWENTY BLOCKS.

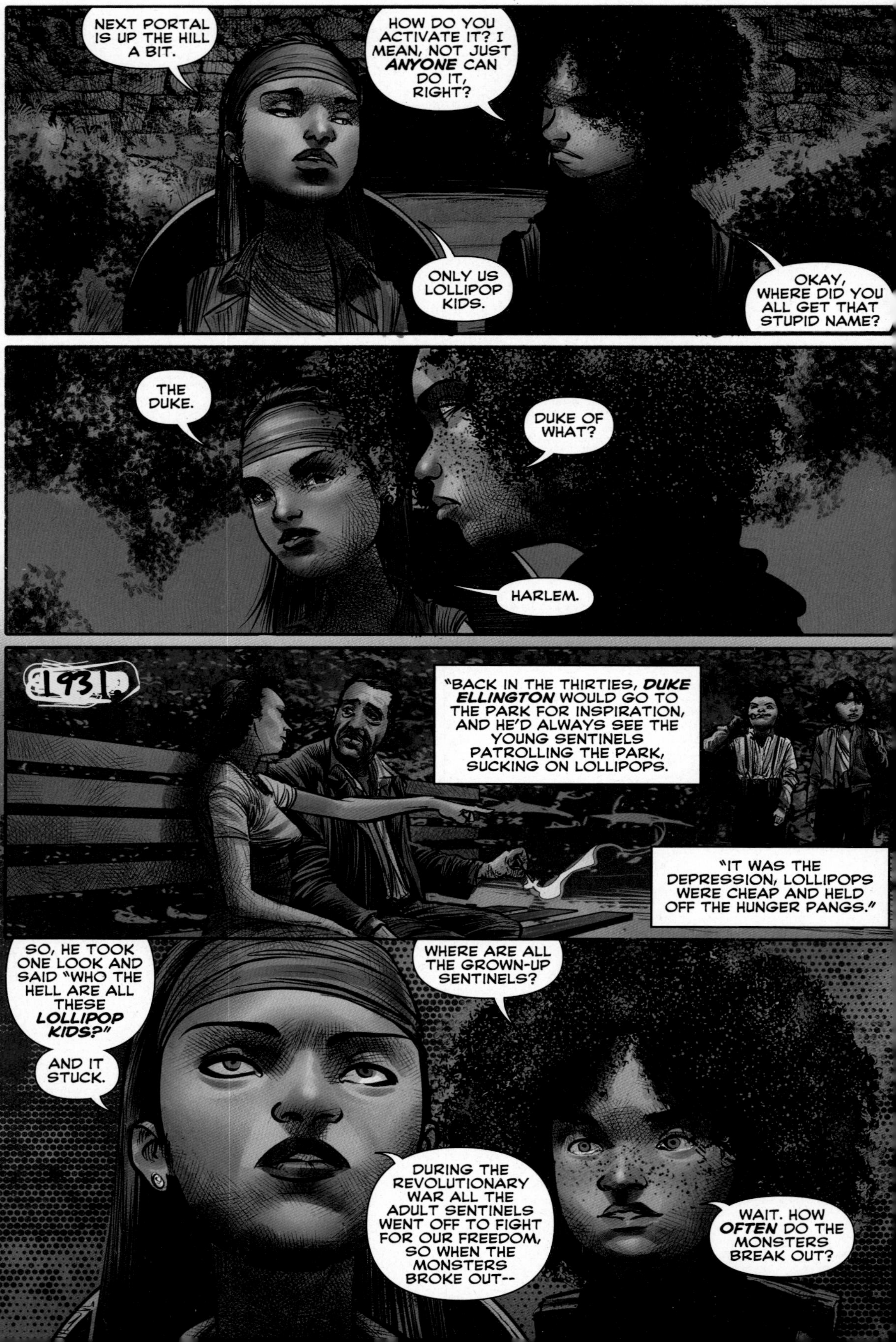
NEXT PORTAL IS UP THE HILL A BIT.
HOW DO YOU ACTIVATE IT? I MEAN, NOT JUST ANYONE CAN DO IT, RIGHT?
ONLY US LOLLIPOP KIDS.
OKAY, WHERE DID YOU ALL GET THAT STUPID NAME?
THE DUKE.
DUKE OF WHAT?
HARLEM.
1931
"BACK IN THE THIRTIES, DUKE ELLINGTON WOULD GO TO THE PARK FOR INSPIRATION, AND HE'D ALWAYS SEE THE YOUNG SENTINELS PATROLLING THE PARK, SUCKING ON LOLLIPOPS.
"IT WAS THE DEPRESSION, LOLLIPOPS WERE CHEAP AND HELD OFF THE HUNGER PANGS."
SO, HE TOOK ONE LOOK AND SAID "WHO THE HELL ARE ALL THESE LOLLIPOP KIDS?"
AND IT STUCK.
WHERE ARE ALL THE GROWN-UP SENTINELS?
DURING THE REVOLUTIONARY WAR ALL THE ADULT SENTINELS WENT OFF TO FIGHT FOR OUR FREEDOM, SO WHEN THE MONSTERS BROKE OUT--
WAIT. HOW OFTEN DO THE MONSTERS BREAK OUT?

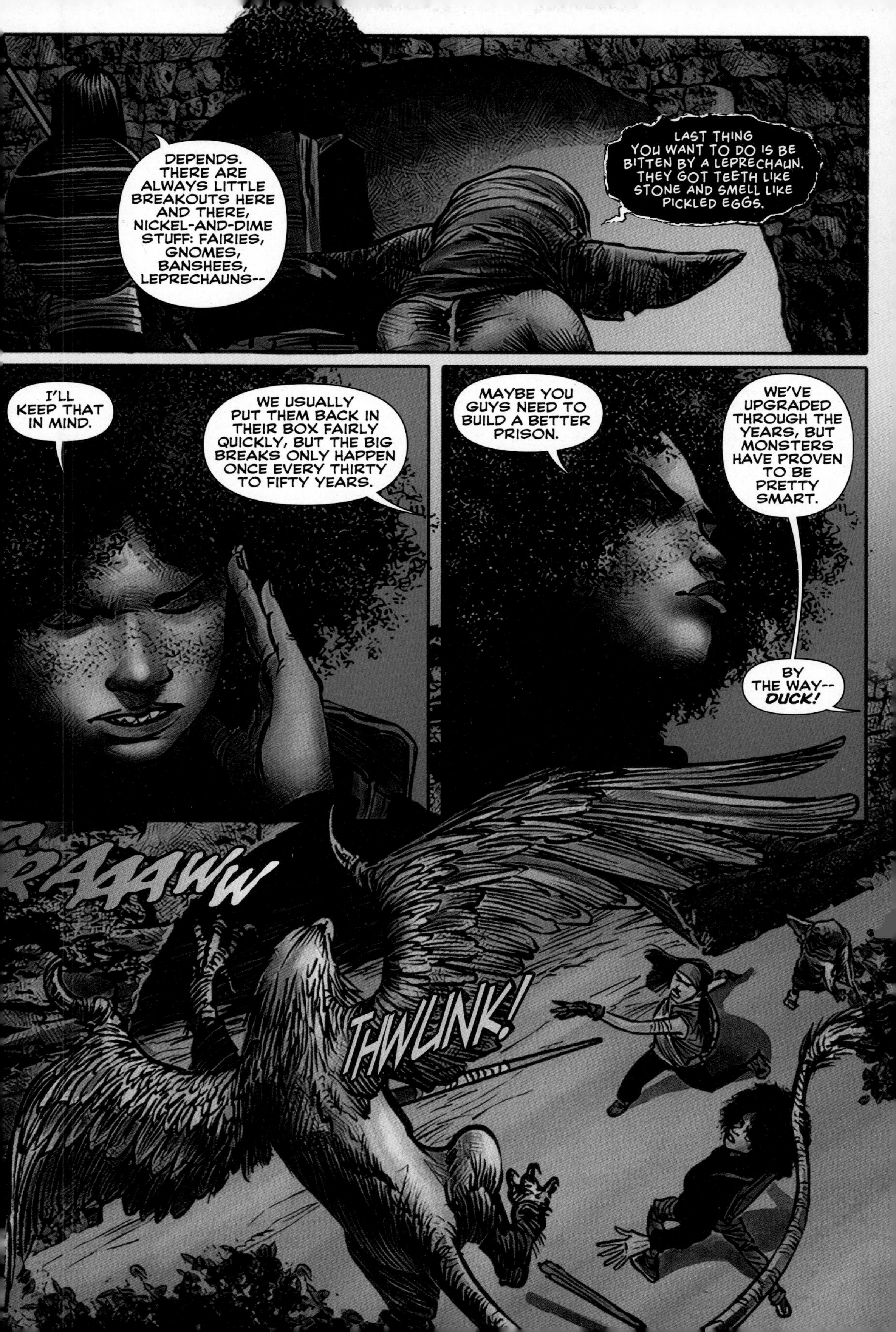
DEPENDS. THERE ARE ALWAYS LITTLE BREAKOUTS HERE AND THERE, NICKEL-AND-DIME STUFF: FAIRIES, GNOMES, BANSHEES, LEPRECHAUNS--
LAST THING YOU WANT TO DO IS BE BITTEN BY A LEPRECHAUN. THEY GOT TEETH LIKE STONE AND SMELL LIKE PICKLED EGGS.
I'LL KEEP THAT IN MIND.
WE USUALLY PUT THEM BACK IN THEIR BOX FAIRLY QUICKLY, BUT THE BIG BREAKS ONLY HAPPEN ONCE EVERY THIRTY TO FIFTY YEARS.
MAYBE YOU GUYS NEED TO BUILD A BETTER PRISON.
WE'VE UPGRADED THROUGH THE YEARS, BUT MONSTERS HAVE PROVEN TO BE PRETTY SMART.
BY THE WAY-- DUCK!
RAAAAWW
THWUNK!

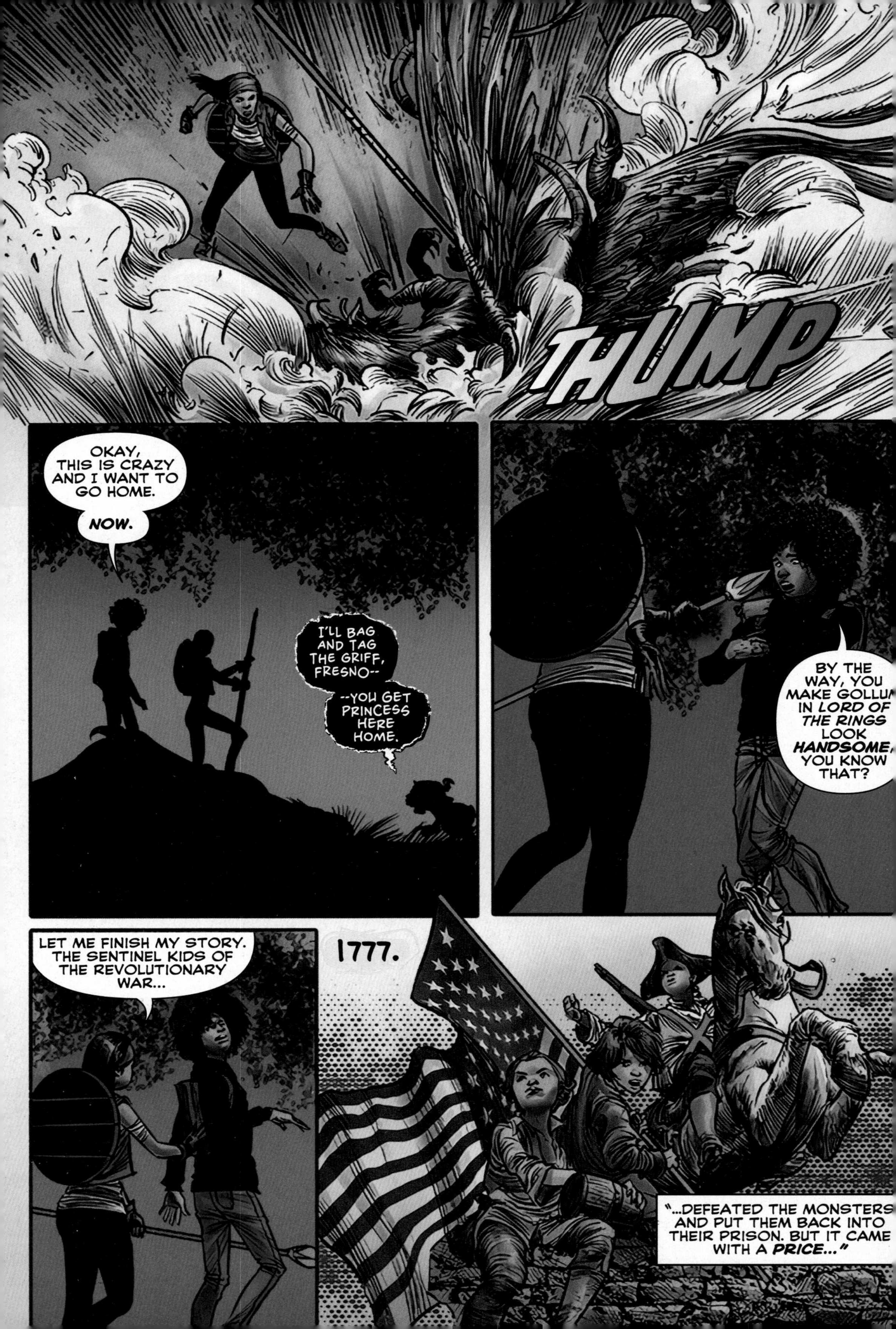

THUMP
OKAY, THIS IS CRAZY AND I WANT TO GO HOME.
NOW.
I'LL BAG AND TAG THE GRIFF, FRESNO--
--YOU GET PRINCESS HERE HOME.
BY THE WAY, YOU MAKE GOLLUM IN LORD OF THE RINGS LOOK HANDSOME, YOU KNOW THAT?
LET ME FINISH MY STORY. THE SENTINEL KIDS OF THE REVOLUTIONARY WAR...
1777.
"...DEFEATED THE MONSTERS AND PUT THEM BACK INTO THEIR PRISON. BUT IT CAME WITH A PRICE..."

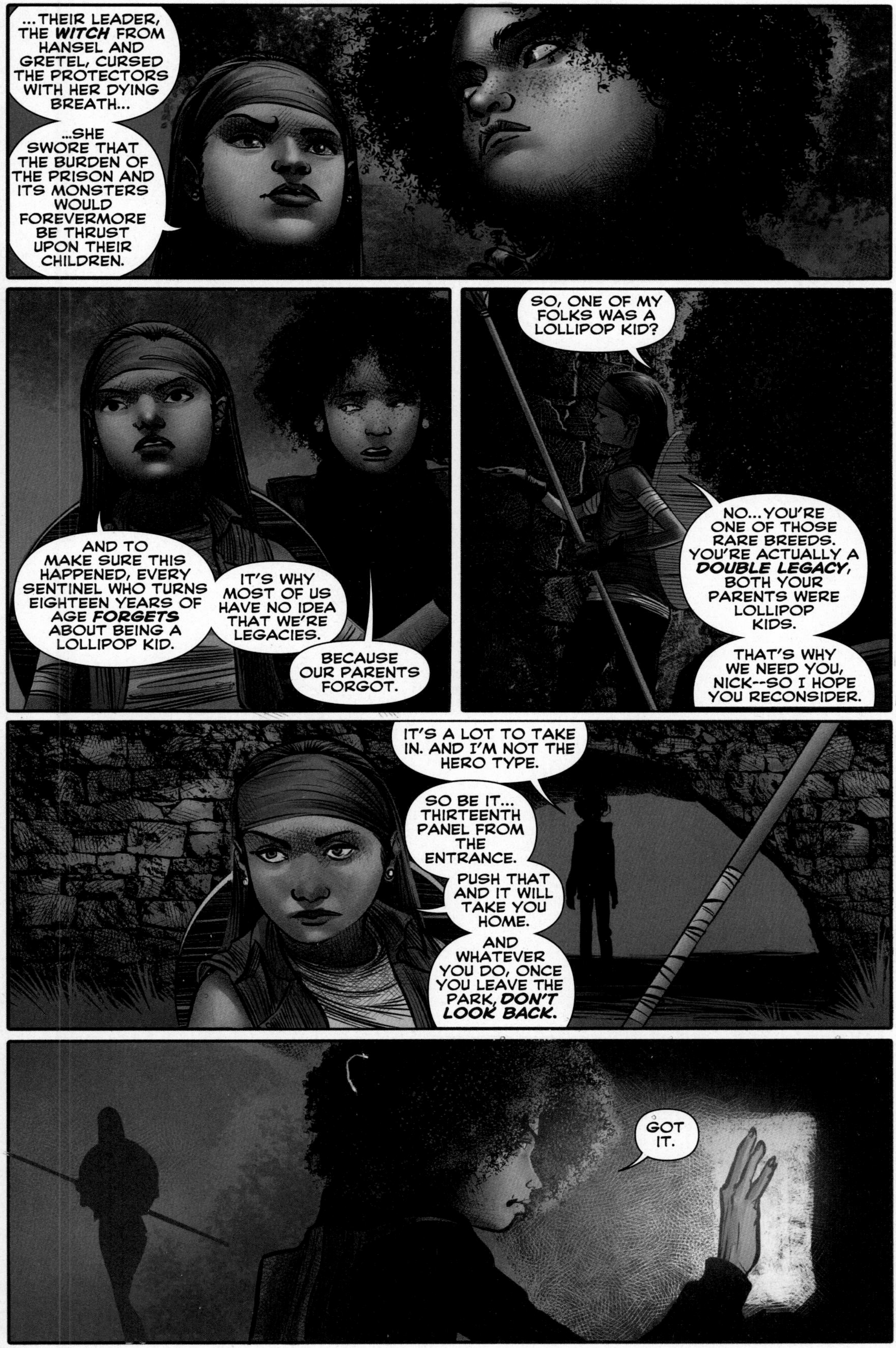
...THEIR LEADER, THE WITCH FROM HANSEL AND GRETEL, CURSED THE PROTECTORS WITH HER DYING BREATH...
...SHE SWORE THAT THE BURDEN OF THE PRISON AND ITS MONSTERS WOULD FOREVERMORE BE THRUST UPON THEIR CHILDREN.
AND TO MAKE SURE THIS HAPPENED, EVERY SENTINEL WHO TURNS EIGHTEEN YEARS OF AGE FORGETS ABOUT BEING A LOLLIPOP KID.
IT'S WHY MOST OF US HAVE NO IDEA THAT WE'RE LEGACIES.
BECAUSE OUR PARENTS FORGOT.
SO, ONE OF MY FOLKS WAS A LOLLIPOP KID?
NO...YOU'RE ONE OF THOSE RARE BREEDS. YOU'RE ACTUALLY A DOUBLE LEGACY, BOTH YOUR PARENTS WERE LOLLIPOP KIDS.
THAT'S WHY WE NEED YOU, NICK--SO I HOPE YOU RECONSIDER.
IT'S A LOT TO TAKE IN. AND I'M NOT THE HERO TYPE.
SO BE IT... THIRTEENTH PANEL FROM THE ENTRANCE.
PUSH THAT AND IT WILL TAKE YOU HOME.
AND WHATEVER YOU DO, ONCE YOU LEAVE THE PARK, DON'T LOOK BACK.
GOT IT.

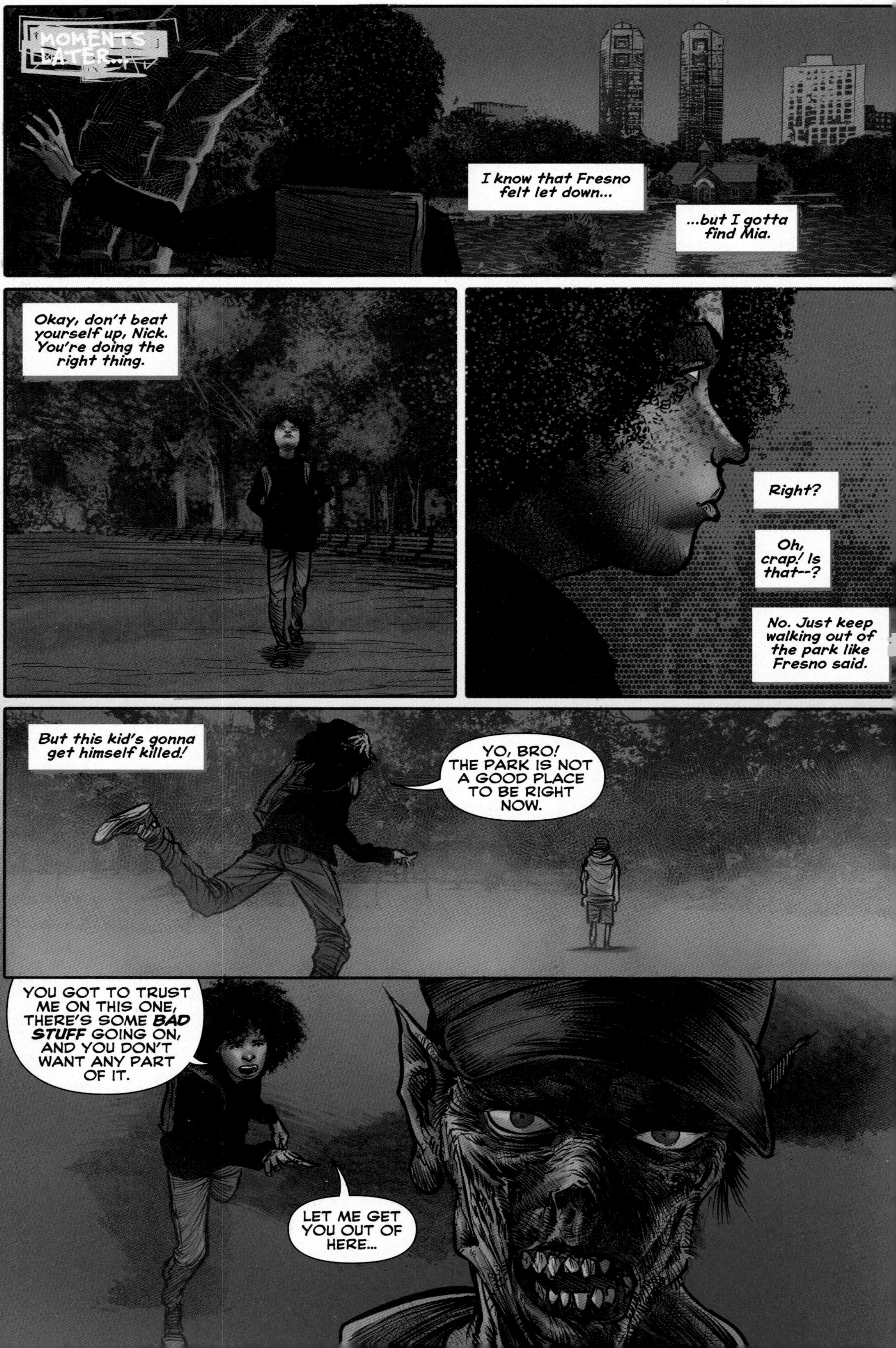
MOMENTS LATER...
I know that Fresno felt let down...
...but I gotta find Mia.
Okay, don't beat yourself up, Nick. You're doing the right thing.
Right?
Oh, crap! Is that--?
No. Just keep walking out of the park like Fresno said.
But this kid's gonna get himself killed!
YO, BRO! THE PARK IS NOT A GOOD PLACE TO BE RIGHT NOW.
YOU GOT TO TRUST ME ON THIS ONE, THERE'S SOME BAD STUFF GOING ON, AND YOU DON'T WANT ANY PART OF IT.
LET ME GET YOU OUT OF HERE...

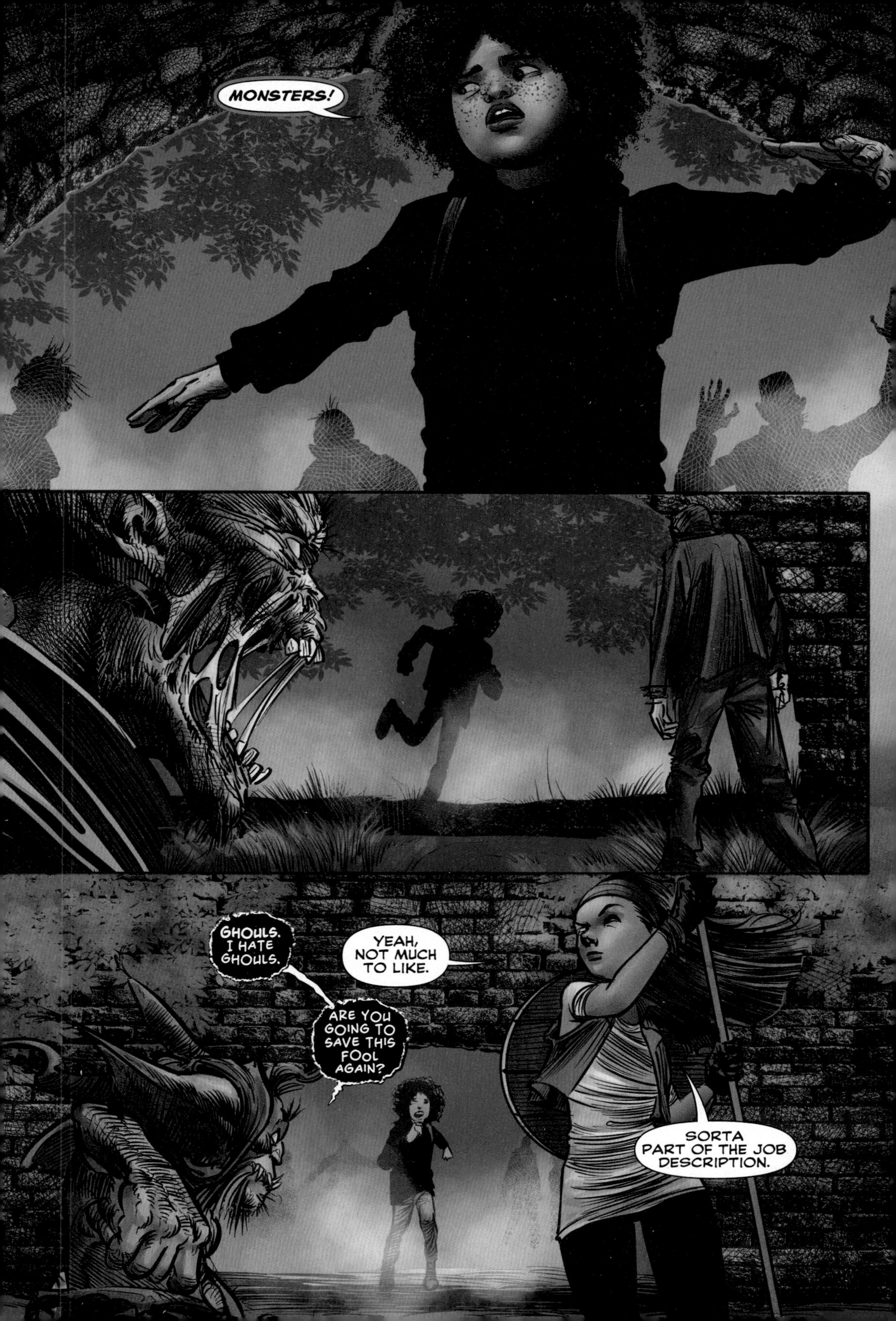
MONSTERS!
GHOULS. I HATE GHOULS.
YEAH, NOT MUCH TO LIKE.
ARE YOU GOING TO SAVE THIS FOOL AGAIN?
SORTA PART OF THE JOB DESCRIPTION.

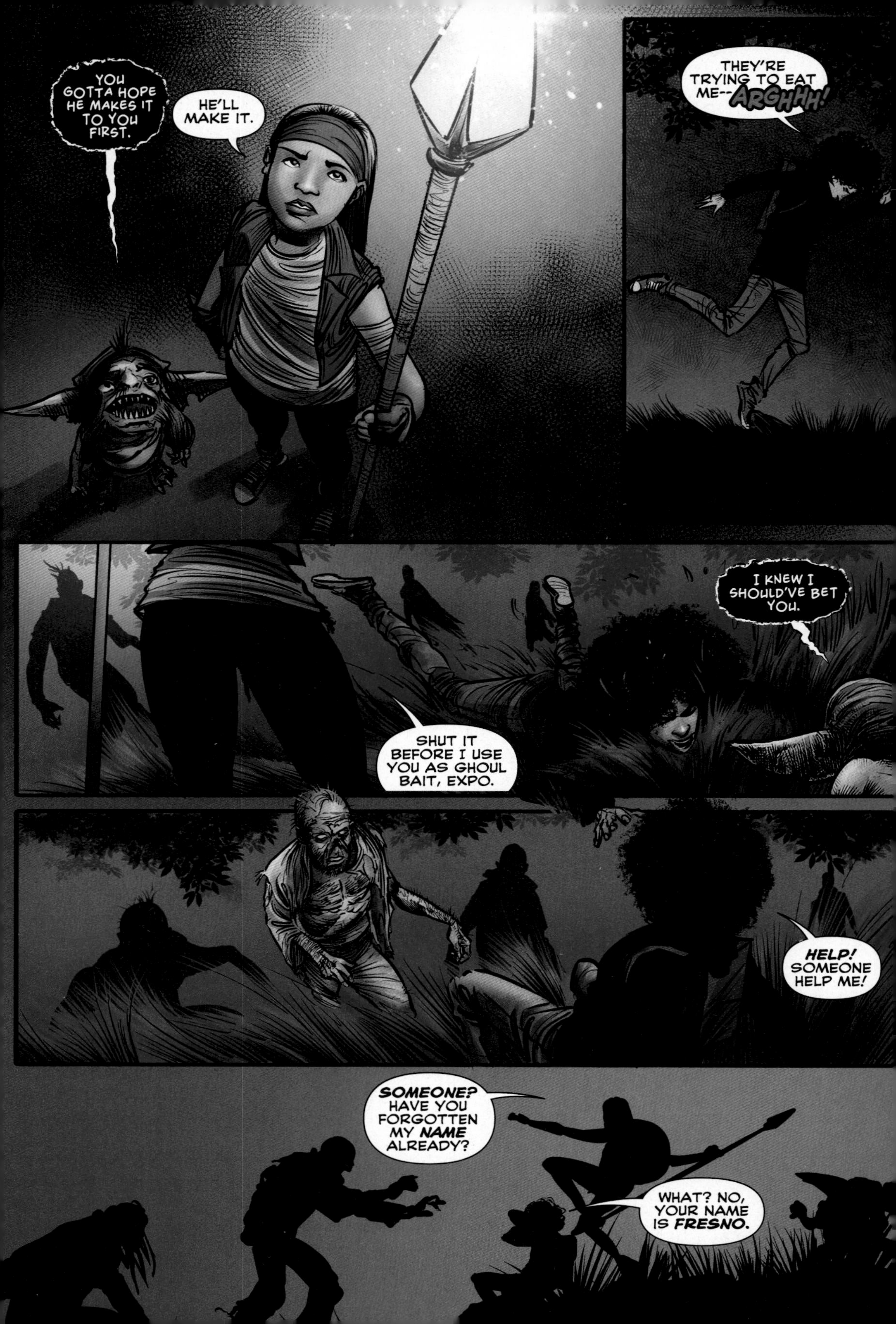
YOU GOTTA HOPE HE MAKES IT TO YOU FIRST.
HE'LL MAKE IT.
THEY'RE TRYING TO EAT ME--ARGHHH!
I KNEW I SHOULD'VE BET YOU.
SHUT IT BEFORE I USE YOU AS GHOUL BAIT, EXPO.
HELP! SOMEONE HELP ME!
SOMEONE? HAVE YOU FORGOTTEN MY NAME ALREADY?
WHAT? NO, YOUR NAME IS FRESNO.

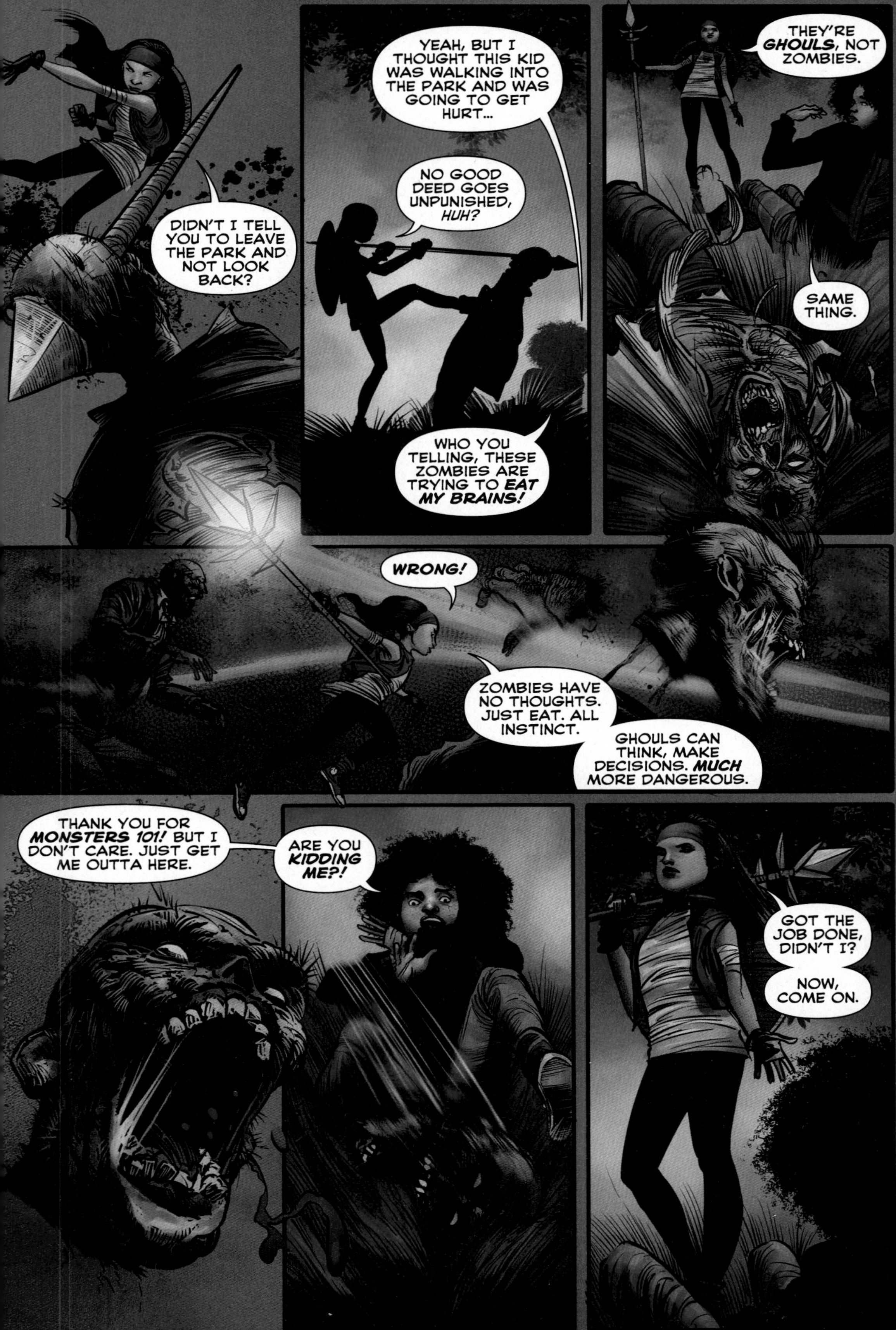
DIDN'T I TELL YOU TO LEAVE THE PARK AND NOT LOOK BACK?
YEAH, BUT I THOUGHT THIS KID WAS WALKING INTO THE PARK AND WAS GOING TO GET HURT...
NO GOOD DEED GOES UNPUNISHED, *HUH?*
WHO YOU TELLING, THESE ZOMBIES ARE TRYING TO **EAT MY BRAINS!**
THEY'RE **GHOULS**, NOT ZOMBIES.
SAME THING.
WRONG!
ZOMBIES HAVE NO THOUGHTS. JUST EAT. ALL INSTINCT.
GHOULS CAN THINK, MAKE DECISIONS. **MUCH** MORE DANGEROUS.
THANK YOU FOR **MONSTERS 101!** BUT I DON'T CARE. JUST GET ME OUTTA HERE.
ARE YOU **KIDDING ME?!**
GOT THE JOB DONE, DIDN'T I?
NOW, COME ON.

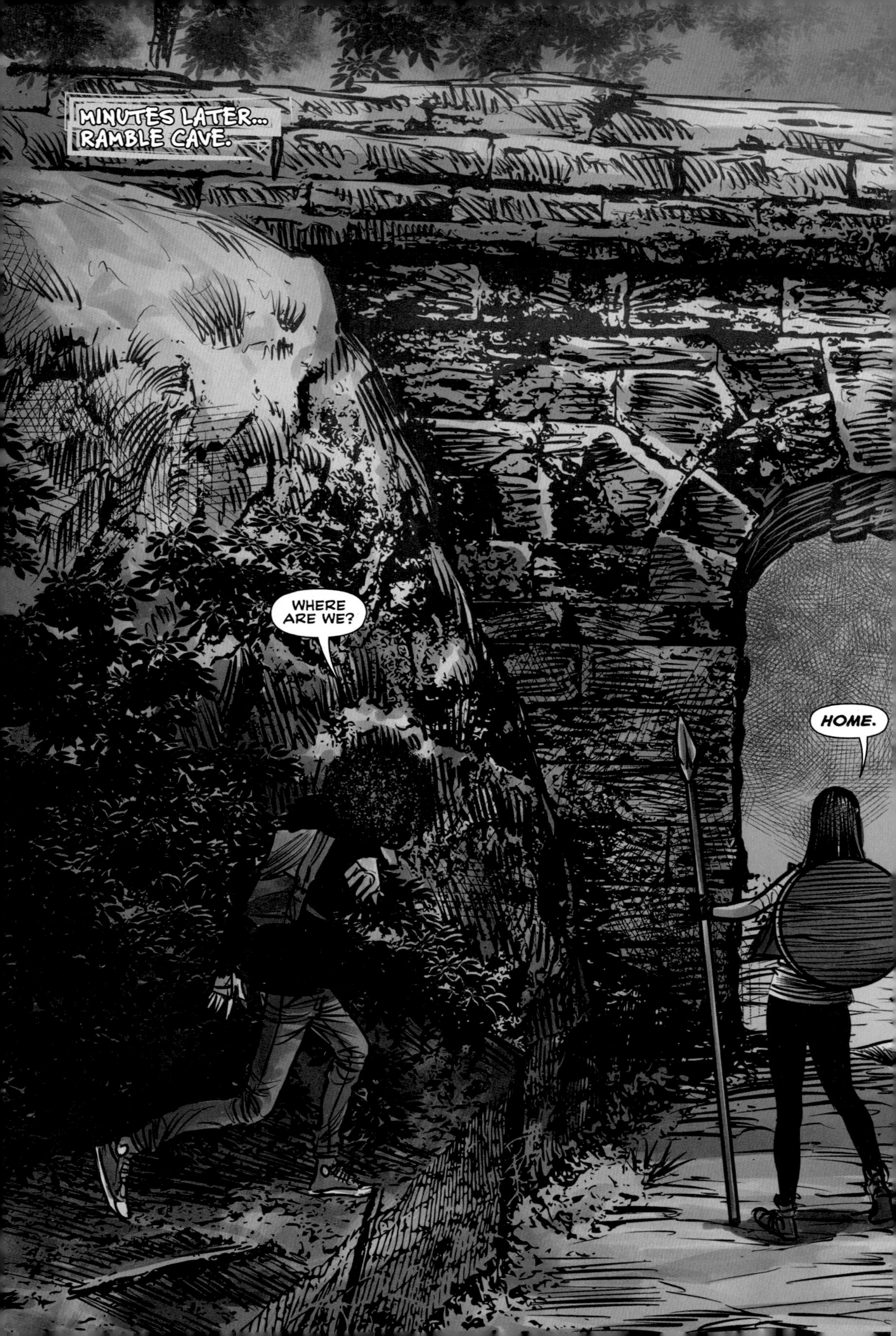

MINUTES LATER...
RAMBLE CAVE.
WHERE ARE WE?
HOME.

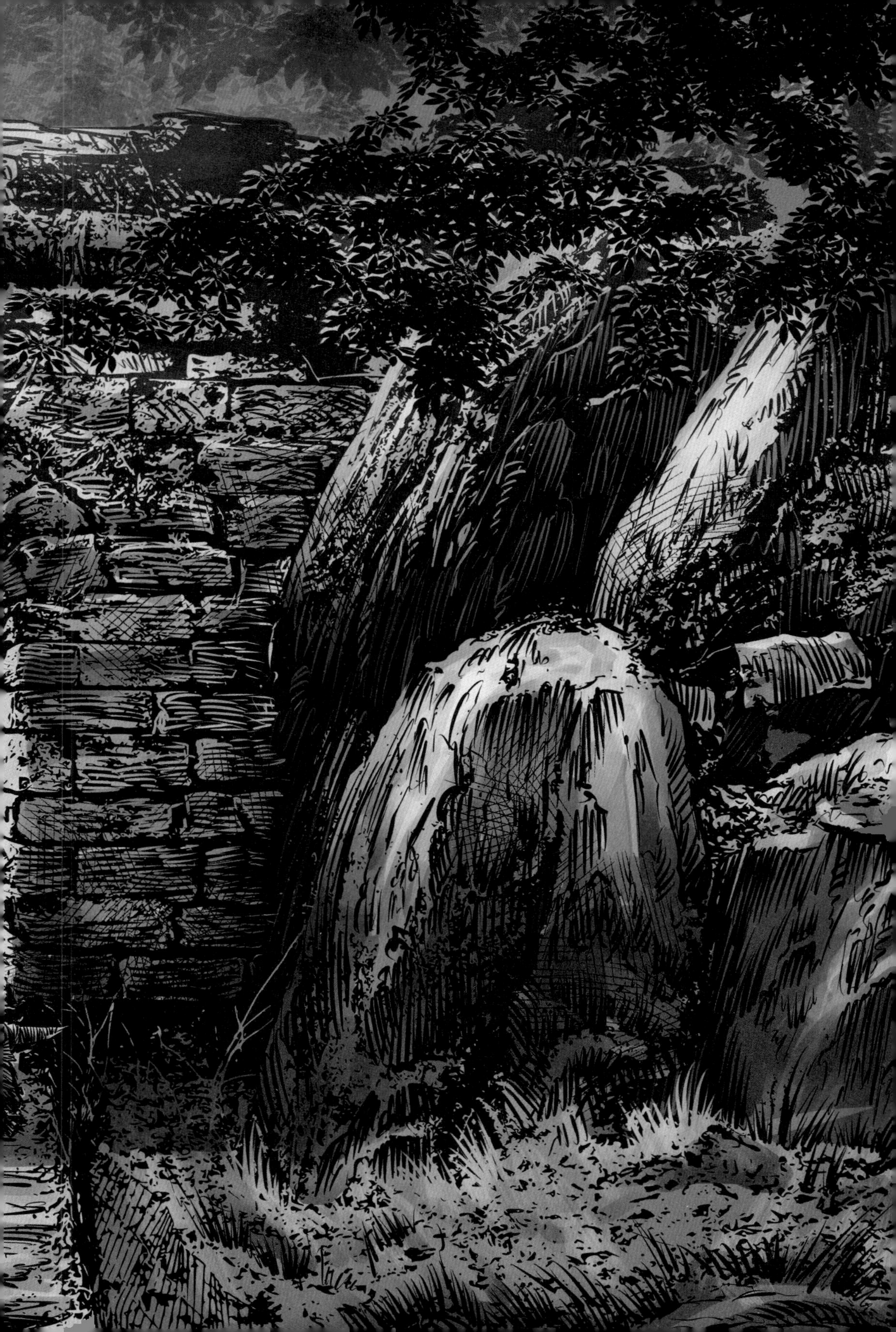

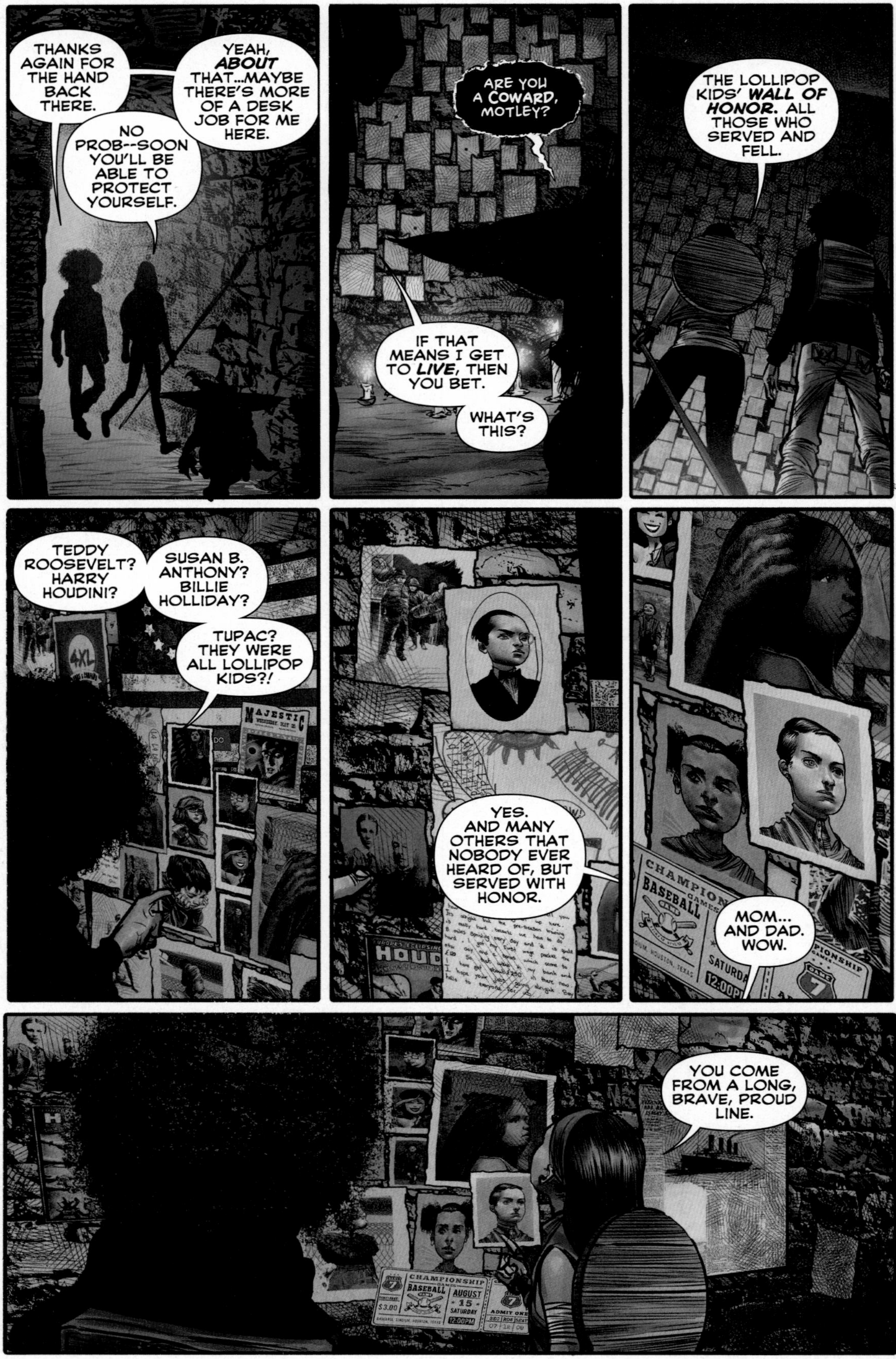
THANKS AGAIN FOR THE HAND BACK THERE.
NO PROB--SOON YOU'LL BE ABLE TO PROTECT YOURSELF.
YEAH, ***ABOUT*** THAT...MAYBE THERE'S MORE OF A DESK JOB FOR ME HERE.
ARE YOU A COWARD, MOTLEY?
IF THAT MEANS I GET TO ***LIVE***, THEN YOU BET.
WHAT'S THIS?
THE LOLLIPOP KIDS' ***WALL OF HONOR.*** ALL THOSE WHO SERVED AND FELL.
TEDDY ROOSEVELT? HARRY HOUDINI?
SUSAN B. ANTHONY? BILLIE HOLLIDAY?
TUPAC? THEY WERE ALL LOLLIPOP KIDS?!
YES. AND MANY OTHERS THAT NOBODY EVER HEARD OF, BUT SERVED WITH HONOR.
MOM... AND DAD. WOW.
YOU COME FROM A LONG, BRAVE, PROUD LINE.

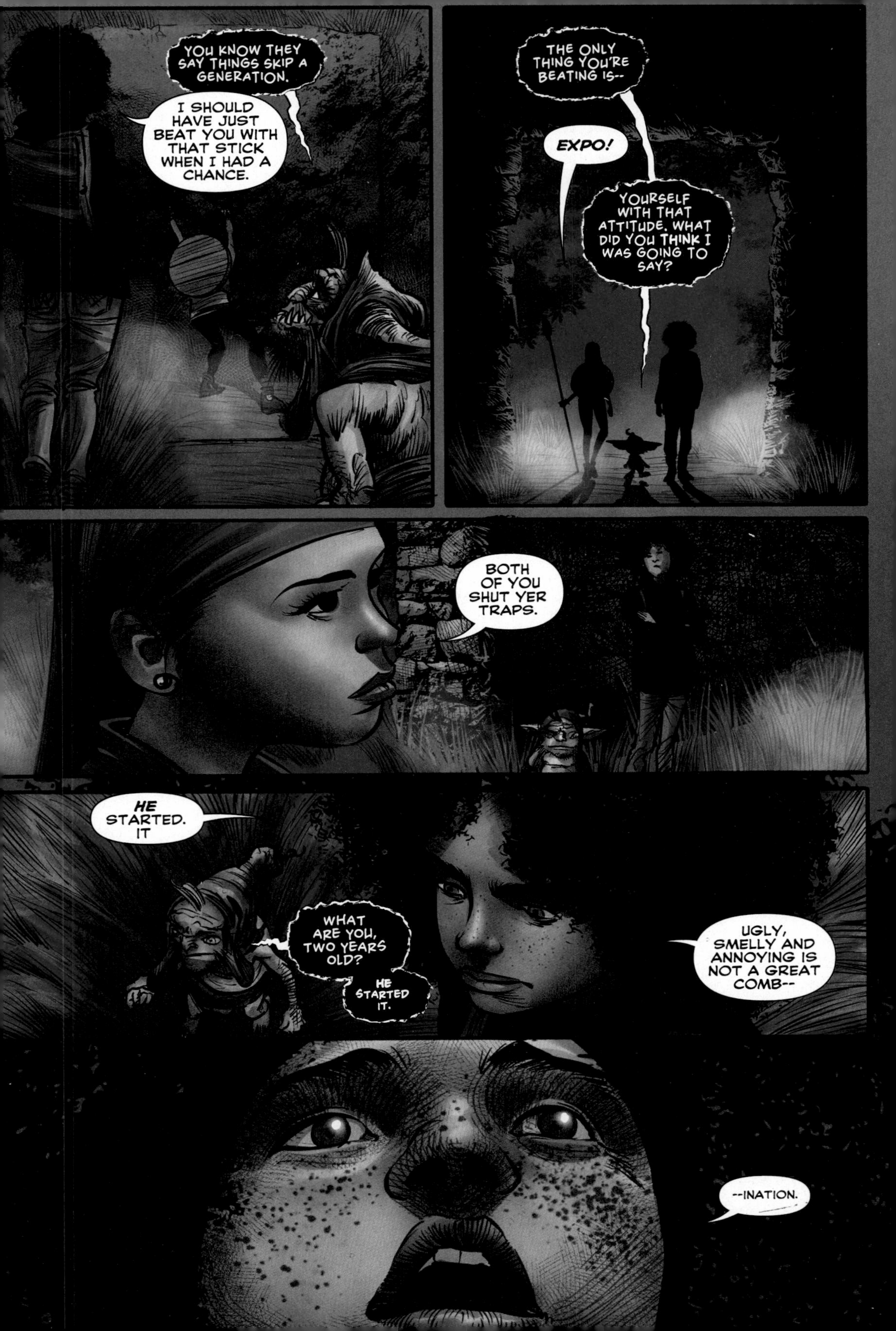
YOU KNOW THEY SAY THINGS SKIP A GENERATION.
I SHOULD HAVE JUST BEAT YOU WITH THAT STICK WHEN I HAD A CHANCE.
THE ONLY THING YOU'RE BEATING IS--
EXPO!
YOURSELF WITH THAT ATTITUDE. WHAT DID YOU THINK I WAS GOING TO SAY?
BOTH OF YOU SHUT YER TRAPS.
HE STARTED. IT
WHAT ARE YOU, TWO YEARS OLD?
HE STARTED IT.
UGLY, SMELLY AND ANNOYING IS NOT A GREAT COMB--
--INATION.

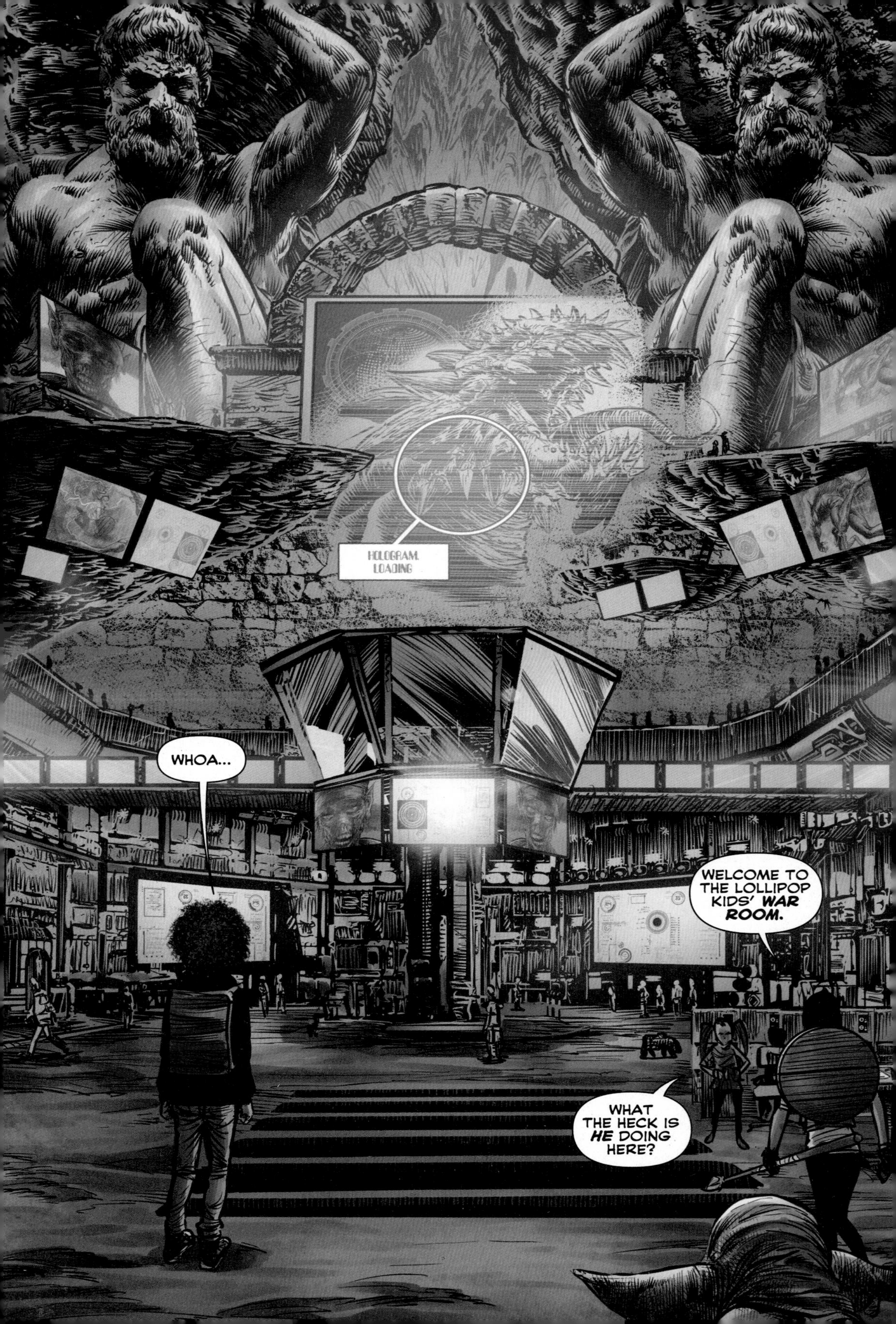
HOLOGRAM LOADING
WHOA...
WELCOME TO THE LOLLIPOP KIDS' WAR ROOM.
WHAT THE HECK IS HE DOING HERE?

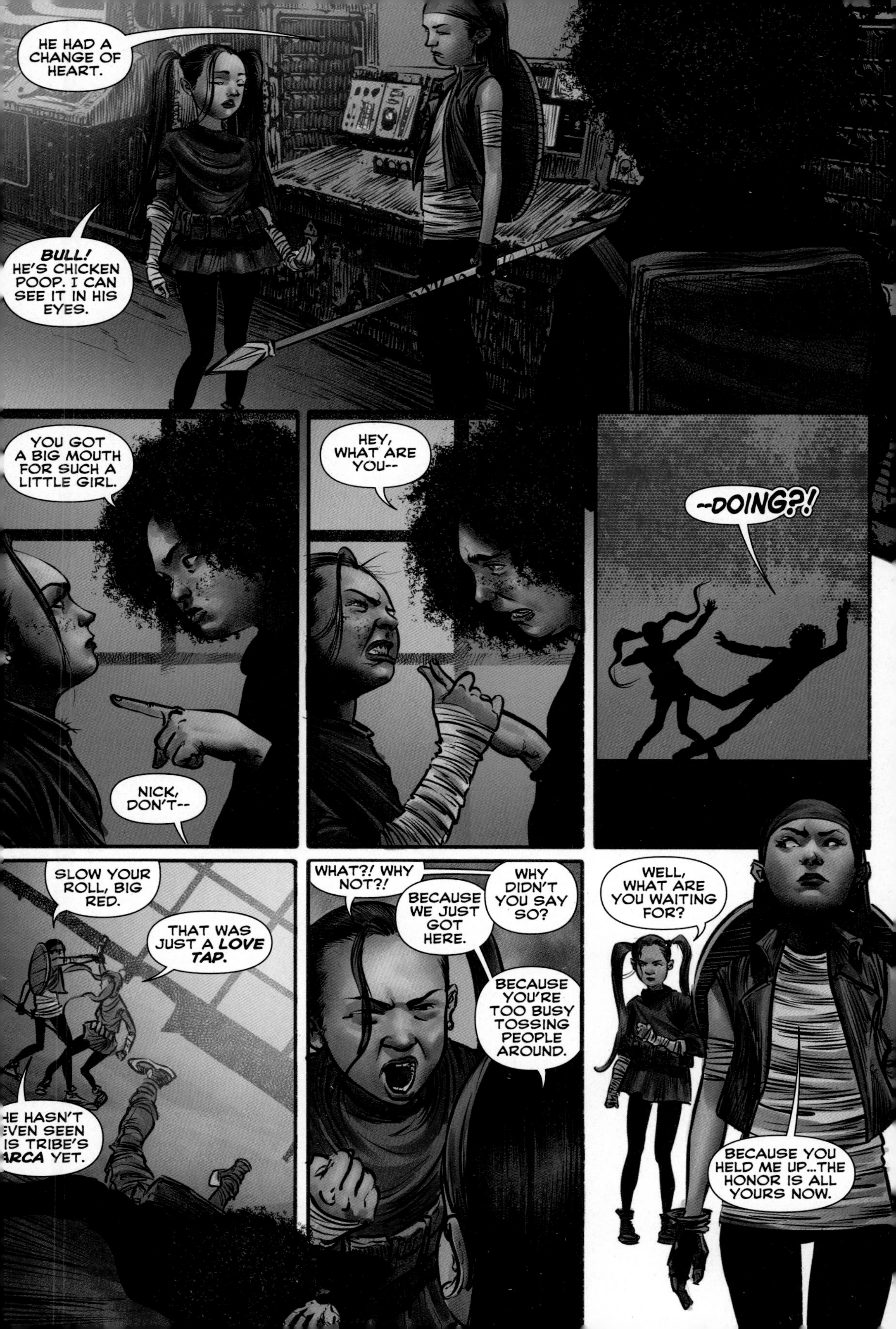

HE HAD A CHANGE OF HEART.
BULL! HE'S CHICKEN POOP. I CAN SEE IT IN HIS EYES.
YOU GOT A BIG MOUTH FOR SUCH A LITTLE GIRL.
NICK, DON'T--
HEY, WHAT ARE YOU--
--DOING?!
SLOW YOUR ROLL, BIG RED.
THAT WAS JUST A ***LOVE TAP.***
HE HASN'T EVEN SEEN IS TRIBE'S ***ARCA*** YET.
WHAT?! WHY NOT?!
WHY DIDN'T YOU SAY SO?
BECAUSE WE JUST GOT HERE.
BECAUSE YOU'RE TOO BUSY TOSSING PEOPLE AROUND.
WELL, WHAT ARE YOU WAITING FOR?
BECAUSE YOU HELD ME UP...THE HONOR IS ALL YOURS NOW.

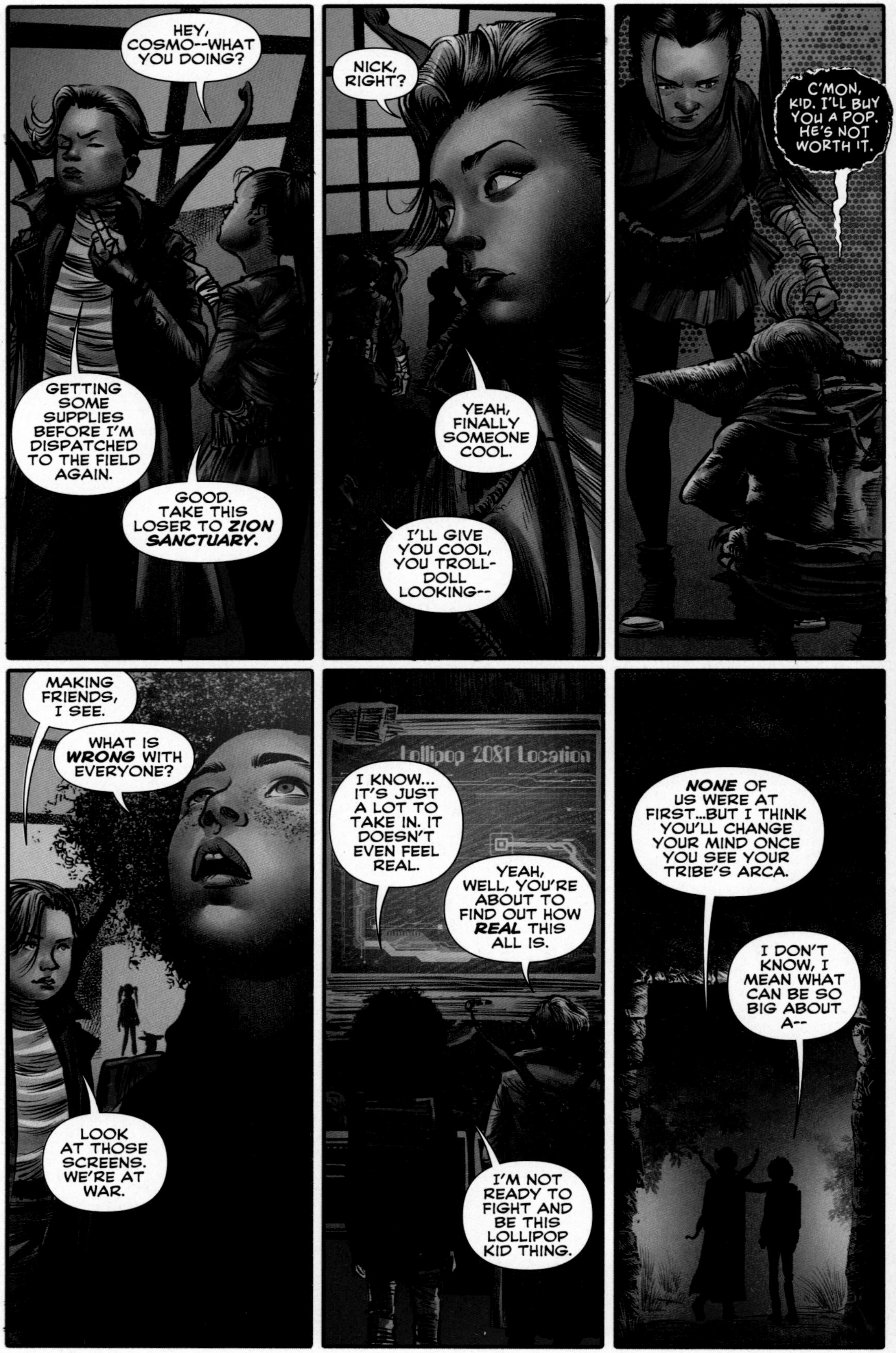
HEY, COSMO--WHAT YOU DOING?
GETTING SOME SUPPLIES BEFORE I'M DISPATCHED TO THE FIELD AGAIN.
GOOD. TAKE THIS LOSER TO ZION SANCTUARY.
NICK, RIGHT?
YEAH, FINALLY SOMEONE COOL.
I'LL GIVE YOU COOL, YOU TROLL-DOLL LOOKING--
C'MON, KID. I'LL BUY YOU A POP. HE'S NOT WORTH IT.
MAKING FRIENDS, I SEE.
WHAT IS WRONG WITH EVERYONE?
LOOK AT THOSE SCREENS. WE'RE AT WAR.
Lollipop 2081 Location
I KNOW... IT'S JUST A LOT TO TAKE IN. IT DOESN'T EVEN FEEL REAL.
YEAH, WELL, YOU'RE ABOUT TO FIND OUT HOW REAL THIS ALL IS.
I'M NOT READY TO FIGHT AND BE THIS LOLLIPOP KID THING.
NONE OF US WERE AT FIRST...BUT I THINK YOU'LL CHANGE YOUR MIND ONCE YOU SEE YOUR TRIBE'S ARCA.
I DON'T KNOW, I MEAN WHAT CAN BE SO BIG ABOUT A--

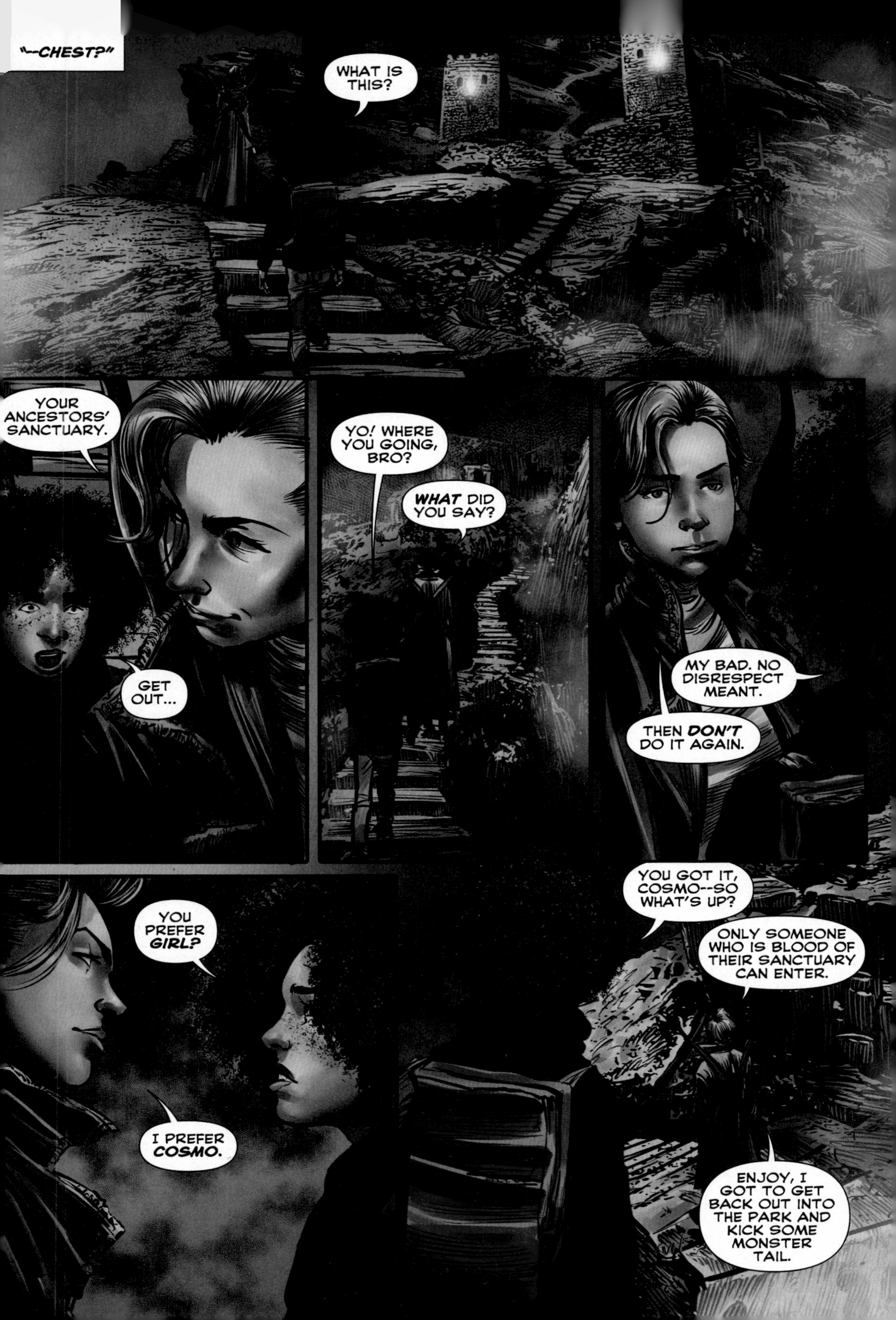
"--CHEST?"
WHAT IS THIS?
YOUR ANCESTORS' SANCTUARY.
GET OUT...
YO! WHERE YOU GOING, BRO?
WHAT DID YOU SAY?
MY BAD. NO DISRESPECT MEANT.
THEN DON'T DO IT AGAIN.
YOU PREFER GIRL?
I PREFER COSMO.
YOU GOT IT, COSMO--SO WHAT'S UP?
ONLY SOMEONE WHO IS BLOOD OF THEIR SANCTUARY CAN ENTER.
ENJOY, I GOT TO GET BACK OUT INTO THE PARK AND KICK SOME MONSTER TAIL.

"BLOOD OF THEIR SANCTUARY"...? ARE THESE CATS FOR REAL?

WHAT THE HECK?

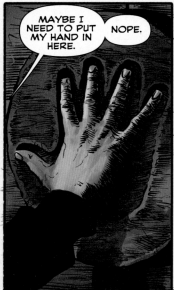

MAYBE I NEED TO PUT MY HAND IN HERE.

NOPE.

They got to be kidding me?

It couldn't be this easy, could it?

I CAN'T BELIEVE I'M DOING THIS...

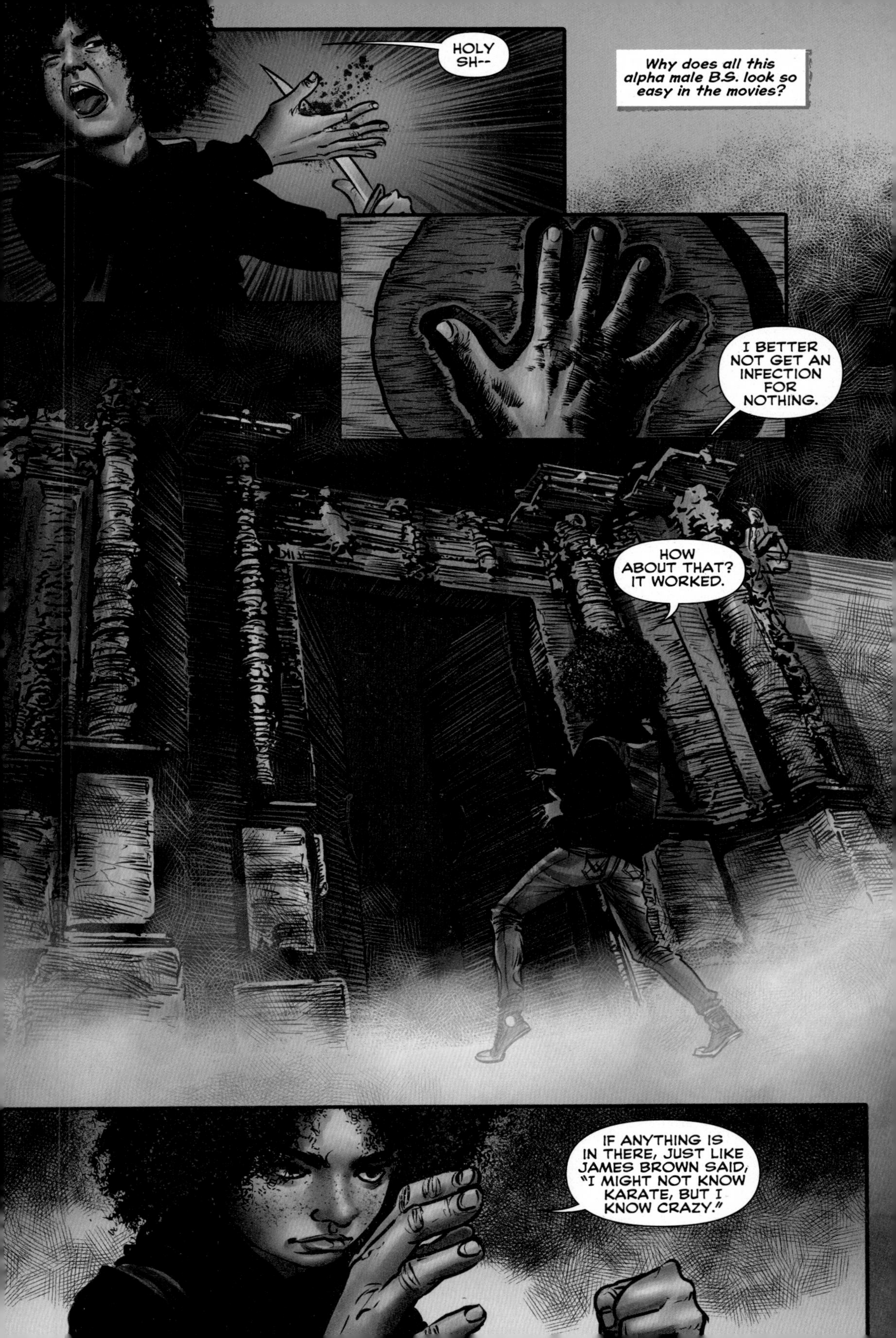
HOLY SH--
Why does all this alpha male B.S. look so easy in the movies?
I BETTER NOT GET AN INFECTION FOR NOTHING.
HOW ABOUT THAT? IT WORKED.
IF ANYTHING IS IN THERE, JUST LIKE JAMES BROWN SAID, "I MIGHT NOT KNOW KARATE, BUT I KNOW CRAZY."

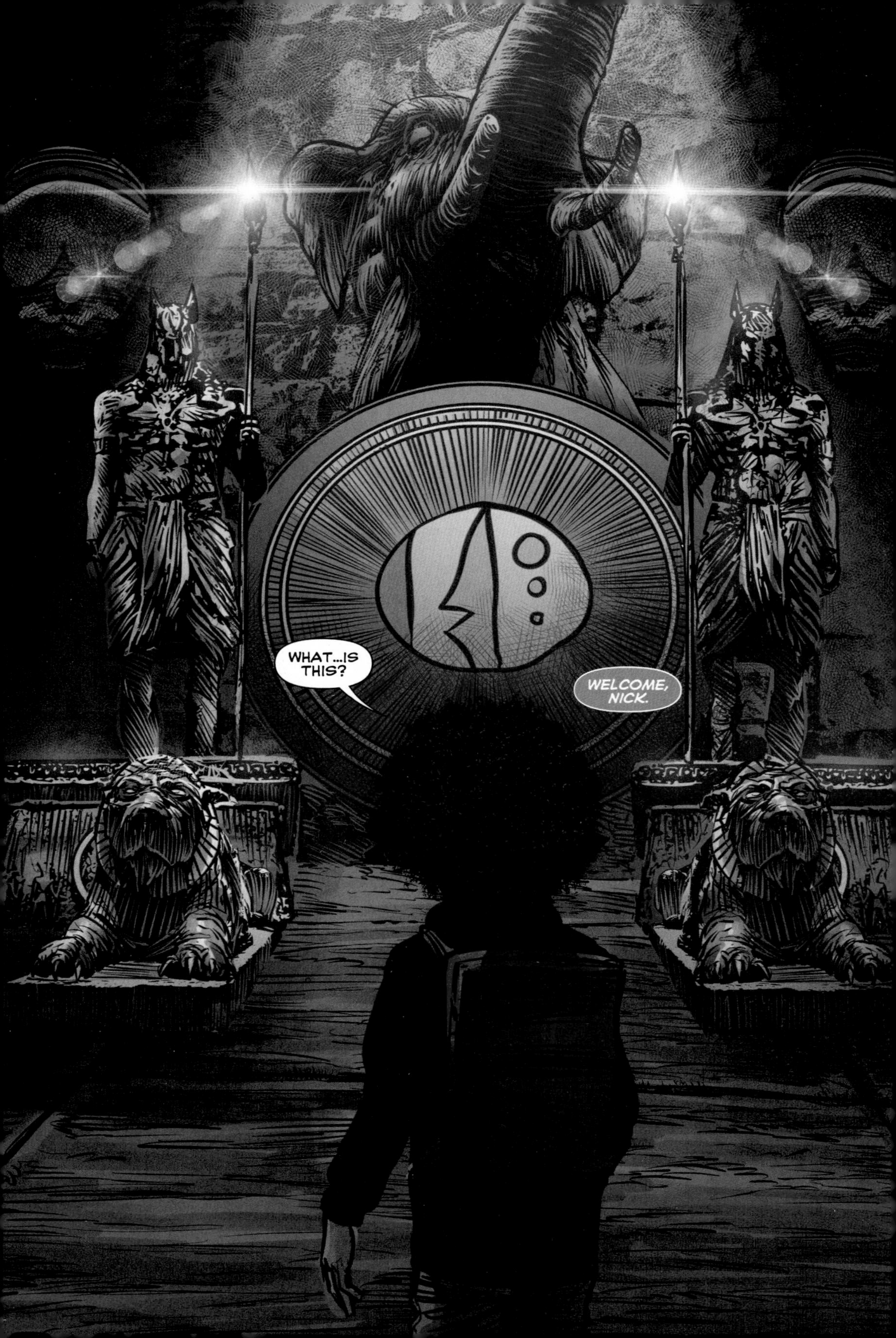
WHAT...IS THIS?
WELCOME, NICK.

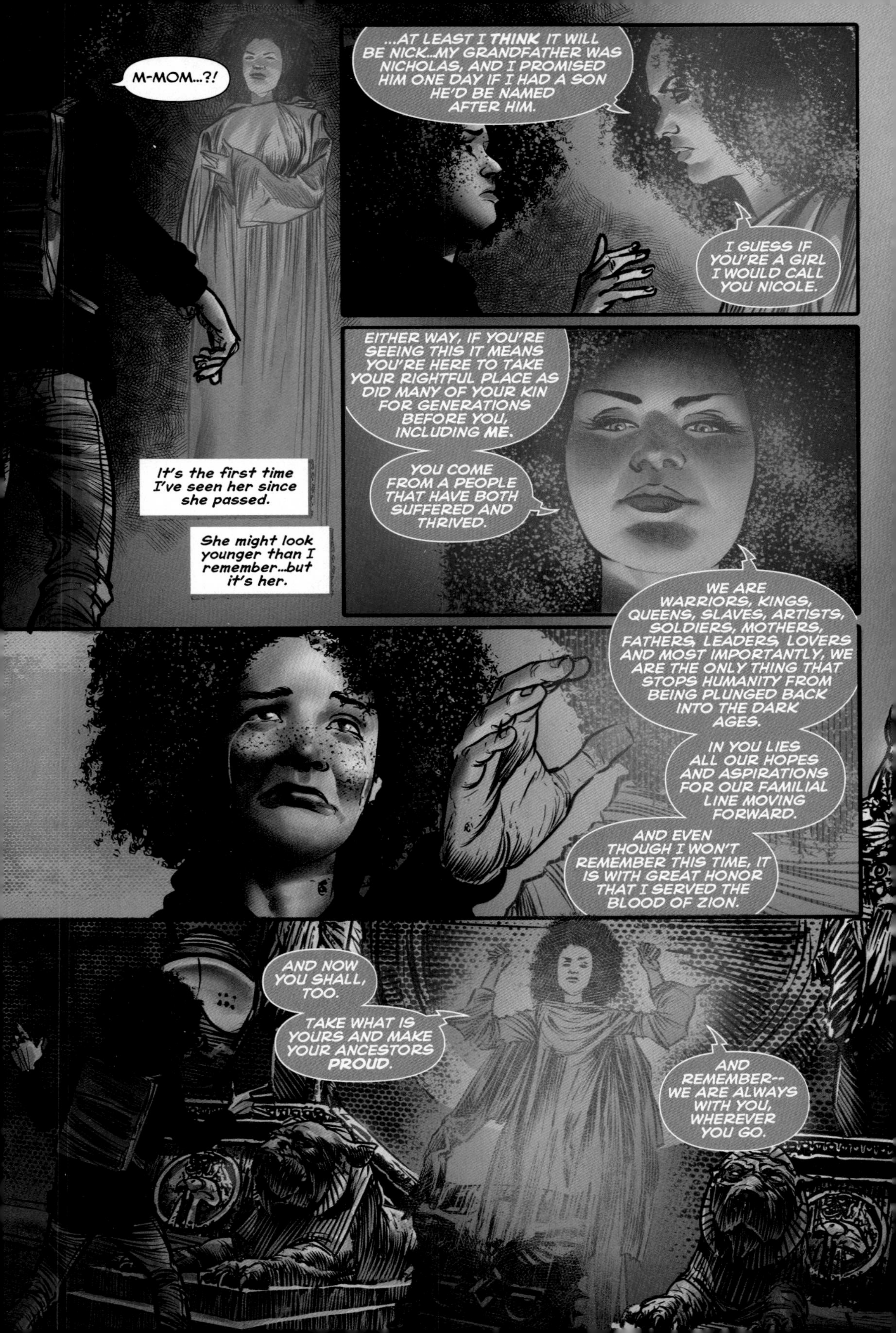
M-MOM...?!
...AT LEAST I THINK IT WILL BE NICK...MY GRANDFATHER WAS NICHOLAS, AND I PROMISED HIM ONE DAY IF I HAD A SON HE'D BE NAMED AFTER HIM.
I GUESS IF YOU'RE A GIRL I WOULD CALL YOU NICOLE.
It's the first time I've seen her since she passed.
She might look younger than I remember...but it's her.
EITHER WAY, IF YOU'RE SEEING THIS IT MEANS YOU'RE HERE TO TAKE YOUR RIGHTFUL PLACE AS DID MANY OF YOUR KIN FOR GENERATIONS BEFORE YOU, INCLUDING ME.
YOU COME FROM A PEOPLE THAT HAVE BOTH SUFFERED AND THRIVED.
WE ARE WARRIORS, KINGS, QUEENS, SLAVES, ARTISTS, SOLDIERS, MOTHERS, FATHERS, LEADERS, LOVERS AND MOST IMPORTANTLY, WE ARE THE ONLY THING THAT STOPS HUMANITY FROM BEING PLUNGED BACK INTO THE DARK AGES.
IN YOU LIES ALL OUR HOPES AND ASPIRATIONS FOR OUR FAMILIAL LINE MOVING FORWARD.
AND EVEN THOUGH I WON'T REMEMBER THIS TIME, IT IS WITH GREAT HONOR THAT I SERVED THE BLOOD OF ZION.
AND NOW YOU SHALL, TOO.
TAKE WHAT IS YOURS AND MAKE YOUR ANCESTORS PROUD.
AND REMEMBER-- WE ARE ALWAYS WITH YOU, WHEREVER YOU GO.

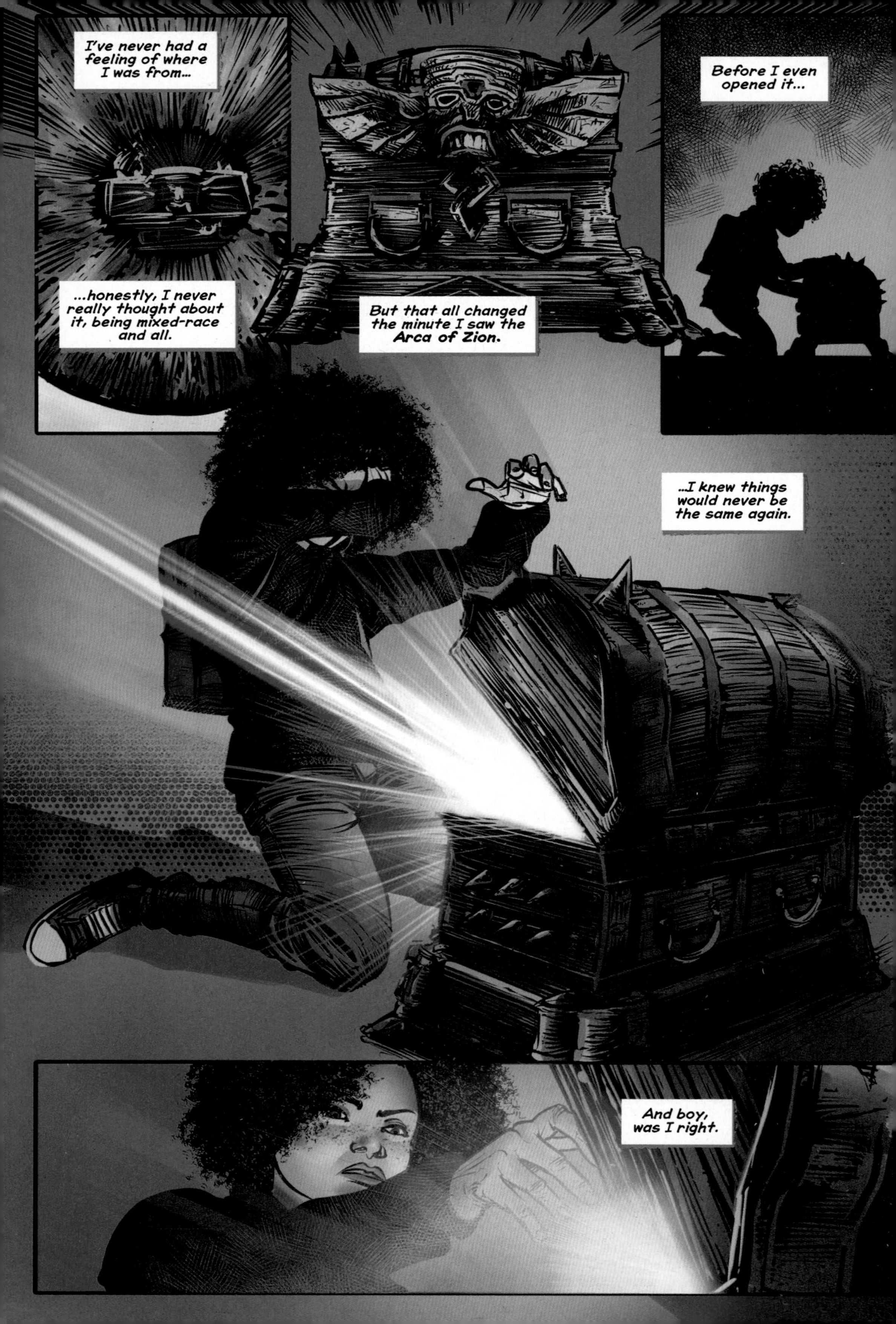

I've never had a feeling of where I was from...
...honestly, I never really thought about it, being mixed-race and all.
But that all changed the minute I saw the Arca of Zion.
Before I even opened it...
...I knew things would never be the same again.
And boy, was I right.

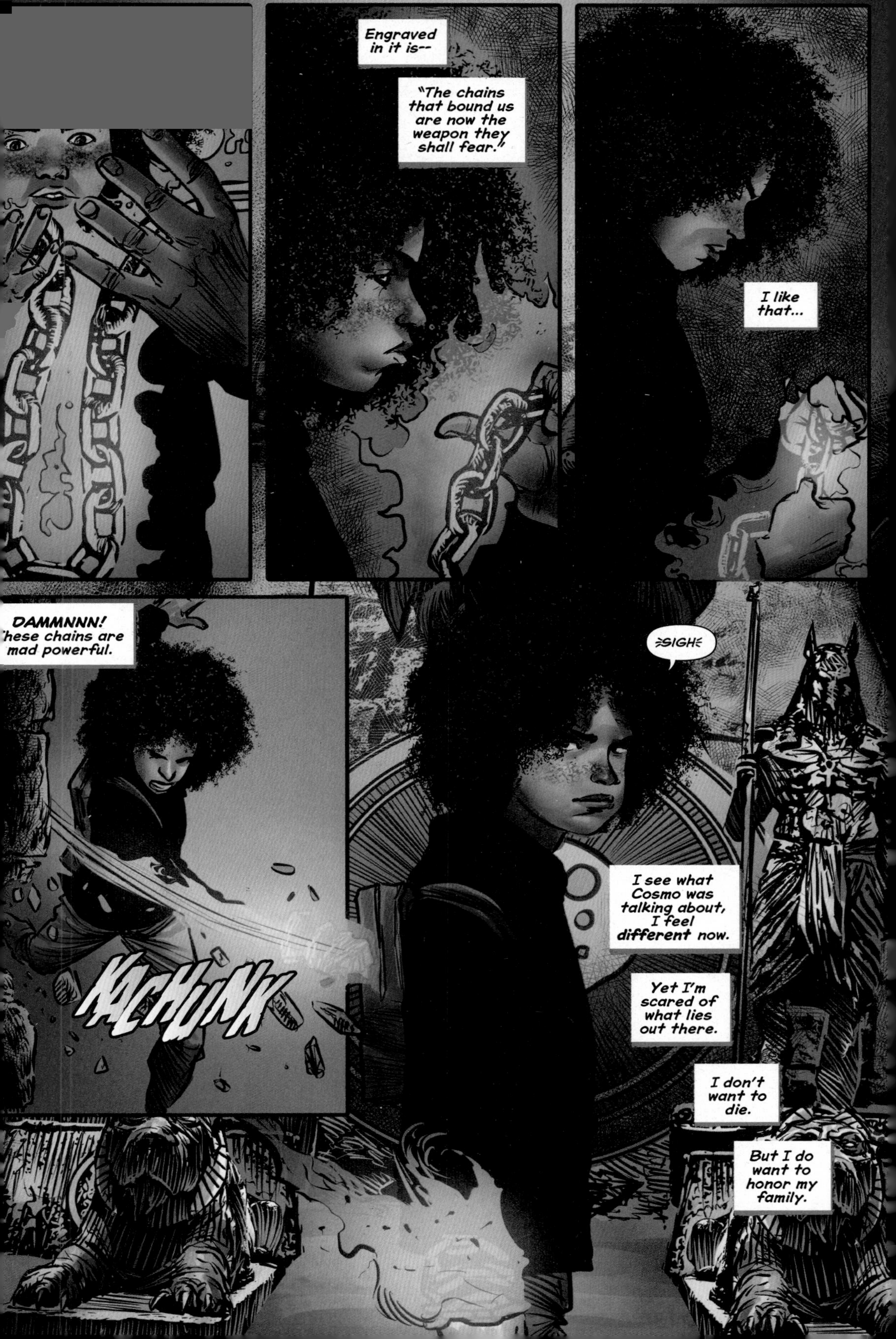

Engraved in it is--
"The chains that bound us are now the weapon they shall fear."
I like that...
DAMMNNN! hese chains are mad powerful.
KACHUNK
SIGH
I see what Cosmo was talking about, I feel different now.
Yet I'm scared of what lies out there.
I don't want to die.
But I do want to honor my family.

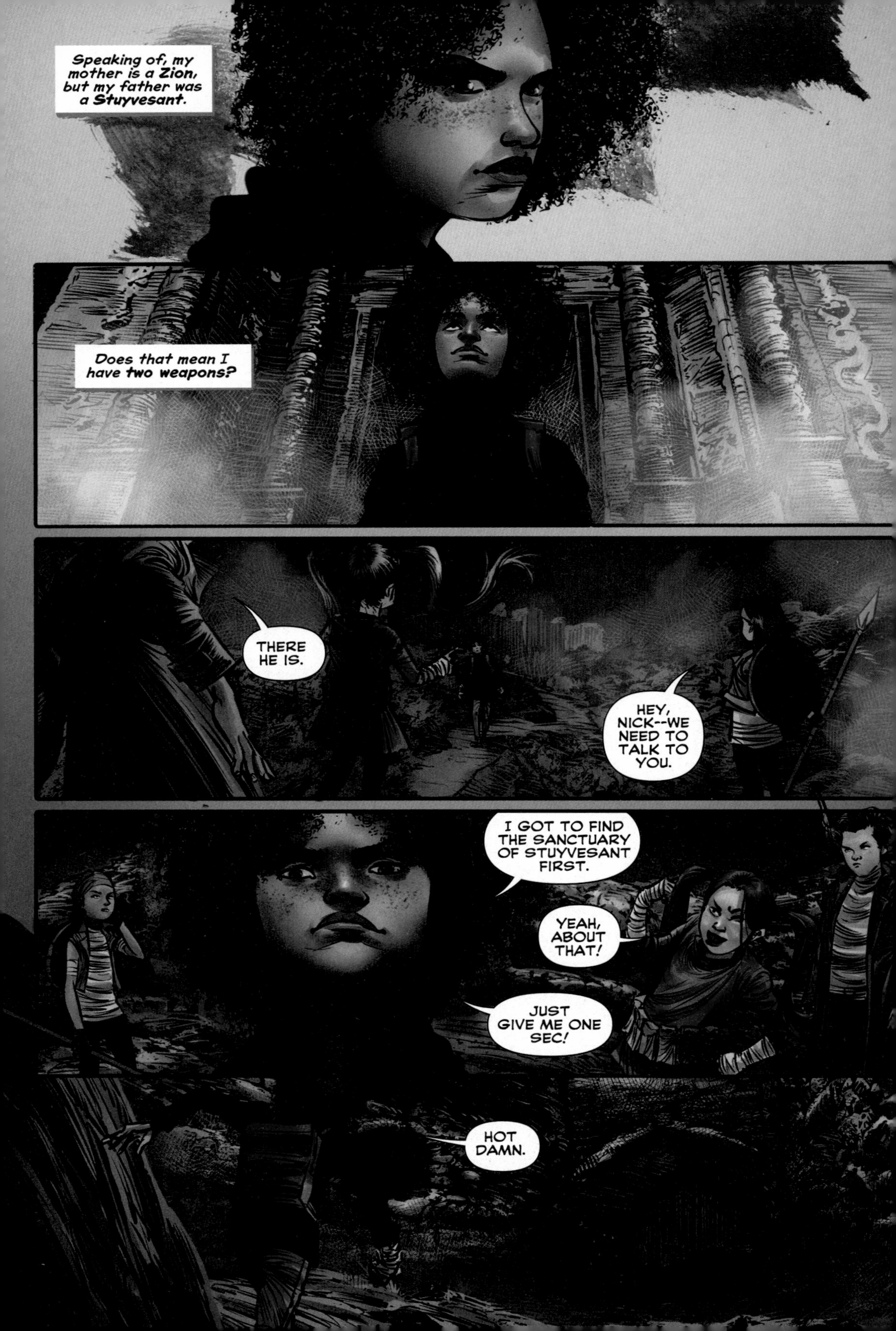
Speaking of, my mother is a Zion, but my father was a Stuyvesant.
Does that mean I have two weapons?
THERE HE IS.
HEY, NICK--WE NEED TO TALK TO YOU.
I GOT TO FIND THE SANCTUARY OF STUYVESANT FIRST.
YEAH, ABOUT THAT!
JUST GIVE ME ONE SEC!
HOT DAMN.

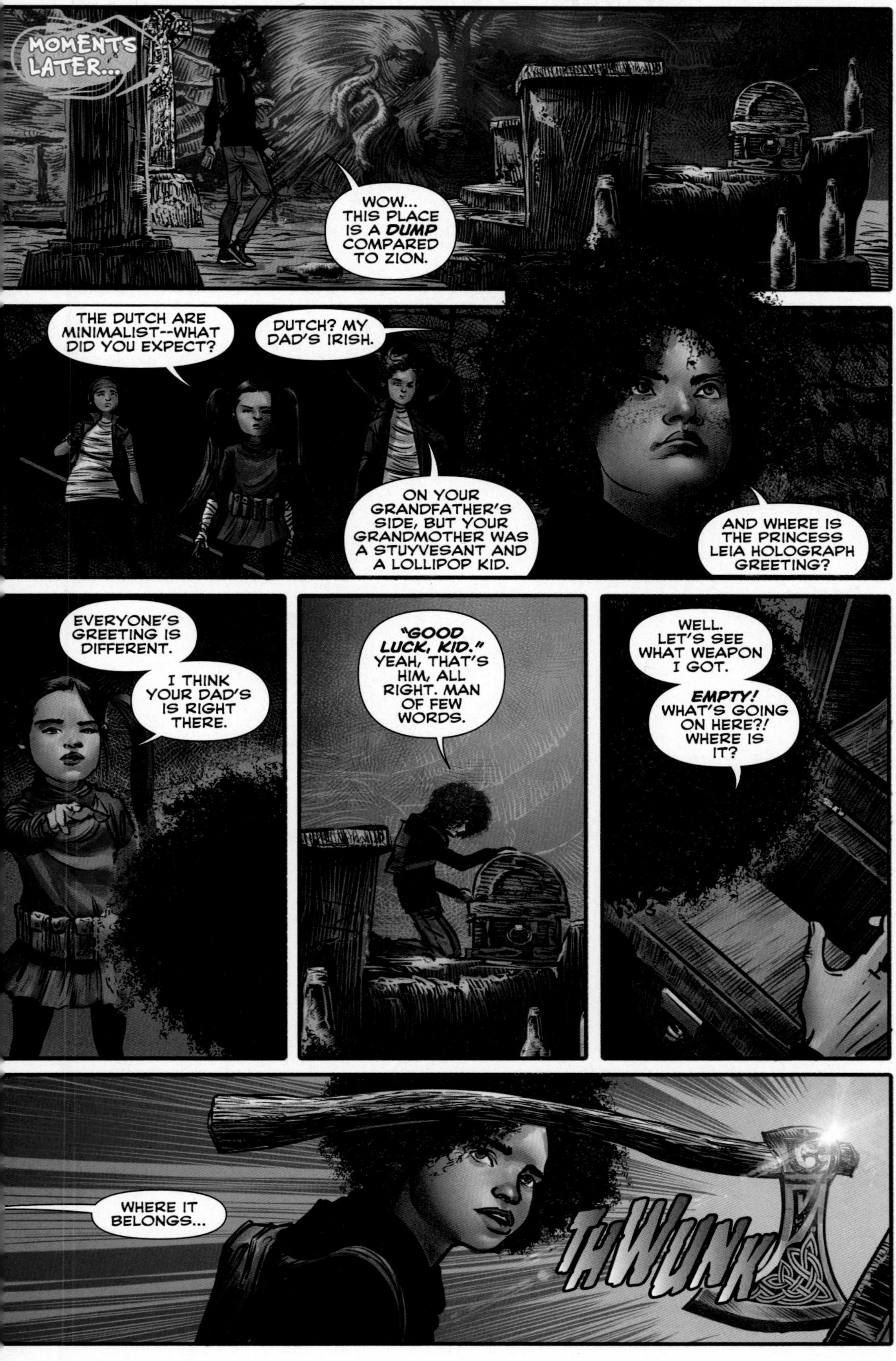
MOMENTS LATER...
WOW... THIS PLACE IS A **DUMP** COMPARED TO ZION.
THE DUTCH ARE MINIMALIST--WHAT DID YOU EXPECT?
DUTCH? MY DAD'S IRISH.
ON YOUR GRANDFATHER'S SIDE, BUT YOUR GRANDMOTHER WAS A STUYVESANT AND A LOLLIPOP KID.
AND WHERE IS THE PRINCESS LEIA HOLOGRAPH GREETING?
EVERYONE'S GREETING IS DIFFERENT.
I THINK YOUR DAD'S IS RIGHT THERE.
"GOOD LUCK, KID." YEAH, THAT'S HIM, ALL RIGHT. MAN OF FEW WORDS.
WELL. LET'S SEE WHAT WEAPON I GOT.
EMPTY! WHAT'S GOING ON HERE?! WHERE IS IT?
WHERE IT BELONGS...
THWUNK

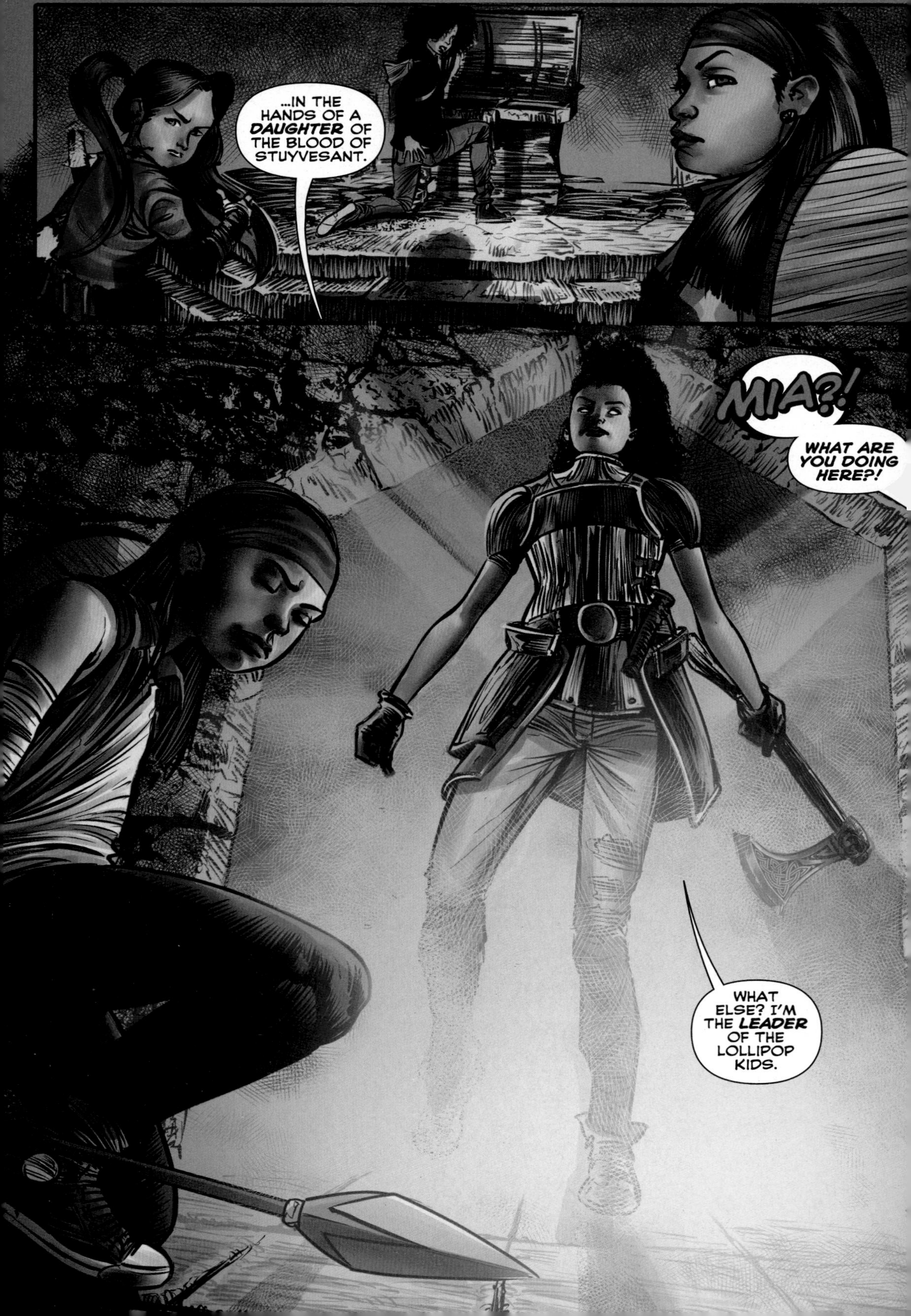

...IN THE HANDS OF A DAUGHTER OF THE BLOOD OF STUYVESANT.
MIA?!
WHAT ARE YOU DOING HERE?!
WHAT ELSE? I'M THE LEADER OF THE LOLLIPOP KIDS.

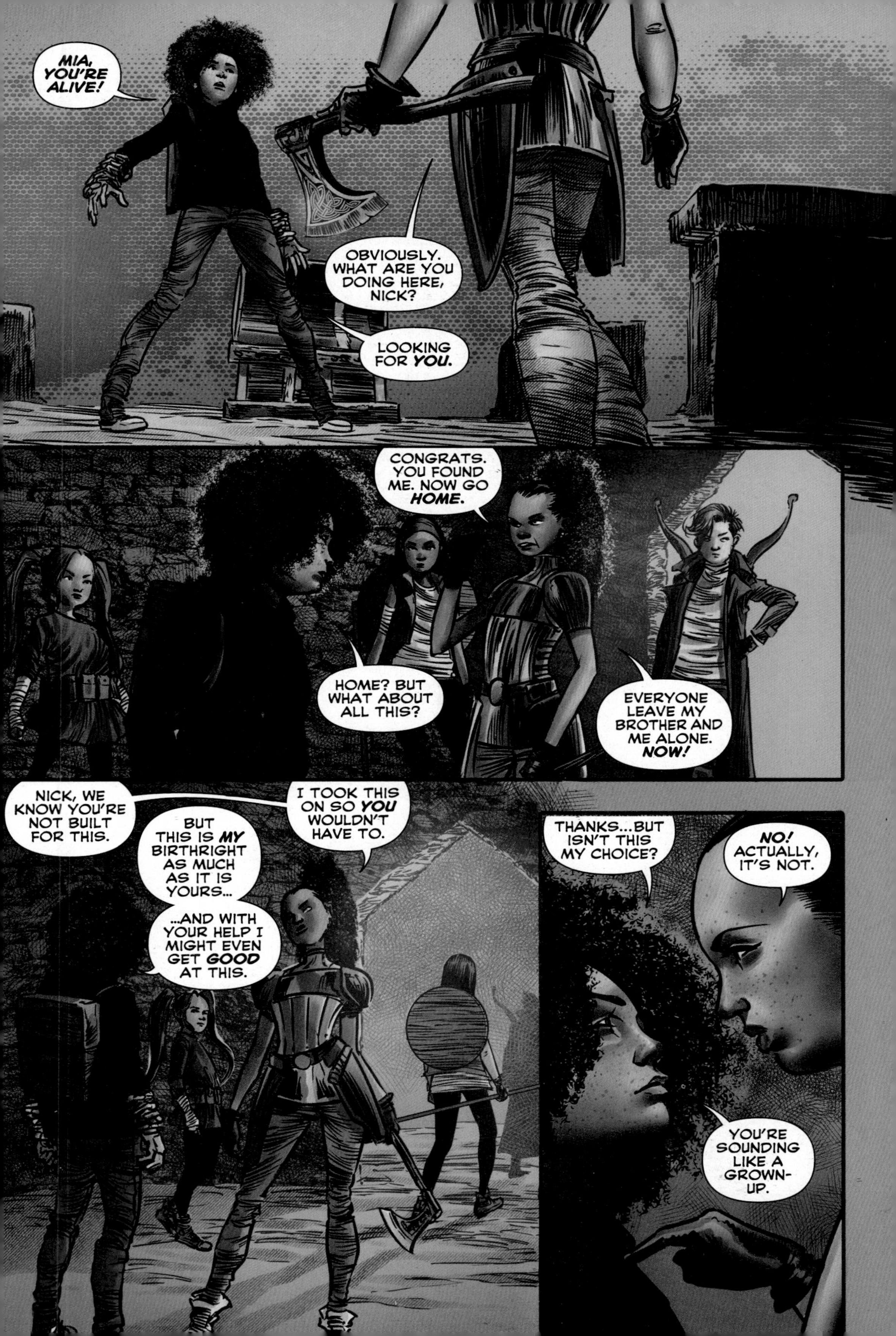
MIA, YOU'RE ALIVE!
OBVIOUSLY. WHAT ARE YOU DOING HERE, NICK?
LOOKING FOR YOU.
CONGRATS. YOU FOUND ME. NOW GO HOME.
HOME? BUT WHAT ABOUT ALL THIS?
EVERYONE LEAVE MY BROTHER AND ME ALONE. NOW!
NICK, WE KNOW YOU'RE NOT BUILT FOR THIS.
I TOOK THIS ON SO YOU WOULDN'T HAVE TO.
BUT THIS IS MY BIRTHRIGHT AS MUCH AS IT IS YOURS...
...AND WITH YOUR HELP I MIGHT EVEN GET GOOD AT THIS.
THANKS...BUT ISN'T THIS MY CHOICE?
NO! ACTUALLY, IT'S NOT.
YOU'RE SOUNDING LIKE A GROWN-UP.

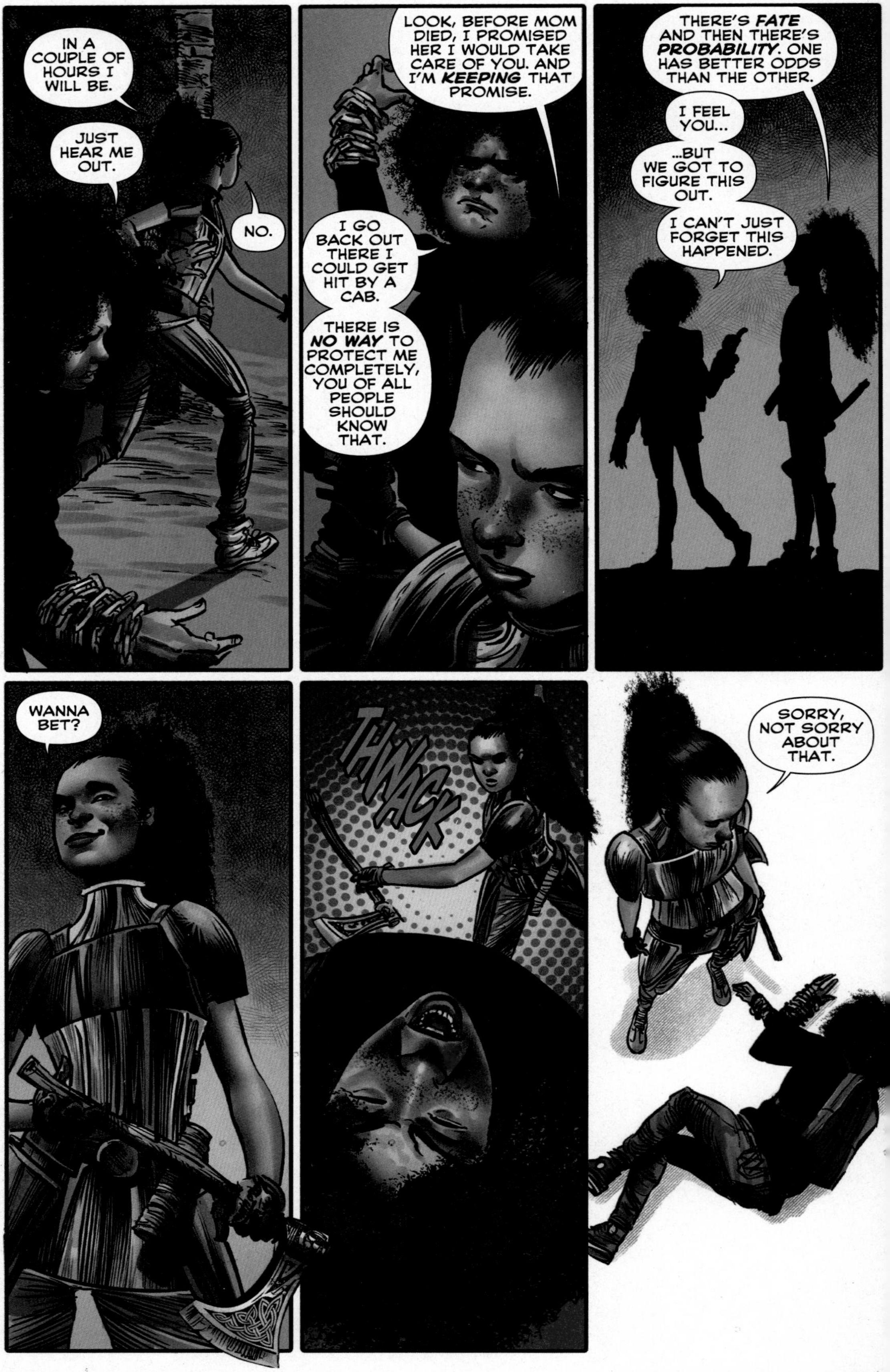
IN A COUPLE OF HOURS I WILL BE.
JUST HEAR ME OUT.
NO.
LOOK, BEFORE MOM DIED, I PROMISED HER I WOULD TAKE CARE OF YOU. AND I'M KEEPING THAT PROMISE.
I GO BACK OUT THERE I COULD GET HIT BY A CAB.
THERE IS NO WAY TO PROTECT ME COMPLETELY, YOU OF ALL PEOPLE SHOULD KNOW THAT.
THERE'S FATE AND THEN THERE'S PROBABILITY. ONE HAS BETTER ODDS THAN THE OTHER.
I FEEL YOU...
...BUT WE GOT TO FIGURE THIS OUT.
I CAN'T JUST FORGET THIS HAPPENED.
WANNA BET?
THWACK
SORRY, NOT SORRY ABOUT THAT.

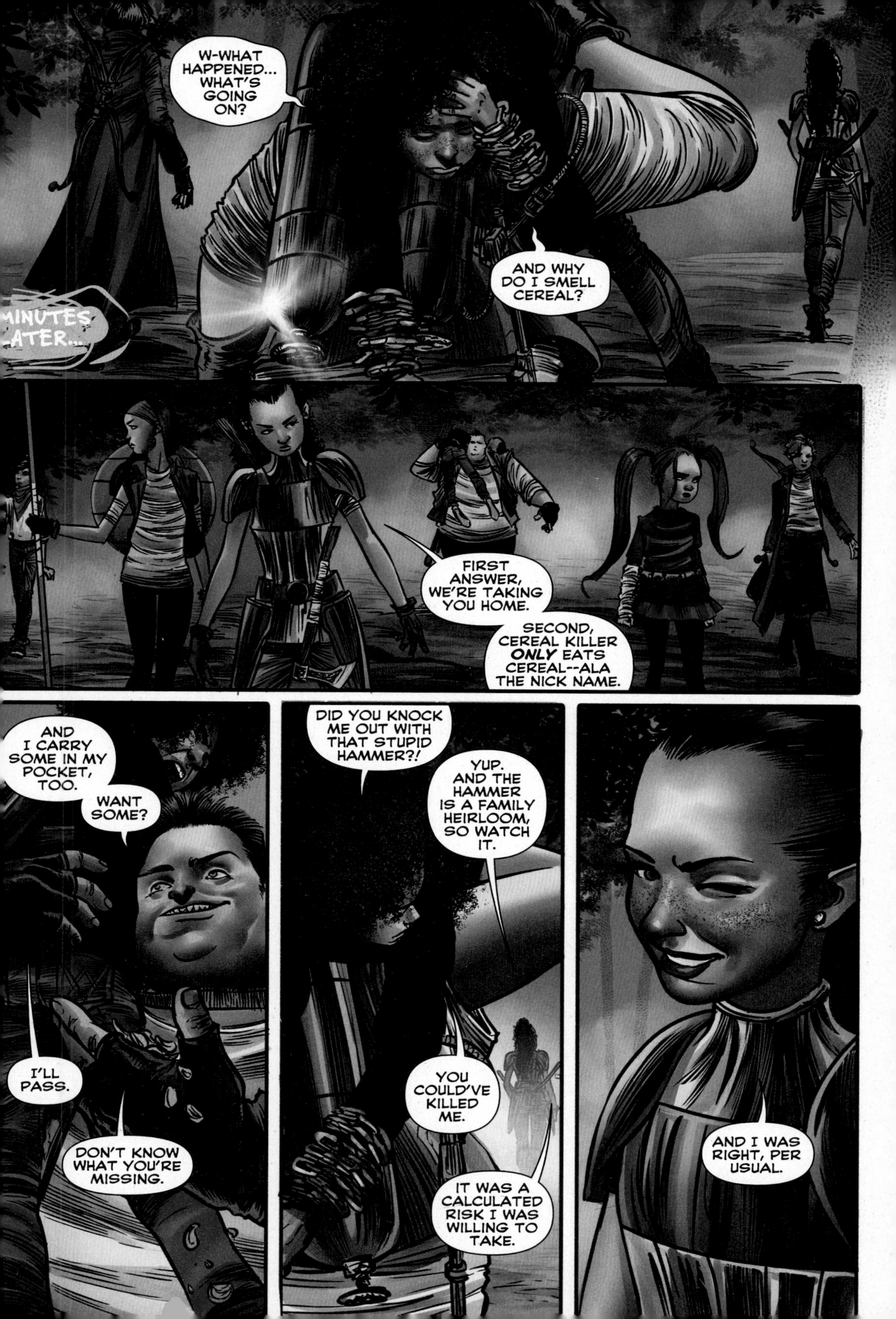
W-WHAT HAPPENED... WHAT'S GOING ON?
MINUTES LATER...
AND WHY DO I SMELL CEREAL?
FIRST ANSWER, WE'RE TAKING YOU HOME.
SECOND, CEREAL KILLER ONLY EATS CEREAL--ALA THE NICK NAME.
AND I CARRY SOME IN MY POCKET, TOO.
WANT SOME?
I'LL PASS.
DON'T KNOW WHAT YOU'RE MISSING.
DID YOU KNOCK ME OUT WITH THAT STUPID HAMMER?!
YUP. AND THE HAMMER IS A FAMILY HEIRLOOM, SO WATCH IT.
YOU COULD'VE KILLED ME.
IT WAS A CALCULATED RISK I WAS WILLING TO TAKE.
AND I WAS RIGHT, PER USUAL.

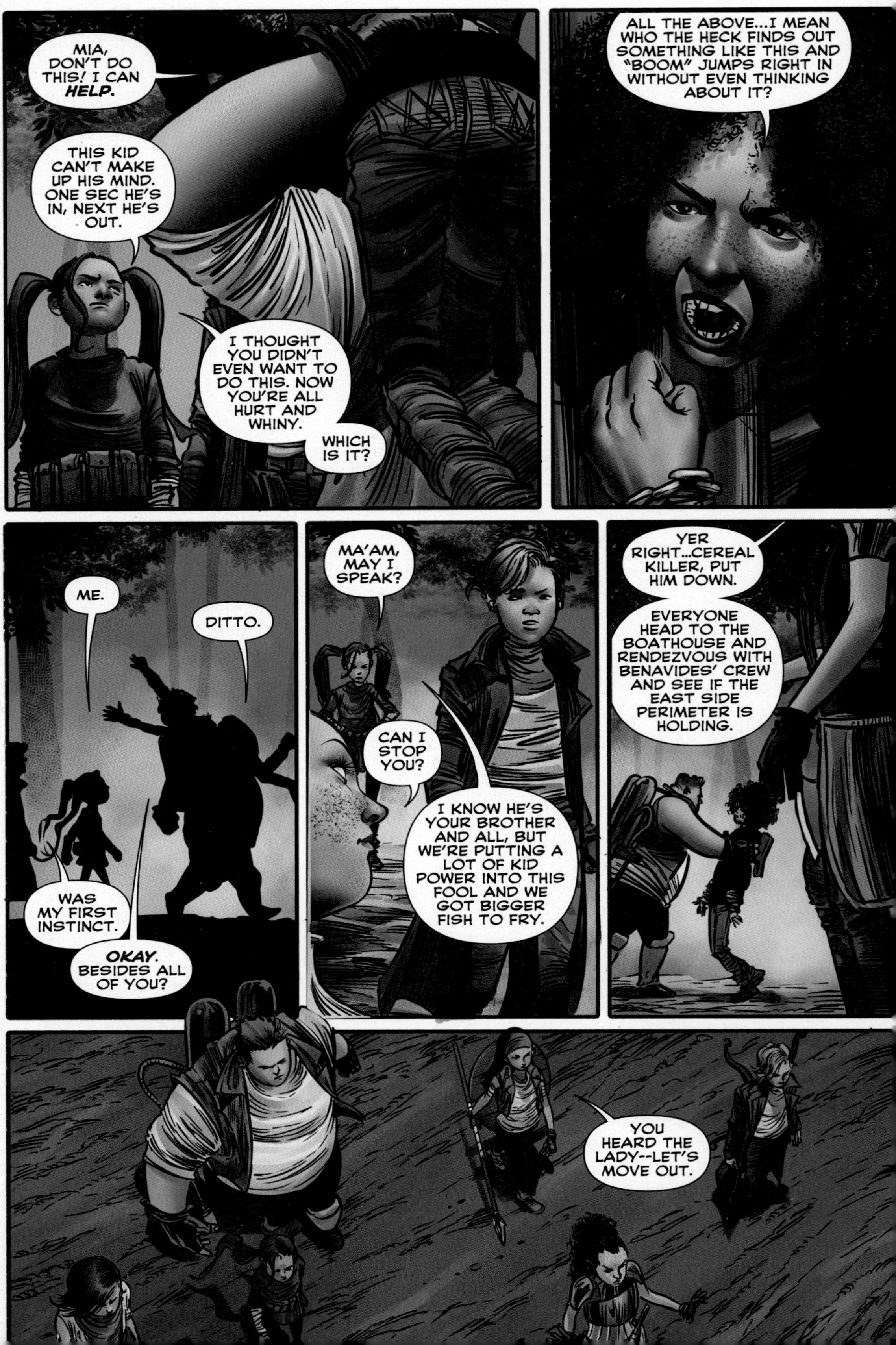
MIA, DON'T DO THIS! I CAN *HELP*.
THIS KID CAN'T MAKE UP HIS MIND. ONE SEC HE'S IN, NEXT HE'S OUT.
I THOUGHT YOU DIDN'T EVEN WANT TO DO THIS. NOW YOU'RE ALL HURT AND WHINY.
WHICH IS IT?
ALL THE ABOVE...I MEAN WHO THE HECK FINDS OUT SOMETHING LIKE THIS AND "BOOM" JUMPS RIGHT IN WITHOUT EVEN THINKING ABOUT IT?
ME.
DITTO.
WAS MY FIRST INSTINCT.
OKAY. BESIDES ALL OF YOU?
MA'AM, MAY I SPEAK?
CAN I STOP YOU?
I KNOW HE'S YOUR BROTHER AND ALL, BUT WE'RE PUTTING A LOT OF KID POWER INTO THIS FOOL AND WE GOT BIGGER FISH TO FRY.
YER RIGHT...CEREAL KILLER, PUT HIM DOWN.
EVERYONE HEAD TO THE BOATHOUSE AND RENDEZVOUS WITH BENAVIDES' CREW AND SEE IF THE EAST SIDE PERIMETER IS HOLDING.
YOU HEARD THE LADY--LET'S MOVE OUT.

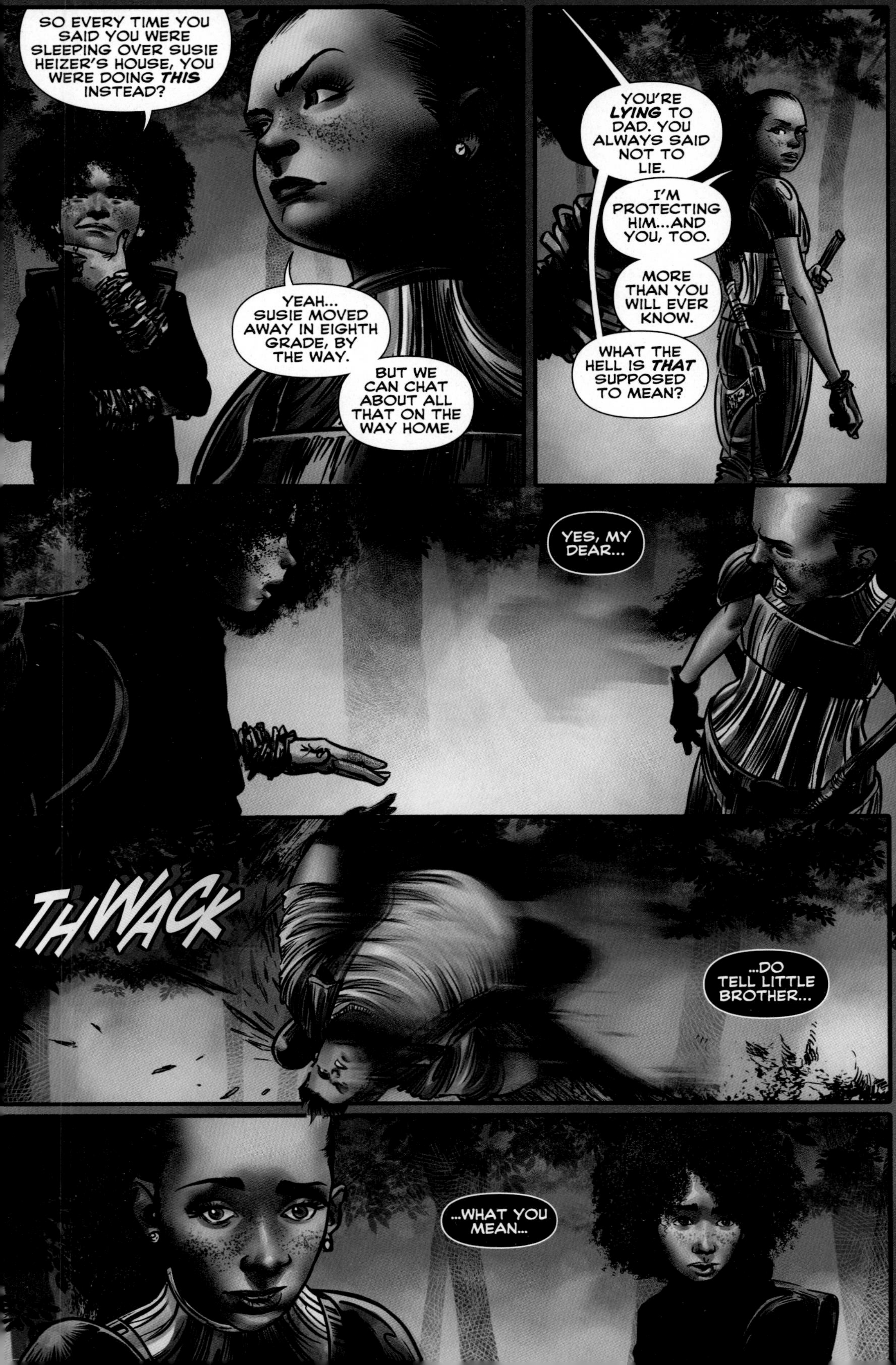
SO EVERY TIME YOU SAID YOU WERE SLEEPING OVER SUSIE HEIZER'S HOUSE, YOU WERE DOING *THIS* INSTEAD?
YEAH... SUSIE MOVED AWAY IN EIGHTH GRADE, BY THE WAY.
BUT WE CAN CHAT ABOUT ALL THAT ON THE WAY HOME.
YOU'RE *LYING* TO DAD. YOU ALWAYS SAID NOT TO LIE.
I'M PROTECTING HIM...AND YOU, TOO.
MORE THAN YOU WILL EVER KNOW.
WHAT THE HELL IS *THAT* SUPPOSED TO MEAN?
YES, MY DEAR...
THWACK
...DO TELL LITTLE BROTHER...
...WHAT YOU MEAN...

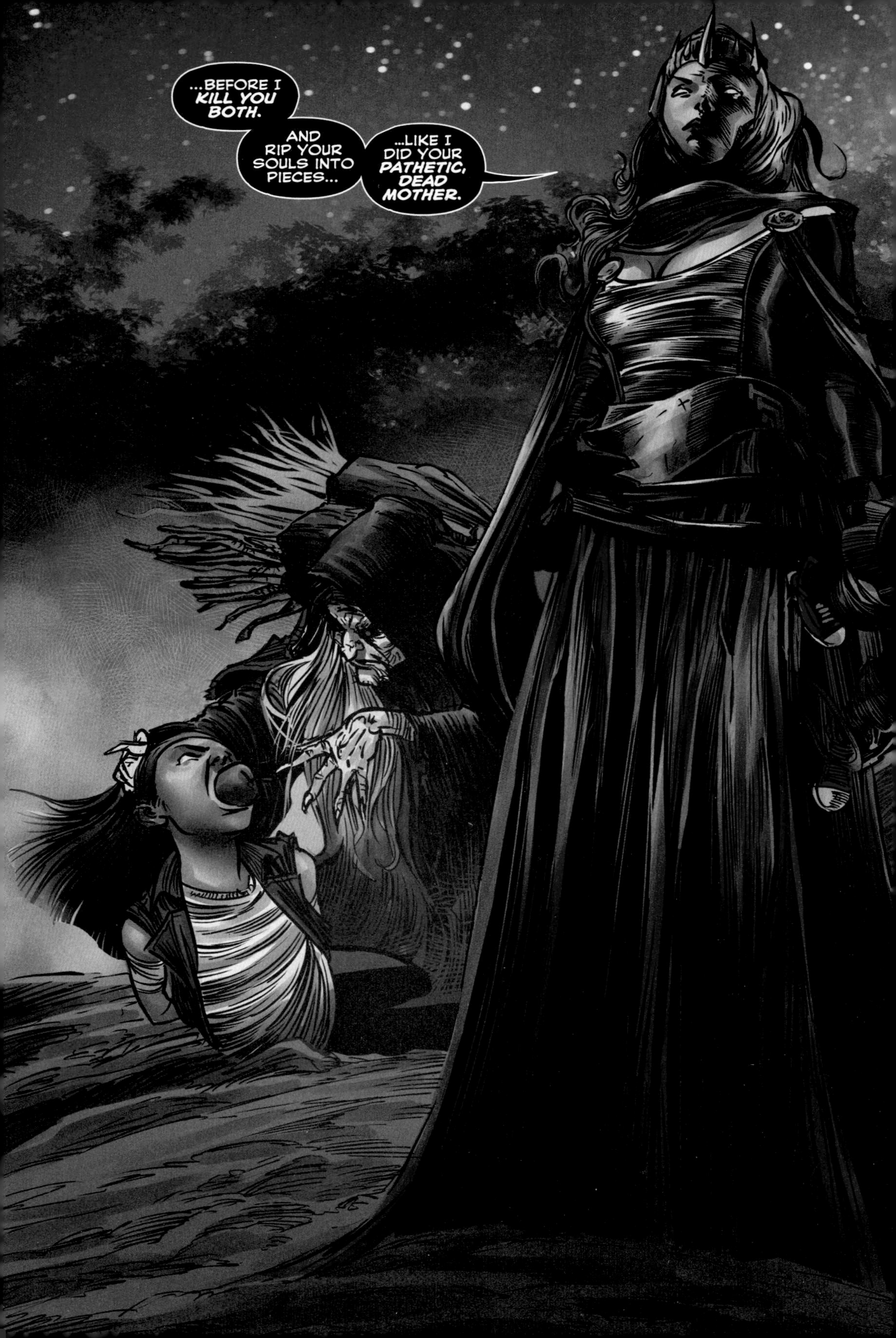
...BEFORE I KILL YOU BOTH.
AND RIP YOUR SOULS INTO PIECES...
...LIKE I DID YOUR PATHETIC, DEAD MOTHER.

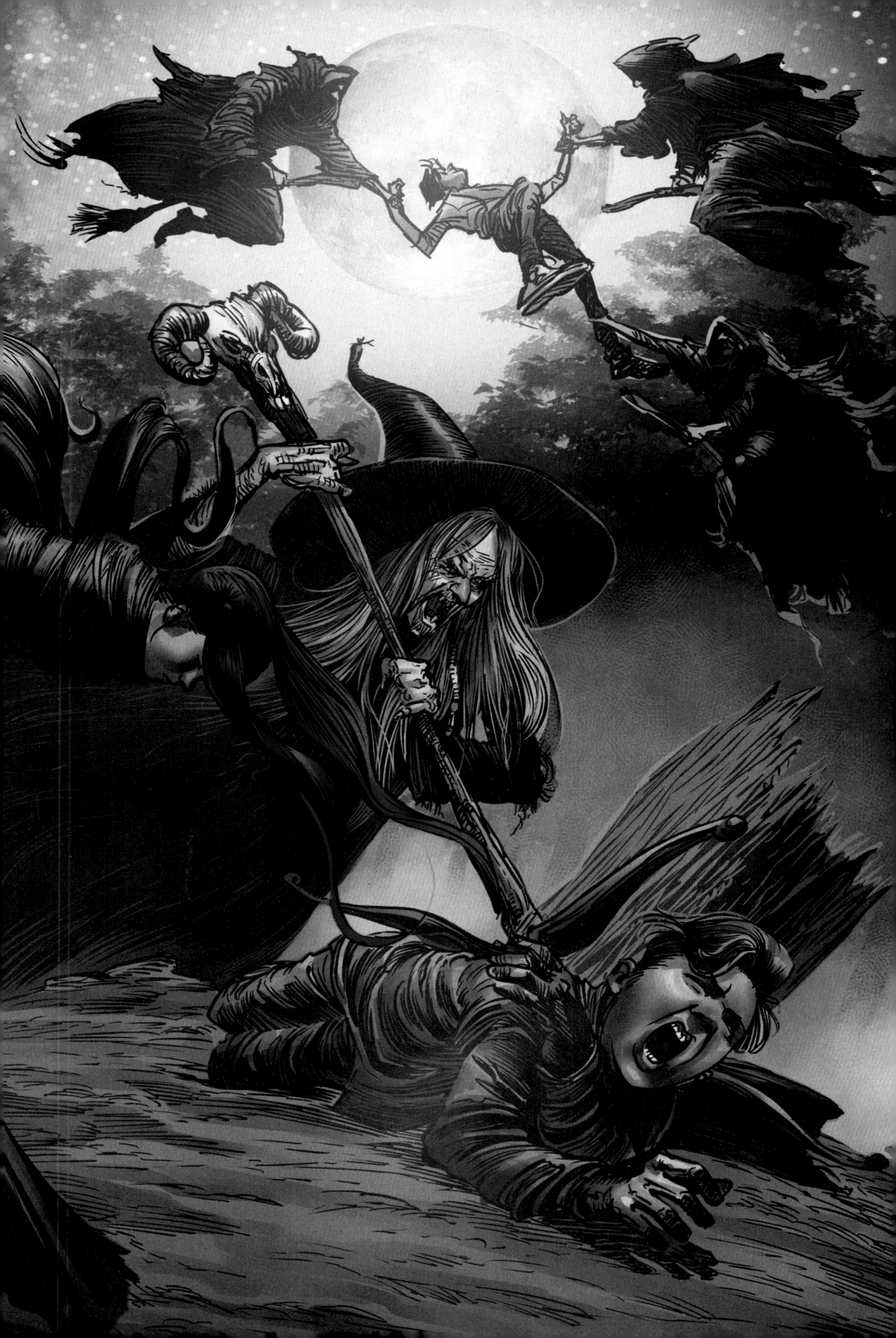

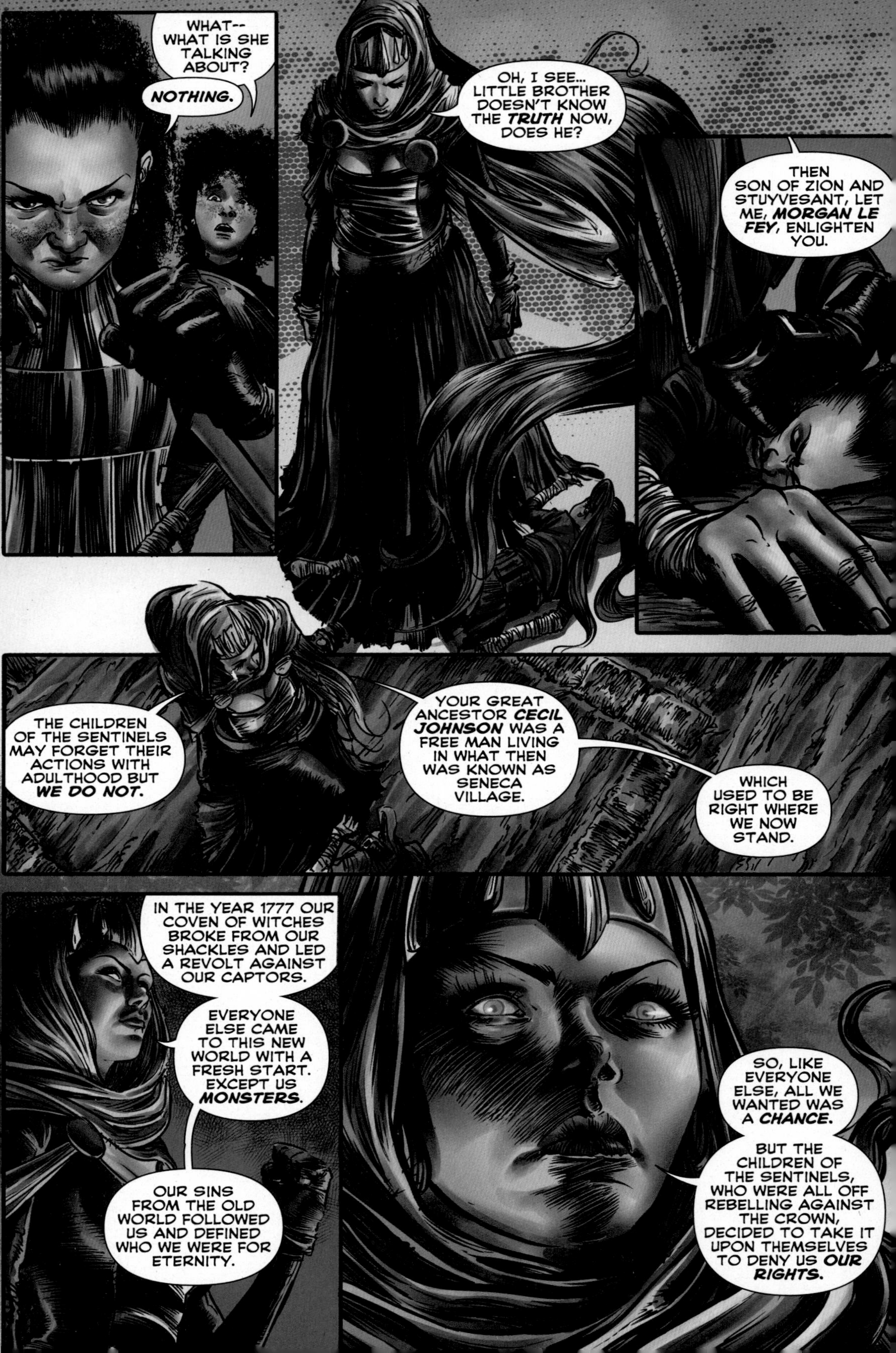
WHAT-- WHAT IS SHE TALKING ABOUT?
NOTHING.
OH, I SEE... LITTLE BROTHER DOESN'T KNOW THE TRUTH NOW, DOES HE?
THEN SON OF ZION AND STUYVESANT, LET ME, MORGAN LE FEY, ENLIGHTEN YOU.
THE CHILDREN OF THE SENTINELS MAY FORGET THEIR ACTIONS WITH ADULTHOOD BUT WE DO NOT.
YOUR GREAT ANCESTOR CECIL JOHNSON WAS A FREE MAN LIVING IN WHAT THEN WAS KNOWN AS SENECA VILLAGE.
WHICH USED TO BE RIGHT WHERE WE NOW STAND.
IN THE YEAR 1777 OUR COVEN OF WITCHES BROKE FROM OUR SHACKLES AND LED A REVOLT AGAINST OUR CAPTORS.
EVERYONE ELSE CAME TO THIS NEW WORLD WITH A FRESH START. EXCEPT US MONSTERS.
OUR SINS FROM THE OLD WORLD FOLLOWED US AND DEFINED WHO WE WERE FOR ETERNITY.
SO, LIKE EVERYONE ELSE, ALL WE WANTED WAS A CHANCE.
BUT THE CHILDREN OF THE SENTINELS, WHO WERE ALL OFF REBELLING AGAINST THE CROWN, DECIDED TO TAKE IT UPON THEMSELVES TO DENY US OUR RIGHTS.

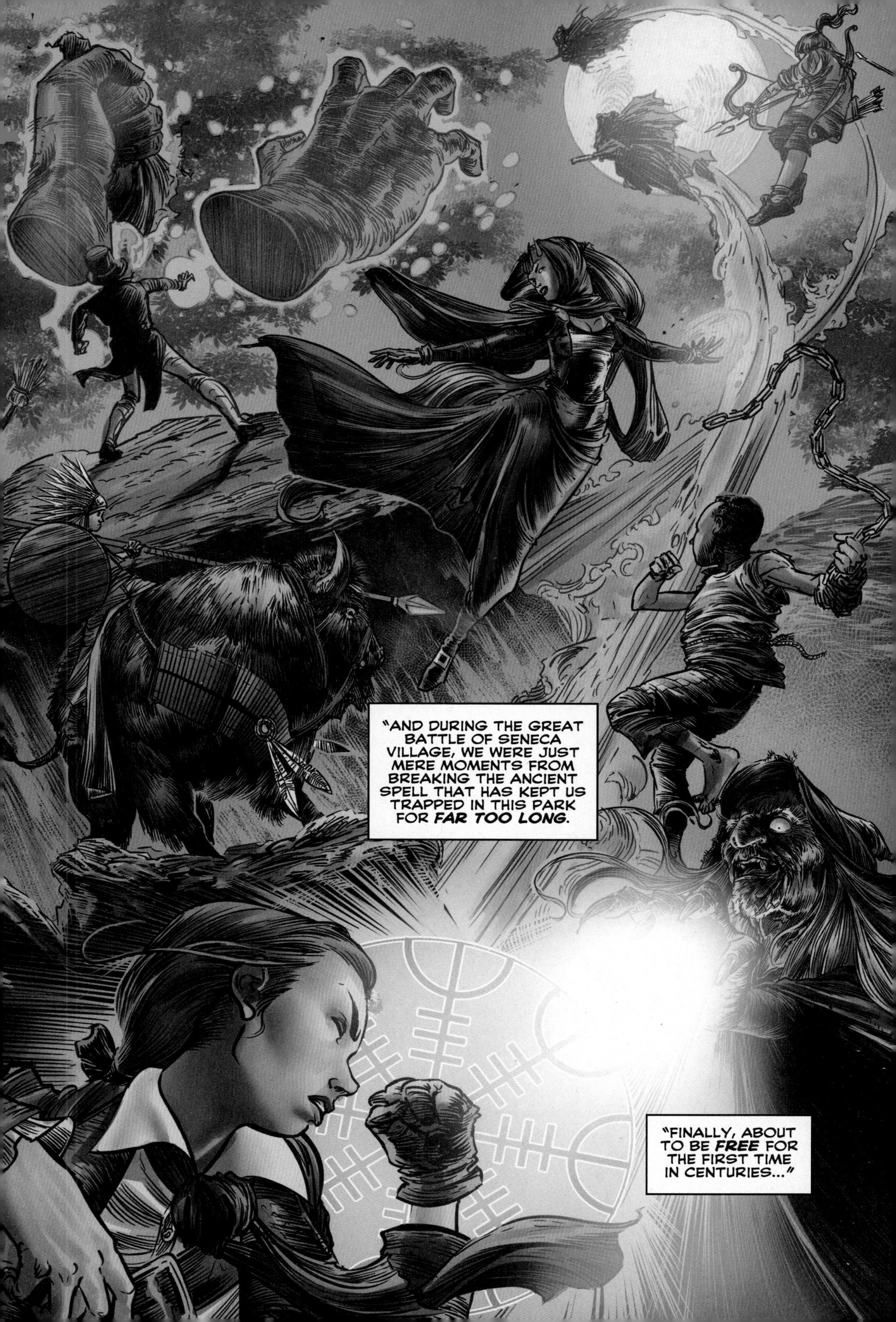
"AND DURING THE GREAT BATTLE OF SENECA VILLAGE, WE WERE JUST MERE MOMENTS FROM BREAKING THE ANCIENT SPELL THAT HAS KEPT US TRAPPED IN THIS PARK FOR ***FAR TOO LONG***.
"FINALLY, ABOUT TO BE ***FREE*** FOR THE FIRST TIME IN CENTURIES..."

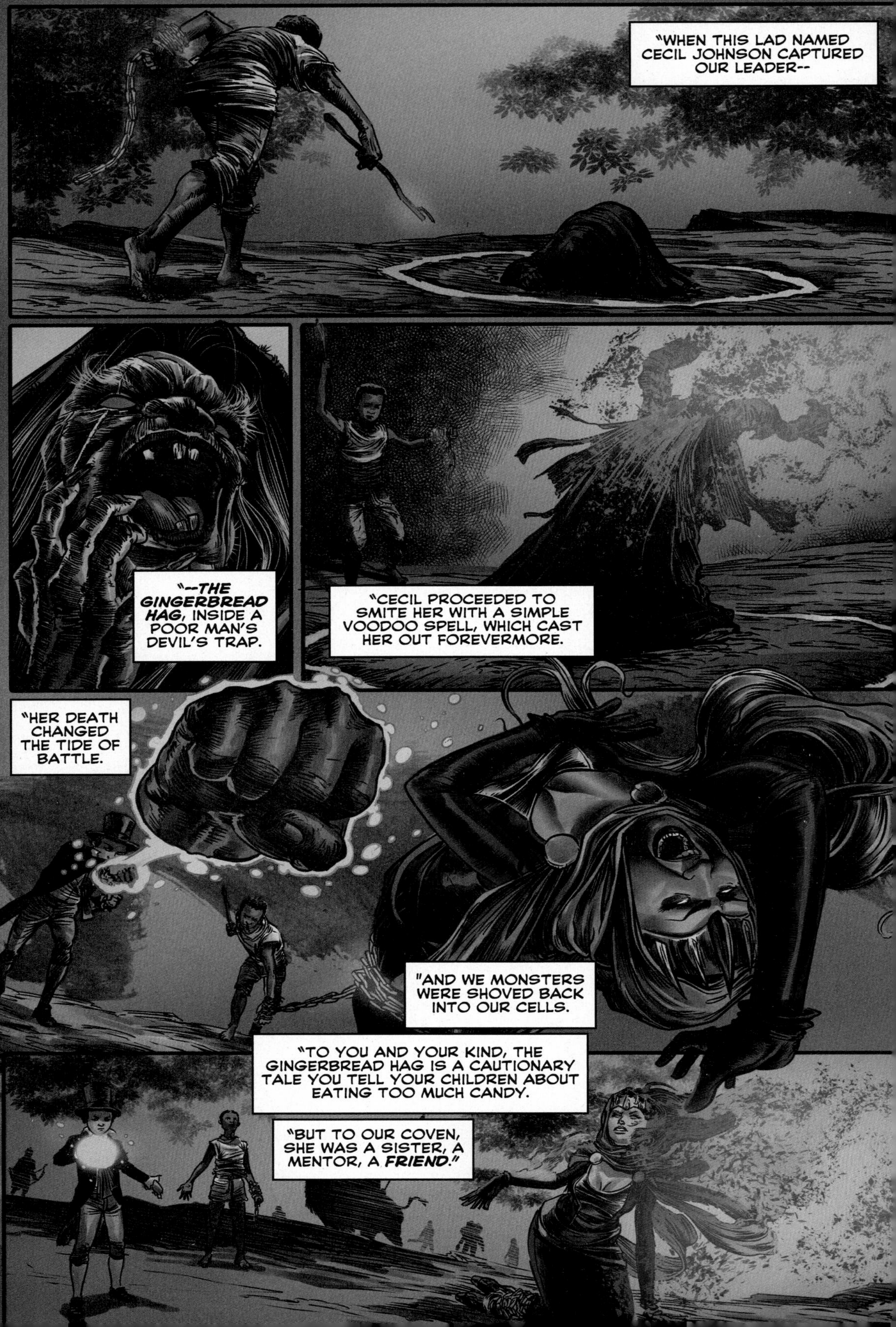
"WHEN THIS LAD NAMED CECIL JOHNSON CAPTURED OUR LEADER--
"--THE GINGERBREAD HAG, INSIDE A POOR MAN'S DEVIL'S TRAP.
"CECIL PROCEEDED TO SMITE HER WITH A SIMPLE VOODOO SPELL, WHICH CAST HER OUT FOREVERMORE.
"HER DEATH CHANGED THE TIDE OF BATTLE.
"AND WE MONSTERS WERE SHOVED BACK INTO OUR CELLS.
"TO YOU AND YOUR KIND, THE GINGERBREAD HAG IS A CAUTIONARY TALE YOU TELL YOUR CHILDREN ABOUT EATING TOO MUCH CANDY.
"BUT TO OUR COVEN, SHE WAS A SISTER, A MENTOR, A ***FRIEND***."

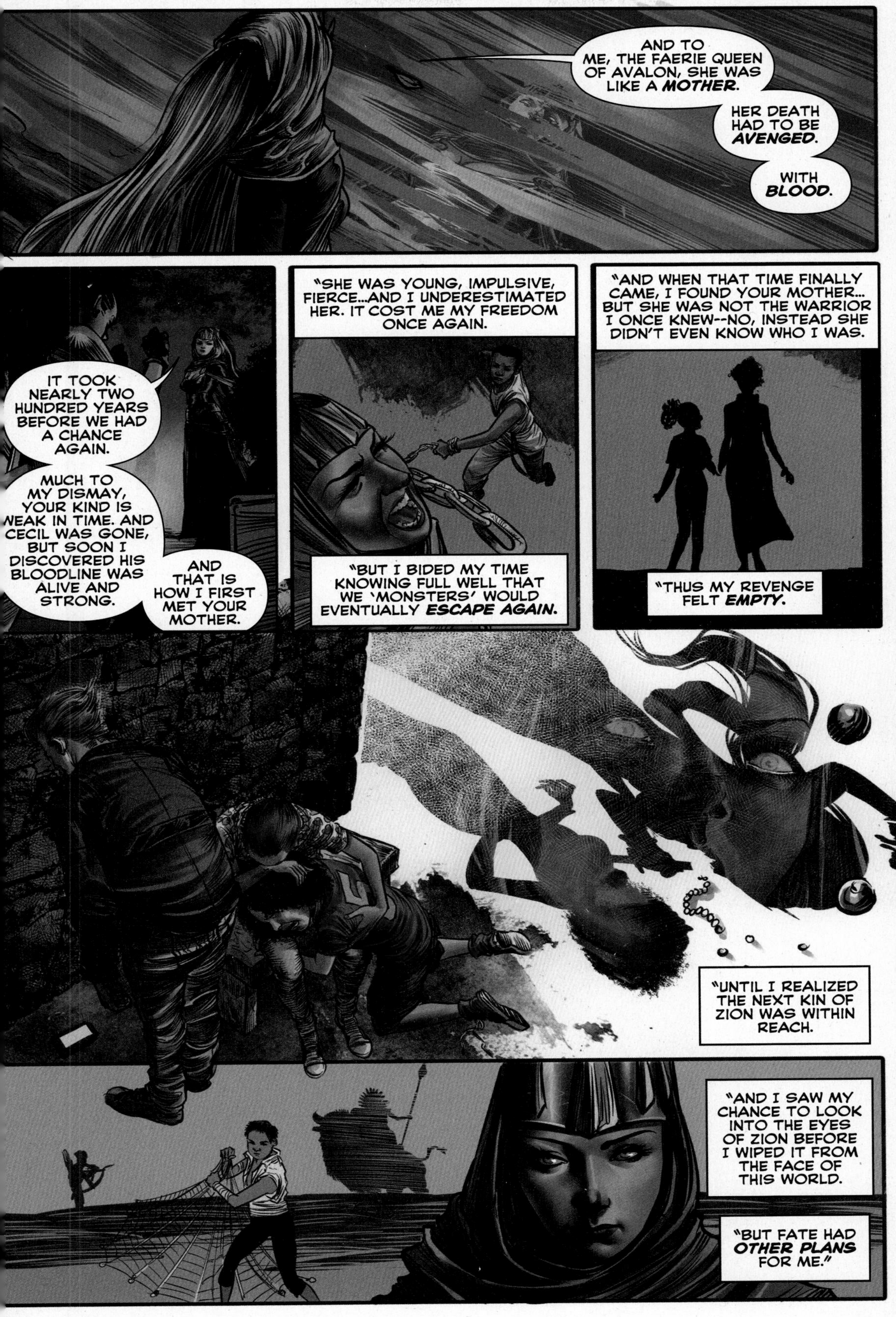
AND TO ME, THE FAERIE QUEEN OF AVALON, SHE WAS LIKE A *MOTHER*.
HER DEATH HAD TO BE *AVENGED*.
WITH *BLOOD*.
IT TOOK NEARLY TWO HUNDRED YEARS BEFORE WE HAD A CHANCE AGAIN.
MUCH TO MY DISMAY, YOUR KIND IS WEAK IN TIME. AND CECIL WAS GONE, BUT SOON I DISCOVERED HIS BLOODLINE WAS ALIVE AND STRONG.
AND THAT IS HOW I FIRST MET YOUR MOTHER.
"SHE WAS YOUNG, IMPULSIVE, FIERCE...AND I UNDERESTIMATED HER. IT COST ME MY FREEDOM ONCE AGAIN.
"BUT I BIDED MY TIME KNOWING FULL WELL THAT WE 'MONSTERS' WOULD EVENTUALLY *ESCAPE AGAIN*.
"AND WHEN THAT TIME FINALLY CAME, I FOUND YOUR MOTHER... BUT SHE WAS NOT THE WARRIOR I ONCE KNEW--NO, INSTEAD SHE DIDN'T EVEN KNOW WHO I WAS.
"THUS MY REVENGE FELT *EMPTY*.
"UNTIL I REALIZED THE NEXT KIN OF ZION WAS WITHIN REACH.
"AND I SAW MY CHANCE TO LOOK INTO THE EYES OF ZION BEFORE I WIPED IT FROM THE FACE OF THIS WORLD.
"BUT FATE HAD *OTHER PLANS* FOR ME."

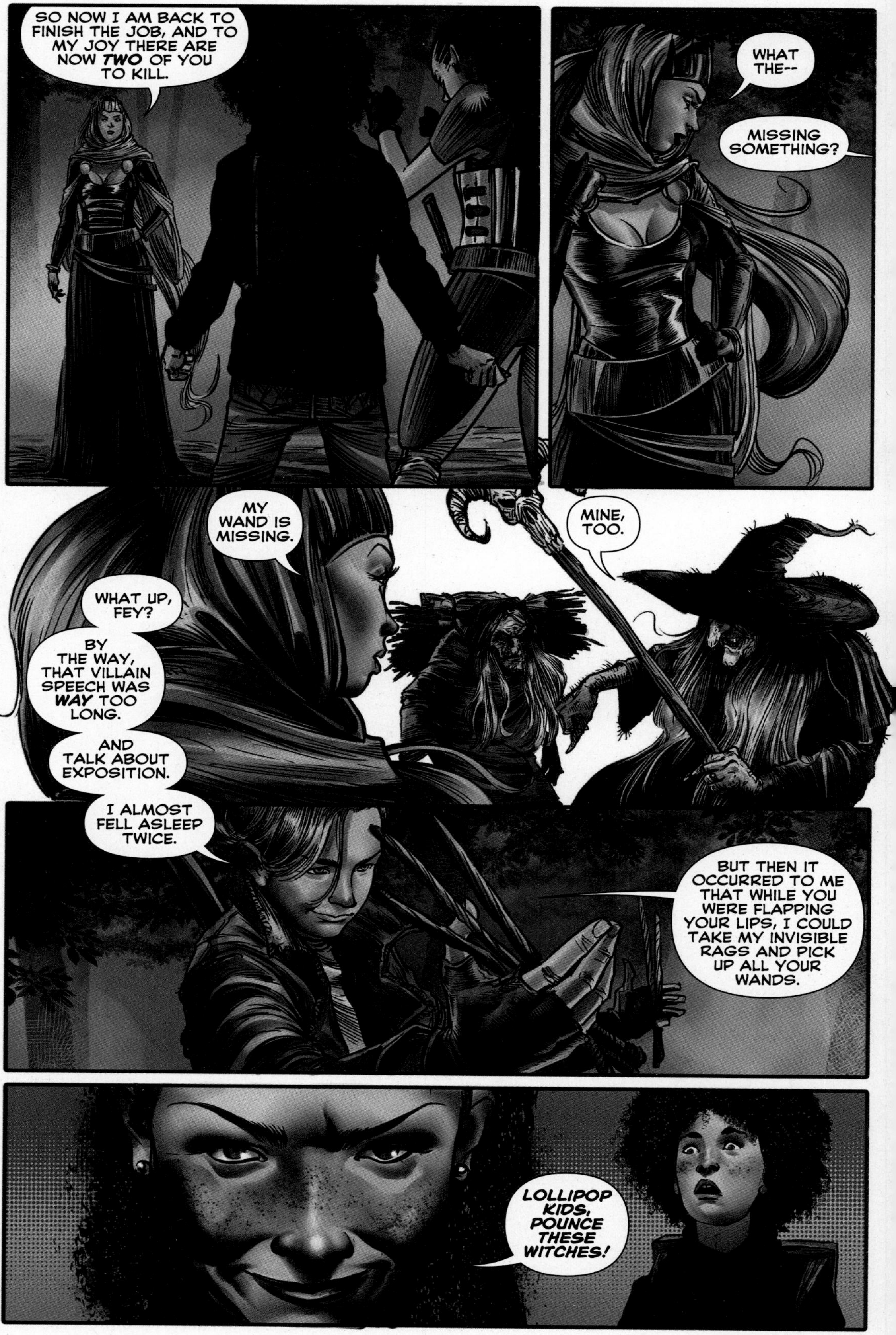
SO NOW I AM BACK TO FINISH THE JOB, AND TO MY JOY THERE ARE NOW **TWO** OF YOU TO KILL.
WHAT THE--
MISSING SOMETHING?
MY WAND IS MISSING.
MINE, TOO.
WHAT UP, FEY?
BY THE WAY, THAT VILLAIN SPEECH WAS **WAY** TOO LONG.
AND TALK ABOUT EXPOSITION.
I ALMOST FELL ASLEEP TWICE.
BUT THEN IT OCCURRED TO ME THAT WHILE YOU WERE FLAPPING YOUR LIPS, I COULD TAKE MY INVISIBLE RAGS AND PICK UP ALL YOUR WANDS.
LOLLIPOP KIDS, POUNCE THESE WITCHES!

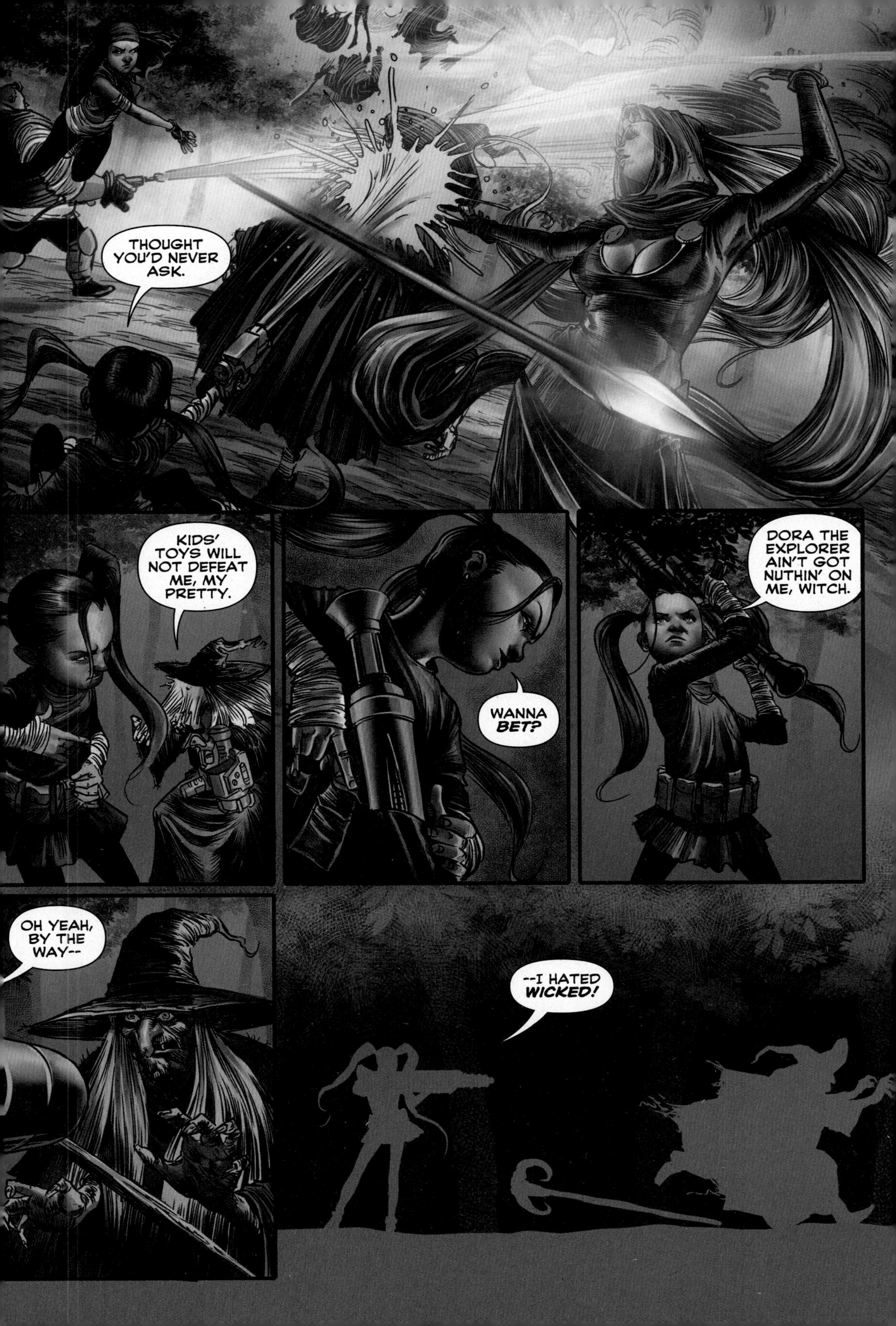
THOUGHT YOU'D NEVER ASK.
KIDS' TOYS WILL NOT DEFEAT ME, MY PRETTY.
WANNA BET?
DORA THE EXPLORER AIN'T GOT NUTHIN' ON ME, WITCH.
OH YEAH, BY THE WAY--
--I HATED WICKED!

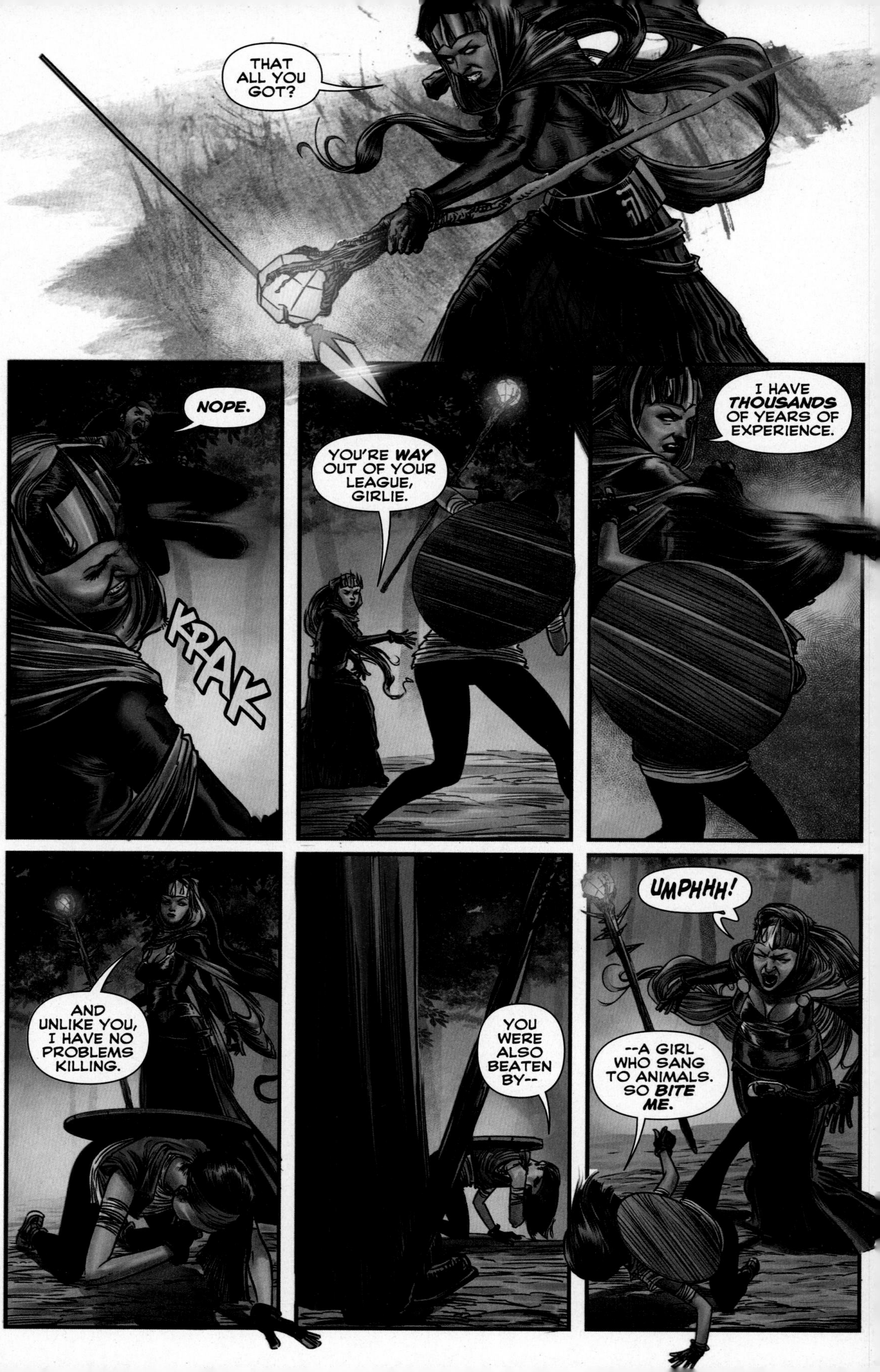
THAT ALL YOU GOT?
NOPE.
KRAK
YOU'RE WAY OUT OF YOUR LEAGUE, GIRLIE.
I HAVE THOUSANDS OF YEARS OF EXPERIENCE.
AND UNLIKE YOU, I HAVE NO PROBLEMS KILLING.
YOU WERE ALSO BEATEN BY--
UMPHHH!
--A GIRL WHO SANG TO ANIMALS. SO BITE ME.

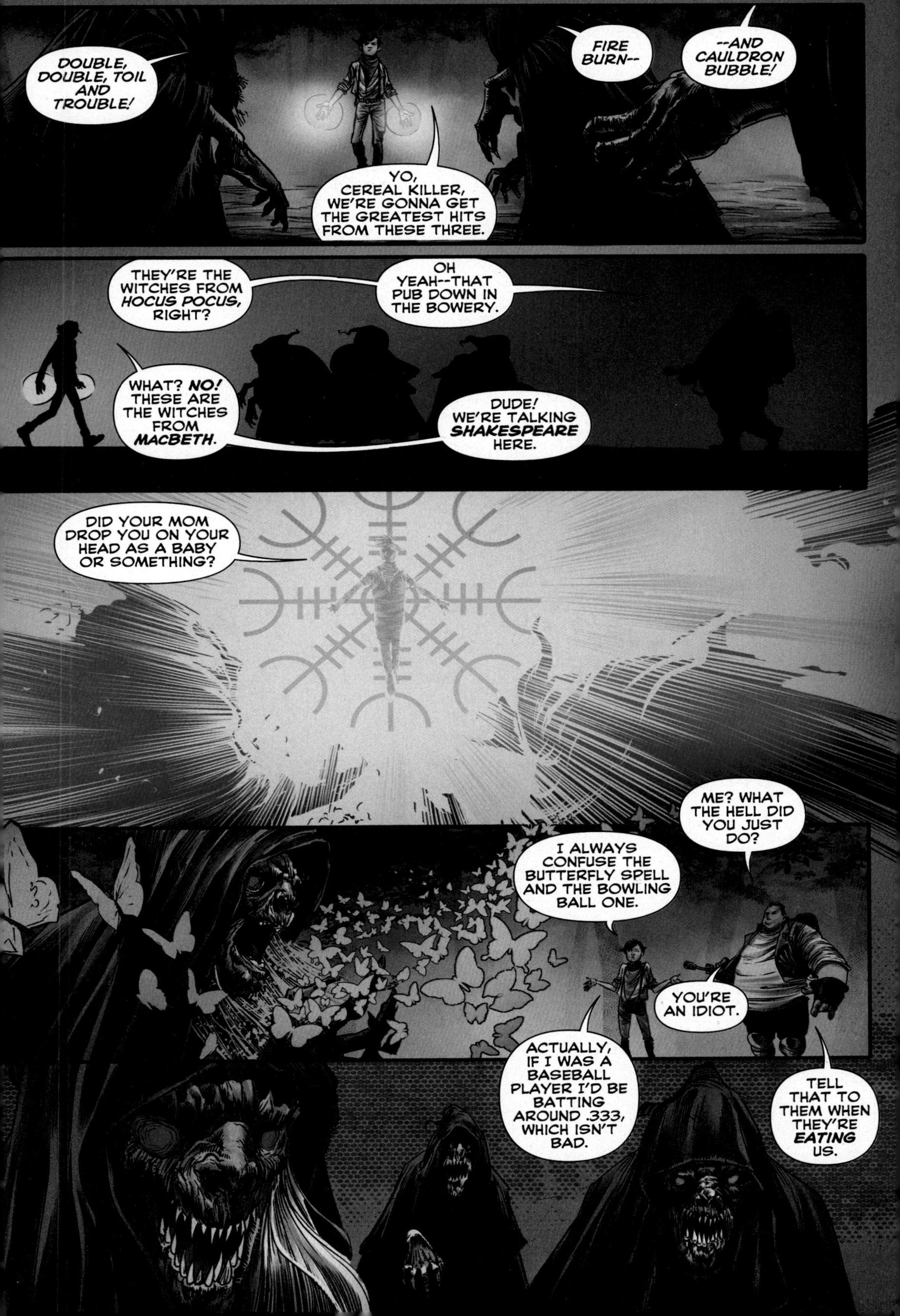
DOUBLE, DOUBLE, TOIL AND TROUBLE!
YO, CEREAL KILLER, WE'RE GONNA GET THE GREATEST HITS FROM THESE THREE.
FIRE BURN--
--AND CAULDRON BUBBLE!
THEY'RE THE WITCHES FROM HOCUS POCUS, RIGHT?
OH YEAH--THAT PUB DOWN IN THE BOWERY.
WHAT? NO! THESE ARE THE WITCHES FROM MACBETH.
DUDE! WE'RE TALKING SHAKESPEARE HERE.
DID YOUR MOM DROP YOU ON YOUR HEAD AS A BABY OR SOMETHING?
ME? WHAT THE HELL DID YOU JUST DO?
I ALWAYS CONFUSE THE BUTTERFLY SPELL AND THE BOWLING BALL ONE.
YOU'RE AN IDIOT.
ACTUALLY, IF I WAS A BASEBALL PLAYER I'D BE BATTING AROUND .333, WHICH ISN'T BAD.
TELL THAT TO THEM WHEN THEY'RE EATING US.

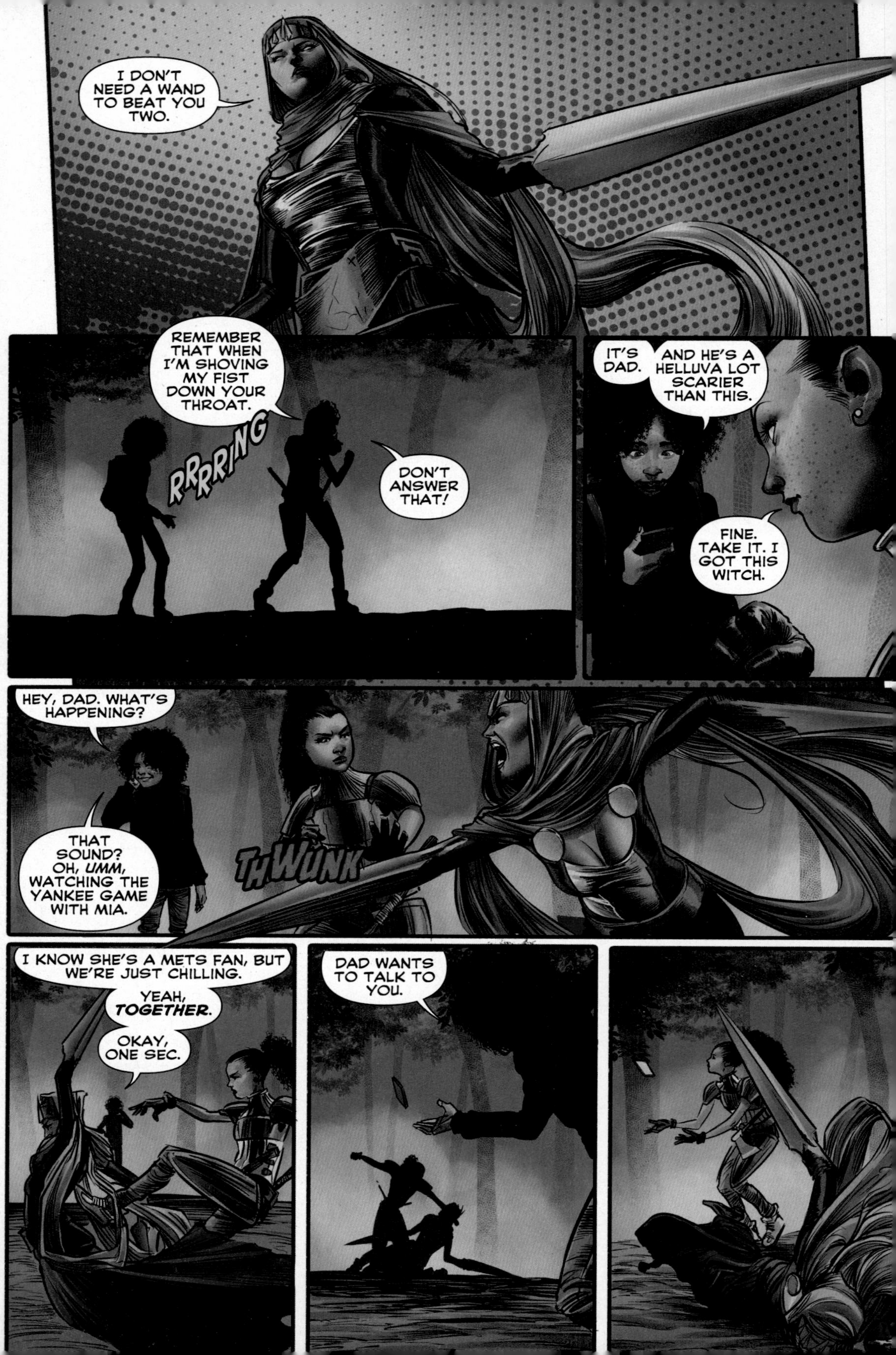
I DON'T NEED A WAND TO BEAT YOU TWO.
REMEMBER THAT WHEN I'M SHOVING MY FIST DOWN YOUR THROAT.
RRRRING
DON'T ANSWER THAT!
IT'S DAD.
AND HE'S A HELLUVA LOT SCARIER THAN THIS.
FINE. TAKE IT. I GOT THIS WITCH.
HEY, DAD. WHAT'S HAPPENING?
THAT SOUND? OH, *UMM*, WATCHING THE YANKEE GAME WITH MIA.
THWUNK
I KNOW SHE'S A METS FAN, BUT WE'RE JUST CHILLING.
YEAH, **TOGETHER**.
OKAY, ONE SEC.
DAD WANTS TO TALK TO YOU.

HEY, POPPA. I MISS YOU, TOO.

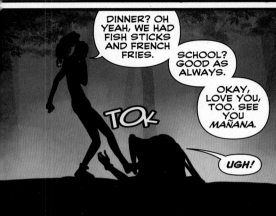

DINNER? OH YEAH, WE HAD FISH STICKS AND FRENCH FRIES.

SCHOOL? GOOD AS ALWAYS.

OKAY, LOVE YOU, TOO. SEE YOU MAÑANA.

UGH!

TOK

YO NICK, DAD WANTS TO SHOUT AT YOU.

I'M BACK.

I ALREADY SHOWERED.

WHO'S WINNING? YANKEES.

THANKS... HAVE A GOOD SHIFT. SEE YOU IN THE MORNING.

JUST FOR KICKS, WHEN I'M DONE KILLING YOU I'M GOING TO GO FIND YOUR FATHER AND RIP HIS *HEART* OUT OF HIS *CHEST* AND *EAT* IT.

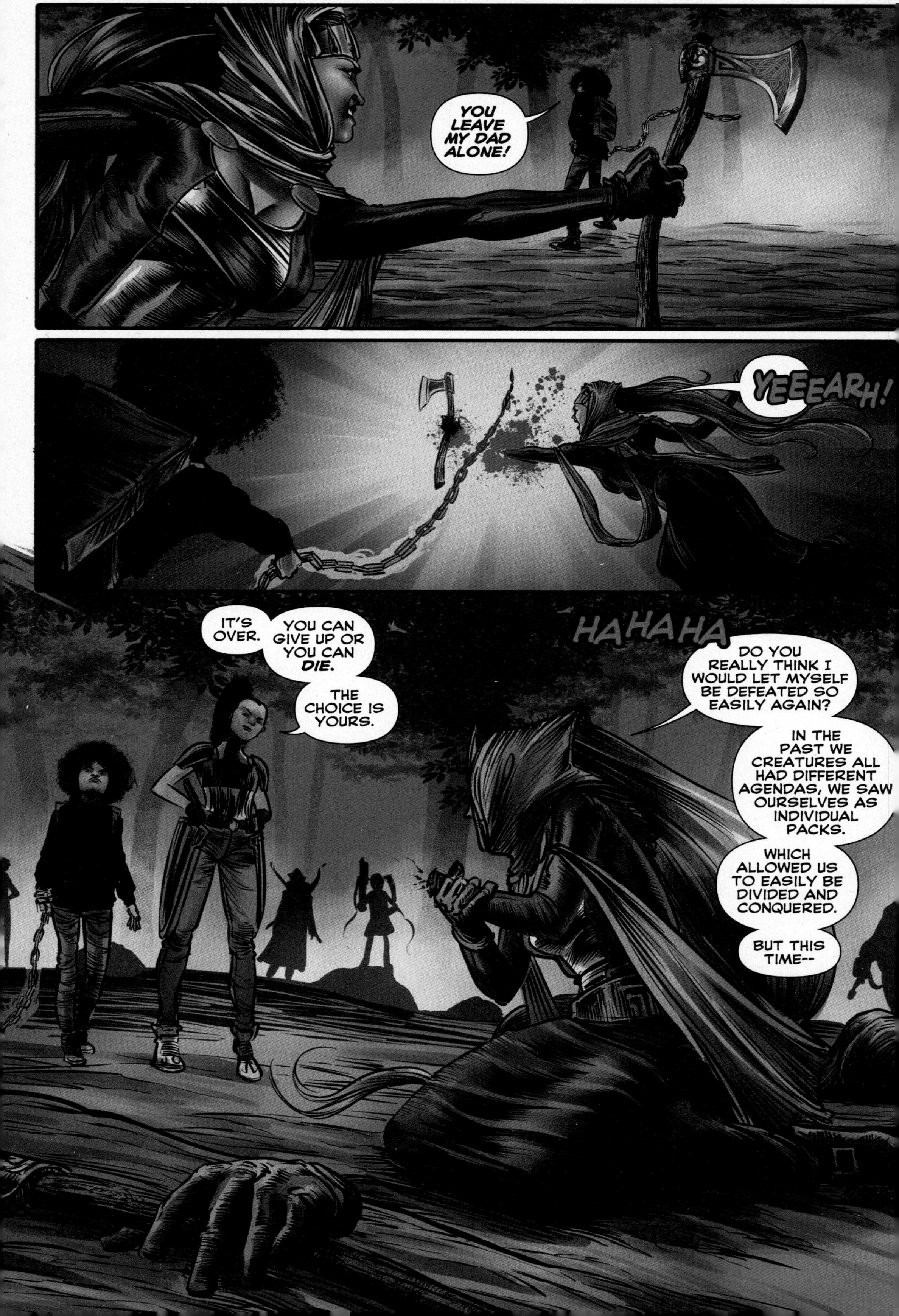
YOU LEAVE MY DAD ALONE!
YEEEARH!
IT'S OVER.
YOU CAN GIVE UP OR YOU CAN DIE.
THE CHOICE IS YOURS.
HAHAHA
DO YOU REALLY THINK I WOULD LET MYSELF BE DEFEATED SO EASILY AGAIN?
IN THE PAST WE CREATURES ALL HAD DIFFERENT AGENDAS, WE SAW OURSELVES AS INDIVIDUAL PACKS.
WHICH ALLOWED US TO EASILY BE DIVIDED AND CONQUERED.
BUT THIS TIME--

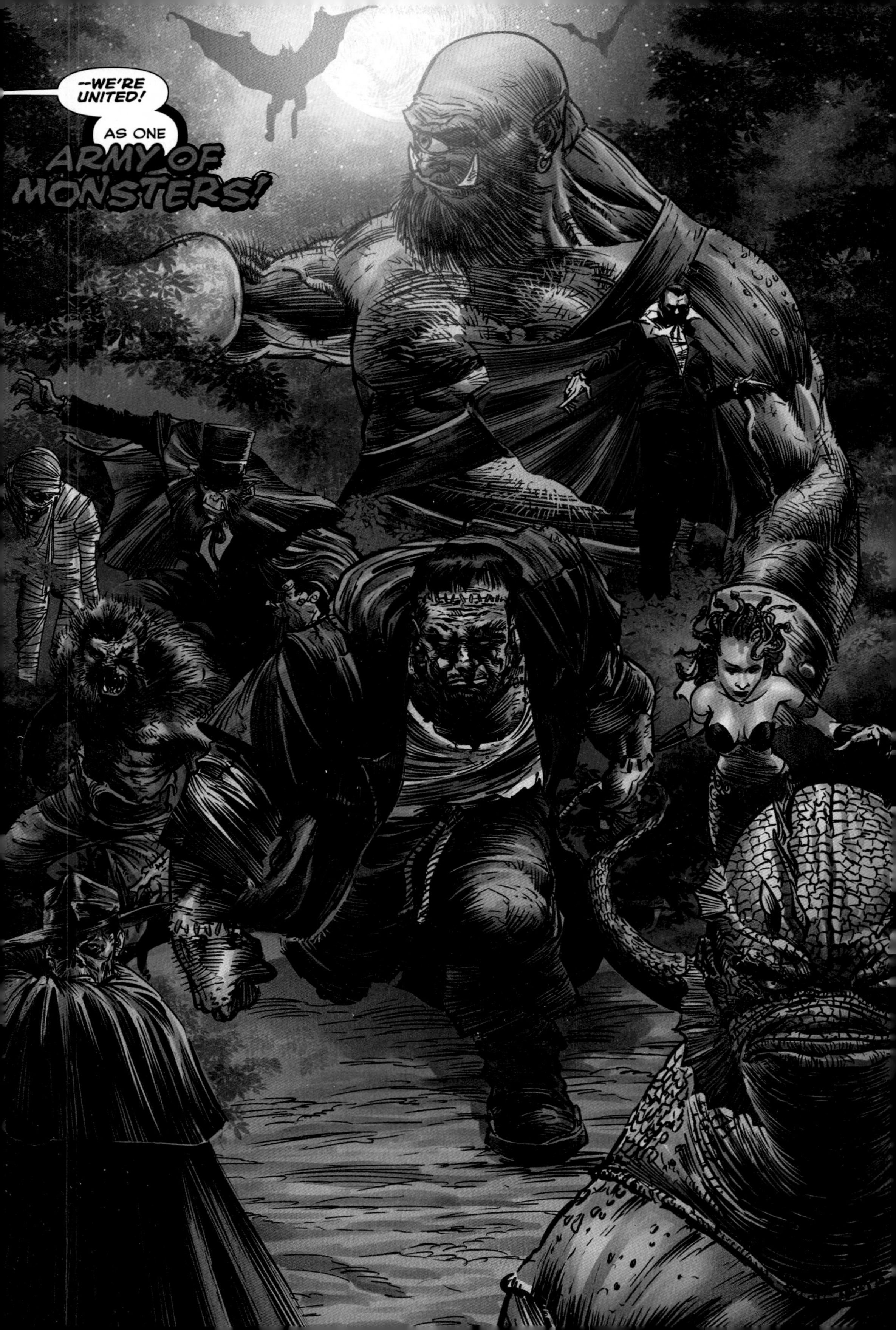
--WE'RE UNITED!
AS ONE
ARMY OF MONSTERS!

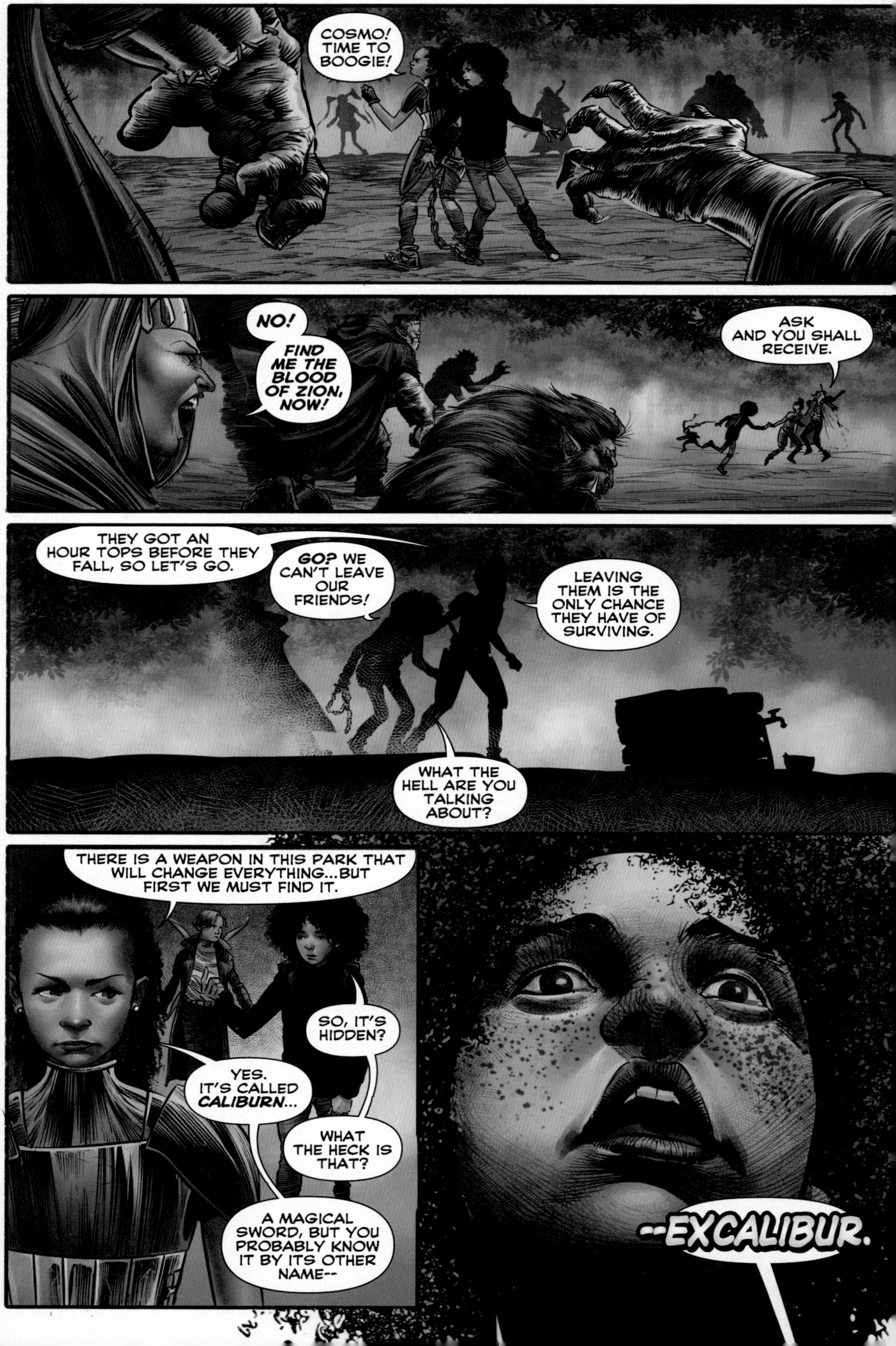
COSMO! TIME TO BOOGIE!
NO!
FIND ME THE BLOOD OF ZION, NOW!
ASK AND YOU SHALL RECEIVE.
THEY GOT AN HOUR TOPS BEFORE THEY FALL, SO LET'S GO.
GO? WE CAN'T LEAVE OUR FRIENDS!
LEAVING THEM IS THE ONLY CHANCE THEY HAVE OF SURVIVING.
WHAT THE HELL ARE YOU TALKING ABOUT?
THERE IS A WEAPON IN THIS PARK THAT WILL CHANGE EVERYTHING...BUT FIRST WE MUST FIND IT.
SO, IT'S HIDDEN?
YES. IT'S CALLED CALIBURN...
WHAT THE HECK IS THAT?
A MAGICAL SWORD, BUT YOU PROBABLY KNOW IT BY ITS OTHER NAME--
--EXCALIBUR.

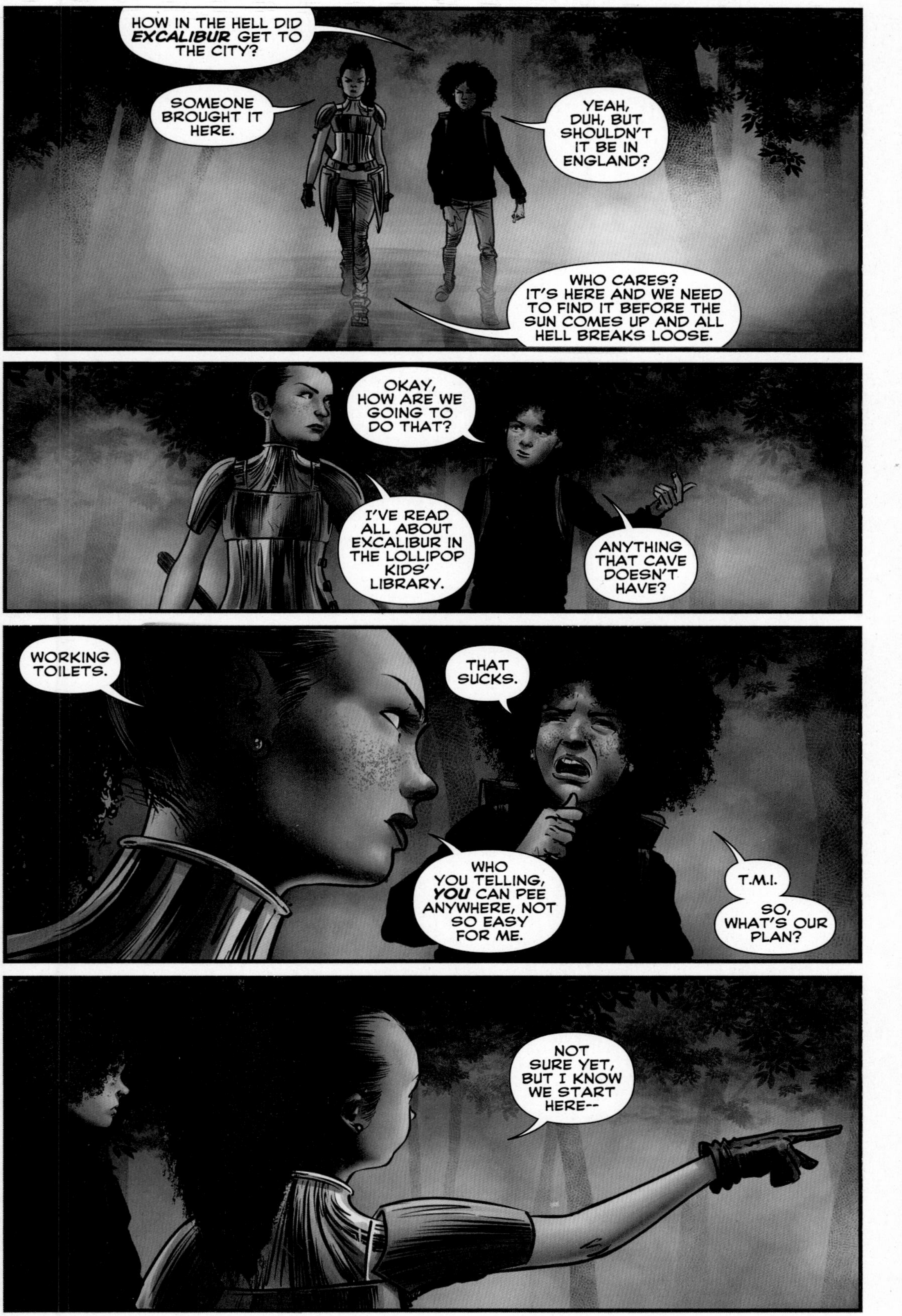

HOW IN THE HELL DID **EXCALIBUR** GET TO THE CITY?
SOMEONE BROUGHT IT HERE.
YEAH, DUH, BUT SHOULDN'T IT BE IN ENGLAND?
WHO CARES? IT'S HERE AND WE NEED TO FIND IT BEFORE THE SUN COMES UP AND ALL HELL BREAKS LOOSE.
OKAY, HOW ARE WE GOING TO DO THAT?
I'VE READ ALL ABOUT EXCALIBUR IN THE LOLLIPOP KIDS' LIBRARY.
ANYTHING THAT CAVE DOESN'T HAVE?
WORKING TOILETS.
THAT SUCKS.
WHO YOU TELLING, **YOU** CAN PEE ANYWHERE, NOT SO EASY FOR ME.
T.M.I.
SO, WHAT'S OUR PLAN?
NOT SURE YET, BUT I KNOW WE START HERE--

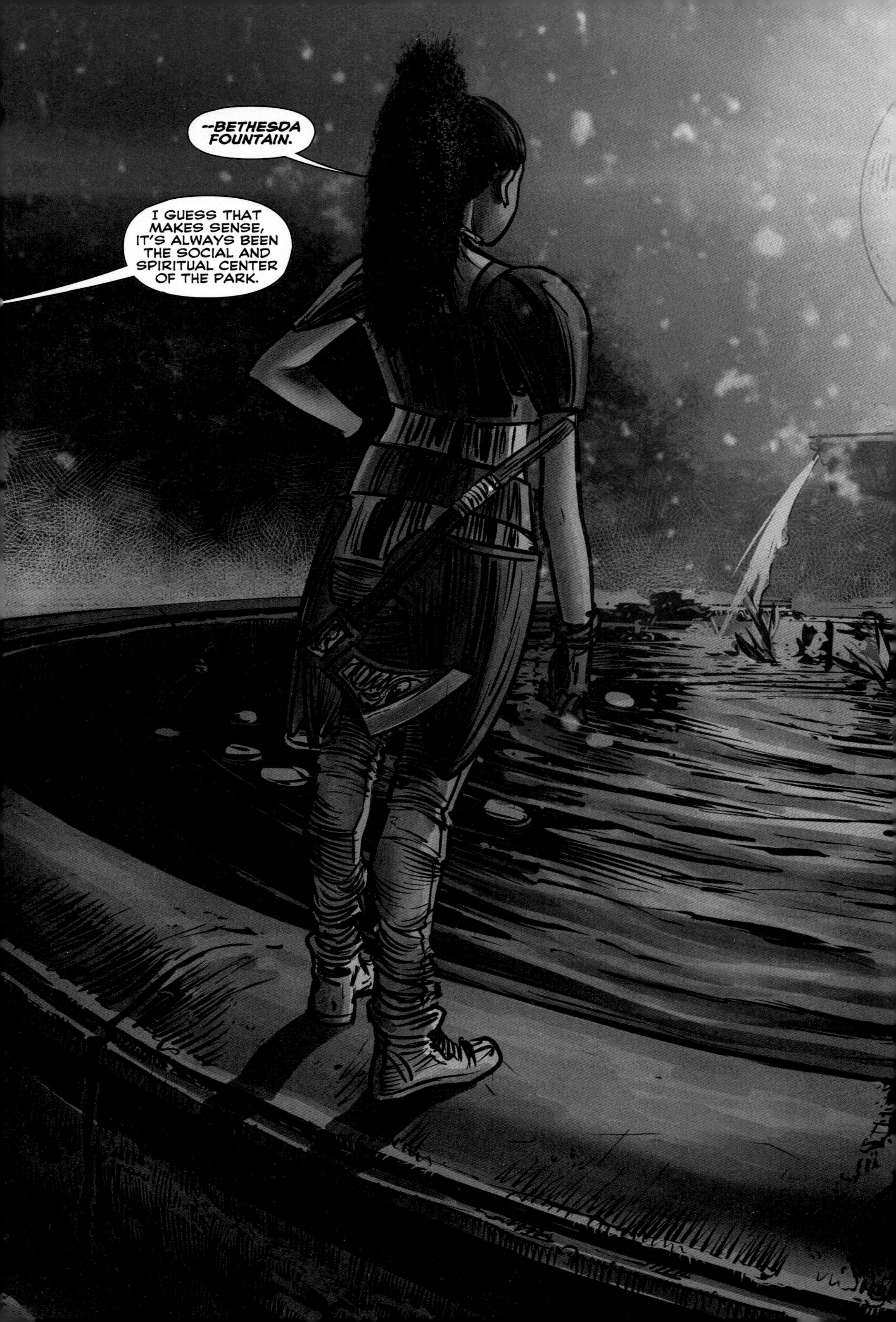
--BETHESDA FOUNTAIN.
I GUESS THAT MAKES SENSE, IT'S ALWAYS BEEN THE SOCIAL AND SPIRITUAL CENTER OF THE PARK.

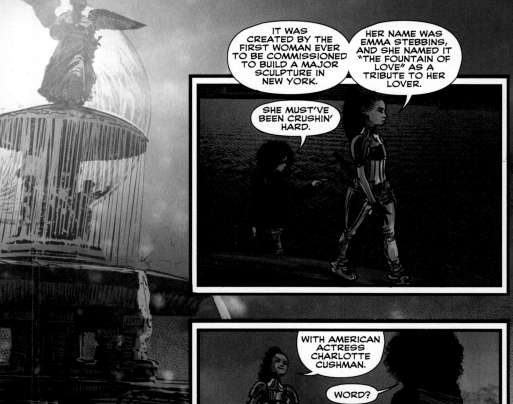

IT WAS CREATED BY THE FIRST WOMAN EVER TO BE COMMISSIONED TO BUILD A MAJOR SCULPTURE IN NEW YORK.

HER NAME WAS EMMA STEBBINS, AND SHE NAMED IT "THE FOUNTAIN OF LOVE" AS A TRIBUTE TO HER LOVER.

SHE MUST'VE BEEN CRUSHIN' HARD.

WITH AMERICAN ACTRESS CHARLOTTE CUSHMAN.

WORD?

YEAH, BUT BACK IN THOSE DAYS THEIR RELATIONSHIP WAS ILLEGAL SO THE FOUNTAIN WAS A WAY FOR EMMA TO PROFESS HER LOVE.

AS MUCH AS I'M LOVING THE HISTORY LESSON WITH THE SOCIALLY CONSCIOUS MESSAGE, WHAT DOES ANY OF THIS HAVE TO DO WITH EXCALIBUR?

EMMA WAS A LOLLIPOP KID.

HER FAMILY WAS THE ONE WHO BROUGHT THE BLADE HERE FROM ENGLAND

AND IT'S BELIEVED SHE WAS THE ONE WHO HID THE SWORD, SO IT WOULDN'T FALL INTO THE WRONG HANDS.

BUT KNOWING SHE WOULD FORGET IT WHEN SHE TURNED EIGHTEEN, EMMA DESIGNED CLUES OF ITS WHEREABOUTS IN HER ART, JUST IN CASE THE LOLLIPOP KIDS EVER NEEDED IT AGAIN.

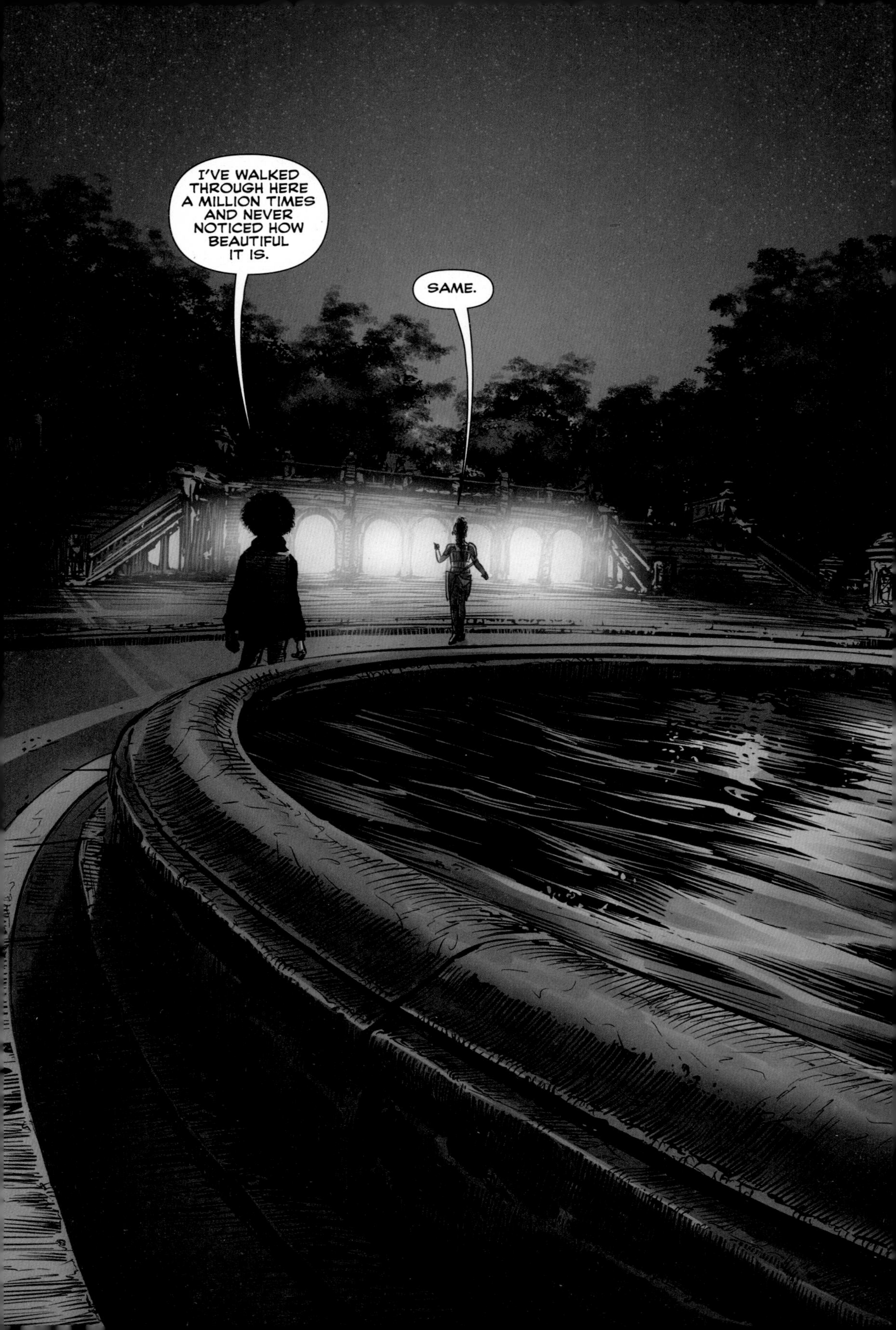
I'VE WALKED THROUGH HERE A MILLION TIMES AND NEVER NOTICED HOW BEAUTIFUL IT IS.
SAME.

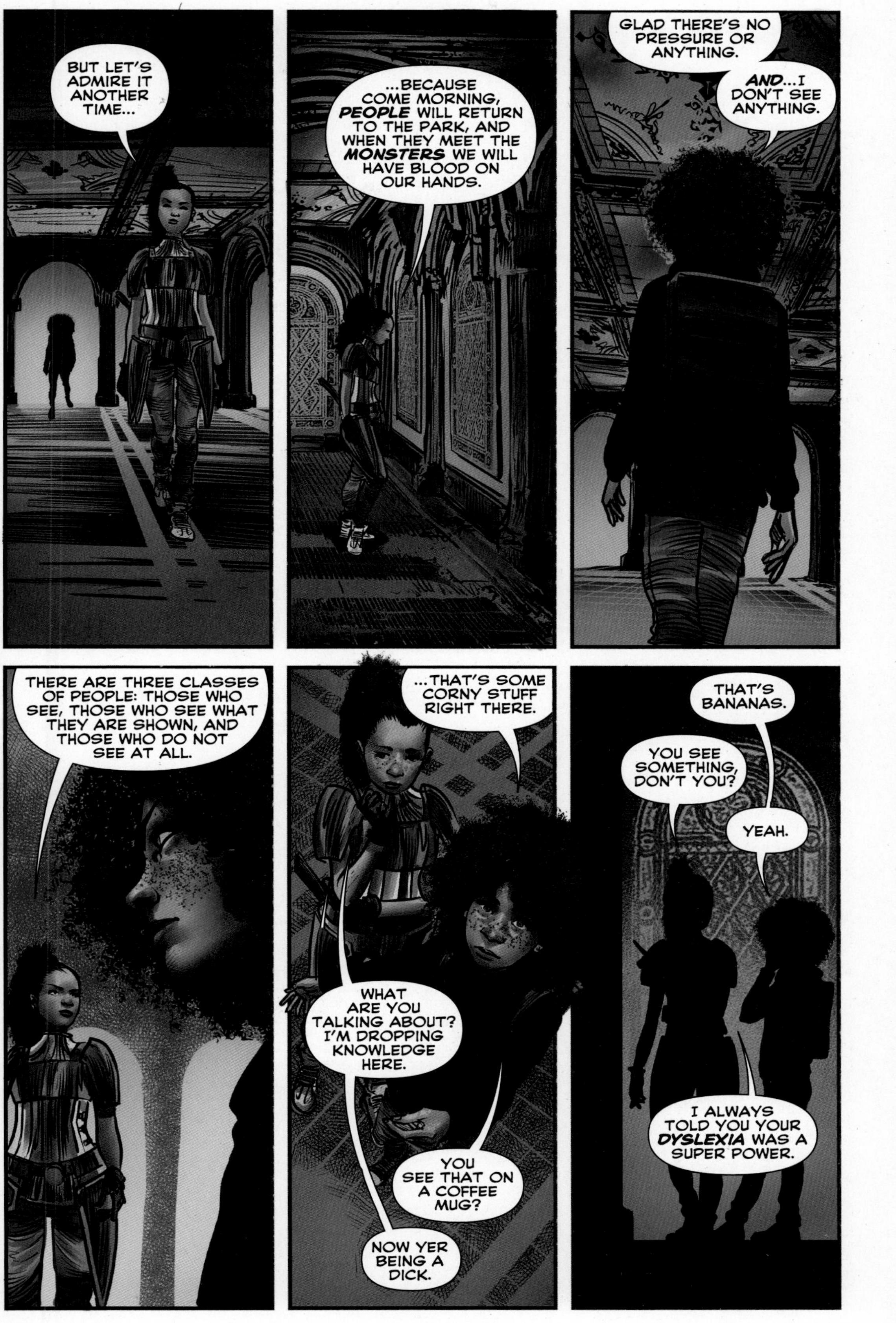
BUT LET'S ADMIRE IT ANOTHER TIME...
...BECAUSE COME MORNING, PEOPLE WILL RETURN TO THE PARK, AND WHEN THEY MEET THE MONSTERS WE WILL HAVE BLOOD ON OUR HANDS.
GLAD THERE'S NO PRESSURE OR ANYTHING.
AND...I DON'T SEE ANYTHING.
THERE ARE THREE CLASSES OF PEOPLE: THOSE WHO SEE, THOSE WHO SEE WHAT THEY ARE SHOWN, AND THOSE WHO DO NOT SEE AT ALL.
...THAT'S SOME CORNY STUFF RIGHT THERE.
WHAT ARE YOU TALKING ABOUT? I'M DROPPING KNOWLEDGE HERE.
YOU SEE THAT ON A COFFEE MUG?
NOW YER BEING A DICK.
THAT'S BANANAS.
YOU SEE SOMETHING, DON'T YOU?
YEAH.
I ALWAYS TOLD YOU YOUR DYSLEXIA WAS A SUPER POWER.

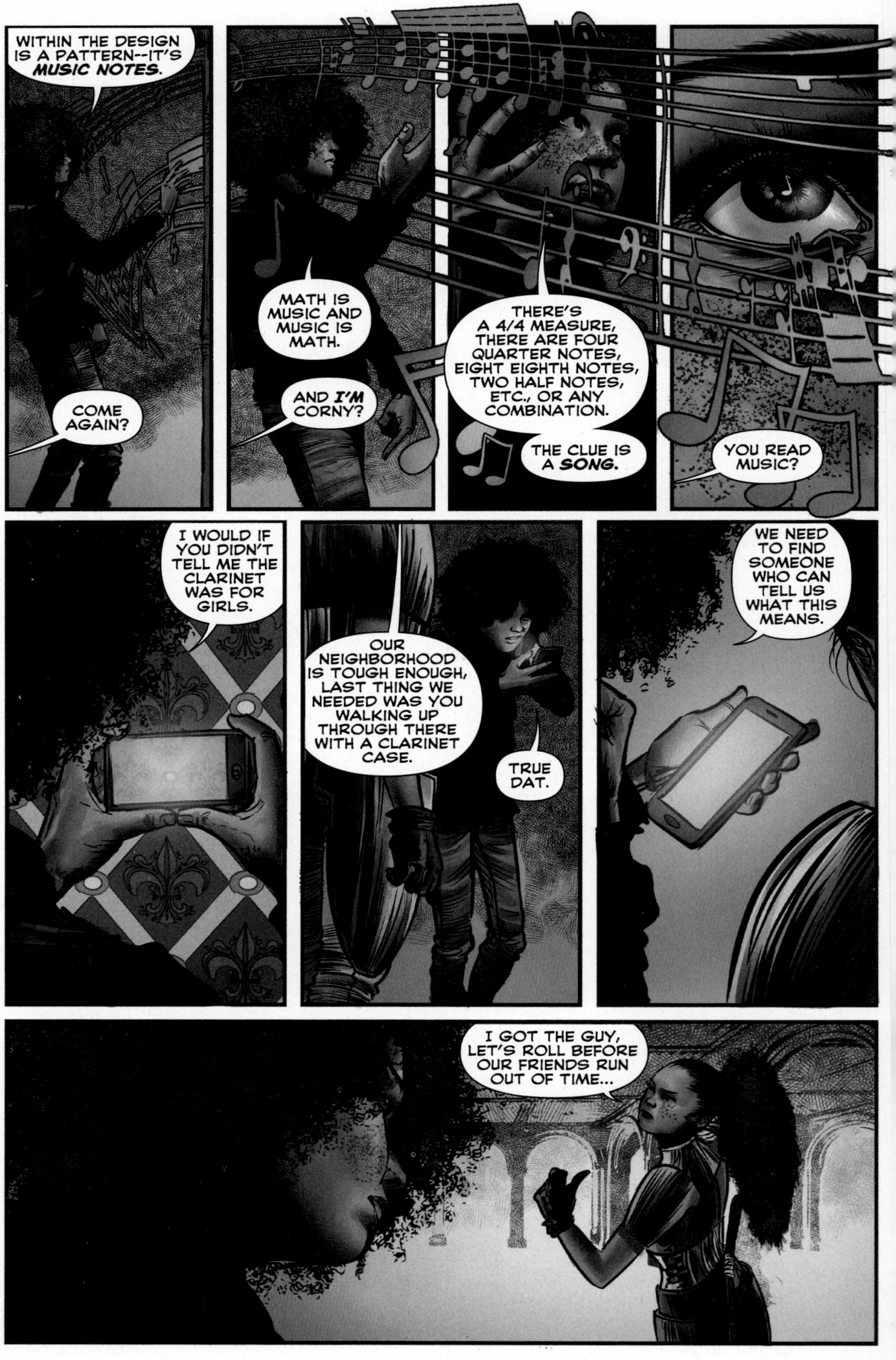
WITHIN THE DESIGN IS A PATTERN--IT'S *MUSIC NOTES*.
COME AGAIN?
MATH IS MUSIC AND MUSIC IS MATH.
AND *I'M* CORNY?
THERE'S A 4/4 MEASURE, THERE ARE FOUR QUARTER NOTES, EIGHT EIGHTH NOTES, TWO HALF NOTES, ETC., OR ANY COMBINATION.
THE CLUE IS A *SONG*.
YOU READ MUSIC?
I WOULD IF YOU DIDN'T TELL ME THE CLARINET WAS FOR GIRLS.
OUR NEIGHBORHOOD IS TOUGH ENOUGH, LAST THING WE NEEDED WAS YOU WALKING UP THROUGH THERE WITH A CLARINET CASE.
TRUE DAT.
WE NEED TO FIND SOMEONE WHO CAN TELL US WHAT THIS MEANS.
I GOT THE GUY, LET'S ROLL BEFORE OUR FRIENDS RUN OUT OF TIME...

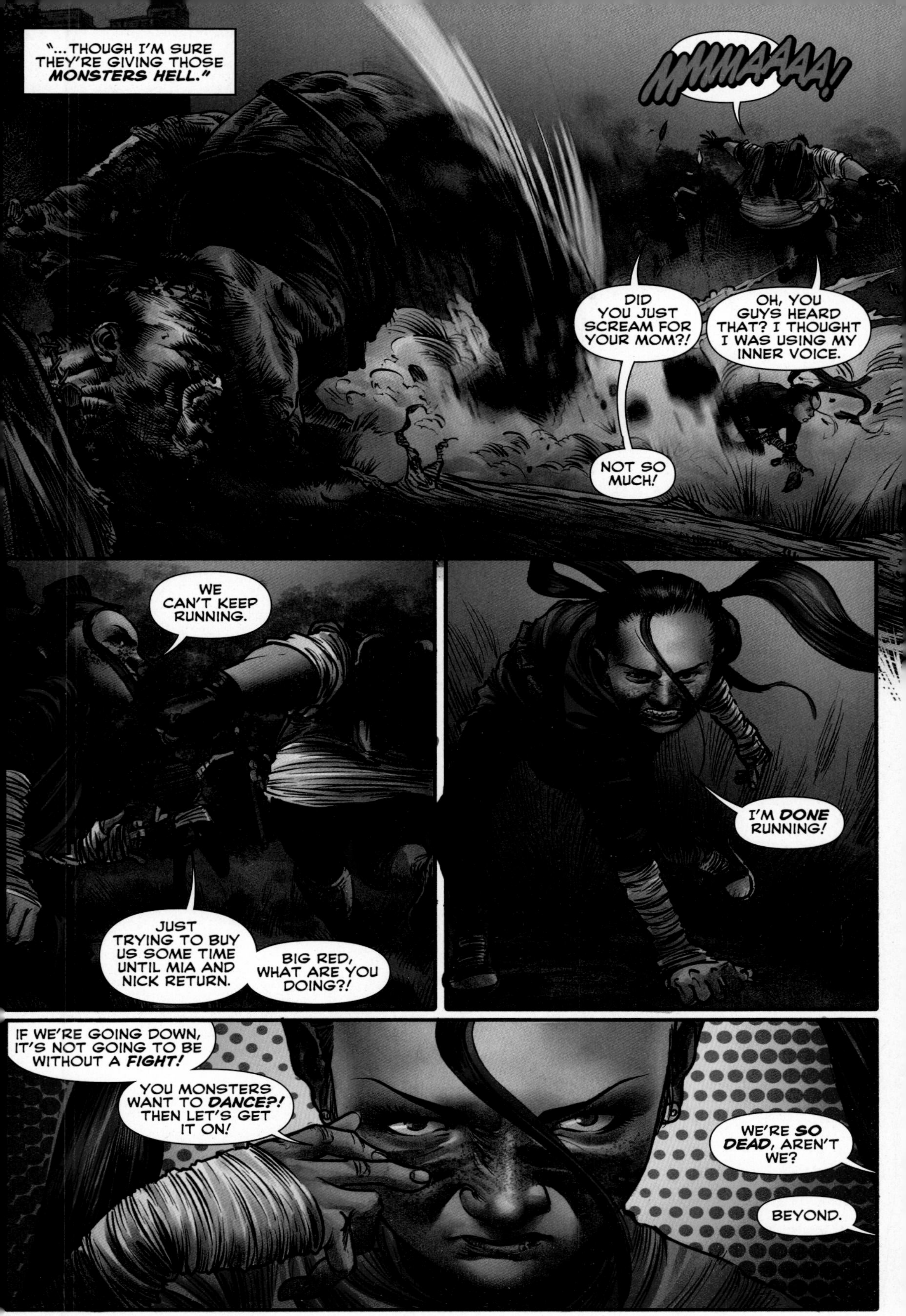
"...THOUGH I'M SURE THEY'RE GIVING THOSE MONSTERS HELL."
MMMAAAA!
DID YOU JUST SCREAM FOR YOUR MOM?!
OH, YOU GUYS HEARD THAT? I THOUGHT I WAS USING MY INNER VOICE.
NOT SO MUCH!
WE CAN'T KEEP RUNNING.
JUST TRYING TO BUY US SOME TIME UNTIL MIA AND NICK RETURN.
BIG RED, WHAT ARE YOU DOING?!
I'M DONE RUNNING!
IF WE'RE GOING DOWN, IT'S NOT GOING TO BE WITHOUT A FIGHT!
YOU MONSTERS WANT TO DANCE?! THEN LET'S GET IT ON!
WE'RE SO DEAD, AREN'T WE?
BEYOND.

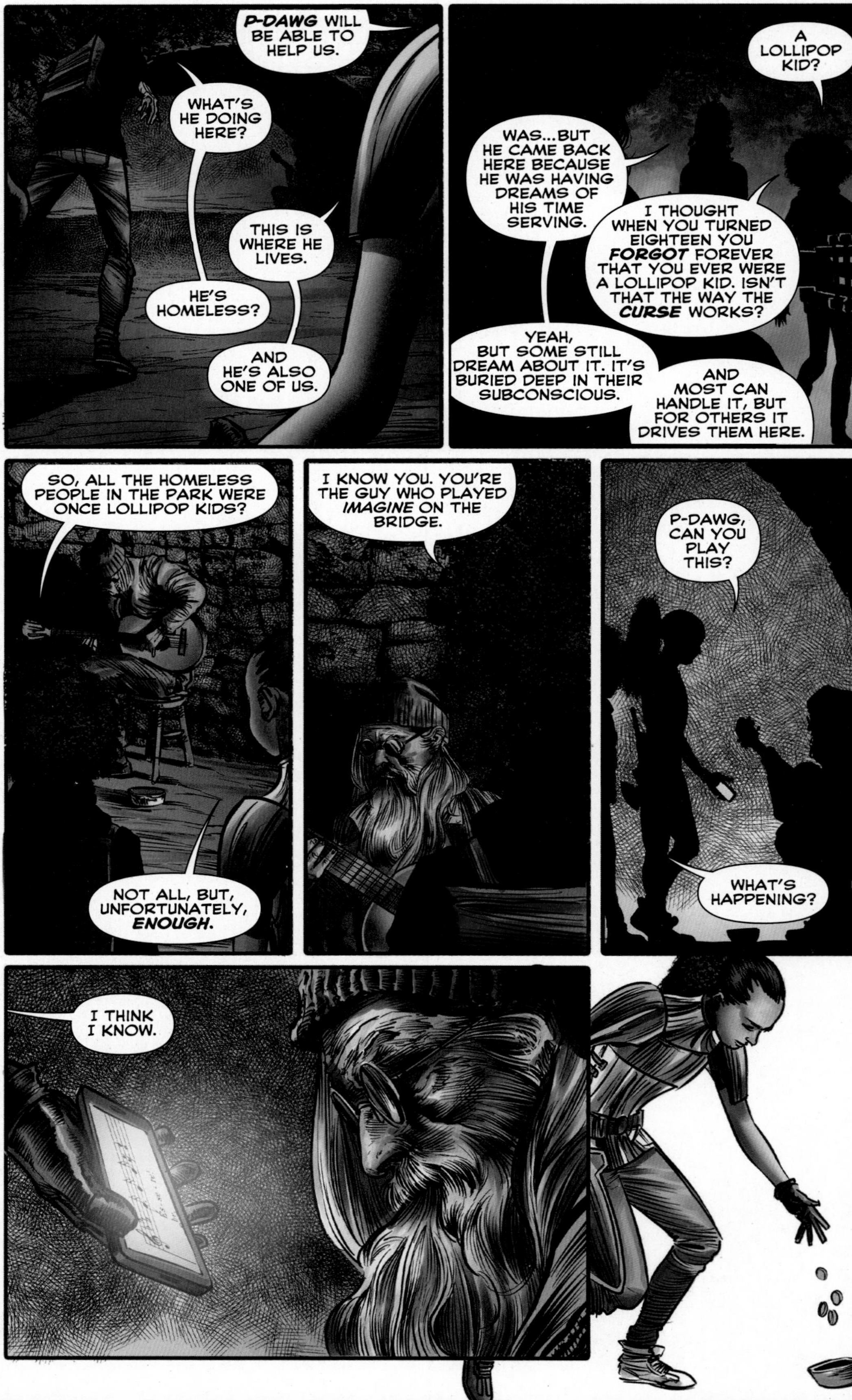
P-DAWG WILL BE ABLE TO HELP US.
WHAT'S HE DOING HERE?
THIS IS WHERE HE LIVES.
HE'S HOMELESS?
AND HE'S ALSO ONE OF US.
A LOLLIPOP KID?
WAS...BUT HE CAME BACK HERE BECAUSE HE WAS HAVING DREAMS OF HIS TIME SERVING.
I THOUGHT WHEN YOU TURNED EIGHTEEN YOU FORGOT FOREVER THAT YOU EVER WERE A LOLLIPOP KID. ISN'T THAT THE WAY THE CURSE WORKS?
YEAH, BUT SOME STILL DREAM ABOUT IT. IT'S BURIED DEEP IN THEIR SUBCONSCIOUS.
AND MOST CAN HANDLE IT, BUT FOR OTHERS IT DRIVES THEM HERE.
SO, ALL THE HOMELESS PEOPLE IN THE PARK WERE ONCE LOLLIPOP KIDS?
NOT ALL, BUT, UNFORTUNATELY, ENOUGH.
I KNOW YOU. YOU'RE THE GUY WHO PLAYED IMAGINE ON THE BRIDGE.
P-DAWG, CAN YOU PLAY THIS?
WHAT'S HAPPENING?
I THINK I KNOW.

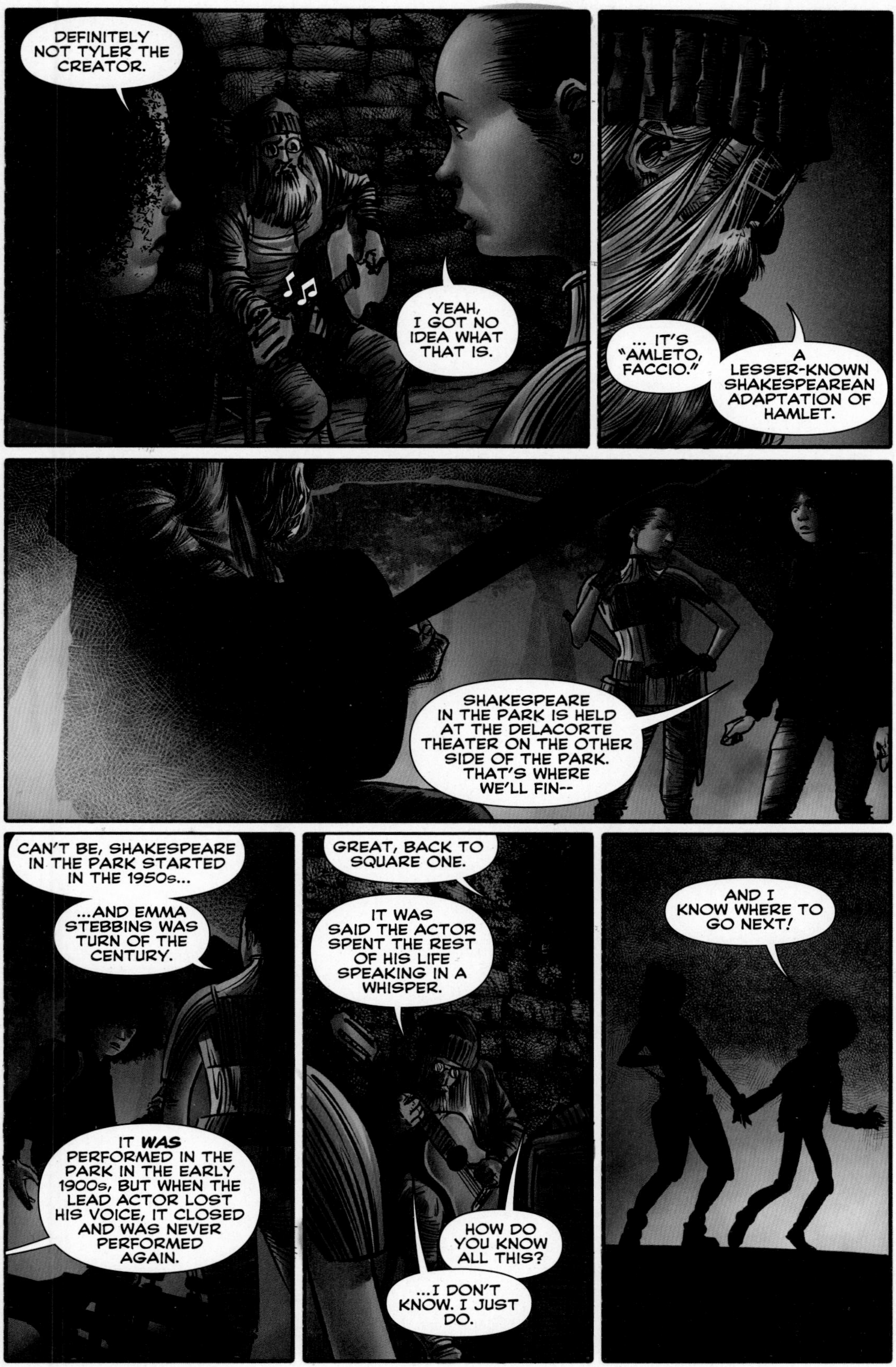
DEFINITELY NOT TYLER THE CREATOR.
YEAH, I GOT NO IDEA WHAT THAT IS.
... IT'S "AMLETO, FACCIO."
A LESSER-KNOWN SHAKESPEAREAN ADAPTATION OF HAMLET.
SHAKESPEARE IN THE PARK IS HELD AT THE DELACORTE THEATER ON THE OTHER SIDE OF THE PARK. THAT'S WHERE WE'LL FIN--
CAN'T BE, SHAKESPEARE IN THE PARK STARTED IN THE 1950s...
...AND EMMA STEBBINS WAS TURN OF THE CENTURY.
IT ***WAS*** PERFORMED IN THE PARK IN THE EARLY 1900s, BUT WHEN THE LEAD ACTOR LOST HIS VOICE, IT CLOSED AND WAS NEVER PERFORMED AGAIN.
GREAT, BACK TO SQUARE ONE.
IT WAS SAID THE ACTOR SPENT THE REST OF HIS LIFE SPEAKING IN A WHISPER.
HOW DO YOU KNOW ALL THIS?
...I DON'T KNOW. I JUST DO.
AND I KNOW WHERE TO GO NEXT!

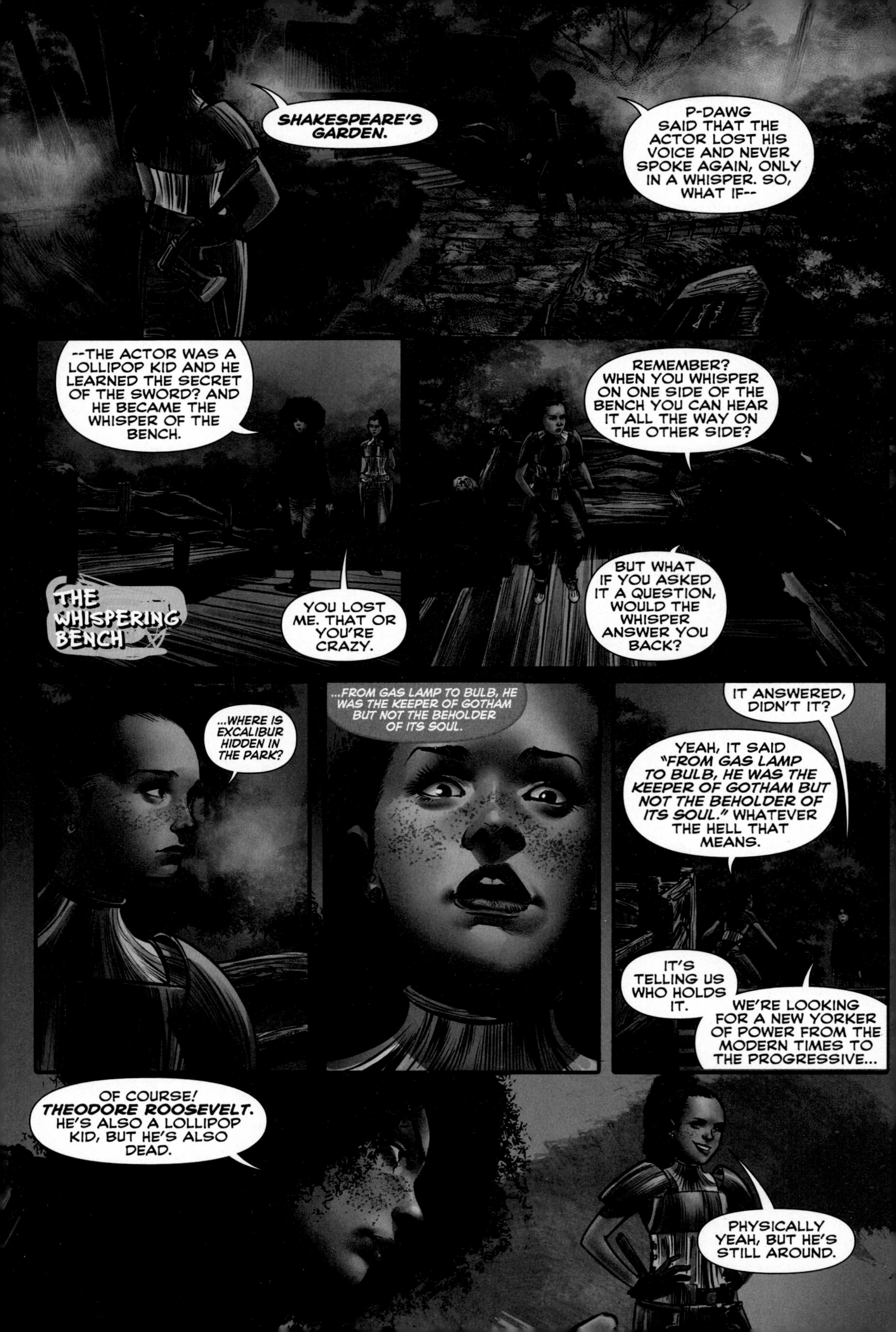

SHAKESPEARE'S GARDEN.
P-DAWG SAID THAT THE ACTOR LOST HIS VOICE AND NEVER SPOKE AGAIN, ONLY IN A WHISPER. SO, WHAT IF--
--THE ACTOR WAS A LOLLIPOP KID AND HE LEARNED THE SECRET OF THE SWORD? AND HE BECAME THE WHISPER OF THE BENCH.
THE WHISPERING BENCH
YOU LOST ME. THAT OR YOU'RE CRAZY.
REMEMBER? WHEN YOU WHISPER ON ONE SIDE OF THE BENCH YOU CAN HEAR IT ALL THE WAY ON THE OTHER SIDE?
BUT WHAT IF YOU ASKED IT A QUESTION, WOULD THE WHISPER ANSWER YOU BACK?
...WHERE IS EXCALIBUR HIDDEN IN THE PARK?
...FROM GAS LAMP TO BULB, HE WAS THE KEEPER OF GOTHAM BUT NOT THE BEHOLDER OF ITS SOUL.
IT ANSWERED, DIDN'T IT?
YEAH, IT SAID "FROM GAS LAMP TO BULB, HE WAS THE KEEPER OF GOTHAM BUT NOT THE BEHOLDER OF ITS SOUL." WHATEVER THE HELL THAT MEANS.
IT'S TELLING US WHO HOLDS IT.
WE'RE LOOKING FOR A NEW YORKER OF POWER FROM THE MODERN TIMES TO THE PROGRESSIVE...
OF COURSE! THEODORE ROOSEVELT. HE'S ALSO A LOLLIPOP KID, BUT HE'S ALSO DEAD.
PHYSICALLY YEAH, BUT HE'S STILL AROUND.

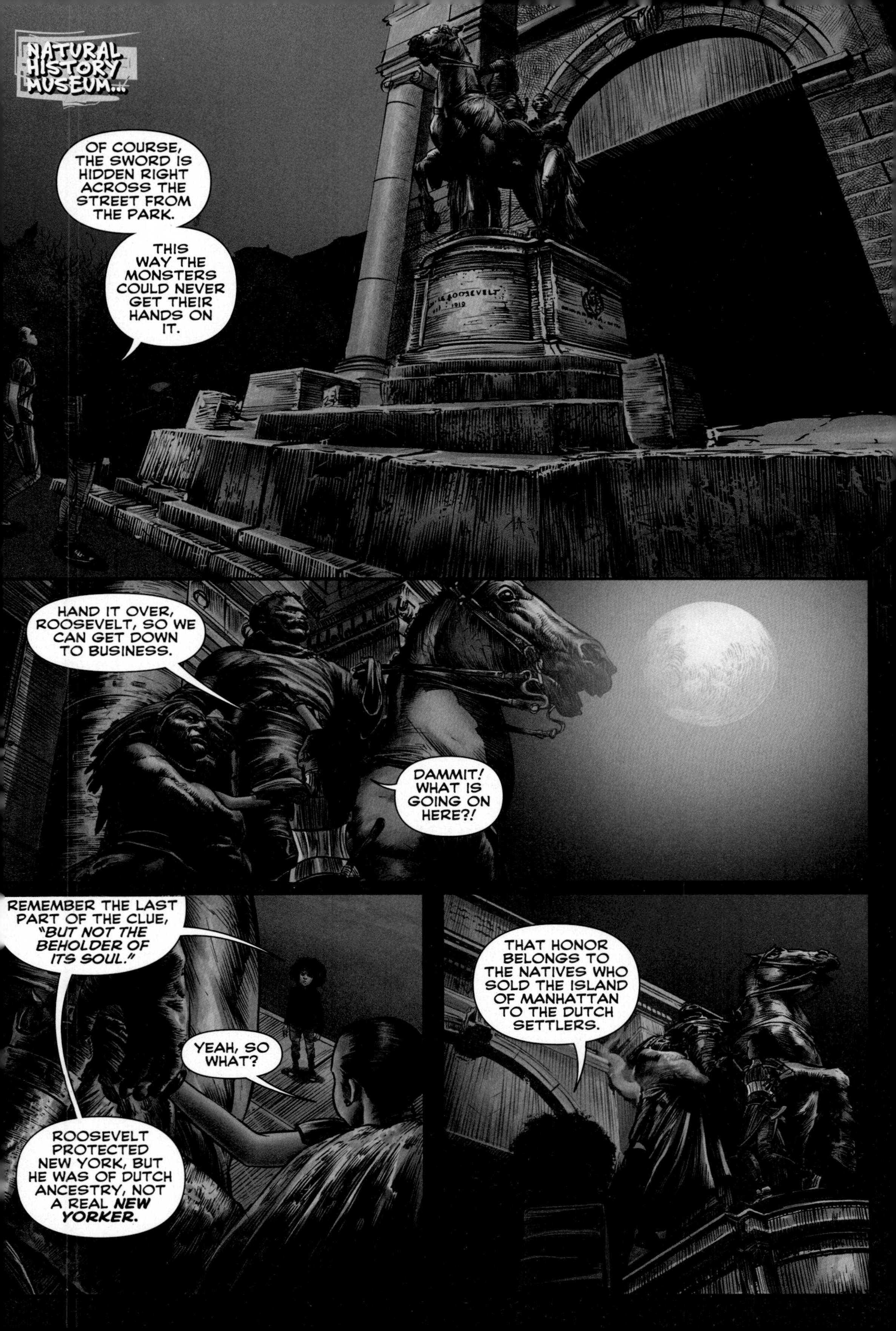
NATURAL HISTORY MUSEUM...
OF COURSE, THE SWORD IS HIDDEN RIGHT ACROSS THE STREET FROM THE PARK.
THIS WAY THE MONSTERS COULD NEVER GET THEIR HANDS ON IT.
HAND IT OVER, ROOSEVELT, SO WE CAN GET DOWN TO BUSINESS.
DAMMIT! WHAT IS GOING ON HERE?!
REMEMBER THE LAST PART OF THE CLUE, *"BUT NOT THE BEHOLDER OF ITS SOUL."*
YEAH, SO WHAT?
ROOSEVELT PROTECTED NEW YORK, BUT HE WAS OF DUTCH ANCESTRY, NOT A REAL ***NEW YORKER***.
THAT HONOR BELONGS TO THE NATIVES WHO SOLD THE ISLAND OF MANHATTAN TO THE DUTCH SETTLERS.

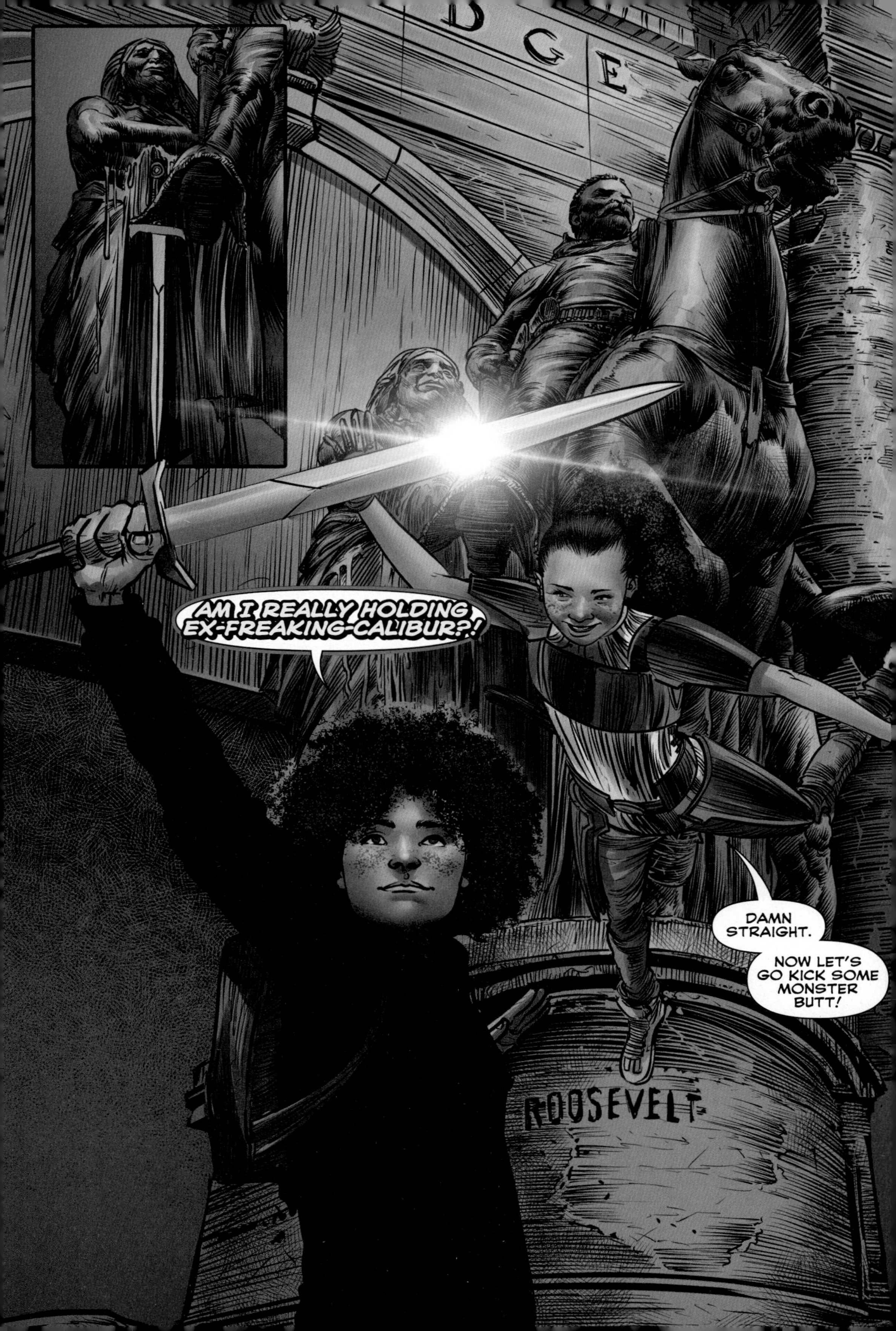
D G E
AM I REALLY HOLDING EX-FREAKING-CALIBUR?!
DAMN STRAIGHT.
NOW LET'S GO KICK SOME MONSTER BUTT!
ROOSEVELT

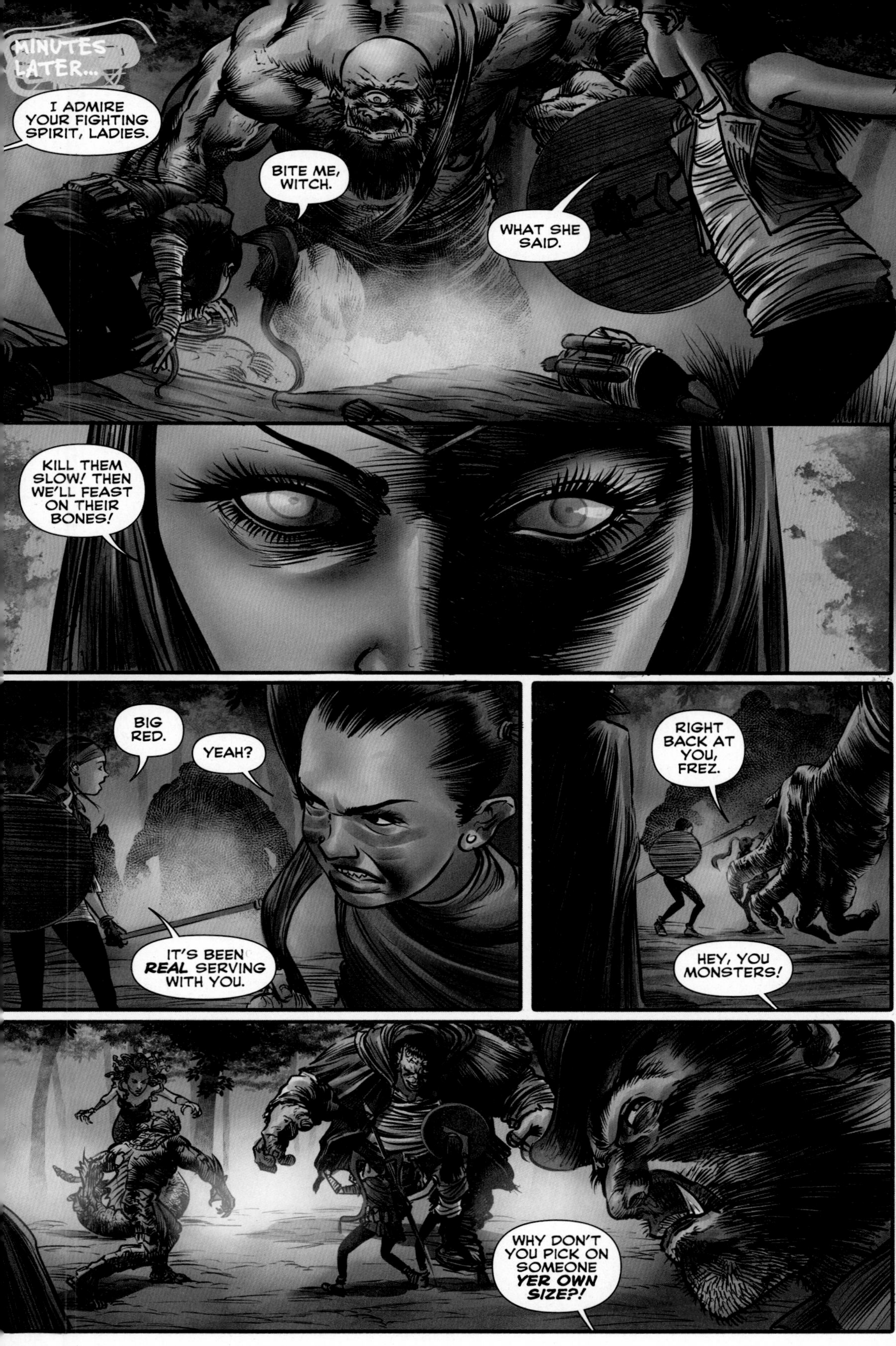
MINUTES LATER...
I ADMIRE YOUR FIGHTING SPIRIT, LADIES.
BITE ME, WITCH.
WHAT SHE SAID.
KILL THEM SLOW! THEN WE'LL FEAST ON THEIR BONES!
BIG RED.
YEAH?
IT'S BEEN REAL SERVING WITH YOU.
RIGHT BACK AT YOU, FREZ.
HEY, YOU MONSTERS!
WHY DON'T YOU PICK ON SOMEONE YER OWN SIZE?!

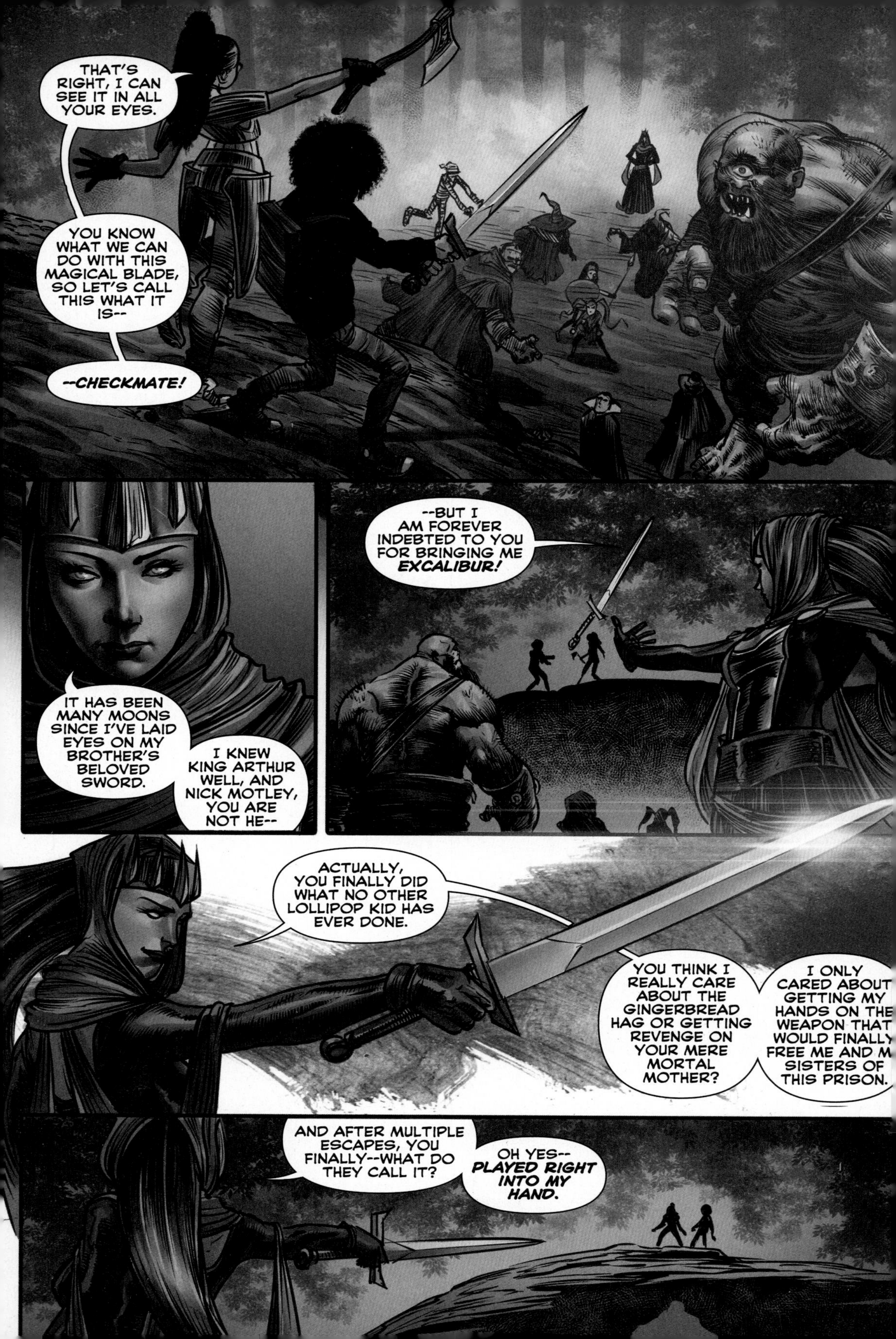
THAT'S RIGHT, I CAN SEE IT IN ALL YOUR EYES.
YOU KNOW WHAT WE CAN DO WITH THIS MAGICAL BLADE, SO LET'S CALL THIS WHAT IT IS--
--CHECKMATE!
IT HAS BEEN MANY MOONS SINCE I'VE LAID EYES ON MY BROTHER'S BELOVED SWORD.
I KNEW KING ARTHUR WELL, AND NICK MOTLEY, YOU ARE NOT HE--
--BUT I AM FOREVER INDEBTED TO YOU FOR BRINGING ME EXCALIBUR!
ACTUALLY, YOU FINALLY DID WHAT NO OTHER LOLLIPOP KID HAS EVER DONE.
YOU THINK I REALLY CARE ABOUT THE GINGERBREAD HAG OR GETTING REVENGE ON YOUR MERE MORTAL MOTHER?
I ONLY CARED ABOUT GETTING MY HANDS ON THE WEAPON THAT WOULD FINALLY FREE ME AND M SISTERS OF THIS PRISON.
AND AFTER MULTIPLE ESCAPES, YOU FINALLY--WHAT DO THEY CALL IT?
OH YES-- PLAYED RIGHT INTO MY HAND.

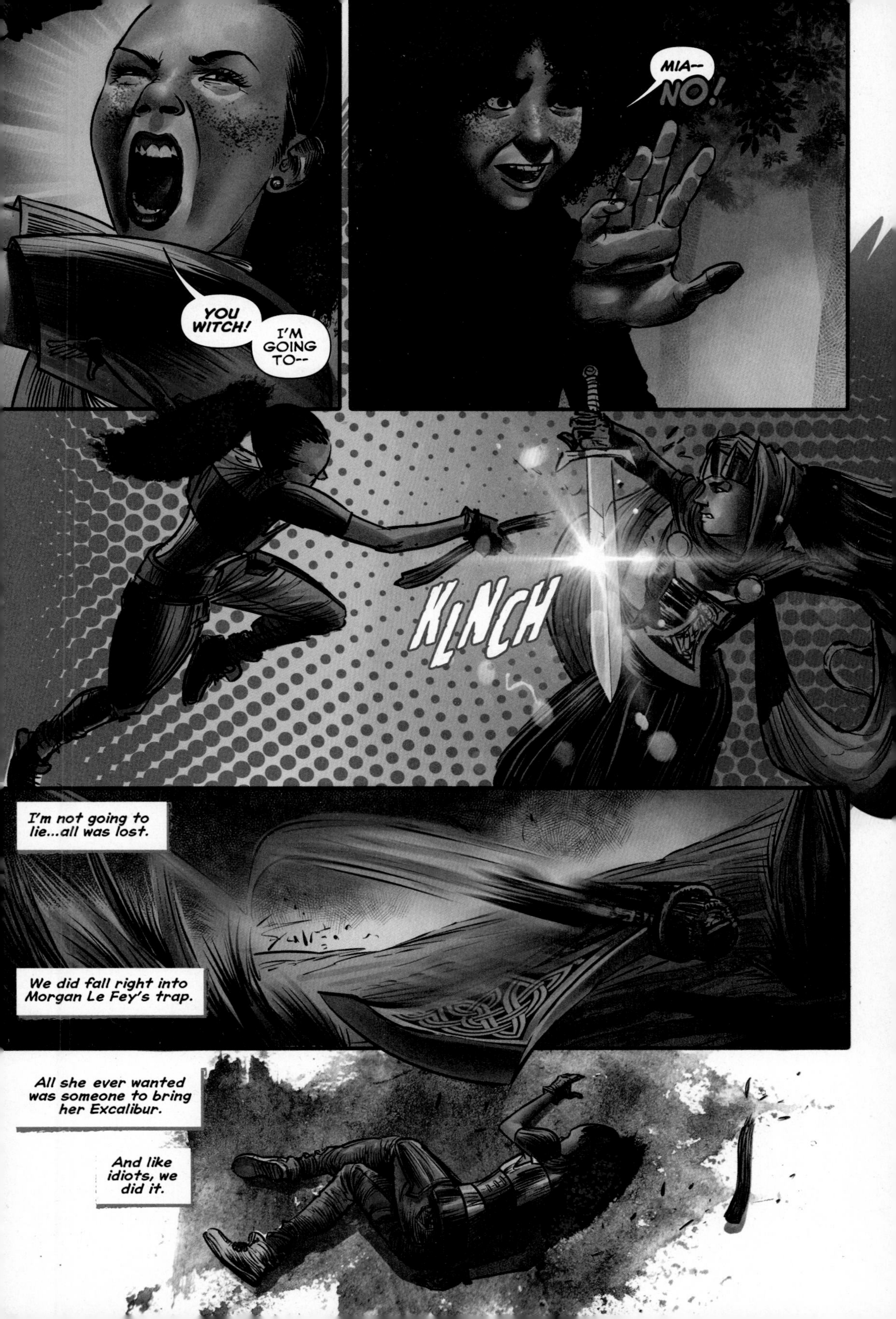
YOU WITCH!
I'M GOING TO--
MIA-- NO!
KLNCH
I'm not going to lie...all was lost.
We did fall right into Morgan Le Fey's trap.
All she ever wanted was someone to bring her Excalibur.
And like idiots, we did it.

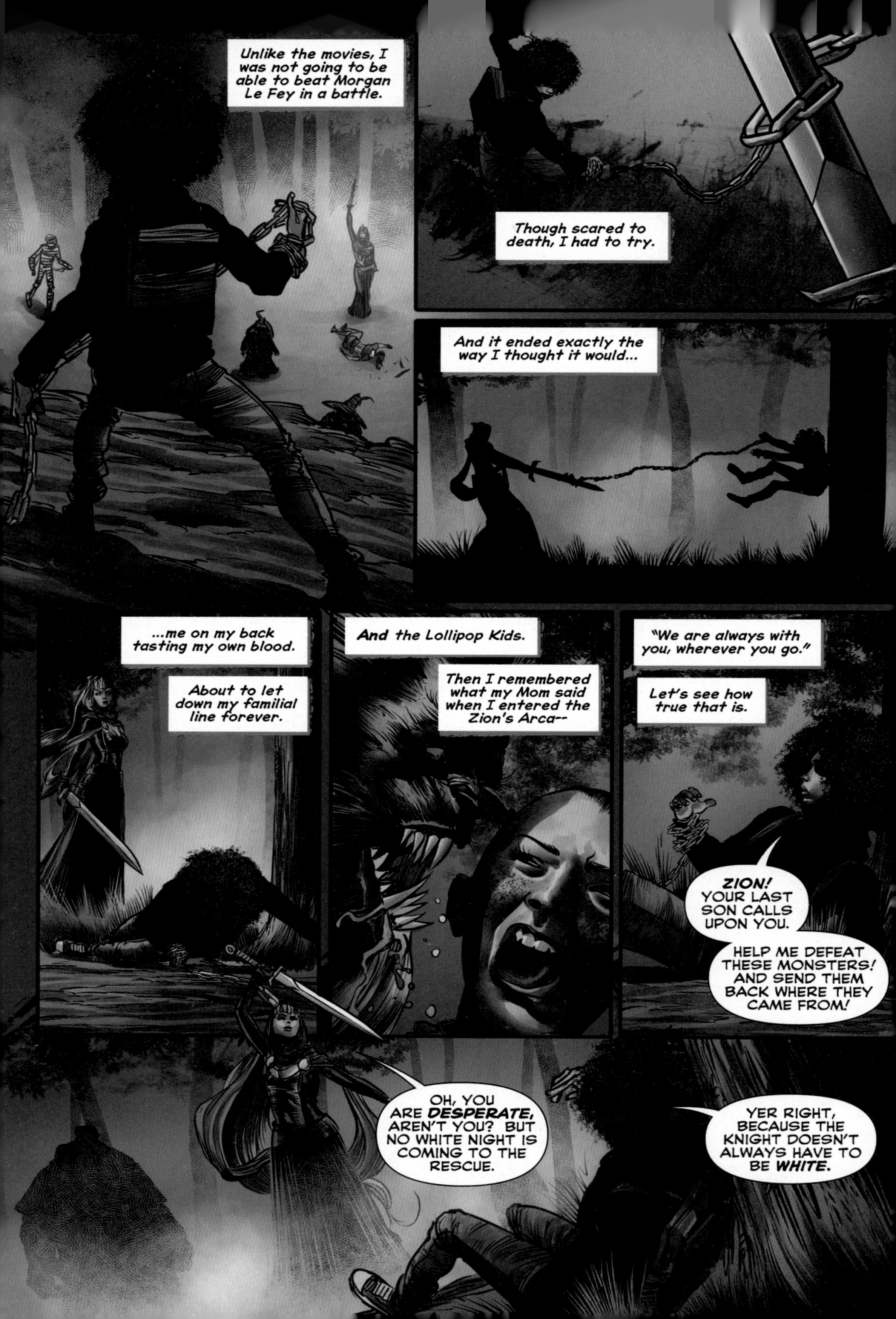

Unlike the movies, I was not going to be able to beat Morgan Le Fey in a battle.
Though scared to death, I had to try.
And it ended exactly the way I thought it would...
...me on my back tasting my own blood.
About to let down my familial line forever.
And the Lollipop Kids.
Then I remembered what my Mom said when I entered the Zion's Arca--
"We are always with you, wherever you go."
Let's see how true that is.
ZION! YOUR LAST SON CALLS UPON YOU.
HELP ME DEFEAT THESE MONSTERS! AND SEND THEM BACK WHERE THEY CAME FROM!
OH, YOU ARE DESPERATE, AREN'T YOU? BUT NO WHITE NIGHT IS COMING TO THE RESCUE.
YER RIGHT, BECAUSE THE KNIGHT DOESN'T ALWAYS HAVE TO BE WHITE.

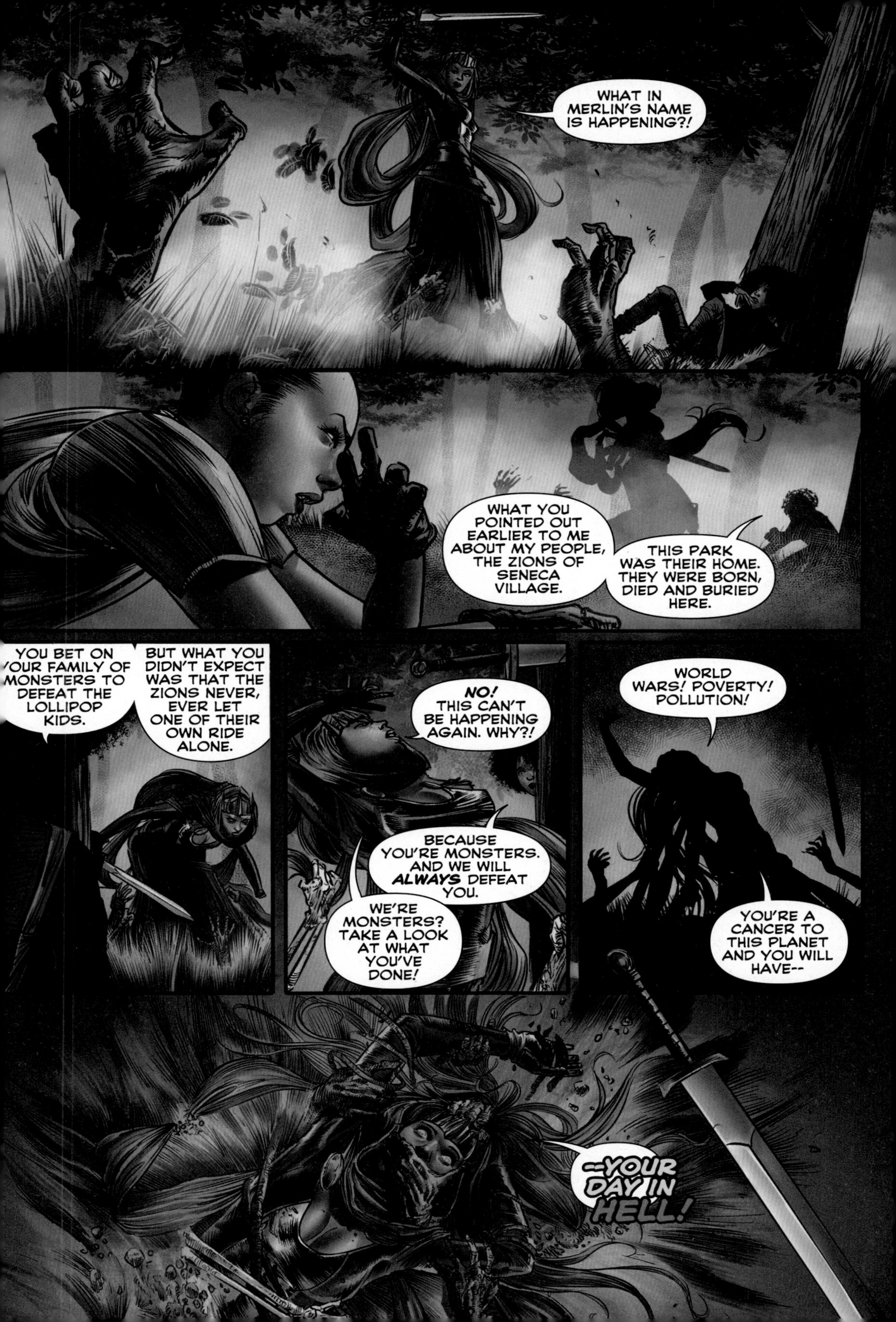
WHAT IN MERLIN'S NAME IS HAPPENING?!
WHAT YOU POINTED OUT EARLIER TO ME ABOUT MY PEOPLE, THE ZIONS OF SENECA VILLAGE.
THIS PARK WAS THEIR HOME. THEY WERE BORN, DIED AND BURIED HERE.
YOU BET ON YOUR FAMILY OF MONSTERS TO DEFEAT THE LOLLIPOP KIDS.
BUT WHAT YOU DIDN'T EXPECT WAS THAT THE ZIONS NEVER, EVER LET ONE OF THEIR OWN RIDE ALONE.
NO! THIS CAN'T BE HAPPENING AGAIN. WHY?!
BECAUSE YOU'RE MONSTERS. AND WE WILL ALWAYS DEFEAT YOU.
WE'RE MONSTERS? TAKE A LOOK AT WHAT YOU'VE DONE!
WORLD WARS! POVERTY! POLLUTION!
YOU'RE A CANCER TO THIS PLANET AND YOU WILL HAVE--
--YOUR DAY IN HELL!

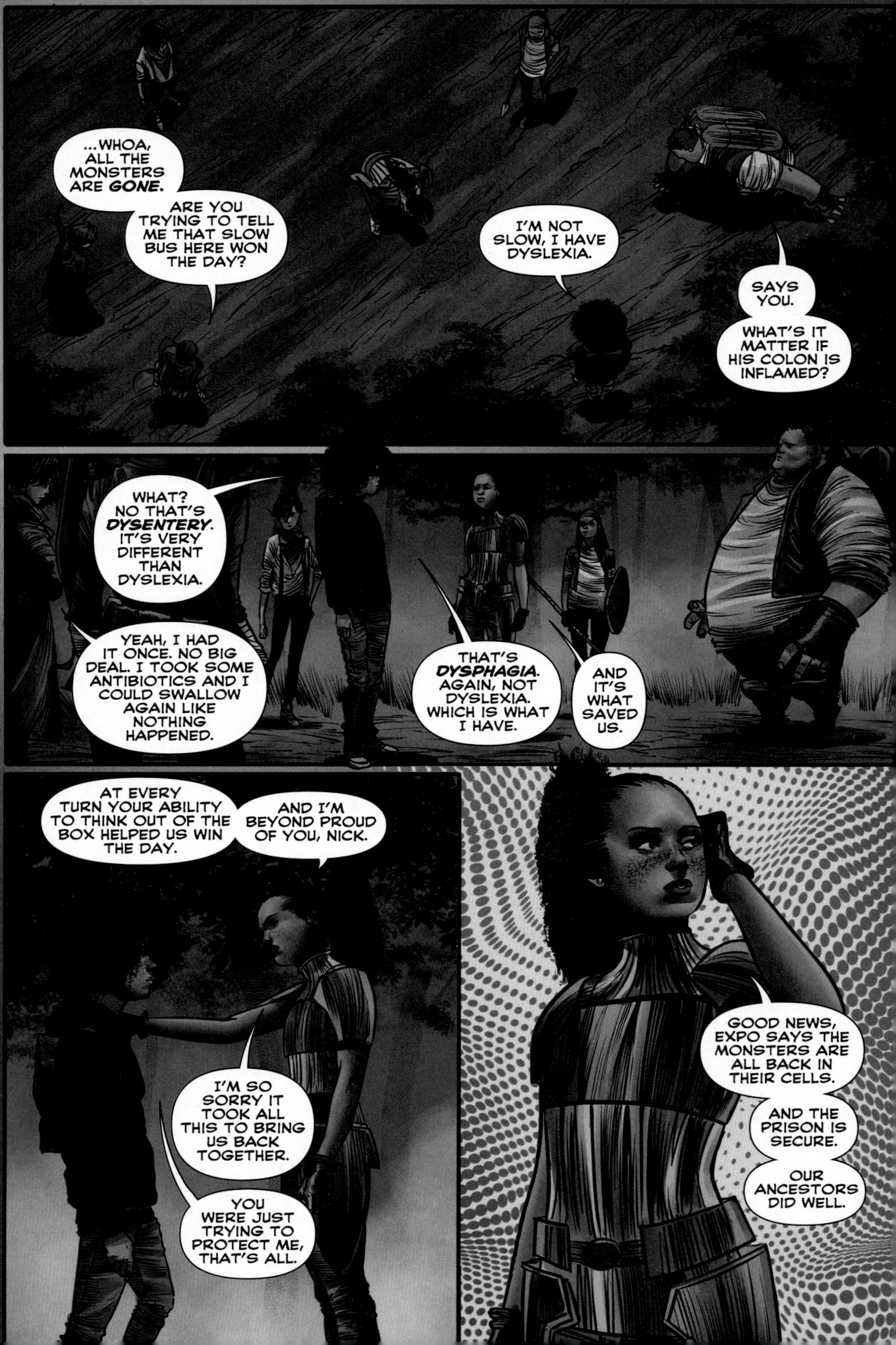
...WHOA, ALL THE MONSTERS ARE **GONE**.
ARE YOU TRYING TO TELL ME THAT SLOW BUS HERE WON THE DAY?
I'M NOT SLOW, I HAVE DYSLEXIA.
SAYS YOU.
WHAT'S IT MATTER IF HIS COLON IS INFLAMED?
WHAT? NO THAT'S ***DYSENTERY***. IT'S VERY DIFFERENT THAN DYSLEXIA.
YEAH, I HAD IT ONCE. NO BIG DEAL. I TOOK SOME ANTIBIOTICS AND I COULD SWALLOW AGAIN LIKE NOTHING HAPPENED.
THAT'S ***DYSPHAGIA***. AGAIN, NOT DYSLEXIA. WHICH IS WHAT I HAVE.
AND IT'S WHAT SAVED US.
AT EVERY TURN YOUR ABILITY TO THINK OUT OF THE BOX HELPED US WIN THE DAY.
AND I'M BEYOND PROUD OF YOU, NICK.
I'M SO SORRY IT TOOK ALL THIS TO BRING US BACK TOGETHER.
YOU WERE JUST TRYING TO PROTECT ME, THAT'S ALL.
GOOD NEWS, EXPO SAYS THE MONSTERS ARE ALL BACK IN THEIR CELLS.
AND THE PRISON IS SECURE.
OUR ANCESTORS DID WELL.

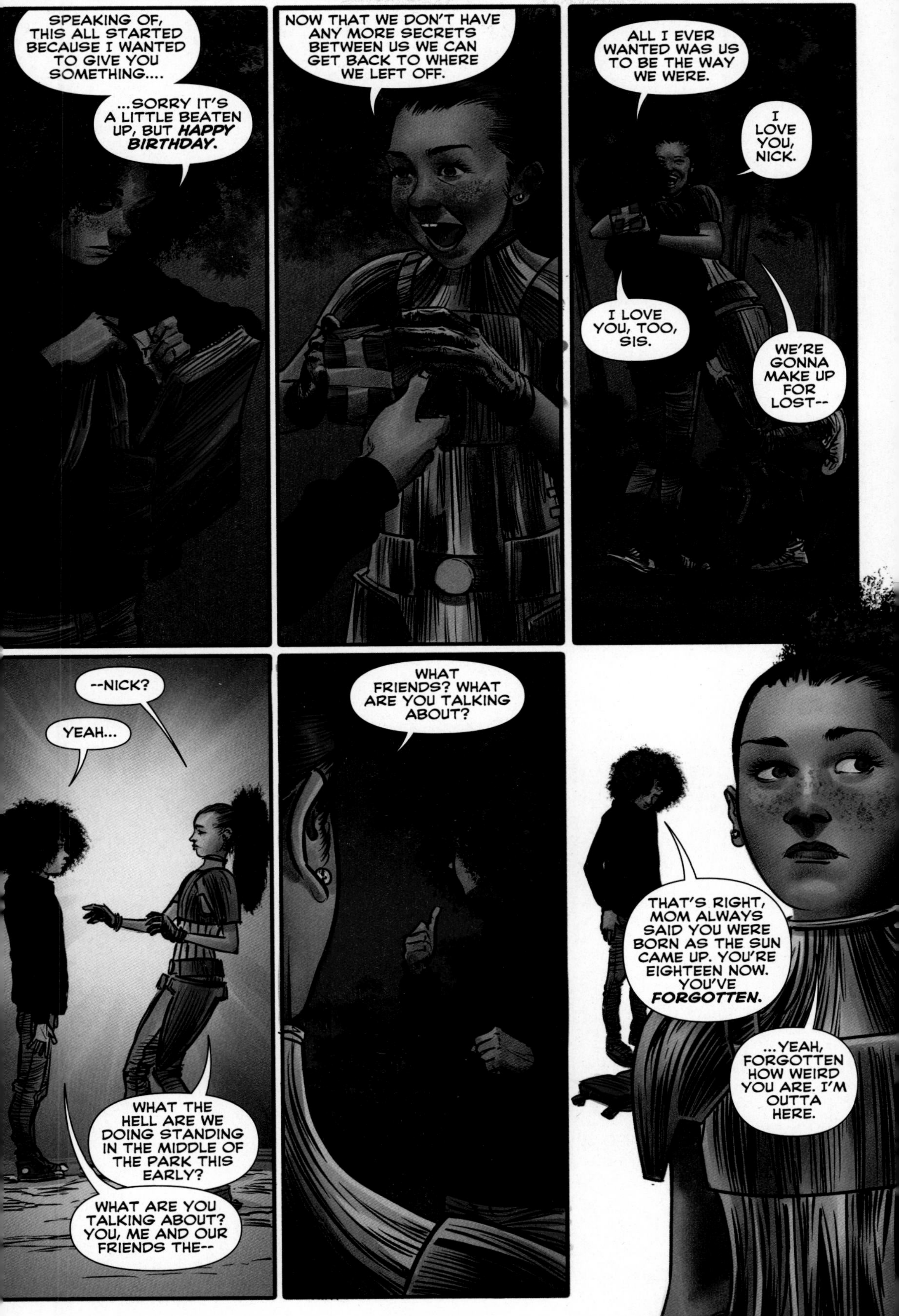
SPEAKING OF, THIS ALL STARTED BECAUSE I WANTED TO GIVE YOU SOMETHING....
...SORRY IT'S A LITTLE BEATEN UP, BUT *HAPPY BIRTHDAY*.
NOW THAT WE DON'T HAVE ANY MORE SECRETS BETWEEN US WE CAN GET BACK TO WHERE WE LEFT OFF.
ALL I EVER WANTED WAS US TO BE THE WAY WE WERE.
I LOVE YOU, NICK.
I LOVE YOU, TOO, SIS.
WE'RE GONNA MAKE UP FOR LOST--
--NICK?
YEAH...
WHAT THE HELL ARE WE DOING STANDING IN THE MIDDLE OF THE PARK THIS EARLY?
WHAT ARE YOU TALKING ABOUT? YOU, ME AND OUR FRIENDS THE--
WHAT FRIENDS? WHAT ARE YOU TALKING ABOUT?
THAT'S RIGHT, MOM ALWAYS SAID YOU WERE BORN AS THE SUN CAME UP. YOU'RE EIGHTEEN NOW. YOU'VE *FORGOTTEN*.
...YEAH, FORGOTTEN HOW WEIRD YOU ARE. I'M OUTTA HERE.

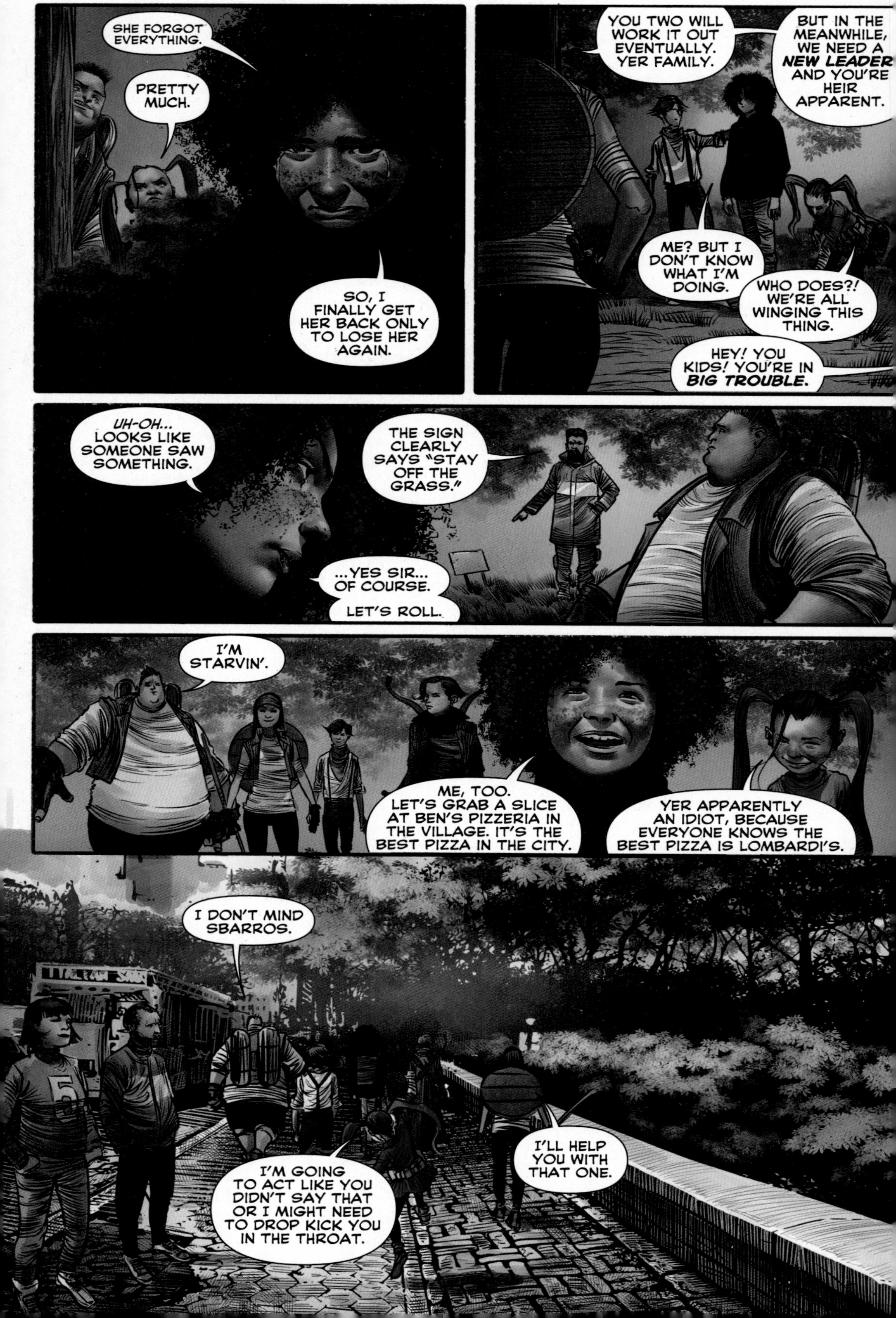
SHE FORGOT EVERYTHING.
PRETTY MUCH.
SO, I FINALLY GET HER BACK ONLY TO LOSE HER AGAIN.
YOU TWO WILL WORK IT OUT EVENTUALLY. YER FAMILY.
BUT IN THE MEANWHILE, WE NEED A *NEW LEADER* AND YOU'RE HEIR APPARENT.
ME? BUT I DON'T KNOW WHAT I'M DOING.
WHO DOES?! WE'RE ALL WINGING THIS THING.
HEY! YOU KIDS! YOU'RE IN *BIG TROUBLE*.
UH-OH... LOOKS LIKE SOMEONE SAW SOMETHING.
THE SIGN CLEARLY SAYS "STAY OFF THE GRASS."
...YES SIR... OF COURSE.
LET'S ROLL.
I'M STARVIN'.
ME, TOO. LET'S GRAB A SLICE AT BEN'S PIZZERIA IN THE VILLAGE. IT'S THE BEST PIZZA IN THE CITY.
YER APPARENTLY AN IDIOT, BECAUSE EVERYONE KNOWS THE BEST PIZZA IS LOMBARDI'S.
I DON'T MIND SBARROS.
I'M GOING TO ACT LIKE YOU DIDN'T SAY THAT OR I MIGHT NEED TO DROP KICK YOU IN THE THROAT.
I'LL HELP YOU WITH THAT ONE.

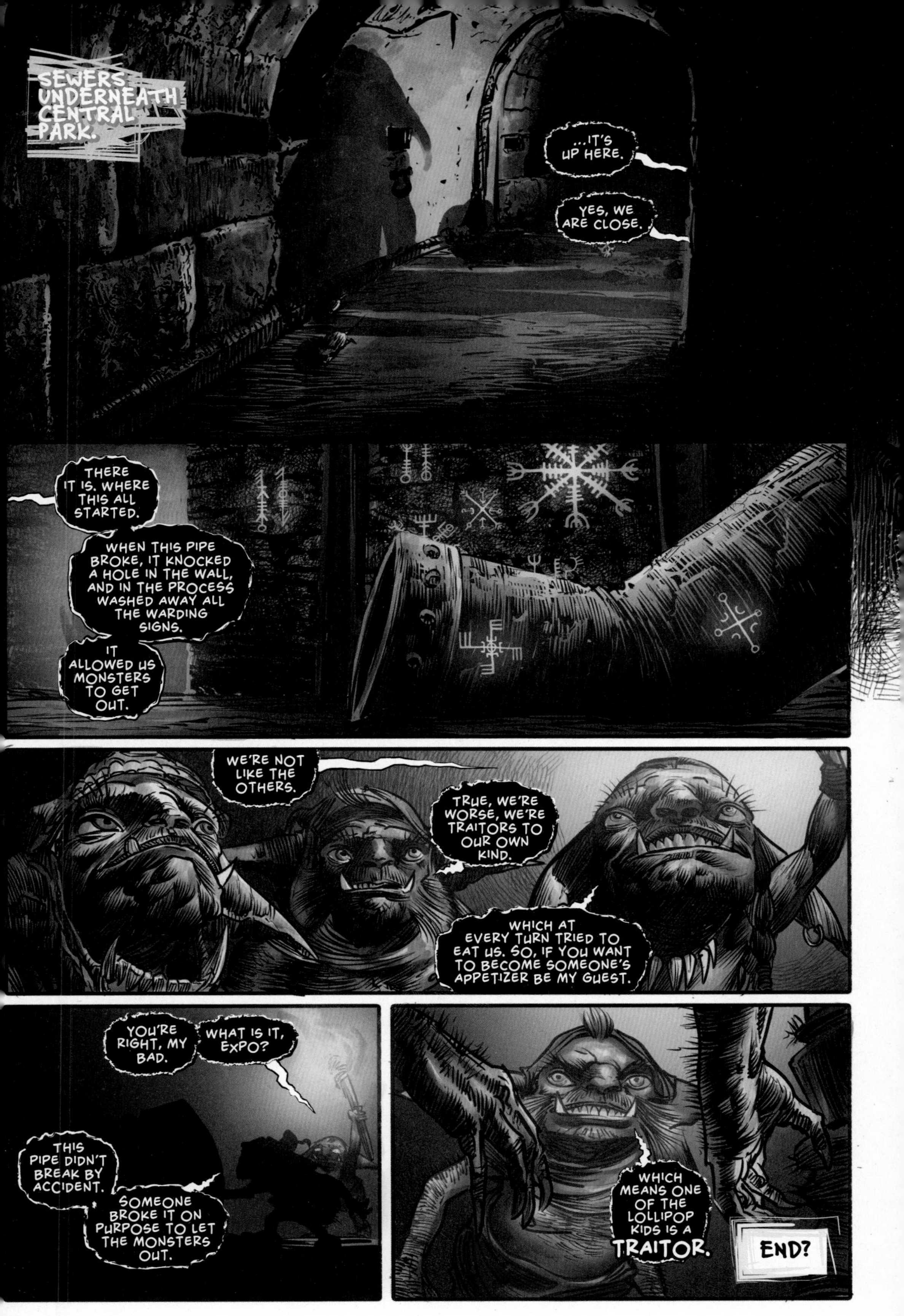
SEWERS UNDERNEATH CENTRAL PARK.
...IT'S UP HERE.
YES, WE ARE CLOSE.
THERE IT IS. WHERE THIS ALL STARTED.
WHEN THIS PIPE BROKE, IT KNOCKED A HOLE IN THE WALL, AND IN THE PROCESS WASHED AWAY ALL THE WARDING SIGNS.
IT ALLOWED US MONSTERS TO GET OUT.
WE'RE NOT LIKE THE OTHERS.
TRUE, WE'RE WORSE, WE'RE TRAITORS TO OUR OWN KIND.
WHICH AT EVERY TURN TRIED TO EAT US. SO, IF YOU WANT TO BECOME SOMEONE'S APPETIZER BE MY GUEST.
YOU'RE RIGHT, MY BAD.
WHAT IS IT, EXPO?
THIS PIPE DIDN'T BREAK BY ACCIDENT.
SOMEONE BROKE IT ON PURPOSE TO LET THE MONSTERS OUT.
WHICH MEANS ONE OF THE LOLLIPOP KIDS IS A TRAITOR.
END?

Q&A WITH CREATOR AIDAN GLASS

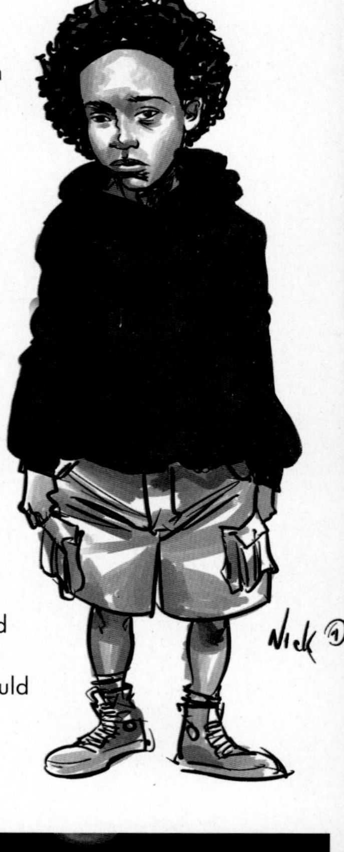

Nick

Seismic Press: You have grown up around comic and film/television scripts your whole life; at what age did you first realize your dad's job differed from your classmates?

Aidan Glass: I found myself on studio lots and sound stages at a young age, witnessing all the movie magic and, honestly, it just felt normal. But it hit home for me when I was in Vancouver on the *Supernatural* set with Sam (Jared) and Dean (Jensen), who I'd watch at home on TV. That's when I realized my Dad has a super awesome job. And still, to this day, nothing makes me happier than going on a set. I'm very fortunate.

SP: Where did the story for THE LOLLIPOP KIDS come from?

AG: Bedtime stories! I was diagnosed with dyslexia at a young age, and reading was hard for me then (not anymore). So, instead of reading books, my family and I would create our own adventures. And THE LOLLIPOP KIDS was one of them. It's a story that kept developing each night until one day when I was older, I said to my Dad, "We should turn this into a comic book."

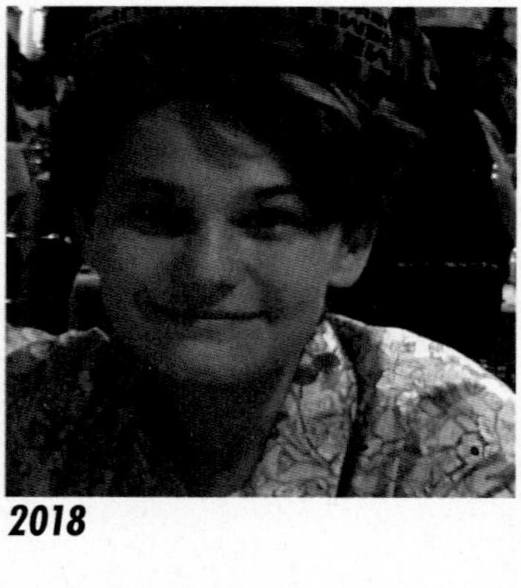

2018

SP: What was it like to co-create a comic book at fourteen-years-old?

AG: For any fourteen-year-old who loves comics, it was nothing but fun. Creating bigger plots and enough twists and turns to last twenty pages was challenging, but thankfully my Dad was there to help me build it, and I learned so much.

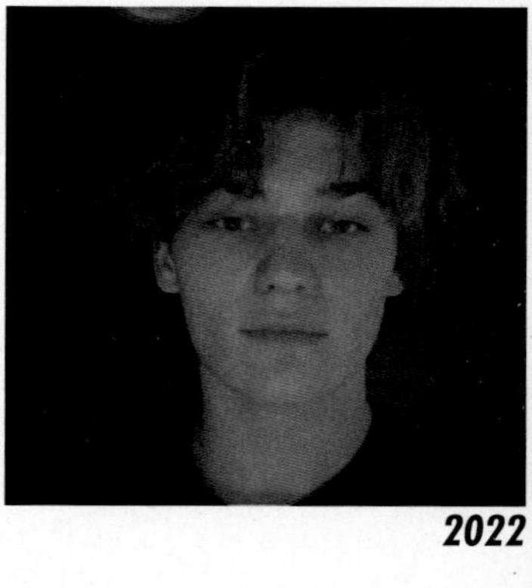

2022

SP: One of the major themes in THE LOLLIPOP KIDS is Nick's dyslexia. How did your personal experience with dyslexia influence Nick's story?

AG: Nick's character is full of many great things; he's adventurous, witty and intelligent. But I wanted to give him something that people can relate to or even understand. Everyone's journey with dyslexia is different, but I found it an outlet to make new friends for me.

SP: Any advice for young adults who want to become a comic book creator?

AG: Draw until your hands fall off. Write so many stories that your head hurts. This is the world you're making, and have fun with it. There are always people who'll not like the stuff you do but none of that matters; if you genuinely believe in what you're doing, that's enough.

SP: Finally, if you could take Expo anywhere in New York City, where would you take him and why?

AG: When I was a kid, I loved Central Park, and still do, but now I'd probably take Expo to the Lower East Side because there are so many hole-in-the-wall stores that sell vintage clothes, records, books, etc., and like in THE LOLLIPOP KIDS, there is a long immigrant history down there. So many people came to this country and started their new lives in Manhattan—you can still feel that when you visit.

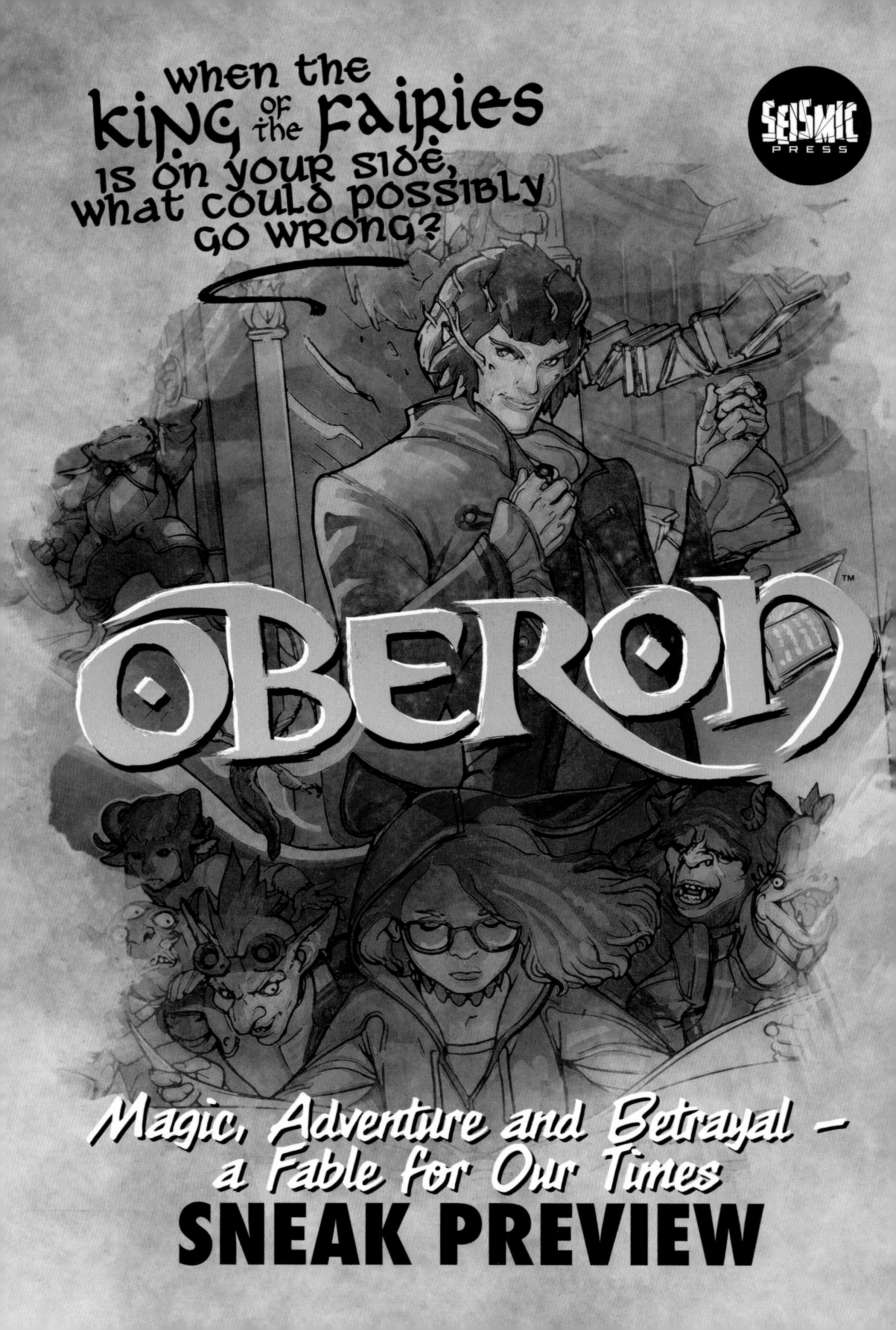
when the KING of the FAIRIES is on your side, what could possibly go wrong?
SEISMIC PRESS
OBERON™
Magic, Adventure and Betrayal – a Fable for Our Times
SNEAK PREVIEW

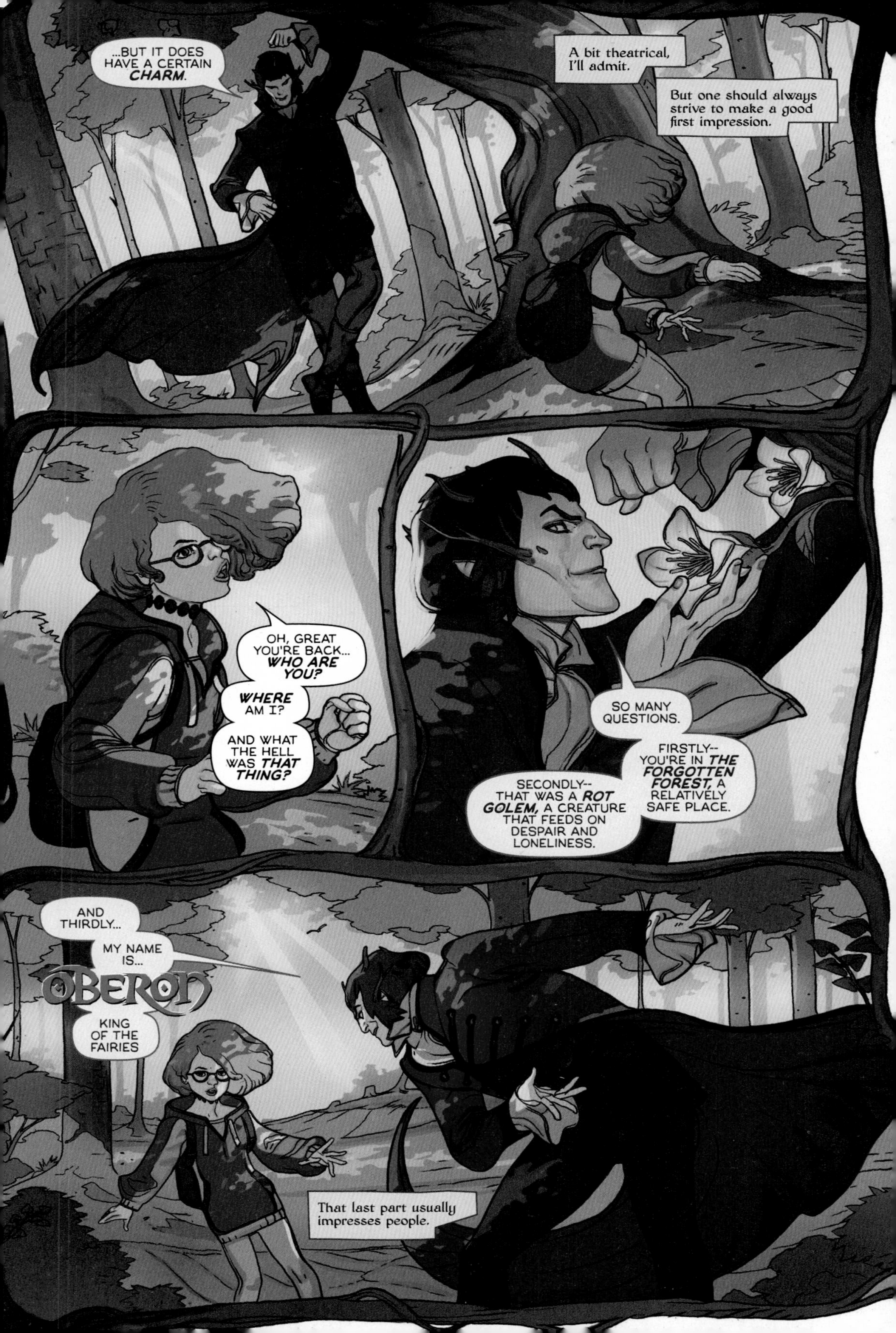
...BUT IT DOES HAVE A CERTAIN *CHARM*.
A bit theatrical, I'll admit.
But one should always strive to make a good first impression.
OH, GREAT YOU'RE BACK... ***WHO ARE YOU?***
WHERE AM I?
AND WHAT THE HELL WAS ***THAT THING?***
SO MANY QUESTIONS.
FIRSTLY-- YOU'RE IN ***THE FORGOTTEN FOREST,*** A RELATIVELY SAFE PLACE.
SECONDLY-- THAT WAS A ***ROT GOLEM,*** A CREATURE THAT FEEDS ON DESPAIR AND LONELINESS.
AND THIRDLY...
MY NAME IS...
OBERON
KING OF THE FAIRIES
That last part usually impresses people.

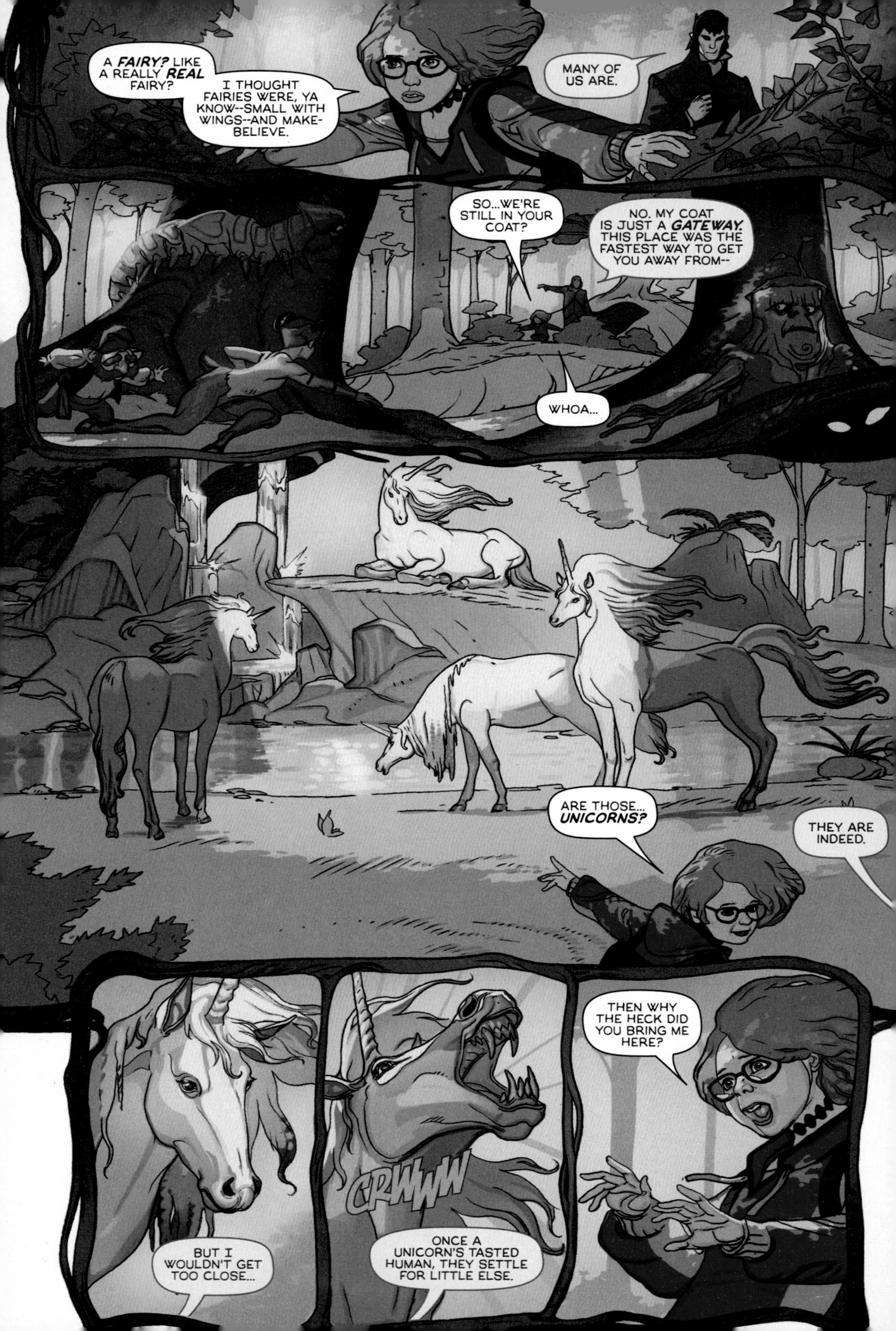
A **FAIRY?** LIKE A REALLY **REAL** FAIRY?
I THOUGHT FAIRIES WERE, YA KNOW--SMALL WITH WINGS--AND MAKE-BELIEVE.
MANY OF US ARE.
SO...WE'RE STILL IN YOUR COAT?
NO. MY COAT IS JUST A **GATEWAY.** THIS PLACE WAS THE FASTEST WAY TO GET YOU AWAY FROM--
WHOA...
ARE THOSE... **UNICORNS?**
THEY ARE INDEED.
BUT I WOULDN'T GET TOO CLOSE...
CRWWW
ONCE A UNICORN'S TASTED HUMAN, THEY SETTLE FOR LITTLE ELSE.
THEN WHY THE HECK DID YOU BRING ME HERE?

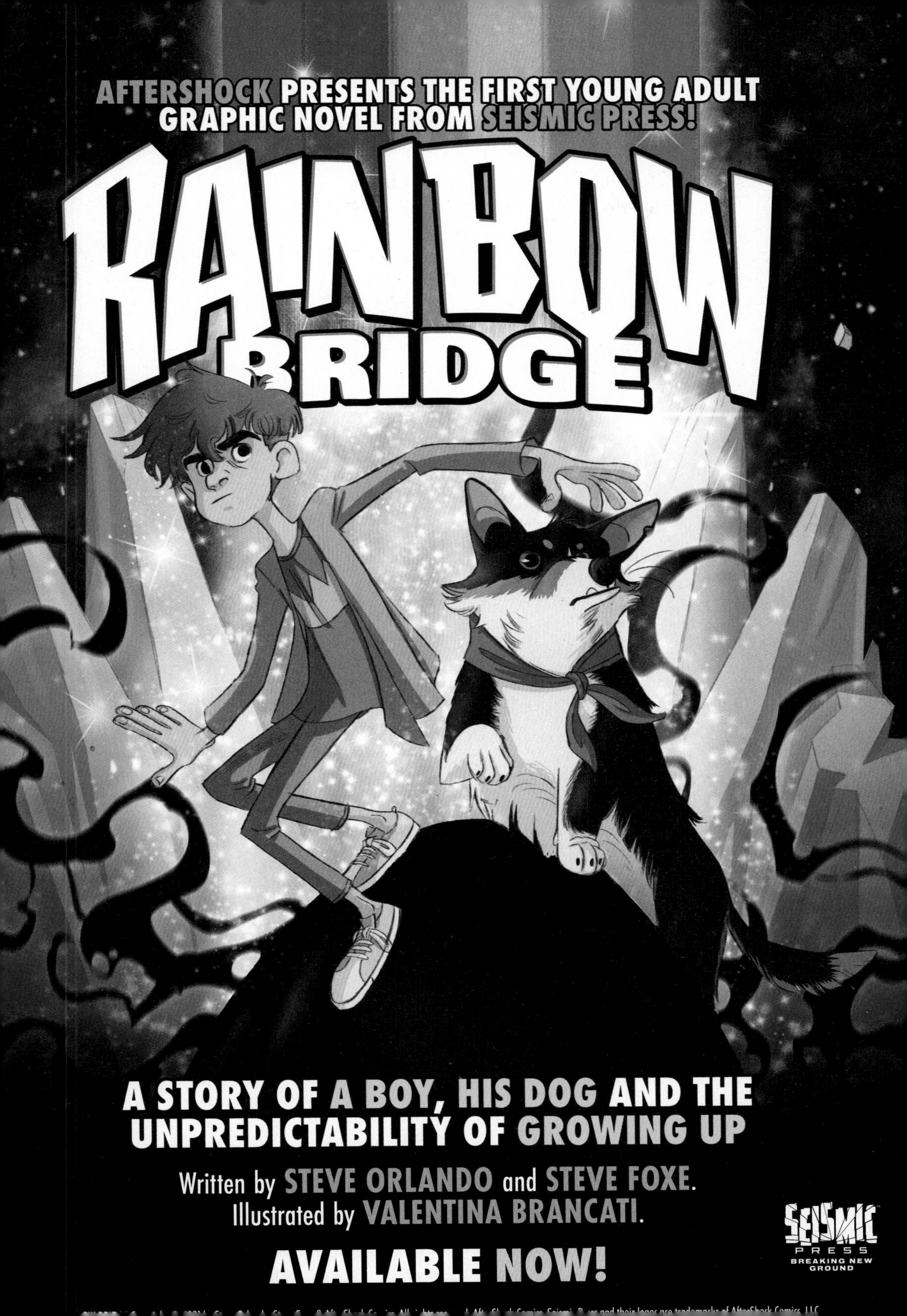
AFTERSHOCK PRESENTS THE FIRST YOUNG ADULT GRAPHIC NOVEL FROM SEISMIC PRESS!
RAINBOW BRIDGE
A STORY OF A BOY, HIS DOG AND THE UNPREDICTABILITY OF GROWING UP
Written by STEVE ORLANDO and STEVE FOXE.
Illustrated by VALENTINA BRANCATI.
AVAILABLE NOW!
SEISMIC PRESS
BREAKING NEW GROUND

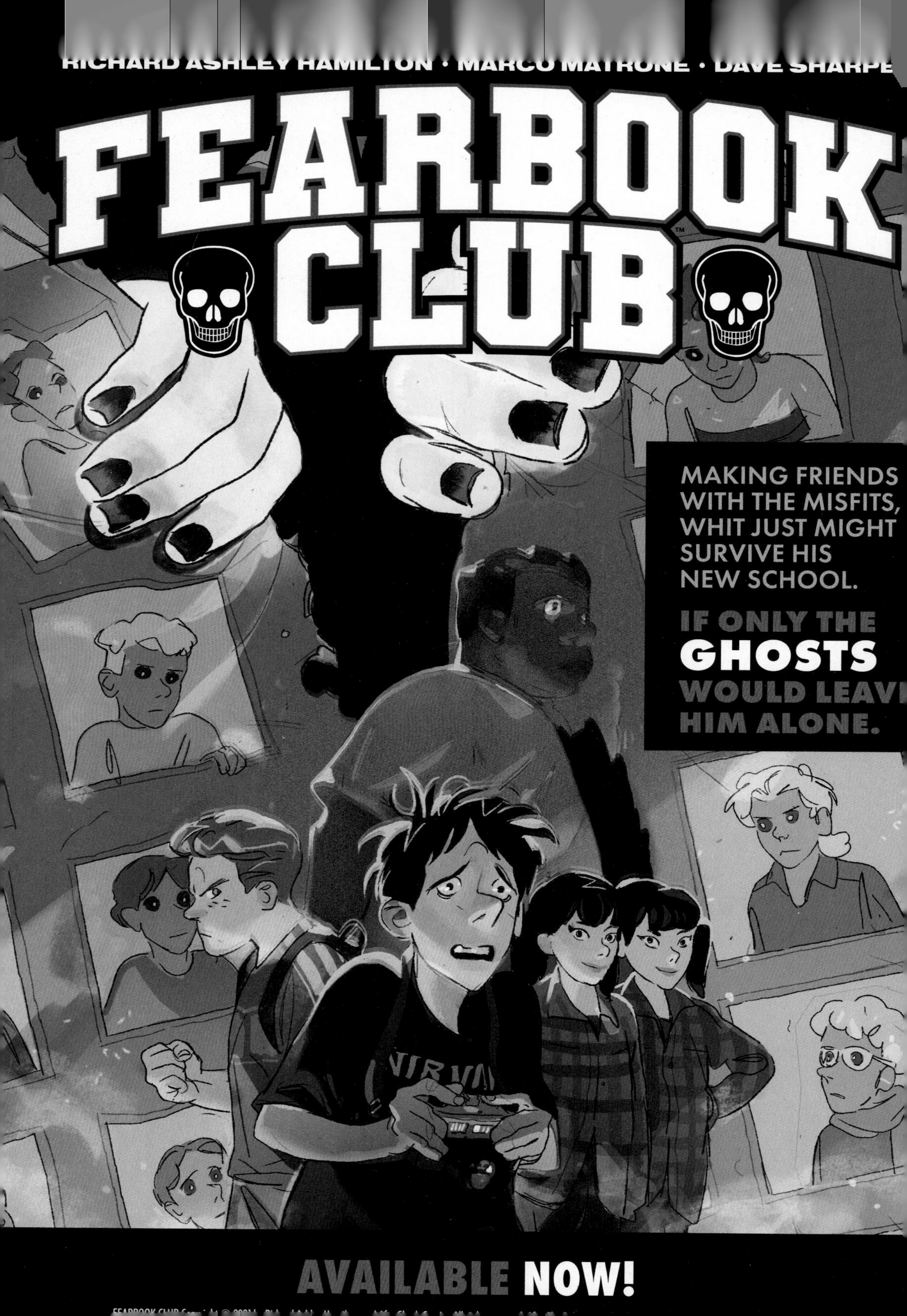

RICHARD ASHLEY HAMILTON · MARCO MATRONE · DAVE SHARPE
FEARBOOK CLUB™
MAKING FRIENDS WITH THE MISFITS, WHIT JUST MIGHT SURVIVE HIS NEW SCHOOL.
IF ONLY THE GHOSTS WOULD LEAVE HIM ALONE.
NIRVANA
AVAILABLE NOW!

HAVE SOMETHING TO SAY?! SPEAK SEISMICALLY

SAY IT HERE
@SeismicComics

OR HERE
@SeismicPress

OR EVEN HERE
@SeismicPress

SEE WHAT WE'RE SAYING?

SEISMIC PRESS

ABOUT THE CREATORS

ADAM GLASS
writer

Though NYC will always be home, Adam resides in Los Angeles and is a TV Writer/Executive Producer of such shows as *Supernatural, Cold Case* and *Criminal Minds: Beyond Borders* on CBS. When Adam is not writing for TV or films, he's writing graphic novels. Some of these titles include: Marvel Comics' *Deadpool: Suicide Kings* and DC Comics' *Suicide Squad*—all of which were NY Times bestsellers. Other books Adam has written or co-written for Marvel are *Deadpool: Pulp, Luke Cage: Noir, Deadpool Team-Up* and *Luke Cage: Origins.* And for DC, *JLA Annual* and the Flashpoint series *Legion of Doom.*

AIDAN GLASS
story

Hailing from Las Angeles, Aidan's love for comic characters began at age three and a half, when his sister changed the channel one afternoon and *Batman: The Animated Series* appeared on screen. Costumes, books and movies followed. While THE LOLLIPOP KIDS is Aidan's first time co-creating a book, he had the most awesome experience co-creating two hero characters, Iceberg and Roundhouse, for his father Adam Glass' reimagining of DC Comic's New 52 *Suicide Squad* and 2018's reboot of *Teen Titans.*

DIEGO YAPUR
artist

Diego Yapur is an Argentinian comic artist, born in Belén, Catamarca. He started his comics career drawing The Night Projectionist´s *Studio 407* in 2008. He has also done work for Jamestown Education, Bluewater Productions, Tokyopop and Valiant. In Argentina, he has collaborated with La Snob, Terminus, UMC, La Murcielaga, Random and others, and now he's bringing his unique style to THE LOLLIPOP KIDS.

DC ALONSO
colorist

DC Alonso is passionate about classical art, especially painting. In his colors, he tries to capture things he's learned from great painters. Alonso has worked for companies like Blizzard, IDW, Lion Forge, but where he's done the most work is in independent comics—coloring comics for authors who have trusted him. THE LOLLIPOP KIDS is his first AfterShock collaboration.

SAL CIPRIANO
letterer

Brooklyn-born/coffee-addicted Sal Cipriano is a freelance letterer and the former Lettering Supervisor for DC Comics. His previous position at DC coupled with experience in writing, drawing, coloring, editing, designing, and publishing comics gives him unique vision as a freelancer. Sal is currently working with — amongst others — DC, Skybound, Lion Forge, Stela, and now AfterShock! Better fire up another fresh pot!